The Daily Diner

M. Marmer Verhoeff

ISBN: 1523462590

ISBN 13: 9781523462599

Library of Congress Control Number: 2016901021
CreateSpace Independent Publishing Platform
North Charleston, South Carolina

For father-in-law Bram,
who gave me an empty journal
and urged me to write

Acknowledgments

A heartfelt thank-you to Cantor Michelle Rubin for sharing her personal experiences as a female student in a male-dominated seminary as well as information about being educated and trained as a hazzan. I could not have created the character Daniella without her help.

Likewise, a special thank-you to Rabbi Adam Baldachin for helping me to understand Conservative theology, including its similarities and differences when compared to Orthodox and Hasidic interpretations. Our discussions were extremely helpful to me.

My character Benny is the result of my in-depth interview with Esther Gaines. I am especially grateful that Esther was willing to share the joy and tragedy that was part of her family's history in Greece. Also, that she took the time to share information about Jewish Greek cuisine, customs in the context of religious practice, and most important, how difficult it was to be a minority Greek Jew in a country where the religion was not favored.

A very special thank-you to Ilan Nifco, who had worked in the diamond industry for years and was willing to sit down with me and share his experiences as well as his knowledge of the industry. Also, to Steve and Sue Matero of Matero Fine Jewelry, who indulged me with information about gems, and especially the peridot. The information from all these individuals was crucial for creating Adam's career in the story.

Thank you to Jenny Kalsner for sharing her stories of childhood in Antwerp, Belgium, and her descriptions of streets, ports, parks, and buildings, all of which helped to create the Gvirzman neighborhood and provide me with a better understanding of the Antwerp diamond district.

Thank you to Bruce Levine for sharing his knowledge of Jewish history and for his own personal stories of life in an Orthodox setting.

My deepest gratitude to Dino Kiryacou and Billy Rodopoulos for granting me permission to photograph their place of business, the Airmont Diner in Airmont, New York. Likewise, to artist Elisa Marmer for using the photograph as inspiration for creating the painting that eventually became the perfect design for my book cover. I wish to also thank Jeremy D. Hembree, photographer, for his editing work, which transformed the painting into a completed book cover design.

Heartfelt admiration and affection for Susan Ecker, my honest and constructive proofreader and, more important, good friend.

All of the individuals listed in this acknowledgment were part and parcel of the creation of this story, and I couldn't have written it without their help.

Last, but never least, thank you to my entire family for constant support and especially to my husband, Ray, who is always my second pair of eyes and the best assistant in manuscript preparation that a person could ask for.

In the town of Airmont, New York, a community icon known as the Airmont Diner sits quietly on the northwest corner of a four-way intersection. Right off a major thoroughfare, it is a stopping ground for the locals as well as the commuter who needs a rest stop on the way up or down state.

Partners Dino Kyriacou and Billy Rodopoulos meet and greet the patrons who come through their doors. They are the salt and pepper, the frick and frack—whatever dynamic duo you can name as the glue that holds an establishment together. Their children, too, have taken post as meeters and greeters to the world. Their waitstaff are equally mindful of taking care of the regulars and providing good customer service.

The allure does not come from the food or the ambience. The diner is just a diner. It comes from a communal atmosphere that is quite hard to articulate. Everyone seems to go there! They have meetings, postgame parties, lunches with friends, or serious talks, knowing all the while that they won't be rushed to leave. There is that certain something in the way Dino says, "Nice to see you again," or in Billy's "Hello, dear." You feel welcomed.

The goings-on at the Airmont Diner inspired me to write this fictional work about an establishment known as the Daily Diner and those who might come through its doors. What might it be like if the owner got tangled up in the lives of his customers? What would happen if an owner got particularly close to one of his or her waitstaff? My diner owner is Greek, and the Daily Diner rests on a corner just off a major highway, but the similarities to the Airmont Diner end there. The characters and the goings-on in their lives are completely fictional, and any resemblance to real people and their own lives is sheer coincidence.

To that end, I thank Dino and Billy and the entire staff of the Airmont Diner, not only for making me feel special each time I come through the doors, but for inspiring me to dream up this unique story.

As an added note: although perhaps not necessary, I have italicized every Yiddish and Hebrew word in the text just to indicate that a language different from English is in use.

Benny's Diner

shoe is a shoe. A feather, a feather. Even a leaf, for all its biological beauty, is simply a leaf. A diner, well, that's a microcosm of the world. It's a truck stop par excellence. A girls' night out. A business meeting over coffee. A communal experience like no other. A global miniature, ever changing and constantly evolving. A place that houses the perplexing beings known as people. Benny had relished the concept as far back as he could remember.

In the dreary cold of the morning, those were the thoughts that came into his head as he pulled into his parking spot aside the restaurant known as the Daily Diner. He looked up through the car glass and smiled at the place he called his second home. The pitter-patter of drizzle obstructed his view through the glass, but Benny smiled despite its obscuring presence. The smile was the result of realizing how much he epitomized the phrase "pride in ownership." Benny sighed with contentment as he prepared to begin yet another workday in his prized establishment.

Benny pulled his raincoat tighter around his neck and skooched over to the edge of the car seat for a quick getaway into the warmth of the restaurant's interior. The chill of the morning was raw despite the prediction of fifty-eight-degree weather by midday. The forecast called for rain. The blessed droplets would bring a damp and dreary day. That would mean a good influx of patrons hoping to get some relief from the nasty weather. Benny would make sure all the coffee urns were running full speed this morning.

After assuring himself that the car was locked, Benny took the short but quick-paced walk to the front door of his place of business. Having moved to Epson County years ago, way back in 1964, to be exact, he'd been in business for a very long time. So much so that he acted by rote, freeing up his mind to think about other things as he headed toward the door.

Fumbling with his key ring, Benny located the master key that unlocked the gateway to his beloved restaurant. He opened the door, his thoughts already centered on supply replenishment and menu changes. After hanging up his coat, Benny began his daily routine, which always started by ensuring the coffee urns were filled and ready for the morning customers. In a matter of minutes, Benny was ready to start his day.

It was as busy a day as Benny knew it would be. The rain was a good friend that way. Patrons came in from the damp chill as if the raindrops actually pushed them through the doors. Each person desperate for that hot bowl of soup or cup of coffee that would warm the bones. Benny was more than grateful when his partner Nate arrived to help with the hustle and bustle of the restaurant.

Good old Nate. Benny couldn't have asked for a better business partner. Kind and quiet, Nate was the calming presence that Benny needed to run things efficiently. On a dreary day like today, Nate's presence was paramount to running the restaurant like clockwork. Benny didn't even have to ask and Nate was already headed to the kitchen to allow Benny to focus on ringing up the customers at the register.

In Nate's case, his day was destined to be easy and his work, straightforward. If Benny knew what the evening had in store for him, he might have never come to work that day. He might have asked Nate to take over and give him a chance to escape before destiny pulled him in as an unwitting player in a love story that would metaphorically shake the foundation of the restaurant.

The dinner hour would arrive in the guise of fate. Benny's heart and mind would be touched by love he thought impossible to exist. Old wounds would be torn apart in order that they could heal. Benny's soul would be challenged and tested. Sadly for Benny, he didn't know that it would all come about, the moment he greeted his favorite group of patrons who had just come through the restaurant doors.

Daniella

"*T*here they are. Welcome, ladies. Nice to see you, as always. Right this way." Benny swept his arm outward as he bowed slightly. "I have your booth ready and waiting for you."

"Benny, you are so good to us," Marcia chirped.

"And why shouldn't I be? You ladies are such good customers, coming in every first Tuesday of the month to have your meetings. Such patronage! Besides, you're such beautiful women. How could I not be nice to such lovelies?"

A hushed laughter, reminiscent of the lighthearted giggles from blushing brides, rose from the clustered four. The women were unbuttoning coats and pocketing scarves near the front entrance of the restaurant.

"Benny, you're such a flirt," Marcia added as she hung up her coat. Being the strong-minded one in the group, she had no qualms about pointing that out to Benny. Despite that, she was quick to add, "That's why we all love you so much!" She gave Benny a warm-hearted smile for good measure.

The foursome followed him to their little corner of the diner. Marcia, Rena, Ruth, and Vonnie all settled themselves within the confines of their special booth, pocketbooks and loose-leaf binders in hand. The paraphernalia took up every last inch of the leathered seats. They made themselves comfortable as each grabbed a menu from the stack Benny had placed on the table.

Marcia took note of the subtle chuckle that escaped Benny's lips as he watched them settle in. She decided to tease him about it.

"What's so funny, Benny? Don't you know we practically own this booth? It's private and the fact that it's toward the back of the restaurant, where quiet reigns, is a bonus for our meetings."

The women were preparing for yet another of their sisterhood meetings. The Daily Diner provided an excuse for a girls' night out. The place was easily accessed, just off the highway. It was the ideal spot for their important get-togethers. Kosher to boot, so no one could point a finger and say they were conducting synagogue business in an unkosher establishment.

Women's League for Conservative Judaism was a nationwide organization. Regional branches throughout the United States and even the world ran the organization like clockwork. It was a stronghold for many women in the Conservative branch of Judaism. At the local level, Women's League was affectionately called Sisterhood and more often than not, each sisterhood formed the backbone of its synagogue.

Marcia served as the current president of her syna-gogue's sisterhood. Rena, Ruth, and Vonnie were vice president, corresponding secretary, and ways and means chair. Tonight's meeting was an important one. They needed to plan the spring event. It was still February, a long way off from the end-of-year dinner, but the spring gala event involved a fashion show, and that meant early planning. The ladies needed to be on top of things and avoid a last-minute sense of panic. In order to plan the perfect event, they needed to decide on details as simple as whether Vonnie should use Yvonna instead of her nick-name on the invitations.

Benny found himself glancing at the booth from time to time, same as he always did. He smiled; the wom-en were quite adorable in how serious they were. How committed they were. He knew the synagogue they hailed from. It was a strong and vital house of worship, quite likely because of all their hard work and efforts.

Benny himself did not frequent that particular Con-servative synagogue. More often than not, he drove into the city with Rose prior to the onset of a holiday or the Sabbath. They loved to spend time with family and at-tend the Greek synagogue of his youth. It was simply a matter of what was familiar. Admittedly, his childhood synagogue was truly a second home.

On rare occasion, he'd stay up in the county and at-tend services in the smaller Orthodox synagogue that was a walkable distance from his home. At those times, Rose always cooked a superb Sabbath meal for Friday night. They'd be sure to have Helen, Iris, and Rhoda join them if possible—his darling daughters. Two of them were already married. Rhoda would find her beau soon enough. Of that, Benny was sure. It was simply a matter of time and God's design.

Benny glanced at the booth again. The ladies were deep in discussion, but if he didn't know any better, he'd swear they were stealing glances at him as well. They seemed to be sharing secrets. Could they be scheming about him? *That's crazy, Benny. You're working too hard.* He was sure he was letting his imagination get wild. Most likely they were heavily involved with their meeting and were only looking at him in the same way he was looking at them.

The fatigue caused by Benny's long hard workday was catching up with him that Tuesday evening. Usually, he was right on the money when he summed up folks or their motivations and overall behavior. Sadly for him, his fatigue was victor and he was not adept at reading the ladies correctly on that particular night. Had he done so, he would have surely walked away before Marcia approached him at the register.

"Can I speak with you a moment, Benny?"

Benny gave Marcia a one moment signal with his hands, indicating he needed to finish writing some information into one of his ledgers at the register.

As Marcia waited, she replayed her conversation of moments ago, silently in her mind.

"Marcia, are you sure you want to ask Benny?" Vonnie had leaned in close as she whispered her question.

"Why not? He's known us long enough. I know he likes me as a person. Why shouldn't I ask him this favor? Daniella could use a job, and he has a great establishment. It's a possibility I don't want to pass up."

"But, Marcia, he's not hiring. There's no sign in the window that says he's looking for help. You're being a bit *chutzpadik,* don't you think?"

Marcia made a dismissing gesture with her hand as she said, "You're being silly, Vonnie. I'll only seem ballsy if I present myself that way." She thought about it further and continued, "OK, so maybe it's a bit pushy, and I don't even know how Daniella will feel about my asking, but...I think I'm going to do it anyway."

Benny put his pen down and smiled. "What's up, lovely lady?"

Marcia leaned in and rested her elbows on the countertop. She spoke in a whisper, as if she were about to share a great secret.

"Benny, my daughter Daniella is about to turn twenty, and she's attending college in the city, so she's a commuter. I mention this because everything, and I mean everything, is more expensive in the city. She has a little over a year left before she graduates, and she keeps telling me she's dreaming of something big."

Marcia leaned in closer. "Benny, you're always so nice to me. I'm hoping you could extend that kindness just a bit. My daughter, well, she's too old for babysitting and has been dropping comments about getting a part-time job so she can fund this big dream of hers. She hasn't told me yet what that dream is, but she keeps promising she will soon. The fact that she wants to fund it, well... it must be as big as she says. Who wouldn't want the pocket money? Especially a college student. Anyway, do you think you could do me a favor and give her a job?"

"I'm not hiring."

"I know, I know. It's just that she's been talking about it so much lately—part time, mind you—because she has to attend school. You were one of the first people I thought of."

Marcia decided to throw in some bait.

" I'm a decent person. Don't they say the fruit doesn't fall far from the tree? She's a good worker; I can promise you that. You see how I run my meetings here. I'm telling you, Benny, she's just like me that way. Efficient and organized. And she really is a nice person."

"I don't know." Benny's tone made clear that he'd rather not oblige the request.

"Benny, please. What harm could it do to interview her? If you don't like what you see, you'll just say no."

Benny thought about it some more. Marcia and her group were regular patrons, supporting his business. Couldn't he return the favor somehow? He caved in.

"I'll tell you what…have her stop by tomorrow evening, let's say about seven, and I'll talk to her then. No promises, though. You understand? No promises."

"Benny, you're an angel. You won't regret it."

Somehow, he already did.

"Danny, can you spare a minute? I have some good news."

Marcia had waited until she heard a break in Daniella's piano playing. She knew by now that her daughter would be extremely upset if she interrupted her in the middle of a piece of music. Marcia had timed her question to begin the moment Daniella struck her ending chord.

Daniella turned herself around on the piano bench and looked up at her mother. "Sure. You can share your good news. I was just finishing, anyway."

"Honey, please don't be mad at me. I know you were thinking about employment, and so I got brave and asked Benny if he'd consider hiring you. He's willing to speak to you tomorrow evening at seven. It could mean a job, sweetheart."

"Mom, I'm a big girl. Benny's going to think I'm a baby or something, getting my mother to do what I should be doing."

"I don't think he was thinking that. If anything, he was probably thinking I'm a meddling mother."

Daniella looked at her mother pensively. After some quick thinking, she decided anger was inappropriate. Her mother had been attempting to save her the hassle of trying to find work, and everyone said that Benny was a doll. Wouldn't that make him a great boss? Think of the tips she could earn!

"I'm not mad, Mom. Thanks for doing that. I'll definitely go and give it my best shot." Daniella gave her mother a juicy hug.

Marcia never knew with her kids. One minute they loved her, and the next minute they were demons, hell-bent on making her miserable. Daniella was a young lady though, and Marcia's gut instinct had proved correct. Daniella's childish behaviors were mostly a thing of the past. Marcia's darling little girl was now just two weeks shy of twenty, and the proof was in the pudding. More and more, Daniella handled herself in a mature manner.

Realizing her role of meddling mother had morphed into that of helpful mom, Marcia planted a kiss on Daniella's cheek.

"That's about it, then. I don't want to keep you from anything, honey. Just be sure to keep me posted." Marcia went into the kitchen to resume her dinner preparations.

Daniella turned to leave the den. As she walked past the piano, she softly stroked the keys above high C. She closed the piano's lid with the gentlest of movements and stepped outside onto the family's deck.

The air outside was becoming colder by the minute, but she didn't mind at the moment, despite the fact that she had no sweater on. She breathed in the crisp oxygen, noting how it lifted the scent of the neighbor's fireplace from next door. Sighing in response to the heavenly smell, Daniella couldn't help but think, *If Benny gives me a job, my problems will be solved.*

A sense of calm wrapped itself around her, and she sat down on the nearby deck chair to enjoy the peacefulness of the outdoors, despite the biting chill in the air. She hugged herself with her arms to keep warm. She'd be brief. Just a moment alone so she could gather her thoughts, and then she'd go back inside.

She still wasn't quite ready to divulge the reason behind her eagerness to gain employment. She sat there and contemplated it once more, as she'd done so many times before. Eventually, she'd have to come clean and be honest with her family. Eventually, she'd have to be brave and tell her parents she planned to become a cantor.

All through her high school years, Daniella had been sure she'd become a music teacher. She had been blessed with a rich alto voice that people said flowed like cream. Several folks even insisted she sounded like an angel. Her music teachers told her she had perfect pitch and was a mezzo-soprano extraordinaire. They encouraged her, actually begged her, to take voice lessons and fine-tune her voice to perfection.

She had always loved to listen to music, to perform it, and even to practice it for as far back as she could remember. Most likely, she had inherited the musical gift from her father. How many times had his violin playing brought her to tears? Ira Sobler could pick up his violin at a moment's notice and play right alongside someone—anyone, for that matter—without ever glancing at the music. He'd just listen and begin to play, same key, same style, same everything. Sheer unadulterated notes fell on the ears of all who listened to him play. For him, it was just a hobby. For Daniella, it was bittersweet, knowing he could have done so much more with his talent. Regardless, she adored his God-given gift. She could do no more than thank the Almighty regularly that fate allowed her to inherit at least some of his talent.

Lately, Daniella had serious thoughts about teaching music in a much less expected way. Her dream of becoming a cantor was solidifying in her mind daily, and she knew in her heart it was the path she wanted to take. She had always been spiritual, and she'd had a deep sense of belief in God even from a young age. Now, those thoughts and feelings were guiding her in a very specific direction.

It had only been a matter of time before she processed those feelings and realized they resided at the very core of her being. How wonderful, then, if she could praise God with the very gift given to her by the master of the universe. If she could help others feel praise through her voice, she would achieve her deepest desire—to feel connected to the ineffable essence that was God, simply through the sound she could create. She could think of nothing more fulfilling, and she wanted it more than ever.

Cantorial training was far from inexpensive. Daniella knew her parents could handle the cost, but not without some difficulties. David had just finished school, and Miriam, being the youngest, would be entering college in the fall. Daniella herself still had a little over a year to go. Wouldn't it be wonderful if she could help even in a small way? A job down at the Daily would most definitely help fill the kitty. If she got a job and earned great tips, she could save her pennies over the next year and help fund her dream.

For the time being, the family thought she was finishing her third year of college with the intention of graduating after one more. She would earn a bachelor's degree in music education and the necessary teaching credentials that went with it. A teaching job would come next, and to ensure she could make ends meet, she'd provide private music instruction to increase her income. That had been the plan.

Daniella would come clean soon. She had to. It would be unfair to misguide the family. She just didn't want to catch her parents off guard. Hopefully, they wouldn't fret too much about it, thinking that she'd get all religious on them. Daniella was too steeped in her Conservative upbringing to ever suddenly believe that, as a woman, she couldn't take on the role of cantor.

She looked upward and said a quick silent prayer of thanks for her placement in the Sobler family. In the Orthodox world, her dream would be next to impossible. At least in the Conservative world it stood a chance. In any case, the journey was about to begin. Step one, get a job. Step two, break the news to her parents as soon as possible. Step three, start to save all the money she could and, hopefully, obtain loans for cantorial training. Step four, hope and pray that her dream would come true. Sometime in the year ahead, she'd know for sure if she was about to begin a cantorial career.

Daniella got up from the deck chair and went back inside to work on the paper that was due in class next Thursday. As she climbed the steps to her room, she began to hum her favorite Purim tune. The holiday wasn't until the middle of March, but Daniella was feeling the spirit.

Marcia Sobler apparently overheard her daughter and shouted out to Daniella's retreating figure. "You're making me want to spin a *grogger* and eat *Hamantaschen*."

Daniella smiled, thinking to herself, *Isn't that what a cantor is supposed to do? I'm invoking the holiday spirit of Purim and making you want to be a part of it!* She responded to her mother's comment with a simple word.

"Good."

*D*aniella walked through the doors of the Daily Diner at 7:00 p.m. She spied Nate leaning against the cashier counter, flipping through a newspaper. Daniella supposed that with the dinner hour winding down, the evening rush was over and Nate was free to relax. Indeed, the restaurant was rather empty at the moment. Enough that the phrase "hear a pin drop" would likely prove correct if Nate had bothered to drop one.

He was absorbed in some personal inner space at the moment. Flipping pages one after the other, he bent his head far enough forward that he did not see Daniella's entrance in his peripheral vision. Daniella's friendly demeanor broke the spell as she walked over and began to speak.

"Mr. Holmes, I'm so sorry to disturb your reading. I'm Daniella Sobler. I'm supposed to meet with Mr. Kalabokas and talk about employment."

Nate knew all about the planned meeting. It didn't matter to him one way or the other, so he was just as happy to let Benny deal with it. He closed the paper as he replied, "Well, hello. Didn't see you come in. Welcome. Benny is in the kitchen. I'll go get him for you. Why don't you have a seat in the booth over there while you're waiting."

Nate exited through the kitchen doors. When he returned and resumed his post at the front counter, he spoke loudly enough for Daniella to hear across the small span between her booth and the front register.

"He'll be right with you, dear. Probably no more than a minute or two."

Having declared that, Nate was more than surprised when Benny came through the kitchen doors, took one look at Daniella sitting in the booth, and then turned with a look of shock on his face that harbored shades of despair. Benny was heading for the spare room in the back of the restaurant, and his pace indicated there was a problem. Nate was hard pressed to figure out what it could be. The restaurant was running like clockwork that evening. There had been no arguments, no back orders, no nothing. The problem couldn't possibly be the melody the young woman was humming under her breath, could it?

Nate heard the distant thud of the office door. It meant Benny had slammed the door shut. Whatever the problem was, it was huge. Nate was not about to head down there and try to comfort his partner with, "What's wrong, Benny? Are you all right?" He'd give Benny five minutes for solace before heading back to the office. In the meantime, he'd do what the two had done countless times. He'd have Benny's back. Nate walked over to Daniella's booth.

"Benny must have discovered some type of issue in the kitchen. He's gone to the office to take care of it. I'm sure he won't be long. Are you in a rush?"

Daniella stopped her wordless tune and replied, "No, not at all."

"Fine, fine. Can I get you something?"

"No, thank you. I'll just wait."

Nate smiled and returned to the front counter. Once more, he flipped pages as Daniella sat patiently and hummed her little tune. The melodic thrum was so soft that Nate could barely hear it, yet he enjoyed the pleasant tune just the same, thinking to himself that she had a lovely voice.

Benny had cloistered himself in the safety of his office. When he had exited the kitchen, he had glanced over to Daniella, and the vision had shaken him to the core. He had wanted an initial look at the young lady who Marcia Sobler insisted was a real gem of a girl, and instead, he got the surprise of his life. Emotion had a field day, and he could barely catch his breath.

A young woman with deep brown wavy hair and a slightly sallow complexion, not unlike that of many a Greek, was sitting at the booth. She was humming a mindless tune while she sat and waited. He could hear it despite the distance between them. The melody was pleasant, and Benny could swear he heard tones reminiscent of Middle Eastern music.

She had a pretty face, with full cheeks and a slender, Romanesque nose that ended with a soft, rounded tip. Benny noted that she had a slight resemblance to the actress Hedy Lamarr. A very pretty Hedy Lamarr. For Benny, that meant a resemblance to his mother. The young lady's soft humming clinched the resemblance, and Benny was overwhelmed.

Benny went over to his desk to sit down. He picked up the small double frame that rested at the corner of his desk and looked at the photos of his mother and father. His eyes watered up as he held the frame in his hand and recalled the soft humming he had just heard outside. For sacred moments, Benny stepped back in time. He was resting in the nook of his mother's arms as they lay together in his bed.

"My sweet Benjamin, you mean more to me than life itself. Tonight will be the last time I can tuck you into bed."

"Why, Mama?"

"Things are very bad in Greece. Things are bad all over Europe. Especially for the Jews. Your father and I are sending you and your sister somewhere safe."

"Why can't you come with us?"

"I know it sounds crazy, but you'll actually be safer without us. You must promise me to pretend you're Greek Orthodox. Learn whatever rituals or prayers you can from the people who will take care of you. You must fool everyone into thinking you are a Greek Orthodox child. Keep your Jewishness secret. Help Hannah. She will be too young to understand."

Benny began to cry. "Mama, I don't want you to leave me."

"I know, my little darling. I don't want to either, but this is for the best. I'll tell you what. Whenever you feel sad, remember this moment right now. Remember me holding you just like this and how much I love you. Remember how proud I am of you. Always hear me telling you, you can do anything, my beautiful son. Never let anyone tell you otherwise. Remember, sweetheart, my love is stronger than anything in this whole wide world. It will help you when you feel sad."

With that, she began a wordless humming lullaby and rocked Benny as her own eyes welled up with tears. He even felt one of the salty droplets fall into his hair and find its way down his own cheek. He fell asleep in the comfort of his mother's arms.

When Benny awoke the following morning, bags had already been packed for him and Hannah. His clever mother had sewn the small double frame into the lining between suitcase and interior. She had also sewn in a locket with two small pictures, which Benny instinctually knew was meant for Hannah to wear. Those items eventually became the only pieces of testimony to prove his parents had ever existed. They had become his only way of recalling the faces of his mother and father.

Still clutching the delicate frame, Benny closed his eyes and began to relive his own history. Benny descended from Romaniote ancestry. His family hailed from the Jews of Ioannina, a Romaniote community in northwest Greece near Albania. The Jews of that region had preserved traditional values and maintained an immensely strong connection to them. They kept their values intact, in fact, until the Nazis took it all away.

Approximately 90 percent of his family's community perished because of animals who dared to call themselves human beings. They were nothing more than thugs and murderers that stole Benny's childhood right out from under him. Only by God's good graces did he, his uncle, and his sister survive. Benny's stomach began to churn as he recalled his past. He could practically taste the bile building in his gut.

A mere stroke of luck had his uncle up in the hills and away from the rest of the family when the Nazis came trudging through. His uncle had gone to help a local farmer review his finances from the past year and project his financial needs for the coming year. Uncle Solomon was good that way. A whiz with numbers, despite any formal training.

The locals knew it. They appreciated Solomon's honesty and the modest sum he requested as payment for his services. They considered him an exception among Jews. Many of the locals who were outwardly anti-Semites admitted deep down that he was good, kind, and all the things a decent human being should be.

The family who had hired him on simply lied when the Nazis inquired as to who he was. He was a cousin, they said. He was a farmer just like them, they said. His classic Greek features did not look different from those of the folks who had hired him. The soldiers, who had little if any understanding of Greek, accepted the information after testing Solomon with basic Greek questions.

In later years, Uncle Solomon always found that part of their personal history laughable. In his opinion, their mispronunciation and poor accent should have made them the ones to be arrested for their inability to speak the local dialect. Uncle said they sounded foolish. He thought it shameful to see men following orders by rote, giving no thought as to what they had been asked to do.

During one of their many reminiscing sessions, Uncle had told Benny that the Nazis actually seemed relieved to finally leave the Greek hills. It was difficult to navigate the many rolls and ridges of their area in Greece, and the Nazis were not familiar with the lay of the land. It was too bad that they hadn't used that reason to refuse to invade the area in the first place. The outcome might have been different.

The Nazis' inability to speak Greek beyond the basics made them irritable and nasty. They often took their frustrations out by pulling some helpless Jew aside and shooting him or her right there on the road. They were especially fond of doing this when they were in the more populated areas. They seemed to relish forcing people to witness their power and control. Uncle had told him more than once that it was a blessing that Benny didn't witness these sad events.

As for Benny and his sister, Uncle Solomon had eventually told him that his parents had begged acquaintances from another area to take the children and keep them safe until things settled down. Once again, a combination of kindness and language barrier formed the winning hand in keeping them alive and well and far removed from Nazi clutches. That, and a sense that Jewish children were somehow exempt from the stereotypes their Greek neighbors placed onto their adult counterparts.

Thinking on it now, Benny could still recall that his caretakers never belittled him or Hannah. They didn't make him feel poorly about being Jewish and they certainly never tried to force him to convert to their religion. Perhaps his mother and father had known they were kind that way. Perhaps, it was just dumb luck.

Benny realized he would never know. His conclusion caused him to refocus on his memories of his past.

By some great miracle, Uncle Solomon located the children when the Great War was about to become a thing of the past. At that time, Benny learned he and Hannah were orphans. There he was, a young boy who was simply trying to make his way in life, and in an instant he took on the role of orphan and head of his family. In late 1944, Benny was a mere boy of ten, and his sister, Hannah, was only seven.

When the end of the war finally came in 1945, both youngsters felt as if childhood had perished too. To this very day, Benny's ire over what was stolen from him, burned inside of him like a raging fire. Feeling the sensation building up, he worked to calm himself and turned his thoughts to how his life continued from that point.

Uncle Solomon made clear they would fight tooth and nail to gain passage to the United States and leave Greece altogether. The homeland, he said, was nothing more than a place of memories filled with misery. He and the children were ghosts who no longer belonged there.

Uncle's passion lay in Palestine, but the Middle East still contained too much unrest after the war. The fighting was bad enough, and the poor treatment of Jews by Arabs, and even by the British, left a bad taste in his mouth. It reminded him too much of the horrors they had finally escaped. Much as the promise of a future Jewish homeland enticed him, Uncle Solomon had had enough of brutality, and he knew he had to place his hopes elsewhere.

Uncle could not bear the thought of living in tents on a territory that was still not the land of the Jews.

With Hitler dead and gone (*he should rot in hell, him and every Nazi that ever lived*), Uncle Solomon felt they would only feel safe in the States. There, they could be free, and they could build a new life far away from the evils of Europe.

True to his word, Uncle Solomon achieved the seemingly insurmountable goal of emigration. All three family members gained passage to the States. They did so through the help of members from a Greek community that lay in the heart of the city that would eventually become home to Benny.

Earlier in the twentieth century, that unique community had begun to build itself via a small but strong synagogue of Greek Jews. Bless that synagogue forever because they did more than their share to help the orphaned Greek children obtain passage to America.

Uncle had a viable occupation, so he was allowed to sail with Benny and Hannah and gain sponsorship from the synagogue in the United States. Well, Uncle did lie a bit about his work background, but no one asked him to prove he was an accountant in Greece. With all the turmoil, so many records regarding Jews were completely destroyed or simply lost. There was really no way to prove whether Uncle told the truth or not.

Once assured that a new life was underway for the hapless trio, Uncle Solomon extracted promises from Benny and Hannah. All three of them needed to forge ahead, he had said. They needed to rebuild the family and be successful. No one, he had said, had the right to dictate what they could or couldn't be. They would choose their own way, and that's how they would stick it to the Nazis. They would thrive in the United States. Show the bastards that despite their best efforts, Jews remained, alive and successful.

Benny closed his eyes and easily returned to that harbor of long ago. He pictured his uncle bending at the knees, looking up at Hannah and him, as the two youngsters stood side by side. There was uncle, grasping Benny's right arm and Hannah's left one as the two of them pressed together and stared down into Uncle's eyes. Benny could still feel his uncle's hand clutching his bicep and squeezing with intent. The Greek words were emblazoned in his mind.

"Children, you were very good. Especially, when we gave our names. I'm so proud of you!"

It had been the first time the family could proudly declare their given names. They made a pact that when they reached the shores of the United States, they would state their birth names as the first step of many in their new lives. They would declare the names given to them at their births and erase the names forced upon them when they lived in Greece.

Solomon had encountered anti-Semitism many times when he dealt with life in the towns of Greece, and the children had seen their fair share as well, no matter that they were so young at the time. It went all the way down to the use of names. In Greece, outside the confines of their home, they were known as Solon, Bryon, and Ana (which was actually short for Anasthasia). Heaven forbid they proudly display their Judaism. The ridicule and teasing would have been endless. Time in a Greek school and the ability to converse fluently in Greek helped all three to pass for the average citizen and avoid many skirmishes that would have resulted if they had insisted on being overly Jewish.

Benny remembered Uncle's grasp getting even tighter as he continued.

"Children, this is the start of our new life. Always remember what we pledged to do. Never forget. Never ever forget what the Nazis did to the Jews. To our family. And you, Benjamin, you must carry on the name of Kalabokas. I'm your mother's brother, and I can't do that for you. It is your legacy, and a great task you must be sure to complete. Make your parents proud."

Uncle had been young enough himself that he could find a wife and give Benny and Hannah new cousins. Aunt Esther was ten years Solomon's junior, but the age difference ensured they would have a chance to have many children. Indeed, Hannah and Benny had five wonderful cousins. Aunt and Uncle took fantastic care of all the children, providing love and support and, in Benny and Hannah's case, the safety they so desperately needed.

Benny realized he was becoming too engrossed in his yesteryear. He was foolishly opening old wounds and for what reason? It was simply coincidence that the young lady waiting for him resembled his mother. What good does it do to sit and replay painful memories? Benny looked at the clock on his desk. He had been reminiscing for five minutes. He felt terrible about keeping the young lady waiting and knew it was time to leave the office.

Benny took a deep breath, collected his thoughts, and placed the frame back down onto his desk. In fairness, he could not approach the young lady as if she were the ghost of his mother. Wasn't there a saying of some sort that we each have seven doppelgängers in the world? People who genetically end up with a similar combination of DNA that causes resemblance even when they're not related? The girl out there was not his mother.

Benny walked to the booth where Daniella sat. Her eyes met his, and she got up to stand beside the booth. Benny put his hand out for a good shake. The firm grip impressed him, and he pocketed the impression in his mind. A handshake opened a window to a person's character, and hers said she was not a wimp. Marcia had said as much when she commented that her daughter possessed qualities akin to hers.

"Come, let's sit down in the booth and have a good chat. And please, call me Benny."

Once he was seated, Benny shouted loudly, "Marilyn, bring over two teas and a plate of cookies."

Looking at Daniella, Benny asked, "That OK with you?" and he began the same routine he'd used on other potential hires.

"So, you need a job. Tell me why I should give you one." Benny smiled to let Daniella know he was not being facetious. Despite that, her answer practically floored him. It was the last thing he expected to hear.

"I want to be a cantor. I need to earn money so I can help my folks pay for my chance to become one."

That was enough, just then and there. She could have possessed an awful character, and he still would have hired her. *A young lady who dreams of being a cantor. Who could imagine such a thing?* Benny knew egalitarianism was obtaining a stronghold in the Conservative branch of Judaism. Like an oil slick penetrating the surface of an ocean, it had already begun to spread through the Reform movement. It was simply a matter of time before Conservatives embraced it as well.

Yes, he was Sephardic in his own traditions. Yes, he leaned heavily toward Orthodoxy, but that was simply because it resembled the religious belief system of his childhood days in Greece. In many ways, he himself leaned toward Conservative thinking. Despite his upbringing, he knew in his heart that Judaism denied women too many opportunities, and they deserved equal religious rights.

Subconsciously, he was already thinking of his mother and her desire to be somebody in life. He could practically hear her arguing, "Sure, I'm good enough to cook and clean, but head a committee for our village's political rights…Heaven forbid you men admit that women can do much the same as men can and that I'd do a better job than you. That's really what is at the heart of the matter. I know it. You men are just afraid."

Benny knew he supported the idea of allowing women the same rights and privileges that men had. Not only in the workplace and daily life but certainly in the context of religion. Anything, anything to perpetuate Judaism. If a woman must do it, so be it. He already wanted Daniella to succeed.

"If it's not too forward, may I ask why you want to be a cantor?"

"I don't mind your asking. It might be hard to explain, though." Daniella paused. "But I'll try."

"Fine."

"I was blessed with the gift of music. I have perfect pitch. I can put emotion into my music. I know this about myself."

Daniella paused again just to be sure she saw no judgment in Benny's eyes. Her words did sound conceited, after all. She added, "I'm not bragging, Benny. I just know it's true.

"I also know the source of the wonderful gift that is my talent. I want to use my voice to praise the creator of the instrument that is my voice. Hopefully, the bonus will be that people can hear that. Hopefully, it will help others obtain spirituality and beauty in hearing it praise God."

The answer clinched it for Benny. How many times had he reflected on the fact that, as miserable as the Nazi bastards had made his life, those sons of bitches couldn't eradicate him or his people? He was a success despite their assurances that he was subhuman. He took his skills and put them to a productive use. Here was a young lady ready and willing to do the same.

Wasn't he grateful for all the good bestowed upon him through the years? Children, a wonderful wife, his beloved eating establishment. How many times had he thanked God for the gifts he had? That such a young person could understand the source of her entire being… wow! That the essence of the universe, which for lack of a better name we called God, understood Benny and now this young lady, well…

Benny's thoughts began to drift. His mind was racing as it gathered perceptions and feelings from his memory banks. He wanted to compare himself and his own drive to be a success to Daniella Sobler's determination to succeed. For precious seconds, Benny was engrossed in contemplation, sorting out the notions in rapid succession. Luckily, he snapped out of it with the thought that the only thing that was important at the moment, was to hire her.

"That's wonderful, Daniella."

Benny paused before concluding with, "Know what? I'm not even going to ask you anything else. You have a job, young lady. I know I won't be sorry. How soon can you start?"

*B*enny's instincts proved correct. Even during Daniella's first week as an employee, he could see her determination to be a good waitress. He saw snippets of himself in most of Daniella's actions, her jovial manner, and her eagerness to provide good customer service. So much so, that focusing on the papers in front of him proved impossible and Benny found himself remembering how determined he was to succeed as a restaurant owner.

Opening the Daily Diner was likely the best decision Benny had ever made. It did not matter that his homey joint was actually a restaurant. He erected the Daily Diner in the mid-sixties to mimic the look, feel, and dining experience that one could find at a roadside diner. And like a roadside diner, his place had a counter, barstools, and booths for dining. There was even a back room for large parties.

He had built it at a time when folks were moving out of the city in droves. Many insisted that the city was going to pot and that if one were wise, one would leave it behind for the suburbs. Even so, folks craved the comforts of the city life they left behind. They wanted shops and theaters. They required dining experiences and homes that would mimic city standards.

Wasn't a diner the ultimate pit stop? During the sixties, shops, restaurants, churches, synagogues, schools, and so much more were practically mowing down the farms and orchards that stood proudly within the rural strongholds. The Daily Diner was no exception. It stood on what was once an open dirt lot that had housed an annual farmers' market.

Benny had recognized the emptied space for what it was: a crossroads for the world to descend upon. The ideal spot to gather in patrons. As the suburbs had grown, the small roads had turned into main thoroughfares, and Benny's restaurant eventually sat right off the main highway in the busy section of the town.

Benny was one among many in the city's community of Jews who was bold enough to leave the comforts that the city provided. Jews who hoped to start a new community in the surrounding suburbs. Moving far away from the comforts of cloistered neighborhoods was all the rage back in the sixties.

The buzzword rang out in building after building: Move to the country; start life anew. Be bold! Be adventurous! Keep up with the Joneses, and most important, show the world that a Jew can be successful. Every time Benjamin blinked, another so-and-so was leaving. Well, young as he was at that time, he wanted to be a so-and-so too.

He knew that small business stores, the libraries, and even the post offices were places a Jew could enter without fear of affecting their way of life. It was a whole other ball of wax when it came to the markets and restaurants of the suburbs. Jews needed kosher products. They needed restaurants that they could dine in without concern about pork or all things non-kosher. Diet was paramount to living a good Jewish life. A kosher restaurant would be a comfortable blanket around a very young Jewish community. Benny knew that, sure as he knew anything.

In the sixties the suburbs were still part boonies. Acres of land were waiting to be plowed and plundered. Horse farms and orchards filled the area when he and others first started to arrive. He knew the area would grow like a weed and that his fellow Jews would continue to move to the suburbs. They would want places to eat and markets they could shop in, just like any other Joe or Jane in the county. Back then, Benny was more than eager to pursue his dream.

And that had been his big dream! It seemed so long ago now. His restaurant. The space that belonged to him. His Daily Diner. The place where Jews could meet and relax, dine, and feel like royalty. He had dreamed it, and it had come to be.

How good the years had been! Benny chuckled softly and looked upward as he gave God a knowing smile. *I'm a lucky duck, and I know it!* It was yet another moment of confirmation directed specifically toward God's ears. One of Benny's many silent prayers to make sure God knew just how he felt and how grateful he was for the way things worked out. Benny watched Daniella work and he smiled. He could see that she would be an asset to the restaurant.

For a reason he couldn't quite articulate, Benny felt it was Daniella's turn to succeed. He had a strong urge to see that through, though for the life of him, he couldn't quite figure out why. Regardless, he was determined to help her out any way he could and if nothing else, mentor her if the opportunity ever presented itself.

"Daniella, it's almost time to go home. Please ask Marilyn to finish refilling the salt shakers. I want to talk with you about something."

Daniella had been smiling, but her expression changed to a fretful grin as she looked in Benny's direction. Poor kid, she probably thought he had something negative to say about her work. Luckily, he noted the panic etched on her features and felt terrible enough that he fixed the misinterpretation immediately.

"Nothing bad, young lady. Just want to catch up on some things."

"Oh, OK, Benny. I'll finish filling this shaker, but then I'll get Marilyn to do the rest."

When the two were sitting not five minutes later, Benny asked the usual question, which was part and parcel of his style. "Tea and cookies, Daniella?"

"Sure, Benny. I do love those Mexican wedding cake cookies. Could I have two of those?"

"You're proving to be such a good worker. Go ahead, take two. Take three. Take as many as you want!"

Benny gave Daniella's upper back a fatherly pat. "I'll go and get us the tea while you pick out your cookies. Grab me a rainbow cookie while you're at it."

Once they returned to the booth, Benny made clear what catching up meant.

"Daniella, I know we're still getting to know each other, but it has been over three months, and you are quickly becoming very special to me. Something about you, I can't quite explain it. Maybe you remind me of my own three girls. Who knows?"

Benny paused and looked at his young employee. Only his deepest subconscious knew the truth—a truth so overwhelming that it needed to stay hidden and buried. Daniella had drive and ambition like his mother's. She had a face too reminiscent of his mother's. So much so, he had to ignore it altogether.

"I have three daughters, if you can believe it. Anyway, two are already married, and even the third is older than you. It's like I've obtained a fourth daughter all of a sudden. And, of course, I want all my girls to succeed."

Benny paused once more, wondering briefly if he was being too personal. He decided to forge ahead and bring his personal thoughts out into the open.

"I'm trying to say that you're different than the rest of the staff. Most of my waitresses and waiters are older than you. My kitchen staff is all male. Marilyn and Zelda are my only other female servers. A youngster like you is a breath of fresh air here at the Daily Diner.

"But it's more than that. You're also a Jew like me. No, even more than that! You're a Jew that wants to let every last person know you're proud of who you are. In a crazy way, I see myself in you. I would be out in the streets shouting, 'Hooray for Judaism,' if such a thing were acceptable. So, Daniella, I want you to be a success."

"Benny, I barely know what to say. I'm so honored you feel that way."

Benny noticed Daniella's eyes looking misty. He had struck a deep chord. *Amazing*. It made him feel even more committed to the sentiments he had just uttered.

"Well, that's why I want to ask you something. I'm already looking forward to the day I'll be able to call you Cantor Sobler. Think of what you will learn, what you will know. Think of how you can bring Judaism to future generations. It's so wonderful, Daniella."

Benny paused and let a light sigh escape his lips before asking his question.

"I simply wanted to ask if you'd be willing to share your progress in that department. Keep me abreast through the journey. Starting with now. Would that be OK?"

"Of course it would! It means so much that you're even interested."

"Great. Then let's start right now. Have you made any kind of a move in that direction?"

"Yes, I have. In fact, there's a lot to share at this point. So much has happened in the last three months. Can I use the restroom real quick and then catch you up?"

"Of course you can. I'm going to move our things into the extra room. There's no party or meeting at the moment, so we'll have quiet in there. And, Daniella, I really want to thank you. It's I who am honored that you're willing to share your personal life with me."

"Know what? Everyone who is close to me, who is a part of my life, calls me Danny. I'd love it if you called me that too."

"Fine. Danny it is. Now go so we can start talking."

Daniella Sobler was no Sam Greenfeld, one of Benny's favorite customers whose forte was talking shop with Benny. There would be no discussions about running a business or dealing with employees. Daniella represented another aspect of Benny's inner soul. She was the fighter in him. She was the stronghold. For him, the Nazis were the enemy. The Nazis that stole his mother and father right out from under him.

For her, most of Judaism was the adversary, insisting that she couldn't be a cantor. A unique determination set both Benny and Danny apart from everyone else. Both were able to say, and God should forgive the bad language, "Fuck all of you. I'm still here, still determined as ever, and I will get in your face about it. Let God, and not you, judge me. I'm a proud Jew. Deal with it!"

As Benny waited for Daniella's return, he recalled a story he had heard from an elderly woman at his synagogue in the city. A World War II story. The woman said she had always had a good command of the Greek language, and her features were such that it was hard to determine her Greek heritage at all. As a result, during the time of the Nazi occupation, she was sent by a Greek underground movement, a small group at that, to retrieve foodstuffs and bring messages from the nearby main city on more than one occasion.

Eventually, a man named Adamos asked her to travel to other areas in the hopes of passing along information to cities farther out. She told Benny how much she had dreaded riding the train and how much she had feared that she would be found out somehow and then shot on the spot. Whenever a Nazi soldier would enter at a train stop, it was all she could do to stay calm and appear unfazed. She would hold her basket tightly on her lap. Sometimes, she would even offer up a fruit to the soldier as he passed by to check the passengers. She did her best to distract the soldier from intimidating some poor soul.

The fake smile for the soldier, the fake kindness and charm, sickened her to the core. Only God's good graces kept the soldier distracted enough to forego searching the basket for the hidden message resting at the bottom.

The woman spoke of one particular time when she had been on her way to retrieve food from another town, having already passed along several papers earlier that day. She had been far away from home at the time—so far that she feared she would never return to her loved ones.

The train had stopped, and the passenger seated in the same car as her, a woman of Bulgarian origin, had shouted out to the Nazi soldier that had come on board the train. Everyone knew how horrifically anti-Semitic Bulgarians were. It was almost no surprise that the malevolent Bulgarian woman did what she did.

It meant nothing less than doom when the soldier stopped right in front of their car and peered at their seats. The woman told Benny that she could still feel the panicked beating of her heart and the anvil-weighted anxiety as she anticipated her death. Yet, for a reason that the woman said she would never understand to her dying day, the Bulgarian had pointed past her and at a second woman sitting close by the window.

"She's a Jew. I'm sure of it."

Without a single word, the soldier grabbed the poor woman by the arm, brutally pushing her out from the train car. He didn't ask for papers. He didn't ask for an explanation. He didn't question the other woman's accusation or motive. Worst of all, he completely ignored the cries of the captured woman, who consistently and repeatedly declared she was not Jewish at all. That she had no idea why someone would say so.

The poor, frightened woman loosened herself from the soldier's grip and ran to the nearest exit in order to flee the horrendous mistake. All the while, she kept shouting, "I'm not Jewish!" Panic seemed to take hold, and she began to run the moment she stepped onto the platform. The soldier, who ran close behind, stepped down from the train.

It was the next part of the story that always saddened Benny the most. The woman sharing the tale looked up at him with sad eyes. She said, "Benyamin, in that sickened, brainwashed Nazi mind, I am sure the soldier could not comprehend the fact that fear makes people panic. He must have equated the running and screaming with the woman's efforts to sway him from the fact that she was a Jew who was found out. That she was running away to try to save her life. Once he reached that conclusion, the rest was probably easy for him. Nazis thought Jewish life was worthless. You'll never convince me, otherwise. You know that. God was so good to you, Benyamin. You live for that woman and every other Greek Jew lost to the Holocaust."

She continued her story, telling the most gruesome part. Benny remembered the details as if it was a memory of his own.

The unmistakable sound of a gunshot rang out over the click-clacking of the train's wheels as the train slowly pulled away. Without even looking out the window, the woman could picture the collapse of the poor soul to the ground, the astonished looks of the people on the platform. She often wondered if anyone had the courage to speak up. Probably not, and not because they didn't want to but because the soldier had a still-loaded gun in his hand.

In sharing her story, the woman told Benny that she couldn't help but chide the other passenger, who also seemed astonished at the sound of the gunshot. "You must be very proud of yourself. You can go home to your husband, your entire family, and brag about the fact that you just had a hand in murdering an innocent soul. You must feel elated."

The woman knew there was likely a language barrier, and she was determined to get her message across. She stood up as the train rolled gently along, hovered right over the other woman, and kept repeating "Jude" as she pointed with loathing at the Bulgarian woman. In any language, people would understand the word well enough, and she repeated it until she saw the glimmer of fear in the other woman's eyes and the body language that began to acknowledge a recognition of what she had done.

It was the only weapon the woman could use…her words. Yet even on the day she spoke to Benny, it did not seem to be enough. That a person could murder so easily, and for such a meaningless reason, remained beyond anything she could comprehend. To put someone to death for having different religious or cultural beliefs was just as insane as murdering someone for not buttering their muffin at breakfast. She could not comprehend how minor differences could make anyone nonhuman. The thought ate away at her core long ago and festered through the years; she could not process it no matter how hard she tried.

The Bulgarian and the Nazi had both been guilty of murder, plain and simple. At the end of her tale, the woman had asked Benny, "How could no one see that? How could so many people stand idly by?" She had looked at Benny with the saddest eyes he had ever seen since his childhood days. She had concluded with, "That it was acceptable in their eyes is incomprehensible. They were the ones who are not human."

The old Greek woman also told Benny that once she was off the train, she vowed she would never ride one again. To this day, she never boards one. She couldn't understand why she was spared and never would be able to. The guilt of it all was a burden far greater to her than the worst of physical ailments she suffered or the grief over so many lost loved ones. When Benny had heard that, he had felt nothing but gratitude that at least he had been a child at the time and unaware of many of the details of the Nazi occupation throughout Europe.

The worst part of hearing the story had been that the woman who was shot could have easily been Benny's own mother. No one really knew what had happened to either of his parents, only that they had perished. Maybe both his parents' lives came to tragic ends equal to this one.

In any case, the story stuck with Benny and strengthened his resolve of honoring women everywhere, Jewish women more so than others. Of giving them every possible opportunity to live life with safety and comfort. To let privileges be their faithful companions. This was the only way he knew to honor his mother, by helping women stay strong. Maybe that was why God sent him three daughters. Maybe that was why God sent him Daniella. Benny couldn't wait to hear what Daniella would share.

aniella worked backward, so to speak, as she gave Benny her update. She began by letting him know that the reality of confessing her desire to her parents had been far easier than the imaginary version she had built up in her head. They were supportive and actually quite proud of her. Among friends, Marcia in particular was already strutting about her daughter's bravery. About how strong Daniella was given the lack of acceptance of women in Judaic leadership roles.

The concept of a female cantor was still a sore spot in Conservative circles. Even in the Reform movement, women were struggling. In the Conservative movement, however, which in actuality was far closer to Orthodoxy than most would admit, the role of women was contested continually. That fact alone made the Soblers proud of Daniella's conviction.

Benny was quite impressed with the information Daniella shared. She had obviously done her homework. Thinking about it, he was in awe of how complicated things could be in Judaism. For all the uniformity, brotherhood, and common ideology, the dissension in the ranks was over the top.

"This is what I can tell you, Benny. Once my parents gave me the green light to investigate the possibility of cantorial training, I made a lot of phone calls and a lot of inquiries."

Benny found it simply amazing how huge her struggle would be. Daniella had begun by giving him a quick review of the Conservative movement's history, at least in the context of women in leadership roles. She spoke of the Schechters, the couple who were at the forefront of the movement in the early twentieth century. She mentioned that Solomon Schechter had been the president of the esteemed Jewish Theological Seminary from 1902 through 1915 and that his wife, Mathilde, had begun to push for the expansion of women's roles in the synagogue.

"I'm telling you the history Benny, because I'm not sure if many Jews know this. I also found out that the Conservative movement had long advocated equal education for women and equal rights in tending to synagogue viability. I never knew that. Sadly though, it is still grounded in traditional thinking when it comes to the role of rabbi or cantor. Everyone is reluctant to change, aren't they? It means I'm still held back from advancement in the ranks when it comes to all things spiritual in Judaism. Of course, you already know that!"

"Yes. My mother complained about it often enough. Greek Jewish orthodoxy is very clear on suppressing women's roles."

"Well, Mathilde Schechter was determined. She had enabled women to oversee the *kashruth*, the fundraising, and the general business of their synagogues. But nowadays, women like me, and certainly my mother, are far more interested in taking leadership roles than in making sure the congregation is kosher or that the synagogue is viable in terms of business. No disrespect Benny, but it's men that consistently block the way."

Daniella didn't delve into some of the other details she had learned. Even if Benny didn't know the details, he knew the facts. She did want to share one or two extra things, though.

"Benny, there have been some changes that really surprised me. Did you know that in the year 1955, the Conservative movement of Judaism allowed women to be called for an *aliyah*? I certainly didn't!"

The sacred rite of being called up to the Torah was paramount to gaining access to stand on the *bimah* and gaze upon the Torah scroll as another read from it. For someone like Daniella, that was essential.

"Likewise, in 1973, women could be counted in a *minyan*! Even so, my synagogue continues to refute that. It makes me so mad!"

The group of ten men required for saying certain prayers was akin to the cornerstone of an old building. A vital supporting block to say prayers correctly and in the right order. For a woman to be acknowledged in this way and therefore pray alongside men was a huge victory. Yet once again, most conservative synagogues were funded by traditionalists who refused to move with the times.

Judaism always professed the obligations males had to God, to one's fellow man, and to the world. Women, for the first time, could prove they were equally obligated if only they were allowed to do so. It was evident that the struggles would continue.

"Here's something I learned from my cantor. A rabbi by the name of Joel Roth created what was called the Roth *Teshuvah*, which was a responsa to the dilemma of women who wanted to be ordained in the religion. In a nutshell, it made clear that if a woman was fully committed to and willing to take on all those obligations formerly expected only of men, then she should be allowed the privilege of doing so. Timely, for me, wouldn't you say so!

"Anyway, this declaration frustrated enough traditionalists in the Conservative movement that they decided to create yet another group in the world of Judaism. They call themselves the Union of Traditional Conservative Judaism and they're committed to the idea that women cannot take on certain roles. Boy, would I like to give them a piece of my mind!"

Daniella laughed as she relayed that to Benny.

"Of course you know Danny, in the Orthodox movement, none of this is acceptable or possible at all. You know that everything in Orthodoxy is very black and white, and certainly traditional. Follow all the rules, no questions asked!"

Benny knew Daniella well enough to know the result of obtaining this information. It would be the fodder that would push her further to achieve her dream. Nonetheless, he couldn't help but ask how in the world she could make it all happen if so many people thought women couldn't be cantors.

"Danny, what does that mean for you? How will you reconcile the fact that a good part of our people think you're crazy to want to even try to become a cantor?"

"Well, I did do a bit more digging and found out that as far back as 1952, women were being accepted into cantorial and Jewish music programs, but we're still not allowed the privilege of becoming a *hazzan*."

Daniella rolled the *ch* sound classic in so many Hebrew words, slowly and deliberately, as if emphasizing her point. She continued her explanation.

"The diploma for *hazzanut* is given only to men. It's causing a huge uproar at this point in time, and it's being debated hotly even as we speak. I have to believe that someday soon, it will change for the better. After all, how crazy is it to teach women all about *davening* or *Halacha* but withhold a title from them? I can be fully educated in prayer and law, but they won't call me *hazzan*? There can be no such person as Cantor Sobler? That's crazy, Benny."

"So, Danny, what do you do then?"

"Well, I still try to get into some type of program, learn all I can learn, and hope and pray that by the time I'm finished with my education, things will have changed."

"Is that even possible?"

"I think so. I contacted the Jewish Theological Seminary to find out what someone like me needs to do to get into a program, and you know what? It's all doable."

"Meaning?"

"Meaning, I should still get my bachelor's in music education because you have to have a four-year college degree before you apply. I should also try to refresh my studies in basic Hebrew, Judaic history, and any other Jewish subject that might help me get a foot in the door because part of the admission process involves being tested for those things.

"I should apply as I get halfway through my last year of college, and if God is rooting for me, Benny, I'd start the following fall. I'll worry about getting the title of *hazzan* later. For now, let me at least get into a program. It literally gives me about a year to get things going. I already can read and write Hebrew, so I just need to improve my comprehension. I certainly know the flow of services and basic Judaic history. I'm practically fluent in Yiddish, courtesy of my family. That's gotta be a bonus somehow…or at least I hope so."

Daniella laughed. "Wow, who would have thought? Hebrew School and going to *shul* to participate in services paid off after all. I can do it, Benny. I know I can." She gave Benny a look etched with determination.

Benny smiled and replied, "And I believe you will."

Something intangible happened during the conversation over tea and cookies. The dynamic between Benny and Daniella changed permanently. It was as if an invisible thread wove them together to create a sense of family. Common heritage, common ideology, common fortitude to remain strong as the underdog. Ashkenazi and Sephardi united as one for the sake of Judaism.

The notion was laughable to Benny when he thought about it, because it was a longstanding thorn in the side that neither group was fond of the other's practices. Yet now, their differences had been overridden by the simple fact that all Jews were the underdog. He and Daniella were more than employer and employee. They were pals. They were adopted kin.

Benny remained blind to the fact that much of his motivation to care for her welfare stemmed from his subconscious memories. Her thick, wavy hair, her bright eyes, her determination to see things get done. All were morsels that made the image clear in Benny's mind, yet there was no acknowledgement of the parallel's existence. Daniella would succeed. That was all that mattered. Benny's thoughts were interrupted when Daniella came flitting over, happy and chipper.

"How's about another evening of tea and cookies? I'd love a chance to ask you some questions, now. Maybe learn more about your history. What do you think?"

"That sounds nice. Sure, Danny. Just let me know when you're done wiping down the menus."

It was an hour later when Benny and Daniella were sitting in Benny's go-to booth, sipping hot tea and munching on cookies.

"So what did you want to know?"

"Well…, how did it come to be that you decided to open a kosher restaurant in a county that has none except in the ultra-orthodox neighborhoods?"

Benny laughed. "Is that all? I'm happy to tell you the history of my restaurant."

With that, Benny shared his long-winded tale. Oddly enough, Daniella was hanging on every word, quite interested in the story he was willing to share.

"My uncle Solomon's skill with numbers had landed him a job at a small bank about a year or so after we arrived in the United States. As time progressed, Uncle moved up the ladder. It took several years, but eventually he became a successful and vital member of one of the most prestigious banks in the heart of the city. I was very proud of him.

"In fact, it was my uncle's job that helped form the kernel of an idea in my mind about the possibility of owning a restaurant. You know…banks gave loans, and I had the good fortune to personally know a banker."

Benny leaned in closer over the edge of the table as if he were about to share a great secret.

"Actually, I got the initial idea for a restaurant from my surname, of all things! I knew enough about Greek history and language to know exactly what my last name meant. Even how my family likely came to have it.

"There had been an influx of Italians, Sicilian Jews, to be precise, into Greece in the latter part of the fifteenth century. *Kala* means good in Greek, and *boca* means mouth in Italian. Historians surmised that the last name was created to indicate one who was proficient in rhetoric. Add to that the fact that *a-s* and *o-s* were often added to Greek names to Hellenize them, and there you had it: Kalabokas.

"I don't know which ancestor had merited the name, but genetics made me a charmer in my own right."

Daniella interjected. "Everyone knows that, Benny."

"Well, shouldn't a restaurant owner possess such a quality? Talk nice to the customers. That sort of thing.

"Anyway, on a day when I was feeling particularly brave, I approached Uncle Solomon and asked if I could obtain a business loan through the bank. I used my best words to explain that I wanted to open a restaurant that looked like a diner." Benny paused for effect and spoke with the same authority he used all those years ago.

"I said something like this: Diners are iconic in the northeastern United States. Everyone wants to go to one for good eats. The Jews should be able to have a place for good eats too. A kosher restaurant that resembles a diner." Benny laughed, incredulously.

"That laugh was my uncle's response. For awhile there, I thought I wouldn't be able to get through to him."

"So how did you?"

"Well, when my uncle calmed himself, he said, 'Benny, tell me one Greek Jew you know who owns a diner. Greeks who own or manage diners, sure. They're a dime a dozen! But not even one of them is a Jew. You're a Greek who is a Jew...Benjamin, that's like the freak in a sideshow. You'll be an oddity. It's crazy.'

"True to my surname, which I told you means proficient in rhetoric, I began to feed my uncle food for thought with the simple reply: and if I become the main attraction...

"I gave him every possible reason as to why the restaurant would be a success, including a promise that I'd make it classy enough that it would not be much like a diner at all. Only the decor would create a diner-like image. There would be such a homey atmosphere that people would be eager to come in, eat, and relax.

"So here we are, all these years later. Do you think I achieved my goal, Daniella?"

"Absolutely, Benny. The restaurant is wonderful. It's almost magical."

"Now, you're being proficient with words."

"No, really. I can't explain it. There's a certain sense of comfort here."

Hours later, Benny sat in the quiet of his kitchen, Rose having gone to bed fifteen minutes prior. He replayed his conversation with Daniella over in his mind, smiling all the while. There were things he left out. Things he wouldn't share with anyone.

His determination to open the restaurant was for his parents' sake, especially for his mother's. To the rest of the world, he referred to her as *Metera*. Deep inside, the little boy who lost her long ago thought of her only as *Mana*. His mommy. His mommy who always made him believe he could accomplish anything. He could still remember her raven hair falling in soft waves around her shoulders. He loved to touch the soft curls, and he relished the look in his mother's eyes as she told him she loved him more than he could possibly comprehend.

He needed to succeed so that he wouldn't let his mother down. He needed to achieve and do so with pride and conviction. *You were right. I can do anything, Mana.* With no collateral, no personal investments, no equity, no nothing, he used no more than his charm twenty some odd years ago, to get Uncle Solomon to cosign on that loan. Benny sighed as he recalled how he finally convinced his uncle to act on his hopeful whim. He played the conversation over in his mind as he stood to pour himself a glass of orange juice.

"Be a part owner, Uncle. It's the least I can do to say thank you for all you've done for me, and besides, I'd be keeping my promise to you to be a success and show what a Jew can do. I'll make you proud. And think of it, a place for the Jewish community to be able to dine up in the suburbs. The area is growing like a weed, I tell you. I can even make Greek food its specialty. Think of what a novelty the place could be." It took three more years to pass after that fateful conversation, before Benny broke ground for the Daily Diner.

Benny turned his thoughts to Nate. He smiled, thinking of his close friend and partner. Benny and Uncle

Solomon had agreed they needed a third partner if the restaurant was to be truly successful and that was why Nate owned the restaurant with him. They would need an owner who was not bound by Judaic rules and regulations. A person who could handle things when they could not.

Jewish law and tradition took precedence at all times, even when owning a kosher restaurant. On Jewish holidays, better to have a non-Jew overseeing the business, despite the fact that the doors to the establishment would be closed. On those days, Nate would be the go-to man when there was a plumbing disaster or electrical crisis or any other such emergency. It had all worked out so well.

Another thing he didn't bother to tell Daniella was that The Daily Diner was his personal way to perpetuate his Judaism. Uphold the laws at all times, even in the guise of running a restaurant. Judaism was at the forefront for him, always. *How stupid could the Nazis be? In wanting to rid the world of Jews, they made us more determined than ever to thrive.*

He also didn't bother to share that once the contracts were signed, Uncle Solomon confessed that he really had no interest in running a restaurant at all. He wanted Benny and Nate to run it together and leave him to his financial workings.

Forgetting that Rose had gone to bed, Benny began to laugh and stated out loud, "Nate, you have become quite the expert on Judaic laws of *kashruth* and the holidays." Benny shook his head as if to emphasize the conclusion.

Benny was at the restaurant every day except the Jewish Sabbath or other major Jewish holidays that required time off. The restaurant was closed on those days. It was just easier that way. Benny could only imagine...the shame of an establishment touting the fact that it was kosher while remaining open on a Jewish holiday. He would never have heard the end of it, and folks would have been sure to spread the word that Benny talked the talk but didn't walk the walk.

For years now, Nate closed the restaurant on Fridays and Benny would stay home to prepare for the Sabbath. The time of the closing depended on the time of the year, or to be more precise, on the time when the sun set. Nate returned to the restaurant on Saturday evenings about an hour before sunset in order to handle the tasks that would have fallen to Benny any other day of the week. It never failed that, by the dark hours of a Saturday night, the restaurant was once again ready to feed the masses, hopping with activity as folks came in for a bite after shopping or taking in a movie.

Nate was rewarded by having every Sunday off. He could go to church Sunday mornings and have his own share of Sabbath rest. Since the diner closed for Jewish holidays that Nate had never even heard of (at least not initially), he had more than his fair share of time off to relax. The bonus in all the holiday rigmarole was that Easter always fell within the same week as Passover, and that meant an entire week off for Nate and Benny both.

Customers often told both men that they hated the fact that the restaurant closed so many times during the year. It was mostly the non-Jewish customers doing the complaining but occasionally, the Jewish ones did too. The toughest time was always the Passover week. A kosher establishment would not remain open during

Passover unless it had been completely and properly pre-pared for that holiday. The task of preparing a home for Passover was monumental, so to prepare an entire res-taurant would be staggering.

Benny always worked Christmas Eve and Day, which was especially nice for all the Jewish customers who had no place to go. Stores and theaters were closed on Christmas Day in the sixties. Everything in the county closed for Christmas back then. It wasn't until the late seventies that things like movie theaters and restaurants began to stay open. For the longest time, Benny had a grand monopoly. Now it was a thing of the past because everyone stayed open during Christmas, in order to rake in the bucks!

The co-owners split the rest of the calendar year equally, sometimes being in the restaurant together to meet and greet everyone who walked through their doors. Folks seemed to like when they worked side by side. Benny did, too. They were the Mutt and Jeff of res-taurant ownership. Benny had the role of the outspoken one. Nate, the quiet one.

Benny realized he never told Daniella why he chose the name, the Daily Diner. He would be sure to tell her the next time she was scheduled to work. Benny smiled and drank the last two gulps of his juice. He headed down the hall to wash up and get ready for bed. As he stared into the mirror, watching himself brush his teeth, he thought about what he would say to her.

I wanted the restaurant to be a place where people felt they could come any day—every day, in fact. A place where they could come daily. That we were here for them always, open and waiting and welcoming. Even if all that person wanted was a cup of coffee and a kind word, I was ready to give it daily. I'd treat them as if they stepped into a four-star restaurant! And if someone came in every day, weren't they a daily diner? They're a daily diner at the Daily Diner!

Even Nate agreed it was a catchy name. Uncle Solomon had liked it, too. Over time, people began to refer to the restaurant as the Daily. It truly became exactly what Benny had always hoped for. A social haven for the local Jewish community, with assurance that they could eat the food that was served. In essence, then, it was a place where anyone and everyone, in the county or beyond, could feel at home and feed the belly with good, wholesome food.

Benny crawled into bed as quietly as he could. He tried to stop thinking about the restaurant. He tried to stop contemplating the rationale behind so many of the decisions he had made through the years but he was on a roll. His thoughts brought him to his choice of decor and then, to his decisions about the food he served.

The style of the restaurant had been sitting like a solid rock in his brain from the get-go. It was simply a matter of convincing Nate, and Uncle Solomon too, about the practicality of his many ideas. The very first of which was that the restaurant would house a meat kitchen only. Most folk were carnivorous, anyway. There were so many tricks to provide meals that originally contained dairy products that Benny knew it would not be a problem.

You could get a hearty breakfast at the Daily, and the diner even offered vegetarian options. Things like pancakes and waffles were easily made without milk. Eggs or dessert could be served up without dairy ever entering the equation. Vegetable dishes were a cinch to create. He even offered a Jewish version of bacon called beef fry. He provided a nondairy creamer for coffee and used a vegetable-based margarine for toast and cooking. He had the food requirements down to a science.

Rule number one in the laws of *kashruth*, never mix meat and milk together. Clear as day, cited in the Old Testament: Thou shalt not seethe the kid in its mother's milk. Benny had learned this as a child. His mother had explained that the milk may well have come from the cow that had birthed the very meat now masticating in his mouth. What a sin it would be to mock the creature by soaking it in its own mother's milk. Best to avoid the possibility altogether.

Benny, like all Jews, learned to avoid the possibility of ever causing such an insult simply by keeping dairy and meat separate. Benny let his personal thoughts run deeper than that. He felt he was paying the highest possible homage to the animal that nourished him simply by taking the time to bring the entire meal to such a higher moral ground. And that, in turn, he knew was at the heart of the laws of keeping kosher.

Benny lifted the muscles of his cheeks into a giggling smirk as he thought of Nate once more. He loved that guy and couldn't have done it without him. And he knew Nate was no fool. It was Benny's charisma and thick Greek accent that kept customers coming back again and again. Even so, Nate's partnership was priceless. Together they had made dining additions, capacity improvements, and most certainly, an increase in their customer base. They had witnessed entire families growing up together, and their children's children come in to dine. Benny had the daily microcosm of life in Epson County, and daily at that, just as he had hoped for.

Boy, I'm really too wound up, thinking about all this stuff. I have got to stop and try to settle in for sleep.

Despite the effort, Benny had one last round of thoughts. He was thinking way back to 1964 when the restaurant officially opened. He was trying to recall who the first customer was. He couldn't but he did recall that one of the very first ones had been Sam Greenfeld, the head manager over at Zindelman's. He was a tough son of a gun, that one. At least in the business world. They had so much in common, Sam and he. Two businessmen eager for success.

Benny sat and chatted with Sam so many times, he couldn't count them if he tried. They were always talking about the duties and obligations of running a business. That was their thing. Their special thing and always over a cup of coffee and pie. They liked to share strategies and ideas and, as most would say, simply talk shop. He was a likable fellow, and to this day, Sam still came in every other week or so. He'd long since retired, but his business savvy was as sharp as ever. Chatting with Sam was one of Benny's favorite things about the Daily Diner.

Now, another favorite thing was having Daniella work for him. Daniella had a dream, and she needed to make it come true. Hadn't he struggled to transform the idea of the Daily Diner into an actual restaurant? Hadn't it been hard to get there? Wasn't it worth it? Of course it was! Benny couldn't help but feel the strength of the connection. He'd do his best not to play favorites; after all, she was one of many employees.

Despite that, he'd keep an eye on her and support her however he could. He'd be her own personal pep rally. He'd follow her progress and, most certainly, keep her in his employ so she could earn money. Maybe he'd even give her a small *Chanukah* bonus if possible. Not that he'd even tell Nate. It would come from him and not the business. Right out of his own pocket. He'd have to wait and see.

Benny lay in the dark room, staring up at a ceiling he could hardly see. *This is nuts. I have to stop thinking so much.* He yawned deeply and turned to his side. As he drifted off to sleep, he lingered on thoughts about the Hasidim in his county. How they shunned his place as if it were the plague.

They didn't deny that the Daily Diner existed, but they loathed the fact that the restaurant was a kosher establishment outside the confines of their community. More so, that it was run by a Jew who to their thinking was not really a Jew at all because he wasn't a Hasid.

Benny fell into a deep sleep, completely unaware of the omniscient foreshadowing the heavenly realm was trying to divulge in those last moments before he slumbered. Those angels who were trying to prepare Benny about the next in line of those whom Benny called his daily diners.

Adam

*T*zvi Goldfarb had been in the diamond business for years. His eye for a well-cut stone and his own strength of character when dealing with the outside world formed a winning hand in making him a successful businessman. He couldn't help but notice that his nephew Adam had inherited similar qualities.

Adam had a quiet dignity that Tzvi found absolutely delightful. Whenever his nephew spoke and interacted with others, he exhibited a sense of grace. It wasn't feminine. Just an inner calm, manly too, that made him seem wise beyond his years. Adam seemed to mull over every situation he was placed in, evaluate it, and make conclusions as a result. He asked a lot of questions. That skill was essential in the diamond business, and Tzvi wanted Adam to be a part of it.

Actually, as far back as Tzvi could remember, Adam had displayed this particular aspect of his personality. Perhaps Adam was not always appropriate with his questions. Tzvi could easily recall numerous youthful inquiries that bordered on shedding negative light on Hasidism. That had been then, though, and this was now. Adam was a delightful young man, and in the diamond business, constant questioning helped ensure a great sale.

As a bonus, Adam seemed fascinated by diamonds. He would ask Tzvi so many questions about the industry that Tzvi could hardly keep track of them all. How are the facets created? Why are some diamonds brighter than others? All these questions put the kernel of an idea into Tzvi's mind. He should think of Adam in terms of employment. After all, Adam wouldn't be a youngster forever. He would be marriage material in the near future, and a good career would ensure success.

Tzvi could sense the potential and wanted to take advantage of it. Adam was honest to a fault. Wouldn't that be a crucial asset for working in the diamond business? People could trust him. His gut instinct told him that Adam would be a shoo-in if given the opportunity to try out the business. He would fight hard to get his nephew employment in it.

Tzvi had finally mustered up the courage to ask his brother Nachum if they could speak after the Sabbath ended. He had been intent on sharing his idea about Adam. To ensure that he didn't even allude to business at the time of the Sabbath, Tzvi simply asked, "Nachum, could I come by tomorrow night, after *Havdalah*?"

Nachum made it easy, however.

"Tzvi, you and the family live, what? Five, six houses away? What a *meshuggah* question! You're in the confines of the *Eruv*. No traveling is happening here. What, suddenly you don't see the string following the telephone lines, marking the area where you can travel about? Of course you can come! Why are you even asking?"

Apparently realizing that Tzvi wasn't sure if he was joking or not, Nachum grinned ear to ear and gave Tzvi an affectionate grasp of the shoulder.

"Bring everyone, dear Tzvi. We'll say good-bye to *Shabbos* together. It will make saying *Havdalah* that much more special."

Tzvi knew how much his brother Nachum loved his own wife's baking. He was more than grateful that Batya had baked two apple-walnut cakes and brought them over before the Sabbath began. The cakes were a favorite of Nachum's, and Batya had obliged Tzvi's request to bake them on that particular Friday morning. She was in on the scheme, so to speak, and of course, she wanted Nachum to honor Tzvi's request for employing Adam. Just as a good wife should, she was doing her part to ensure her husband's success, no matter how big or small the issue.

They consumed the first cake at Friday night's dinner. They had put aside the second to have with tea after the Sabbath ended. It would help sweeten the proposal that Tzvi wanted to make. Ply his brother with his favorite cake. Appeal to Nachum's sweet tooth and his common sense all in one fell swoop so he would answer yes.

With Nachum's blessing, Adam had been offered a chance to work in the diamond business, and Tzvi's instincts had proved correct. The best part was that Adam had done even better than Tzvi could have imagined.

Adam, presently twenty-three years of age, had become so adept at understanding the nuances of a good business transaction that Tzvi knew beyond a shadow of a doubt that Adam needed to come full force into the fold. He'd taken Adam out to peddle a few stones alongside him, and the feedback had been wonderful. Adam was gracious, dignified, and honest, and quite notably, showed he had a good eye for stones.

Tzvi considered it an art form, just of a different nature. Some people could be a great painter or composer. Adam was one of the lucky few who could view a gemstone with an artist's eye. Blood relative or not, Tzvi wouldn't pass on someone who was adept at understanding and detecting diamond quality. How fortunate for him that he was referring to his nephew as a future permanent employee.

Adam still seemed pleasantly surprised, however, when Tzvi asked him into his office and made the generous offer that would change Adam's future forever.

"Adam, you are such a *mentch*. Everyone talks about what a good soul you are. You know, they're right. I'm very proud of you."

"Thank you, *Feter* Tzvi. I'm learning from the best. Lucky for me, it's my uncle."

That was his nephew. Humble to a fault. *Hashem* forbid he should get cocky even just once and acknowledge the fact that he was a wonder with diamonds.

"I appreciate the compliment, but, Adam, you do have an eye for the business. So much so that I want to make you an offer. I'd like to pay for you to enroll in a diploma program with GIA so you can learn all you can about diamonds. I only ask that when you are finished with the program, you return the favor by continuing to work for me."

Adam's response to the comment was a look of complete surprise. He loved the business for a reason he couldn't explain, and he adored handling diamonds. They fascinated him. Certification from the Gemological Institute of America would be the feather in his cap that would make him a respected diamond dealer in the outside world. He didn't even have to think it over.

"*Feter*, I accept your gracious offer. You have a deal."

It would only be a matter of time before Adam became a bona fide diamond dealer, able to ferret out the best of the best, in all aspects of life.

A year had passed. At the ripe old age of twenty-four, Adam was ready to make his way in the industry. After several discussions with his uncle, they had decided that Adam would work with independent jewelers rather than department-store jewelry departments.

The diamonds that Tzvi imported mostly came from Belgium, South Africa, and Russia, and usually, they went one of two ways: department stores or independent jewelers. Adam's nature made him a shoo-in for dealing with the independents. In the Majors (which was the nickname for the department stores), Adam would have certainly made more money, but his eggs would have been in one basket, so to speak. If he only dealt with one big store, what would happen if the buyer quit or went on leave? It would be just like the story of Joseph in the Bible, then. The new buyer wouldn't know Adam. Even if he or she knew of Adam's reputation, that person still wouldn't know Adam and might not want to work with him. There was no guarantee he or she would continue to keep the connection alive.

Working with independents was better suited to Adam's style. These folks believed strongly in their merchandise and bought for inventory. They needed to be very concerned about keeping their good name in the business, and they didn't have a housewares, shoe, or men's clothing department to compensate for a possibly lackluster jewelry department.

Adam would work on commission no matter which route he took, but he'd make a good salary either way. Tzvi was sure of it. The only tough part would be the travel. Sometimes Adam would have to be gone for two or possibly three weeks at a time, selling diamonds worldwide. Tzvi would get him used to the idea by starting him out with baby steps. He'd send him to several customers in the United States, first. Once Adam really got a foothold in the business, Tzvi would have him take on the international challenges of the industry.

The frightening part of the business was acknowledging that you were flying with millions of dollars in diamonds and you were the party responsible for getting them safely to their destination. Unlike some, Tzvi had great concerns regarding dressing in the Hasidic way when traveling with so many jewels. Too many people equated being a Hasidic male traveler with stowing diamonds in the briefcase that happened to be at that man's side.

Because Adam was only twenty-four and had such a youthful-looking face, Tzvi concocted an unusual idea. A very naive idea. He would suggest that Adam travel in *goyishe* clothes. He'd explain the benefits of traveling in an outfit that would make Adam look like every other youngster on the planet. It would be clever and devious but for the right reasons.

At this early juncture, Tzvi still didn't know just how much Adam was secretly questioning his Hasidic life. Tzvi never gave thought to the possibility that Adam would welcome *goyishe* clothes. He never gave credence to the fact that if anyone found out his crazy idea, everyone would shame and ridicule him for tempting Adam to consider the ways of the outside world.

Tzvi wanted to conceal Adam's Hasidic identity when he traveled simply to maximize the number of diamonds that he could transfer. It would mean that Adam could fly with millions worth of diamonds in tow and be completely ignored. He wanted Adam to travel in clothing that wasn't traditional. Clothing that was strictly forbidden. It would be their little secret. It would throw would-be thieves off the scent.

Adam would be instructed in the subtleties of dressing like a *goy*. He'd have to shed his Orthodox appearance in favor of that of a young man who was as mainstream as the next. Tzvi would take advantage of Adam's youth and make him appear to be the least likely person to be hauling millions. He'd make him look like a college student.

"For example, Adam, you'll wear a sweatshirt and a baseball cap instead of a *yarmulke*. You'll have to tuck your *tzitzit* deep inside your shirt. You can't give away the fact that you're an observant Jew. Your fringes would be a dead giveaway. You know, it's no mystery that Hasidic Jews are in the industry. If people see you on a plane with a briefcase at your side, they may easily deduce you're carrying diamonds. Then, *Hashem* forbid, who knows what could happen."

Tzvi continued. "It's a bit scary at first, knowing you have diamonds worth millions in your possession, but you do get used to it. When you pack your suitcase, you'll have your suit, your *yarmulke* and hat, and all the things you need to be the Adam that represents the business but, more importantly, his Judaism. That Adam can get ready at his hotel! When you fly, however, you have to blend in. *Farshteysts?*"

"Yes, I understand."

"OK, so I have only one more thing to share, and it has nothing to do with the business. At least, not directly. You'll be making many, many trips to the airport, and it so happens there is a restaurant that is just off the highway exit for the city that's actually a kosher establishment. Can you believe such a thing? In the middle of *goyim* central, and yet there it stands.

"It's called the Daily Diner. Strange name, no? Anyway, the bathrooms are clean, and believe it or not, it really does have kosher certification. Who would think you could find a kosher establishment right off the highway like that? Still makes me shake my head in wonder. Anyway...

"I can tell that some of the waitstaff are not Jewish, and I think even one of the two owners isn't either, but somehow, someway, they have kosher certification. So strange!" Tzvi shook his head to emphasize the point.

"Anyhow...they must be doing something right. They've been there for twenty years, and the place is always busy."

Tzvi continued his little speech. "You will rarely, if ever, find the *Hasidim*—or, for that matter, most of the people from the religious neighborhoods—in there. The few of us who have gone in are businessmen on the way to or from the airport who desperately need a bathroom or want a cup of coffee. That's as far as any of us have ever taken it. A meal there would be out of the question."

Tzvi glanced at his nephew, who stood quietly and listened intently. Tzvi didn't bother to explain why a meal would be out of the question, and Adam didn't ask, so Tzvi just continued.

"Especially, if you're taking a night flight and need to stay awake to drive, well, at least you can grab a coffee."

Tzvi was not about to announce that he had actually tried a doughnut once. It was a sin best kept quiet. Instead, he said, "I hear they get the baked goods and the breads from Herschel's Bakery in the city. Herschel's is well known even in our neighborhood, Adam."

Tzvi paused and shook his head again. He was continually amazed by the notion that a Greek Sephardic Jew—and who knew what the other owner was—somehow had obtained such specific kosher connections.

"Anyway, Adam, I do know Herschel's Bakery makes everything *pareve*. The diner only serves meat-based meals, so if the owners are ensuring that the baked goods have no milk ingredients, seems they really do know exactly how to keep kosher. Having a full meal there, well, I don't know. I don't recommend it, and I'd be very careful."

"*Feter*, if they have kosher certification and they deal with Herschel's, what's the problem? What's the big deal?"

There it was again. One of those hard-to-answer questions that Adam spewed out of his mouth. Tzvi did his best, all the while avoiding the heart of the matter.

"You'd be severely ridiculed if you ate a meal there and it was found out. I wouldn't want that to happen to you."

Tzvi evaded the question's true answer: the fact that their entire community had a watchdog mentality and the rules were never, ever to be broken. To ensure that, the community kept claims of the wrath of God constant in all matters. God would be displeased with anything that occurred outside the confines of the neighborhood.

Tzvi softened the blow a bit by adding, "Still, it's good to know the restaurant is there when you need an emergency pit stop late at night or early in the morning."

Tzvi paused once more, realizing he hadn't made his point.

"Look, I'm just trying to say that, fortunately, we have the luxury of a pit stop if need be. Except for those in our neighborhood, it's the only kosher restaurant in all of Epson County. A little haven, if you will. A pit stop if we need it. Apparently, even our non-Jewish neighbors love the place. And that's in spite of it being kosher.

"I think for that reason alone, you should avoid it. I think that's why we all avoid it. Not so much about the certifications. It's about the clientele. Non-Jews from every walk of life. Worse, Jews that have strayed. Jews with crazy ideas about who and what we are. Chatting with the *goyim* can lead to all sorts of problems.

"Listen, I'm telling you all this because I've gone in there myself when I've flown on business and needed a good hot cup of coffee to keep me awake. It's a very long drive to the airport, as you know, and especially boring in the quiet of the nighttime or the monotony of a traffic jam. A hot cup of coffee makes for good company."

Tzvi was almost done with his little speech. He wanted to make one more point.

"The Jewish owner is a good man. Well, so is the non-Jewish man, I suppose, but I'm specifically referring to the Jewish owner right now. I've spoken with him once or twice. He told me that he wanted to have a kosher establishment because if he did, everyone could eat there, observant or not. Very thoughtful, if you ask me. Too bad he continues to live outside the fold. That kind of thinking is the potential for a good Jewish life.

"Hard to explain, but that statement made me feel I could trust him. If he felt concern enough that people like you and me should be able to eat there, well, to me, that's a *mentch* no matter how misguided. Not everyone is that considerate toward others. If you ever go in there..." Tzvi paused and continued with a parental tone, "And that would be for coffee or the bathroom only, Adam." He paused once more. "Tell him you're my nephew. Maybe he'll remember me from the few times I've stopped in for coffee. I have a feeling he might. He'll take good care of you."

dam had flown into the city airport an hour ago. *Schlepping* his suitcase tiredly behind him, he was extremely grateful that he had finally arrived at his parked car in the long-term lot. It wasn't so much that he was physically tired. It was more that he was mentally fatigued. The last two weeks had been filled with harrowing bargaining, and it had taken its toll on him. Arriving home meant a soft, warm bed and the peace and quiet of the nighttime.

Still, the pressures of the job excited him, and this trip in particular had been jam-packed with meetings and exchanges that had been worth every moment of frustration. Adam loved his career. He felt lucky to have the opportunity to be in two worlds, bargaining and selling one minute, cloistered in safety and love the next. It felt very good to know he'd be home soon and able to stay in the area for the next few weeks with family and friends.

While driving, Adam was not feeling the pressures of the job so much as a pressure of a different nature. The kind that comes from family and one's parents in particular. The kind that has a very persistent nature. That awful pressure to marry. Since Adam would be home for the next few weeks, he knew his parents would be pushing the issue.

Rebecca, Malka, Aviva, and Reuben were all married, and his sisters were new mothers as well. Being the baby in his own line of siblings, he felt the full force of the pressure. According to the family, he should have been married already. It was a joyous thing to be able to marry off your last child, especially when you were a member of the Hasidic community. Something his mother reminded him of constantly.

She was particularly eager for the honor that was bestowed on the mother when her last child married. She would sit like a grand duchess as community members hovered around her to bless her on marrying off the last of the children. More than once she had told Adam of the joy she would feel inside as others danced around her and gave her that special blessing.

Adam had caught a bit of a break when everyone was temporarily fussing over his new nephew. Now, his nephew was just another reminder that the clock was ticking. His parents were hounding him about the importance of the covenant of marriage. Actually, everyone in the neighborhood was intent on helping him find his *beshert*.

Adam had often wondered if there really was such a thing as a soul mate, a fated one who completed you. Everyone was on the lookout for the young woman, fated or not, who would be the other half of a *shiddach* meant just for him. As Adam drove along, he could only wonder if that woman was as ignorant as he about the nuances of marriage. As far as he was concerned, he knew very little about relationships. No one ever spoke of them.

Everyone always just said he would find out for himself. Adam couldn't understand why it was such taboo to speak about the intimacies in the partnership called marriage, but it was the Hasidic way. It was only important to understand that the covenant of marriage was sacred. Marriage was the ultimate way to honor and perpetuate *Hashem's* plan for his chosen people.

The thought served only to remind him about how ignorant he was regarding so much else in life. He'd always had questions. They had been present as far back as he could remember. Recently, they had begun to solidify like a rock in his head. It was as if they were amassing into a huge concrete block in the back of his mind. Solid. Tangible.

They solidified because of his career. They solidified because he became part of the bigger world whenever he was working. His job allowed him to mingle in the very thick of it and see that not everything was the way he had been told it should be. He encountered folks from all walks of life when he left his community, and they seemed to function just fine despite Hasidism's assurance they were all doomed.

As Adam drove along, that thought led to yet another one, and this one in particular reminded him of the questions he'd had even as a young boy. Adam remembered a particular scene he'd overheard as he played in the street. It had all centered around his neighbor Naomi, a girl who at the time had been merely ten years old.

Adam was tossing a ball in the air, catching it, and tossing it again when he heard loud ranting coming from

Naomi's house. The noise ended with Mr. Moskovitz storming out and dumping a book into the trash can. Curiosity got the best of him, and Adam waited until evening to sneak over to the garbage pail and see why a book would cause such a stir.

When Adam picked it up, he noticed it had a charming cartoonish cover. The title read *Charlotte's Web*. He also took note of the fact that the binding had a library number on it. Not wanting Naomi to get in any more trouble, he picked it up so he could return it on her behalf. He noticed a torn library card floating in pieces around the remaining trash as he lifted the book up.

He almost couldn't help himself. He snuck into his own house, ferreted a flashlight from the supply closet, ran into his room, and shut the door tight. He began to read the book. There was nothing in it except a story about farm animals. Animals that could talk and think for themselves. When Adam saw Naomi the next day, he noticed that she held her arm closely to her side, as if it ached. He wanted desperately to comfort her, but touching between boys and girls was strictly forbidden.

Instead, he felt helpless and angry. Angry that Naomi had suffered over such an innocent book. Relieved, too, that Mr. Moskovitz didn't go back to the trash can to see if his daughter had tried to retrieve the book. He would have never believed that Naomi had not been the one to take it out of the trash. Yet Adam was torn because he also recalled the words of Naomi's father, shouted out to no one in particular as he threw the book into the trash.

"A book that gives animals the ability to think, to speak, or have any feelings that a person would is a slap in the face towards the Almighty. It belittles everything

Hashem has made sacred. This book will only lead to another and another. That will be the worst crime of all in the face of the Almighty. My own daughter, accepting evil notions into her head."

Perhaps Mr. Moskovitz was right. Still, when Adam returned the library book, he couldn't help but feel that the man was actually wrong. People read books all the time. Wasn't information also education? Even if it was a silly love story or drama of some sort, didn't it help people to learn about themselves? What about all the history books? Wasn't it important to know what was happening in the world around them? What had happened around them before they even existed? Didn't past events shape the future? Arguably, couldn't one take out a book on the history of his own people to learn how they came to be?

Thinking about those questions, Adam could not resist the temptation to get his own library card. To his summation, it was all an act of chivalry and defiance on behalf of Naomi. He would read books to honor her courage. He didn't realize it at that time, but that act was one of the first doors he opened to enter into parts of life strictly forbidden to him. Ultimately, his own fears regarding the sin of reading library books kept his visits to the library infrequent and quite limited in time. It had been safer to limit his visits than to be found out as Naomi had been.

Thinking about the negative memories perked Adam up as he drove. His thoughts energized him, and he found himself drifting from subject to subject as the highway lamps whirred past, one after the other. He smirked, thinking of the lamps shining in his face, urging him to confess his sins as if they were local detectives. Suddenly, his thoughts returned to Naomi, which in turn led to a stark confession. He spoke the confession as he stared out at the highway.

"I think there is an overall unfairness in the way my community treats women as compared to men. Naomi should have been able to read books. We all should be able to read books."

Adam was most bothered by the notion that keeping women away from texts of any kind would guard their modesty. The men in the community had no qualms about ensuring the meekness and obedience of the women. How many times had Adam himself witnessed a male in the community taking advantage when he could? Leering. Flirting in their way. Speaking harshly to re-mind the female who was the boss.

Well, not all the men. That was extremely unfair. Adam knew there were good souls in his community. Righteous men who took good care of their wives and of their daughters. He directed his anger toward the small few who de-clared piety and sinned when no one was looking.

He'd heard his fair share of comments among his peers about the mysteries of women, but they were always vague and guarded, almost as if the men were afraid to be overheard. Secretive comments that, on rare occasion, actually troubled him. Comments about sleep-ing with a prostitute in the city because a wife was now off limits, and after all, a *goyishe* woman hardly counted. To Adam's thinking, all souls counted, and he questioned the possibility that the sin actually was adultery, regard-less of the notion that non-Jewish women didn't count in the eyes of God. Why would God create these women if they didn't count?

Then there was sin of another kind. One that seemed to be swept under the rugs, and the community chided those who spoke of the sins rather than the perpetrators. Adam's thoughts slipped back as he remembered the chilling words of one of the oldest boys in the *yeshiva* he had attended. Adam couldn't remember his name at the moment, but the boy's story was emblazoned in Adam's memory.

The rabbi who instructed the boys about expectations for marriage, the raising of a family, and the ways those corresponded to Jewish law apparently had chosen a select few of the boys, that young student among them, for "special" tutorials.

The rabbi had told that student that because of his rakish good looks, his wife to be was bound to be more than obliging in matters of sex. The rabbi wanted him to understand how wonderful it could all be. In the guise of concerned welfare, the rabbi had the young man expose himself so the rabbi could stroke his penis and show the wonders that would happen. The student told Adam he was petrified but too intimidated to speak up.

When the rabbi grabbed him firmly, the explosion of delightful sensation overwhelmed the young man, and he was too busy experiencing it to feel afraid. The boy described the sensation as something unlike anything he had ever felt in his entire life. It was wonderful beyond all description. He could hardly wait to experience it again with a future wife.

Adam couldn't help but notice that as his fellow student shared the story, the tone of his words, seemingly filled with enthusiasm, didn't quite match the look of distress hidden behind his eyes. Adam never forgot that look, and it always troubled him to think about it.

The rabbi always ended the special sessions by telling the students that the experience was sacred and they should not discuss it lightly. In fact, he said it would be a disgrace to talk of such personal things with one's parents or relatives. He told them that the session was a onetime thing only for the sake of education in marriage, and the boys should just carry on as if nothing had happened. In essence, none of the privileged few spoke of their own incidents when they were in the school courtyard. They certainly never mentioned it to their parents, since they had been told it was too sacred to speak of.

When Adam asked why the young student was telling him, then, the student answered that he had a hunch that Adam was to be next. The young man had noticed the rabbi looking at Adam many times and in a peculiar way. He wanted Adam to know what it meant if he got called into the office. Adam found the thought both frightening and curious all at the same time.

Much as he was eager to know what it must feel like to have sex, Adam was relieved that he had never been called into the office for that special lesson. When the rabbi in question did approach Adam on what might have been a fateful day, he lifted Adam's face and gazed into his eyes.

"Such a shame that you look so much like a girl." The rabbi had shaken his head and tsked. "So much like a girl. All those ringlets of hair, and still not a trace of a beard anywhere on your face. Well, perhaps if you merit the honor of growing into a man, you'll eventually merit a special lesson on the privileges of being a man."

Now, while driving, Adam knew the core of the matter was grievous sin on the part of the rabbi. A rabbi who was so highly respected that no one dared to question his motives or actions. A rabbi who got away with his sin until a massive stroke turned him into a wheelchair-bound vegetable. A rabbi who shunned Adam again just prior to his damning stroke when Adam had just turned seventeen. Adam had been too feminine for his tastes.

What about Mrs. Nussbaum, who often had bruises on her face and arms? What about Mr. Horowitz, who always seemed to walk in a drunken stupor, especially to his own home? Were these the result of marriage? Were these the result of leading a pious life? Were these the result of living a Hasidic life?

He was being silly. Yes, he questioned some things about his upbringing. The very core, however, was a spiritual and holy place filled with good people. People who cared about each other and, most important, about *Hashem*. That was what he kept at the forefront whenever he thought about his life and the fact that it was time to move forward and marry. There were good and righteous people in the sea of folks that formed his community.

Adam brought himself back to his initial thought. Marriage. He was well aware that many mainstream Jews found the notion of matchmaking for marriage old fashioned. He himself wasn't so sure. A *shiddach* took into consideration one's character, intelligence, learning, finances, family, health, appearance, and observance. The list could go on. In essence, he would meet someone who complemented his own qualities. That was a good thing, wasn't it?

Adam laughed as he drove up the highway. How was matchmaking any different from the concept of a blind date? He had heard about youngsters who set up their friends in the hopes of a match. Yet somehow, making a *shiddach* was considered ancient and not in keeping with the times.

In any case, Adam was sure his parents had already contacted the local *shadchan*. Was he ready to deal with the matchmaker? Probably. He did think about a woman to share his life with, to divulge his dreams and hopes for the future to. A companion, a lover. The thought gave Adam a little shiver as he drove. To feel love for a woman. It must feel wonderful.

Adam looked up into the night sky for a brief moment before refocusing on the road. He smiled up at the stars and muttered a quick blessing for the gifts in nature. The distraction was only temporary, however, as Adam found himself thinking about a match once more.

There had been one time—no, two actually—when Adam's parents and two other families had been intent on setting up a *bashow*. Each time, those families, both parents and children, sat together in the living room and talked. Eventually, the parents went into the other room and left the two youngsters to get to know each other a bit. They hoped it would create a match.

The first *bashow* was a washout. The girl seemed nice enough, but there was no spark. She knew it too. Both youngsters told their parents it was a no go. As for the second attempt, well, it took three meetings of the two families before those efforts ended in failure as well. Adam sensed the girl was mildly neurotic, and it was starting to show in a concrete way by the third meeting. He told his parents he just couldn't handle a woman who could potentially become more neurotic through the years.

Then little Yonkele was born, and for a brief time, Adam had a break. *Thank you, nephew!* Now, however, he was the main focus once more, and he knew that a marriage was likely in his future. Deep down, though, he was ready. Admittedly, he was hopeful. He wanted a wife. He wanted love. He could only imagine who she would be and what she would look like.

The reflections about his situation and the empty highway made it a breeze for Adam to cruise along and make good time. Despite that, he was feeling tired again and hungry as well. A bad combination to be sure. He was contending with the grumbles in his gut and the sleepy feeling behind his eyes. The last thing he needed was to get in an accident, especially when he was getting closer to the haven he called home.

Maybe he'd stop at that place *Feter* had told him about. Why not? A cup of coffee would wake him up a bit, and maybe a bit of eggs would ease his hunger. He wouldn't tell anybody about that part. Thinking on it further, Adam decided to stop there before going home. It was only 9:00 p.m. If he was timely, he could eat and still be in bed by 10:45 with the luxury of having someone else to clean up after him. *What have I got to lose?*

Adam kept one hand on the steering wheel as he reached up to check that his *yarmulke* was in place. He took his eyes off the road for mere seconds in order to check and make sure his *tzitzit* were clearly visible over his pant legs. For a reason he couldn't explain, he wanted to put this restaurant to the test. He was merely curious. He had no malicious intent in his heart. If the restaurant was as kosher as *Feter* implied, he wanted to see how they would handle the Hasidic man coming through the doors.

It was Benny's turn to take an evening shift. Nate had taken two nights in a row, and now he wanted to catch up on some sleep. Benny was leaning against the counter, reading the newspaper same as he always did. It was the quiet time of day when he could indulge this personal luxury. Reading a newspaper helped pass the evening hours, however slowly.

Benny had menus at the ready for the few who came to eat a late supper, but the menus had been at his side for thirty minutes now, untouched by the waiting hands of patrons. To make matters worse, he wasn't fond of the local press he happened to be reading. Benny turned the page for what seemed like the millionth time as he looked, desperately searching for a decent article. Maybe he'd try the Jumble printed on the comic page.

The distinct jingle of the bells mounted over the door announced the arrival of a customer. Habit made Benny smile for his patron before he even looked up. The bells were the call to arms. Nate and Benny's cue to prepare to greet a customer. No matter where they themselves happened to be inside their restaurant, the cling clang of the tiny clappers against the metal beckoned. The bells were especially handy during the late hours.

Looking at the young man entering the Daily, Benny was hard pressed to know how his smile was interpreted. The young man looked very tired, which may have explained why he gave no smile in return. Hopefully he would not be dealing with a tired customer who was also rude. Benny couldn't tell yet. But how exciting that he was going to deal with a Hasid. The boy had the look, unfair as the summation might be. He was a black and white silhouette against the colorful diner walls. And the black hat resting squarely atop his head provided further proof. Benny could see *pais* curls tucked behind each ear.

He never knew what to expect from the rare ultra-Orthodox patrons who came through the doors. Some of them were very nice, kind in fact. Some of them made demands, refusing to sit next to a woman at the small counter designed to look like a diner's. God forbid, they couldn't resolve the matter by just sitting at a table instead while they waited for their coffee. Some of the few who came through the doors even challenged him about his knowledge of *kashruth*, almost as if they were afraid to eat there. In fact, the few who had patronized the restaurant had ordered coffee and no more. Only once, one of them had ordered a doughnut.

Are you kidding me? My certification comes from a highly respected mashgiach. *Well known enough that he is respected among the* mashgichim *from the city. You better believe everything is acceptably kosher!*

Benny loved to see the look on the face of the challenger when he shared the name of the *mashgiach*. He had every possible angle covered in ensuring that his establishment was kosher, all the way down to making sure the chefs were Jews. The bus boys, the servers, those people were the regular Joes and Janes in the county. Benny would not be prejudiced that way and refuse to hire someone simply because that person wasn't Jewish. The food, however, was all prepared by the hands of a Jew. It was the accepted way among most reputable *mashgichim*. Benny could do no more than smile when the patron who made the challenge would finally hush up.

It was extremely insulting to have the certification and still be questioned in that way. Benny supposed it was the simple fact that they couldn't believe a restaurant that was in the middle of the county and outside the fold of the Hasidic section—right off a highway, no less—would be so...well, so Orthodox. Benny never gave thought to the fact that anything outside of the Hasidic world, Jewish or not, was strictly off limits to these people.

What hurt Benny most was the fact that those few who did come in never spread the word. He'd been there for twenty years, and still only a small handful stopped by. They mostly wanted to use his bathroom or purchase a coffee. His restaurant was good enough for that. It was always the businessmen, too, the ones on the way into or back from the city, but never, never, the big families coming to dine. Benny would have loved to see their families come and dine as well. *You're my brethren, for crying out loud.*

Benny even covered his bases in terms of ownership. The restaurant closed on all the Jewish holidays, just as any other decent Jewish business would. At Passover time, however, to be sure that he didn't own anything *chametzdik*, Benny went through a yearly ritual with Nate to keep everything, well, kosher. Practically memorized by years of performing it, Benny was hearing it in his head as he stared at his young customer.

"Nate, you know, I've been thinking. Passover is around the corner. I don't want to own the restaurant anymore, since it isn't kosher for Passover. It would be too much to *kasher* it for the holiday. Take it off my hands. I'll sell it to you for whatever you have on you."

Nate would pay out whatever was in his pocket, they'd shake hands, and Benny would leave to go home and be free of owning a business that was filled with all sorts of bread products. Without fail, Benny would come back to the restaurant hours after sundown on the last day of Passover. He'd meet up with Nate, who would just happen to be there.

"I've come in for a cup of coffee, Nate."

"Benny, I'm so glad you stopped by. I have to tell you…I can't do it alone. Please, please, I'm begging you. Reconsider and be in business with me again."

Benny would buy back his share of the restaurant; Nate, more than willing to sell it to him. They'd prepare the restaurant for the onslaught of people sure to come in the morning. Every Jew for miles around had spent the last eight days refraining from bread products, and they would relish a chance to eat out. Best to be ready. The men would be in business together once more, and they would repeat their song and dance next spring.

Benny knew the heart of the matter was simply that the ultra-Orthodox, and certainly the Hasidim, preferred to stay within the confines of their own community. They didn't want to mingle in the outside world any more than they absolutely had to. They followed that particular rule for the sake of being safe. They wanted to keep their own ways and culture intact, unchanged by the outside influences around them. Yet it was still a slap in the face.

Knowing that staring at the young man and thinking about Hasids accomplished nothing, Benny addressed the youngster same as he would any other customer.

"Welcome to the Daily. Come in. Take a load off. Would you prefer the counter, a table, or a booth?"

"I'll sit at a booth, thank you."

Benny grabbed a menu as he stepped outside the confines of the cashier's counter. "Right this way."

As they walked to the booth, Adam asked, "Are you one of the owners?"

"Yes, I'm Benny Kalabokas. Why do you ask?"

"My uncle told me to mention his name to you."

"Who's your uncle?"

"Tzvi Goldfarb."

"Tzvi! Of course I remember Tzvi!" *The only Hasid brave enough to purchase a doughnut, and that's why I remember him.* "If he's your uncle, you're a lucky one. A nice guy. A really nice guy. I wish he'd come in more often. I've rarely seen him in here." Benny paused. "May I ask your name?"

"Adam. Adam Goldfarb."

"Well, Adam, are you here for coffee?"

"No, I'm actually hungry."

Benny thought he had died and gone to heaven. He gave Adam a very joyful response.

"Well, Adam, you just earned yourself the best of the best. I'll have Danny wait on you. My top server. Order whatever you'd like. It's all good, I assure you."

Adam sat down at the booth after placing his black hat on the coat hook attached to the end of the seat. He graciously accepted the menu Benny put into his hands.

"Thanks. Wow, it's a pretty thick menu. Looks like I'll have a lot to choose from."

To make sure his young customer knew from the get-go that he could eat comfortably and safely, Benny added the comment that made clear he understood Jewish protocol.

"Once you've placed your order, there is a washing station in the back. It's outside the restrooms so you can make *bracha*."

Adam looked up at Benny. Astonishment was written on his features, but Benny could see no signs of a challenge etched into the young man's face. Adam was merely surprised by the information. No more, no less. Adam would be able to wash his hands and recite the proper blessing so he could eat, a ritual that only someone well versed in Jewish protocol would know.

"OK, young man. I'll leave you to it. Danny will be right with you."

The restaurant was quiet at the moment. There were only four other folks besides Adam. Two of them looked like truckers, and the other two were women touting Jordache jeans and Members Only jackets. Benny could only imagine what Adam might be thinking because he was certainly staring at them. Maybe he couldn't help but notice the big poufy hairstyles atop the women's heads? Not meaning to be punny, even Benny found the overall look a bit over the top!

Adam was staring at the gaudy makeup and big hair of the two female patrons. It compelled him to reach up and ensure that his black velvet *yarmulke* was still in place. Looking back at the menu, Adam was quite impressed by the selection. A single sheet clipped onto the menu's edge caught his attention. It read: Greek Night, Every First Thursday of the Month. The next line read: Come and enjoy a bit of Greek cuisine. Well, it wasn't the first Thursday of the month, so he'd better seek out something from the main menu. Adam still had that hankering for eggs.

Engrossed in his menu, he hadn't noticed Daniella standing aside the booth. He looked up only after she spoke.

"Good evening. Welcome to the Daily. Can I start you off with something to drink?"

Adam looked up in response to the rich, velvety voice that clearly belonged to a woman. "Mr. Kalabokas said a Danny would be taking care of me."

Daniella smiled, and Adam couldn't help but notice her two very pronounced dimples. They rested on plump, white cheeks that harbored a rosy hue.

"I'm Danny. It's a nickname for Daniella. I'm sorry if that confused you." Looking at the fellow, Daniella couldn't stop herself from thinking, *A yarmulke, pais curls lying gently against the ears, and tzitzit.* She added, "Would you prefer that I get one of our waiters over here?"

Daniella didn't want to be standing over him, pouring water or a drink, or laying down his food with her body tilting in his direction. She knew the drill, and she was mindful of it. Modesty, modesty in all things. Don't entice the man in any way. The last thing she wanted to do was offend the guy. She disagreed with the notion but was respectful of it just the same.

Benny had told her during initial training that they had never had a Modern Orthodox or Hasidic person sit down for an actual meal. Benny had merely been giving her a bit of information about the patronage of the establishment in order that she could be fully knowledgeable regarding the restaurant's history. It meant that this was a first, and Daniella didn't want to mess it up for Benny, or Nate, for that matter. She began to walk away so she could ask Benny what to do. "I'll be right back."

Adam didn't know if she asked because she was Jewish and knew to ask such a question or if the owner had drilled all the staff members in understanding that Orthodox men avoided contact with women who were not their own wives. It didn't matter. He was drawn in by the vision she created just by standing there. He wanted her service. He wanted her near. He was not going to answer, "Yes, I'd prefer a man." He wanted the intimacy of her service for a reason he could hardly explain. He watched her as she spoke with her employer.

Her hair was the color of the darkest cup of coffee he could imagine, which Adam felt foolish for thinking. Yet it was the perfect description because he thought of the velvety richness of coffee beans as he stared at their deep, roasted color. Even the oily shimmer of a roasted bean could be equated to the shimmers in her hair that reflected the lights.

Adam caught her attention and signaled her to come back to the booth. The two green eyes looking down on him highlighted the warmth of her hair color. Peridot gems. Her eyes were like peridot gems. Adam had always been fond of the light-green hue of the August birthstone. Her eyes personified the gem's beauty. Such an unusual shade of green. So kind and warm despite the light color or the fact that green was often associated with jealousy and envy.

The smiling dimples and clear complexion sealed the deal. The waitress was like the Snow White he'd heard of. His sister had once described her. Apparently, when Aviva was little, she had snuck a peek at the character in a book at the supermarket. Her description of what she remembered painted an image of Snow White as an attractive woman with a milky-white complexion and flowing, deep, dark hair. The fairy princess had ruby-colored lips, but this Danny gal had lips that were full and lush pink.

He wanted to keep talking to her simply because the chemical responses within him were already taking charge. It was a new experience for him, and the stirrings felt exciting and good. He'd never had such a reaction to a woman before. Looking at her created butterflies in his stomach. To her question about a change in waitstaff, he could only reply earnestly, "It's not necessary for you to find another server. Not necessary at all. I'm sorry if I implied anything by my actions."

"No apology necessary. What can I get you?"

"Well, I'd like some eggs, but everything looks good."

"How about salami and eggs and a Dr. Brown's cream soda?"

"That actually sounds really good. I'll take it."

Daniella wrote notes on her pad and then reached out to take the menu from Adam's hand. They exchanged a brief glance as their hands rested on opposite corners, each silently reluctant to let go. Subconscious, perhaps, but it allowed for two seconds of the kindling spark that occurs when there is chemistry between two people.

"I'll get that soda to you right away," Daniella added in for good measure.

Adam watched the swish and sway of her slender figure as she walked away. The bow of her apron rested gently against her lower back, and the ends of the bow lay over the top of her buttock cheeks, practically hugging them. It brought Adam's eyes to her hips, which he noticed were full and shapely. *Hashem, forgive me. She's so…so…feminine.* Well, maybe it didn't hurt to take a peek. He wasn't harming anyone by it, after all.

Benny caught sight of the eager glances the young man was casting toward Daniella's retreating figure. He opted not to say anything when the young man passed by to use the washing station for fear that it would reveal he had been watching the exchange between the two youngsters all along. But he opted to make a comment when the young man returned, just for the sake of making friendly conversation. Subconsciously, however, he was already trying to make a match.

"I'm sorry I wasn't clear that Danny was a girl. You were surprised that she was your server. I could see that."

"No apology necessary. I'm really not concerned with who serves me."

Benny couldn't help himself, although why, he wasn't quite sure. It was as if the heavenly realm gave him a gentle push at that moment. They were nudging him, saying, "Play matchmaker."

"She's one of my very few Jewish servers."

And there it was. Benny could see it all over the handsome face. The look of pleasant surprise. Now, Daniella was not just a girl. She was a Jewish girl. Benny continued.

"Well, anyway, go. Sit down. As I said before, Danny will take good care of you."

With that, Benny watched as the drama began to unfold. Even over the distance between booth and cashier counter, Benny could tell that flirtatious conversation had taken over the moment Daniella delivered her plate of salami and eggs. Likely, lighthearted comments that meant nothing but implied everything. If only he could hear them! Benny could even swear he saw the sparks ignite. He stared as if watching a television with the sound muted. He could see that Daniella spoke first.

"Here are your salami and eggs."

Adam smiled at Daniella and said, "Who should I complain to if I don't like them?"

"I suppose that would be me."

"You wouldn't yell at me if I complained, would you?" Adam spoke in a child-like tone.

"I'd give you my best smile and try to deliver eggs that were to your satisfaction."

With that last comment, Daniella gifted Adam with one of her best smiles. She even made a slight dip as if curtsying for approval. Adam couldn't help but say aloud what he was thinking.

"You have an amazing smile. It highlights your eyes."

Much as Daniella was subconsciously hoping for such a comment, she was taken by surprise. The man's frankness caught her off guard just enough, that she felt compelled to leave the table and contemplate the flirting privately.

"I think I'll leave you to your meal. I'll come back in a few minutes to see if you need anything else."

Benny was wise enough not to say anything to Daniella after the young man left that evening. Let the two of them mull over their introduction to each other. Let it register that something had been in the air for them both. Benny knew that it would only be a matter of time before Daniella would begin to talk about the new customer. And the fact that he happened to be Orthodox would be the highlight of her remarks. Benny never bothered to consider how troubling matchmaking between the two might be. He merely waved a goodbye to the young man and shouted out to his retreating figure, "Hope to see you again, soon."

Adam waved in turn as he stood aside his car and put his car key into the lock of the car door. He was happy he had stopped at the Daily. The salami and eggs had been sheer perfection. The salty aftertaste of the hard salami still lingered in his mouth as he drove down the streets that led to home. He would sleep well. *A delicious meal and a beautiful Jewish girl that I would definitely like to get to know better.* Adam said a prayer of thanks into the air.

"*Baruch, Hashem.*" The good Lord should certainly be blessed for the introduction. Adam gave no thought to the fact that she was a mainstream Jewess and therefore hardly a Jew at all. He was too taken by her looks and her kindness to even care about the matter.

Back at the restaurant, Benny told Daniella to finish cleaning up for the night and neither said a word about the customer who had just left. Daniella got busy wiping down the table at the booth that Adam had occupied, thinking her thoughts, smiling all the while.

What a nice man! He seemed so, so... Daniella was looking for the word. *So humble? So dignified?* It would come to her eventually. In any case, he was a gentleman, which in itself was a pleasant surprise. Snubbing had come many a time when she had tried to interact with Hasidic folks. Snubbing under the guise of fear that somehow her corrupt ways (a result of *goyishe* influences) would influence them to stray. The men would turn their backs on her. The women, well, they were harsher. They could use their words to voice their disapproval.

This man was very nice. *Come on, Danny girl, be honest with yourself. He's adorable!* It was the first time she could ever remember being attracted to an Orthodox man. His golden brown hair was a mop of long ringlets about his head, and that was an understatement! Perfect curlicues encased his face, practically engulfing the *pais* curls he wore. In fact, she almost could have missed the *pais* curls by the mere fact that they blended in with the curls that surrounded them. Daniella was convinced they were begging to be pulled straight just so they could prove they would bounce right back. She had, of course, ignored the urge.

Little highlights of blond hugged every last curl. They shimmered in the restaurant's light. Dark-brown eyes in sockets shaped like perfected ovals were as rich as the hue on the shell of a hazelnut. His eyes were so doe-like. His gentle features were, well, they were pretty in a very handsome sort of way. In another life, he could have been a fashion model.

She could only wonder why his face was so clean shaven. Beards were practically a must in Hasidic male circles. Daniella would find out at a much later date that, try as he might, Adam could not grow a full beard. His hairs came in skimpy enough that he found his beard practically shameful. The other men often teased at his inability to grow one and even implied that he might be hairless elsewhere because God had put all the hair on top of his head.

Daniella recalled his parting comment before paying at the register.

"You took good care of me, and for that, I thank you."

Daniella assumed he would know Yiddish. After all, the local Hasidim were fluent in the language, and he was likely from the area, himself. Then again, there were those in the area who couldn't speak the language at all. She hardly knew for sure who was who, which was which, or who hailed from where. She recalled meeting an Orthodox woman from Montreal, Canada, who spoke only French and Hebrew.

Thoughts of that woman reminded her that there were several sects of Hasids in the area, as well as Modern Orthodox people like the French Canadian woman, who were actually Sephardic. That they didn't really mingle with each other or even like each other. Maybe he was one of them. Maybe he didn't know Yiddish at all.

She decided to stick with her original assumption that he most likely spoke the language. It happened that Yiddish was a second language for her as well. Her grandparents spoke it with her mother all the time. She'd heard it repeatedly throughout her childhood, to the point of being fluent in it herself.

To test her assumption, Daniella had taken a chance during their last exchange at the booth, before the good-looking stranger prepared to leave. She had wanted to blurt out something just to prove she had some type of connection to him beyond the fact that she was Jewish. It would be a way to make clear she was worthy of consideration, to indicate she knew more than other mainstream Jews. It would keep the connection alive. *Let him know you can speak Yiddish.*

Daniella had smiled warmly as she placed his check on the table, "*Zei Ga Zind.*"

Indeed, Adam looked at her with surprise and responded, "*Vershtais*, Yiddish?" Daniella chose the phrase because it was a common departing phrase throughout the Jewish neighborhoods, often blurted out without any thought. It meant that nothing should harm or befall the listener.

The underlying message was one of God's protection. *Hashem* should watch over and keep safe the recipient of the phrase, and to the highest degree, as that person departed on his or her journey. His smile told her he understood. She was indicating he already mattered to her.

Daniella responded coyly to his simple question. "*A bissel.*"

She didn't want to sound like a braggart. Better to admit understanding only a little. *Stay modest in his eyes.* Where that thought came from, she couldn't even begin to ponder. She had never bought into the female modesty model touted in Orthodox circles. For some strange reason, she wanted acceptance in that moment.

As she had watched the young man's figure fade into the evening's blackness, practically swallowing up all the black he had been wearing, Daniella could do no more than hope and pray he would return. She didn't even know his name.

~⁀~

Two weeks later to the day, Adam showed up again at the Daily. He arrived late in the evening and was clever enough to have picked the same day of the week as his prior visit, all in the hope that Daniella would be working that shift. He would have liked to have patronized the restaurant sooner, but he didn't want to appear eager to talk to the Jewish girl.

Benny Kalabokas was behind the register just as before, and a smile lit up his face the moment Adam walked through the door.

"Well, look who's back. Nice to see you again. And now that you're here a second time, I just know you're going to become one of my regulars. So at this point, let's start with a formal reintroduction to each other.

"I am Benny Kalabokas, part owner of the Daily Diner, and it is a pleasure to see you again."

Benny held out his hand for a hearty handshake. It was reciprocated in strength and sincerity.

"I'm Adam Goldfarb, gemologist. I'm a buyer and seller of diamonds. I'm happy to be back."

The two men smiled as they shook hands in the traditional greeting rhythm. Benny continued the conversation as their hands released.

"Really? A gemologist. Diamonds, no less. How interesting! I'd love to hear more about that."

Adam hesitated. He could offer up the opportunity to let Benny do just that by suggesting he come and sit for a while, but Adam preferred to be honest about his reason for revisiting the restaurant. All of which became perfectly clear with his simple inquiry. "Is Danny here tonight?"

Adam noted that Benny appeared to be quite pleased by the question.

"Yes, she is. Would you like her to be your waitress?"

Benny didn't even wait for the answer, which was already sitting on the tip of Adam's tongue.

"Follow me, Adam. I'll put you at the best booth in her section."

Once again, Benny did his best to seem disinterested, allowing the two to have their back and forth while he secretly watched from a distance. However, just like a good matchmaker, he could only allow so much. About halfway through the meal, he walked over and sat down in Adam's booth. And really, that wasn't so strange. Benny did it quite often and to so many of his customers.

He had a suspicion about Adam. Something in the way he walked or maybe talked. Benny couldn't be sure. He had a gut feeling that Adam seemed disgruntled about life. The mere fact that he had come in once before, eaten a full meal, and showed an interest in Daniella told Benny that Adam was not happy with his Hasidic upbringing. Perhaps Adam didn't know it himself. Benny decided to put his instinct to the test.

With a hint of cleverness, Benny made sure that the timing of his inquiries of Adam matched Daniella's arrivals to the booth. Each time she came back with an item, Benny posed another question. He figured doing so would afford her a chance to linger and learn more about the young man. Benny began with an inviting phrase.

"Adam, tell us a bit more about yourself."

"Well, I'm a gemologist, as I told you before, Benny." He made sure to express sincere gratitude for his uncle Tzvi's determination to get him involved in the first place.

"I travel the world buying and selling diamonds. My travels are mostly to Belgium and the Netherlands. When I'm home, I'm mostly at home but I do make the occasional trip into the city because I have several jewelers who want to work with me rather than someone else."

Adam realized it sound conceited. He wanted to clarify the statement so that he wouldn't be falsely judged.

"You see, I really enjoy the beauty of the diamond, one of *Hashem's* incredible creations in nature." Adam laughed as he continued to speak. "A diamond is king among the gems. Rubies, emeralds, sapphires, they're just as miraculous, but the diamond is still king. Maybe the jewelers can tell that working with precious stones is my passion."

"I couldn't agree more with you, Adam. I mean, that gems are gorgeous, and it is no wonder that people desire to own them. Beautiful, beautiful things." The comment came from Daniella as she stood at the side of the table.

OK, enough of this! As a matchmaker, it's time to get down to business. Benny needed to give a little push. Benny waited until Daniella poured Adam his cup of coffee and had the pot upright once more. His verbal jostle would likely give her a jolt, and he didn't want her to spill the hot liquid.

"You know, Adam, our Danny here hopes to be a cantor."

As anticipated, the look of shock spread like a malignancy across Adam's face. Daniella's eyes grew as large as saucers, but only in preparation to throw daggers with them as she gave Benny a very angry look. Adam found the thought of any woman wanting to be a *hazzan* outrageous. Daniella stood stoically, admitting to herself that Adam didn't approve. It certainly explained the look of shock on his face.

Benny had gone and done it. She was sure that all hope was lost for any more flirting. Her dream of *hazzanut* was now exposed like an angry wound. Why Benny would do such a thing, Daniella could hardly understand. She opted to ignore the situation altogether and turned to leave so she could return the coffee urn to its resting plate. Her simple turn of the hip denied her the chance to see the relaxing of Adam's features and Benny's feigning oblivion as to what he had just done. Benny continued to speak.

"She is extremely intelligent and is on the threshold of learning so much more, Judaically speaking, that is. If fate is on her side, her dream will come to fruition."

After Daniella walked away in a bit of a huff, Adam's shock turned to curiosity. If the young man were curious enough, he just might want to see her again simply to talk some sense into her. Or, perhaps, to try to understand why she felt that way in the first place. And that meant more discussion between them. A chance to talk about something outside the context of eggs and toast. Benny, happy that he achieved the outcome he had hoped for, knew it was time to excuse himself.

"Adam, I really should be getting back to the register. It was nice chatting with you and learning about your role in the diamond industry. I look forward to seeing you again and soon, I hope."

Benny got up and left before Adam had a chance to say anything.

After steady minutes of interaction, Adam was suddenly alone at his table. He noticed that Daniella was lingering by the shelf stacked with glasses. She was wiping one after the other, seemingly preoccupied by the task. Was she afraid to return to the booth? Adam wondered if she thought he might judge her plans? He hoped not. The notion of her chanting liturgy was completely crazy to Adam's thinking, but he would certainly try to understand why she wanted to become a *hazzan*.

As of late, he himself had begun to question the rules that were part and parcel of his upbringing. Well, the questions had always been there; he knew that. But now he was an adult, and the questions had begun to gel for reasons he still couldn't understand. The push for him to marry had begun juggling the questions around in his head. Round and round, never committing to one line of thinking. It was actually driving him a bit crazy.

With the dining scenario now played out, his questions were more urgent than ever before. Curiosity was piqued. He wanted some answers. Perhaps someone like Daniella could provide food for thought for the many questions he had. After all, she was a Jewish girl, even if of a different kind. She knew much about the bigger world because she was in it. She could teach him how the Jews outside his neighborhood felt. How they acted. Together they could talk about, well, about everything.

The new piece of knowledge about her dreams and wishes offered the perfect segue into asking for permission to see her again. He had a solid reason to get to know her better. To understand her thoughts and feelings about Judaism and about life. It was a chance at the possibility of something between them even though her occupational desire was completely insane. *That could change. Hear her out. Understand her. The door isn't already closed. Maybe, just maybe, it could open up.* Adam got up and walked over to the register.

"Benny, do you think that Danny might be willing to meet with me?"

The look Benny gave Adam made the young man wonder if Benny had somehow planned for him to ask such a question. Adam convinced himself he was being foolish and smiled, awaiting Benny's answer.

"Adam, she has many wonderful qualities, one of which is judging everyone on their own merit. If she's interested, she'd want to get to know you for your own sake and not because you're Hasidic. You two probably have far more in common than you realize. I'm sure she'd be willing to meet with you. I will say one thing though."

Benny paused to gather his words so they would come out in the exact way he meant them.

"I feel very protective of Danny. She's like another daughter to me. If you want to meet up with her, I don't want you doing it in a secret place somewhere because you're ashamed of chasing after a Jew that is outside your fold.

"I insist that you meet with her here. This place is a public, open space and safe for her. If you talk with her and realize that no good will come of things, you changed your mind, whatever it is…better that she is here. You can get up and leave, and that will be the end of it. OK? No meeting in secret."

Benny paused before adding in one last comment.

"Isn't that better for you, anyway? It's not like the Hasidim are rushing to come in here. I'm saying this because I'm assuming you're not about to announce to your family that you're interested in a girl that exposes her upper arms, her legs, sings to men and women, and wants a leadership role. I doubt that Danny's parents would be happy about this either."

Benny was right. He knew how Adam's family would feel about a girl like Daniella, and it wasn't good. The Hasidim viewed all Jews outside their community as doomed beings who fell prey to the demonized world of the non-Jew.

"Benny, I'll honor your request and meet with her here—that is, if she's willing. If anything comes of it, though, I do hope you'll loosen the reins, just a bit. You sound more like a father than a boss." Adam produced a nervous laugh, instantly regretting his comment.

Benny decided to let the disparaging comment be as he continued. "We'll see, Adam. We'll see. I'm going to trust you, though. My heart tells me you'll treat her like…" Benny paused. "Like a diamond." Benny's thoughts strayed briefly.

So it begins. A romance between two of the most unlikely characters who were part of the history of my restaurant. I can hardly believe this. A cantor wannabe and a disgruntled Hasidic gemologist, both intent on making a match despite living in two completely separate worlds.

Benny gave Adam a shoo gesture. "It's now or never, Adam."

It was later that night when Daniella informed Benny that a simple yes on her part, was the response to Adam's request to meet with her.

"We'll have to keep our time together secret because both sets of parents will be mortified if they find out. But Benny, I'm really excited about this. We can have a grand exchange of thoughts, ideas, and feelings. We timed our meeting for the quiet hours when the restaurant has few customers."

"The back booth can be your safe haven. I've never understood why, but all the customers seem hopeful about sitting in it. Maybe it's a lucky booth!"

Benny's nonjudgmental demeanor was like a comfort blanket for Daniella. More so, as those first few meetings occurred. Even Nate knew to seat them in the back corner booth. When the booth happened to be occupied, they would be allowed to sit in the unused back room. Nonetheless, both youngsters and even Benny seemed to forget that the restaurant only protected them in its insular world. It could not protect them from the rest of the world that lay just outside the front doors.

"Tell me, Danny, why a cantor?"

Adam felt he could finally pose the question during their fourth meeting at the Daily in what he now considered their booth. He wasn't sure why he kept calling and asking to come back to see her. Her demeanor? Her attitude toward him in particular? Something about their exchanges was provoking him to delve deeper, which in itself seemed quite odd because she frustrated him with her absurd notions.

Even so, something about her answers caused Adam to reconsider every idea or feeling he'd ever had about life or the reasons people live it. He needed to find out what made her tick. He needed to find out why she gave her way of life more credence than his. As long as he could remember, his community had told him that women tended to be easily befuddled by higher thinking. In essence, that they were less intelligent than men. Yet here she was, spoon-feeding him wisdom beyond that of a simple girl. She had an answer for every new subject he brought up.

Presently, he still feared the very things that were becoming more and more appealing to him. In an effort to lessen that appeal, he planned the evening with a determination to dissuade her from her idea of ever becoming a *hazzan*. If he could do that somehow, she might fit better into his own world.

He should have known better. Not only did her answer surprise him, but it caused what would become their temporary breakup.

"I was blessed with the gift of music. It's that simple, Adam. I can belt it out with the best of them, and I connect with my music on a very soulful level. What better way to show my gratitude for such a blessing than to praise *Hashem* with it?"

Daniella paused. She focused on what she wanted to say next.

"No...more than that. I want to help others connect to their spiritual selves. Too many people don't, and you of all people should know that, being as observant as you are. Too many Jews are losing their way. I want to help guide them in the right direction. Judaism is wonderful, Adam. I can help them see that, feel that...live that."

Adam could see her conviction, practically touch it, as if the passion laced in her words suddenly solidified. What really struck him, however, was that for all intents and purposes she recited the same sentiment that his entire community expressed countless times. *Judaism is wonderful, especially if expressed wholeheartedly.* If anything, it was a connective statement. Why, then, did he still feel worlds apart? Why, then, was he so torn between her views and his own?

He couldn't get past his own upbringing and the ideas that had been emblazoned into the teachings he had learned growing up. His only response to the adorably charming girl across the table was, "What about *Kol Isha?*"

"What about it?"

Adam had been raised to believe that the sound of a woman singing was arousing, and therefore it was a severe distraction from prayer and many other obligations in life. He believed that too. It made perfect sense to him to keep the women separate when praying at *shul* or even in general, lest he or others lose focus. He was willing to admit that the separation was necessary because men were weak at heart when it came to the opposite sex. He knew that being with women, seeing them and hearing them, aroused the *yetzer harah*, a terrible inclination to do evil and sin.

"Danny, women are lovely. Not only their voice in song but everything about them. Better to be safe about meeting our obligations to *Hashem* by keeping the distraction minimal. Even the hair…" Adam paused only a moment before blurting out his compliment.

"Look at yours, for example. Such a unique color, and the way it falls around your shoulders…It's, well…delightful. You look very beautiful, Danny." Adam blushed a deep shade of red.

"Thank you, Adam." Daniella blushed in turn.

There was a substantial shift in Daniella's thoughts at that very moment. However much she relished the compliment and was pleased that Adam found her attractive, she was more concerned about convincing him about the foolishness of forbidding himself to hear a woman's voice in song. Daniella carefully gathered her thoughts and spoke.

"So much of what you said is by rote. Have you ever given any further thought to that conviction, or do you just accept it blindly?"

Daniella shifted in her seat so that she was staring directly into Adam's eyes. She could see that look in them. The one that innocently said, "What do you mean? What are you talking about?" Well, she was determined to explain and make herself perfectly clear.

"I've been doing my homework. Speaking to lots of rabbis and cantors in the area and even some at the seminary on phone call after phone call. I've been preparing as best I can to fulfill my dream. Reading books on all things Judaic so I can be accepted into a cantorial program. My last year of college is starting next week, and by the end of November, I need to apply to the program I have in mind.

"I can read and write Hebrew. I can understand it to a fair extent. I know a lot about our history and rituals, courtesy of years of Hebrew School three days a week. I've attended services so often that I can already chant certain prayers with ease. So, believe you me, I have counter comments about *Kol Isha*."

Her undertone of frustration and anger kept building as she spoke. Suddenly, she had placed Adam into the role of scapegoat for his entire community, and she directed her disgruntlement straight toward him.

"How does the lullaby that your mother sang to you as a young boy suddenly become the potential for sex?

The intent of that song is to soothe a child's fears about sleeping in the dark. A grown man has to run into another room if his mother is singing to a grandchild? *Hashem* forbid, he'll think of sex because he hears his mother's voice? His own mother? That's sick, Adam.

"I'll take it even further. You can listen to your young sister sing prayers at the Sabbath table because you're 'used' to her voice, whatever that means!" Daniella made two very distinct quote marks in the air.

"Somehow, when she turns another year older... boom, the same rule applies to her too. She's forbidden to pray aloud in your presence because of your weakness? Shame on all of you men for putting the onus on women and denying them a chance to praise just as heartily as you."

Adam chimed in. "But they can praise heartily. They just need to do it separately."

"It's all a guise, Adam. A guise to keep women inferior. You've brainwashed every last one of them to believe such nonsense."

Adam began to squirm in his seat.

"Adam, if singing isn't being done for personal enjoyment and the aim of the woman is not to cause enjoyment, don't the rabbis say that in some cases, it's acceptable? Like, maybe, a mortally ill child, for example, who needs his mother's voice to soothe with a lullaby even though men might be in the hospital room alongside her. Why, then, can't the same apply to a woman's prayer? She's not chanting to induce a sexual encounter. She's praying with her heart to *Hashem* in the hopes of connecting with the Almighty. I just don't understand the logic."

Adam could not stand in Daniella's shoes and feel the feelings a woman might feel; he could only respond as a male.

"Danny, logically speaking you make perfect sense. I think many men would possibly agree. Even Orthodox men. But then, put in the fact that we are men. I know enough about biology to tell you that testosterone is the worst *yetzer harah* of all. It's the ultimate test that *Hashem* placed on us males. It's like *Hashem* were saying, 'Let's see if you can overcome all your earthly urges and connect with the realm your soul left behind. Let's play hide and seek. Come find me, but not without obstacles along the way.' Danny, I overheard somewhere that men think about sex every twenty seconds. Know what? I don't doubt it!"

Adam fretted for a moment and paused.

"I'm sorry that I'm speaking so directly to you. This actually feels inappropriate. I should be talking to a man about sex and not you. But if you have the notion to push the issue, I feel I should say something."

"Not talk to me because we're discussing human nature? My gosh, Adam. You and your whole community are backward! You're backward enough to not even realize the issue here is not sex at all. You're talking about men trying to keep control. You're talking about women being second-class citizens. Can't you see that?"

Daniella tried to afford Adam the same courtesy of placing herself in his shoes, but being on the other side, being female and far more worldly, she could not handle the closed-minded thinking that she found to be prevalent among observant Jewish men. And that was even in her own community. When it came to women in public, Hasidic and Orthodox men were in the Stone Age. Conservative men, perhaps just one step ahead of that. Things needed to change, and she was brave enough to argue for the cause. She had more fodder to fuel her argument, and she continued without hesitation.

"You say that talking this way is inappropriate? So why are you speaking to me about anything at all?"

Daniella paused to calm herself, realizing she was getting a bit flustered.

"Don't you see how illogical it is to go to the men in your community to discuss the feelings or issues that are about women? Are they inside the women's brains that they know exactly what is being thought or considered? Mr. So-and-So down the block will do no more than tell you this is all forbidden and you shouldn't be questioning it."

"So now you're an expert on my community?"

"Adam, I know far more about your community than you'll ever know about mine, and you know it! Besides, half the time your community won't even agree with the one next to it, or the rabbis themselves won't agree with each other.

"How many times have different rabbis in different communities had different opinions about *Kol Isha*? One rabbi says men should never hear a woman's voice in song or in prayer. That he'll be aroused no matter what and then he'll lose focus and won't be able to pray or even function at all.

"Another rabbi says you can listen to a song on the radio because then you can't see the woman and so won't have to deal with the possibility of her being attractive." Daniella snorted derisively. "So it's really all about looks and suddenly not about the voice at all.

"Talk about bending the rules! Adam, all I have to do is this, and you still have the same problem." Daniella changed the tone of her voice to make it sound sexy as she lifted her napkin to cover her face. Her voice was suddenly sultry and deep as it traveled through the veil of the napkin and into Adam's ears.

"Today's weather is overcast, with a chance of rain. Perhaps you should consider carrying an umbrella. Better yet, stay indoors."

Daniella dropped her napkin to take a peek at Adam.

"I wasn't singing then, Adam, was I? I was only speaking. What then? Should women never speak at all because they might have a voice that sounds too sexy?"

Adam looked perturbed, but Daniella couldn't tell if that was because the sexual tone in her voice got to him or because he actually grasped the logic of her argument.

"My answer, Danny, is you're intentionally provoking me with that sexy tone."

"That's a cop-out answer, Adam. I'm trying to show you that simply speaking can be just as provoking as singing or anything else. In the same way a woman needs to speak to be understood, she needs to pray and sing to have her chance to connect with *Hashem*. It should be unfettered by rules that men created. Men, Adam. Not *Hashem*.

"The answer you men always seem to come up with is that she should shut herself off from anything that will make you get hot under the collar. It's even more than the voice! She has to wear a wig if she's married because her own hair is too sexually arousing? Come on! Those wigs are just as beautiful, and men look at the women anyway. Cover those elbows and knees because somehow just one inch higher on the hems and sex is in order. Isn't it interesting that the rules always seem to come out in the man's favor? Isn't it interesting that the rules were made by men as well?"

Daniella was visibly angered. Her dimpled cheeks were becoming redder by the minute.

"If you men feel this so strongly, then why aren't we all wrapped up from head to toe with only our eyes showing?" Daniella was practically spewing venom. Adam was trying to stay calm.

"What do you mean by that, Danny?"

"If everything is such a distraction, women should not be seen or heard! Right, Adam? Otherwise, men can't get on with their lives. Isn't that what you're implying?"

Adam guffawed a bit. It bought him precious moments to collect some sort of answer for himself.

"Danny, you're being unfair. And you know what? It is sexy! Blame it on us men. I don't care! We're weak! The more flesh we see, the more we want it."

Daniella interrupted abruptly. "That's because you made women so unreachable. If you lived outside your little bubble, you'd come across women all the time, dressed in all sorts of ways, and you'd see that everyone just gets on with their lives. Men and women both. No one is stopping the other in the streets saying, 'You're too sexy, and you're too sexy.' Pointing each person out so they can hurry home and cover up. You made women like the candy in a shop—the treat that sits high on the shelf. No one can have it, so all of you want it."

"We just can't afford to make women more important than *Hashem*. Now *that* you must surely understand. You, who wants to be a *hazzan*."

Adam ground out the last comment to make it more hurtful, and Daniella felt it. He threatened her conviction of someday being a *hazzan*, and her response came roaring through like an exploding cannonball.

"Adam, put me on the other side of a *mechitzah* or upstairs in a balcony and I'll still praise *Hashem* loud and clear and with all my heart. Who are you to take that away from me? And what? You'll kick me out of the synagogue for praying loudly and with all my heart? Yes, actually, you probably will. Who do you think *Hashem* will judge? Me or you? Me, who wanted to thank God for the blessings of life, or you, who wouldn't let me?"

Adam was now on the defensive, as evidenced by the smack his fist made on the table's edge.

"Danny, you can pray all you want. You just don't understand. I'm telling you, testosterone is a curse. A horrible test that was put on us to see if we make the grade."

"Bull pucky. It's a convenient excuse because you men are afraid to lose your control over everything. You've brainwashed the women in your community to really believe it is their duty to refrain from advancing in the ranks in any way, shape, or form. They actually buy into the notion that they are second class."

Daniella banged her fist on the table's edge as well. As far as she was concerned, she had just gotten to the heart of the matter. Deep down, it was all about control and men knowing full well that women were perfectly capable of taking on leadership roles. Men were afraid to lose their ability to run the show. She would never buy into the idea that men had obligations but women were excused from them so they could raise children and run a home. Men created the rules simply to keep women down. She finished her ranting by adding in one last comment.

"Your half of the species is always insisting you're the superior ones. Yet, you can't even control your urges? Sounds inferior to me!"

Daniella paused in an effort to calm her tone.

"Adam, you will never understand the demeaning gesture of standing up and walking out of a room when a woman opens her mouth to do no more than praise God. It comes across as loathing of a woman. Pure loathing."

The fury in her tone was creeping back in.

"Read your Bible again, Adam! Women received Torah right by man's side. It was given to them too, remember? And equally, as I recall. They weren't asked to stand behind a *mechitzah* so *Hashem* could deliver it to the men first."

She was quoting Bible now. Well, so could he.

"Read your own Bible, Danny! Right at the very beginning. Right in *Bereshit*. Right there in the creation story. *Hashem* is angered by the sin of eating from the Tree of Knowledge. His punishment for the snake is crawling for all eternity in order to live and find sustenance. More so, to be loathed and feared in the eyes of all humans that spy him on the ground.

"For Eve, it is pain in childbearing, but for Adam, however, it is dominion over Eve and the earth. Dominion over women, Danny! Says it right there in the beginning chapters of the Torah."

Adam had no idea why he was dishing out such an open-ended counterpoint. Even he knew his comments were vague and easily arguable. Many components of the creation story could be discussed and debated by any number of people learned in Old Testament text. He supposed he wanted to stump her. Prove that she had no right, let alone any qualifications, to think she could stand in front of a community and be their spiritual leader. He wasn't even sure why he felt that way. Part of him, deep down, was already pondering the possibility and wanting her to succeed.

"I have read my Bible, Adam, and you're leaving out quite a bit. When God made Adam and Eve, they were equals. She was flesh of his flesh, bone of his bone. One and the same material because she came directly from him. No difference, then, in their bodily make up. *Hashem* meant for it to be that way. Two halves of a whole meant to be equal and a complete partnership."

Adam wanted to say something, but Daniella hushed him up instantly by putting her hand up in the classic stop-sign gesture.

"I'm not finished yet. Three creatures sinned in the garden, but of them all, Adam was the guiltiest. *Adam*, Adam. Not anyone else. He had been given the directive not to eat of the tree. It came directly from God's mouth, and he disobeyed it. So God diminished his level of existence.

"He put him below the Godliness that was part and parcel of coexisting with God in the garden. He made it so that Adam would no longer have a life of ease. He'd have to toil, run a household, make sure that everyone and everything was well cared for. He was brought down a peg from the godly realm he once resided in.

"It's only because of Adam's sin that everything came about! Even if Eve ate the apple because she was coaxed, it didn't mean Adam had to. He could have said no. All

Adam did say was, 'She made me do it.' Even back then, Adam...men blaming women for their own mistakes. In fact, *Kol Isha* is simply more of that. It's blatant sexism with the excuse that man is supposed to have the last say.

"Well, know what? I'm proud of my Conservative upbringing. I can't help but feel that we are trying our best to return to the equality that God originally intended. I plan to continue that effort. You're more than welcome to stick with your backward way of thinking and silly notion that women can't do certain things."

The impasse had been reached, and each knew it. The fourth date, made originally because the prior ones had been so wonderfully enjoyable, had now gone sour. Like some giant grandfather clock, the two were standing up now, each body a hand pointing in the opposite direction. Each on separate sides of the table indicating the time had come to end the date.

Daniella put up her hand to indicate to Adam that he should stay put.

"I'm done, Adam. But I have one last thing to suggest before I go. Get educated, Adam. Maybe you should start with psychology one-oh-one."

Daniella produced a chuckling sneer as she stared into his eyes. "You probably don't even know what that means! Oh, and you should probably learn about Brown versus the Board of Education, too! Separate but equal, my as...*tush*!"

She walked away from the table before he could respond. She grabbed her handbag from behind the cashier counter where she had placed it for safekeeping, gave a quick nod to Nate who happened to be on duty that evening, and left without another word. She knew that

Adam could see her through the glass so she rushed to her car and hastily pulled away. She was praying that she didn't look foolish.

As she pulled away, she stole a quick glance into the large window near the back booth. She could see that Adam had sat back down. She muttered a wish that he was sitting there feeling miserable. At least, that he felt as miserable as she.

Daniella arrived home that night feeling emotionally exhausted. How could she have thought for even one moment that she could connect with an ultra-Orthodox man? He lived a cloistered life. She didn't. He had the watchful eyes of his community on him, and constantly at that. She didn't. Her thinking was drenched in influences from the outside world. His was soaked in tradition that was stuck in eighteenth-century Europe.

Sadly, he hailed from a sect known for their over-the-top adherence to some very fanatical notions. Would it have been easier if he had come from one of the groups known to be kinder to outside Jews or to the entire world? If he had been a member of a sect that was even willing to interact with *goyim*? Was there such a thing?

Daniella made a snort of derision. They even thought of her as a *goy*. Any Jew who was not like them was not a true Jew at all. You were only the real deal if you were exactly like them. How pathetic. They were like Dr. Seuss's Sneetches on beaches. The ones with stars upon thars. They were the only kind of acceptable Sneetch. Any Sneetch missing the star was screwed.

Adam's sect wouldn't even know what a Sneetch was or, for that matter, recognize any Dr. Seuss classic. It didn't even matter because all those sects were at odds with each other. Some even had out-and-out dislike for the other. Hasids existed in a world she would never understand.

Despite that, she couldn't help but acknowledge just how attractive she found Adam. Not only physically but in the way he expressed himself and the few times he seemed to agree with her thoughts about their religion. She even wondered what it might be like to kiss him. The notion was crazy, even to her. Especially given what had just transpired. Despite that, she admitted to herself she could easily fall for him, if such a thing were possible.

She felt the chemistry every single time he was near. She was sure he felt it too. That summation made an idea creep into her thoughts...Maybe that was why he answered her the way he did! The possibility made her smile. The very notion that he was attracted to her... *Well, it's all moot now. I think I made clear that he wouldn't be able to get me to think his way, and isn't that a red flag for both of us? Thank goodness I didn't bother to tell Mom or Dad about him. I could just imagine what they would have thought.*

In another place entirely, Adam was sitting in the quiet of his bedroom. He had driven home from the Daily that evening flustered and annoyed. He wanted nothing more than to be left alone. His proof had been right before his eyes the whole time. Validation of the very argument he had given her. He was distracted by the fact that she was so pleasing to look at. Coffee-colored hair, thick with rivulets of shimmers. Bright-green eyes that sparkled with the enthusiasm of her words. Two of the deepest and cutest dimples he had ever seen. Even her nose was as perfect as a rose, long and sleek with a budding tip. She was a Jewess quite unlike any he had ever met. Worse, she made the chemical sparks kindle inside. Even her anger fueled his desire.

Adam couldn't help but believe it was all a test sent from heaven and, somehow, he had just miraculously passed the exam. Even when he was driving home, his hands had clutched the steering wheel tightly to express his frustration. The grip most definitely the result of the anger within. Tight and steadfast. Presently, he clutched his fists once more as Adam suddenly felt an ire of a different kind.

I'm twenty-four, for crying out loud. A grown man. I should be married and out of the house by now. It's time to get on with my life, and not by chasing after some girl with a deep-rooted notion to out-step her bounds.

He thought that, but at his deepest level, the words rang untrue. At this particular juncture, Adam was questioning so much of his own life and she had hit the nail on the head. He was standing close to a crossroads that confused him, and he didn't know which way to turn.

His parents formed a great part of the blockade standing by his imaginary crossroads. His parents loved him and meant well. Adam breathed a heavy sigh. They were intent on keeping him at home for a while longer so his savings could increase a bit more before he married. They wanted to allow him to build up the nest egg so he would be a good provider. That was their credo. It was the Hasidic way. Children should stay in the home until they married and were ready to have a home of their own.

Adam had been moved from his bedroom upstairs into the spare room by the back door once he had completed his training as a gemologist. He would have preferred to live alone in a place of his own and get on with his adult life, but his parents pressured him consistently. They wanted him to stay put and prepare for his future. At least downstairs in the back room, he could feel as if he were in his own little apartment.

Adam thought about Danny, who was certainly not the right material for building a Hasidic life. Yet Adam felt there was so much of her to like. He admired her conviction, and no matter how twisted it was, wasn't her thinking at least in the right direction? She wanted to be a good Jew, didn't she? Wasn't that a good thing? She was just misguided, that's all. *Or am I the misguided one?*

Thank goodness he hadn't mentioned her to his parents. They would have been miserable to deal with if a girl like her had ever come into the picture. She was evil personified as far as his community was concerned. The thought troubled him, and for the briefest of moments, Adam acknowledged that their thinking must be as backward as Daniella had implied.

Adam pulled into the driveway, parked the car, got out and walked to the side door, and turned the lock. He stepped inside and wiped his feet, preparing to remove his shoes so he could enter his bedroom. He was distracted by the sound of his father's footfall as he walked down the hall toward Adam's room.

"Adam, I thought you were home! I'm glad you're here. Would you mind coming into the kitchen? We want to talk with you about something, and we've been quite eager for your arrival. Where were you, anyway?"

It was only 9:00 p.m. The date with Daniella, called for 7:30 p.m., had ended so abruptly that Adam was actually home much sooner than planned. How to answer his parent? It would be no lie to state where he had been, would it?

"I *davened* at six forty-five and then decided to go…"

Instinct made Adam change his mind at the last moment.

"For a ride in the car. I just wanted to enjoy the night air that *Hashem* made so crisp and clear tonight. What better time than right after praising *Hashem* at evening prayers?"

"Suddenly, you're wanting to commune with the stars? Anyway, come into the kitchen. We'll tell you our news. We think you're going to be very excited."

They walked down the hall together. Adam silently asked for forgiveness, having just lied to his father, and quickly changed his thinking to what he already knew lay at the heart of the discussion his father planned. That certain sense of a *shiddach* was brewing in the air. His mother's waiting figure at the kitchen table confirmed it as Adam glanced at her eager face. She had his favorite homemade cookies at the ready.

Well, he was more than primed for meeting a woman, especially one he could connect with in the ways that were right. He would much rather talk about whomever they had in mind than the peculiarity of a kosher restaurant in the middle of nowhere and the very beautiful Jewish girl who was employed at the Daily. As he listened to his parents, he made a mental note to sneak another visit to the library at the east end of the county. He blamed the urge on Daniella. He was very curious to find out what psychology 101 meant or for that matter, Brown vs. the Board of Education.

"Adam, *Tante* Batya and *Feter* Tzvi invited us over for tea to tell us about a young woman." Tsivia Goldfarb could barely contain her enthusiasm as she stated the fact to her son.

Nachum gave the table a gentle rap, indicating he'd take over. "A colleague of Tzvi's told him about another coworker in the industry who resides here in the States but happens to have a niece in Belgium. She's the daughter of his brother, who is a diamond cutter. Maybe you know him? Well, let me continue first.

"The mother, his sister-in-law, is a seamstress. I mention this because his niece is also very talented with needle and thread. The niece is the perfect age for you, has all the makings of a future *balabusta*, and is a pretty and sweet young woman from what I am told."

Nachum wanted to add in a bit more. "He mentioned that she's smart but charming. Just like you, Adam. They say she loves being traditional. Isn't that wonderful, Adam? All those qualities and the makings of a future homemaker as well! Now that's what I call a *balabusta* in the making! Who doesn't want a woman who can cook, clean, and keep a proper home?"

Tsivia Goldfarb piped in. "This colleague told Tzvi he's actually met the girl during his own travels to Belgium. He saw her when he paid a visit to his coworker. He was a guest in the family's home. For *Shabbat*, to be exact. So he was able to see how she functions in a household. He told Papa that she already acts like a *balabusta*. So good to her parents and takes care of the home. Served the meal beautifully. It means she can cook, take care of a house, is good mother material. Just like *Tata* said to you. That makes me happy for you."

Nachum smiled at his wife, rapped the table once more, and began to speak. "She's from the Hasidic community and is observant as a good Jewess should be. And it's Antwerp, Adam. You travel there so often yourself. What do you think? Can we make arrangements for you two to meet when you travel there next? Her parents are willing to consider a long-distance match. We are too, since the prospects here haven't worked out."

Tsivia piped in with a comment of her own but directed it to her husband. "Tell him about your idea."

Nachum nodded and continued. "You know the city well enough that you can plan a date if you meet her and really like her. Think how impressed she'd be that even though you're a foreigner, you know your way around, and besides, you can speak Yiddish with her! That's a bonus right there. *Feter* tells me they speak Flemish in public, but Yiddish is the language at home and around the neighborhood. Out of necessity the children learn French and English, and of course they learn Hebrew, but I suppose you know all that. Five languages, Adam. Five! Impressive! If she speaks Flemish, it means she'll understand Dutch too. That makes six! Sounds to me like she's an intelligent girl. That would be so important in terms of future children."

"What's her name, *Tata?*"

"*Oy*, Adam. I'm so excited about this, I forgot. Her name is Teme. Teme Gvirzman."

Adam smiled at his parents. "Sure, why not. Maybe she's the girl of my dreams."

Teme

Antwerp was the heart and soul of Jewish Orthodoxy in Europe. A long and complicated history had extracted Jews from several areas across Europe, over hundreds of years, to be exact, uprooting and rerouting them throughout the continent. A decent attitude toward Jews eventually placed a large percentage of them in Antwerp.

Edicts that expelled Jews from one place or another—or even worse, denied people the right to be Jewish at all—were practically a constant in Europe's history. Antwerp became the little piece of heaven inside a hellish land. Recognition that Jews were an asset in financial and business matters won out over any other concerns the Antwerp residents may have had, and ultimately, the Jews thrived there.

By the time Teme had been born, the Jewish community had been more than ancient in Antwerp. The only sorrow was that they numbered a lot less courtesy of the evil known as Hitler. Perhaps about fifteen thousand or so remained, but one could not be sure.

The diamond district housed the Jews of Antwerp. It was not accurate to make a blanket statement that the Hasidic people were the sole residents there. However, it was more than accurate to say that many of the different sects that practiced Hasidism or some form of Orthodoxy comprised the melting pot that was Jewish Antwerp. Even Haredi Jews, known for their fervent interpretation of Hasidic life, resided in Antwerp. Some folks were not even part of those communities at all. Some, perhaps, were not even Jewish.

Teme was never quite sure exactly where her family fit in. It seemed that every time she turned around, the rules had changed in her particular sect. One day *Tata* would announce that the rabbi said "A," and so the family had to do "A." Then the following week, when the rabbi said "B," *Tata* would change the rules once more. The only thing she could give credence to was that her family was Hasidic and very traditional in their beliefs.

Teme felt happy being traditionally Orthodox. Deep down, her soul rejoiced over being Jewish. She could have cited many reasons for that feeling, but she thought it was because of her given Hebrew names. It was Ashkenazic tradition to name a child after a deceased relative, and she had been named after two very special ladies.

During the post-Holocaust era, many families insisted on the honor of passing on names of the deceased family members who had perished. They did so for the sake of continuity. This made the children a living testimony that the generations past would not be forgotten. More important, it ensured that their loved ones' names could be carried into the future. This would only change if, God forbid, a close relative like a parent, sibling, or grandparent had passed and so needed the honor instead.

With no recently passed relatives to honor, Teme's parents chose to name her after her great-great-grand-mother's sisters, who, it was surmised, had perished in a government-sanctioned pogrom. No one really knew for sure. They could only be sure that the two women had been erased from existence. That uncertainty alone so-lidified the belief that the deaths had likely been horrific.

Teme would carry on their names and eventually become the mother and wife neither of them could be. Teme didn't know how old the sisters had been—or anything about them, for that matter. One thing in par-ticular, however, resided at the very core of Teme's being. She believed with all her heart and soul that she was des-tined to live a full and joyous Jewish life simply because they could not. It was her sacred duty to be a good Jew to honor their memory.

She became even more convinced as a young teen, when Mama shared the information that both sisters had apparently been seamstresses...just like Teme and her mother. One of them had been particularly adept at bob-bin lacing and tatting, but no one knew which sister that had been. Teme loved to sew alongside her mother, and for a reason she could not place, she could create lace with the best of them. Enough so that by present day she was an expert in the craft, as well as in needle lacing, hairpin lacing, and even filet netting. She was the only one in the family who seemed to have the knack and, most especially, the patience for it.

Teme was sure her talent arose from the hapless soul of her great-great-aunt, whichever one it was, coming through her and begging Teme to create all the things she never could. Teme had already been asked on several occasions to create lace trims for one occasion or another. She had even done lace work for the wedding gowns that her mother had sewn for the local brides. Teme could hardly wait for the day when she would make lace for her own wedding gown.

Since her younger years, she had been determined to live her happy Jewish life as a good Jewish homemaker and eventual mother. She saw herself tatting and doing lacework for others as she perpetuated the traditions that were part of a good Jewish lifestyle. Doing so would ensure a blessing upon the memory of her two special aunts. It was no surprise, then, that Teme was eager to meet potential bridegrooms.

A young man was coming for *Shabbos*. A young man from the United States. He was a buyer and seller of diamonds, and he planned to visit for *Shabbos* after spending time with *Tata* during the week. He had come to discuss potential business deals with *Tata* before he returned to the United States, and *Tata* thought it would be nice if he came for a good *Shabbos* meal before returning to his home across the ocean.

Teme knew better. He was a potential mate, and *Tata* and Mama were both providing an opportunity to meet and evaluate this potential suitor. Admittedly, Teme was excited and hopeful. She was more than ready and willing to consider marriage.

With most of the cooking having been seen to the night before and the cleaning finished up by early morning, the ladies of the house, which included Mama, Teme, and *Bubbe* Yedida, had finished with their preparations. Since it was only midday, Mama and *Bubbe* both suggested that Teme find a pretty outfit to wear for *Shabbos* and make herself presentable for the sake of the family.

It was important to make sure no stone was unturned in presenting the best possible atmosphere for their special guest, and that included the family's appearance. With the men expected soon after evening services, time was of the essence, so best that Teme start to dress early.

"Teme, let me help you with your hair," *Bubbe* Yedida piped in. "So beautiful. I know just the perfect style that will complement your modesty. Come, *Shayna*."

Teme loved that her grandmother thought she was beautiful, but that hardly counted. In matters of making a match, it only mattered that her future prospective bridegroom would think so.

There they were, in the kitchen reviewing and checking that Teme looked perfect. Fussing and clucking like chickens, mother and grandmother insisted that everything must look just right. That included the food, which was now under its third round of inspection. Teme was the first to hear her father's arrival at the door to their home.

"*Shalom*. Hallo. We're here."

She touched her mother's arm in a way that indicated her excitement, dusted off and removed her apron, straightened her dress creases, and looked to both women for one last nod of approval. The women exited the kitchen one by one. They lined up in the front entryway as the men took off their evening coats and hats, and they waited to be formally introduced to their special guest.

"Adam Goldfarb, may I present my wife, Bina, my mother, Yedida, and our daughter, Teme. My sons are grown and married and enjoying *Shabbos* in their own homes. I have four of them, you know. *Hashem* should will it, you can meet with them after services tomorrow. They come by on *Shabbos*, usually in the late afternoon, and they bring the *gantze mishpacha*. Let me tell you, that is a congregation in itself! I have so many grandchildren, I've lost count! I'm a lucky man in that respect. Sons, daughters-in-law, and little ones to add to my *Shabbos* joy!"

Aaron Gvirzman blabbed on and on, oblivious to the fact that very few of his comments penetrated the brain of the young man at his side. The young man who had momentarily lost track of the words because the young woman who was Aaron's daughter had caught his eye with her demure actions.

When Aaron Gvirzman had mentioned Teme's name to Adam, she had given him a quick curtsy and smiled at him rather coyly. She had lowered her head during the deepest part of her bow in order to demonstrate her modesty. Yet she gently lifted her eyes to gaze up at him and send a flirtatious message. The well-rehearsed dance struck Adam like a lightning bolt and he couldn't help but stare. Adam didn't even realize that Aaron Gvirzman had finished his little speech.

"So what do you think, Adam? I have my wonderful ladies here who have completely prepared for the Sabbath and of course, to take care of us all."

Adam simply stated the obvious as he continued to look in Teme's direction.

"Mrs. Gvirzman, Mrs. Gvirzman, Miss Gvirzman. Nice to meet you."

Teme smiled once more as she stood there. "Welcome, Mr. Goldfarb."

Adam took in so much information in that instant that his mind was overloaded with sensation. Two eyes were gazing at him as if he were a prize. They were the color of icy diamonds, blue in hue but so light that he thought they looked like ice crystals on a cold winter's day. He surmised that the young woman had outlined her eyes with deep-brown liner, because her eyes seemed to be encased by a coffee-colored kohl. He concluded he must have a thing for coffee since he was always referencing it as of late when he described women. Only moments later, Adam realized the young woman's lashes were so thick that they traced the shape of her sockets.

Her hair was dripping honey. Deep, dark, amber honey. The cinnamon color framed her face with wisps that loosened from a small chignon that rested at the back of her head atop hanging curls. The long strands wrapped around her shoulders and captured her beauty as if she were inside a picture frame. The vision made Adam think of a cameo. Perfectly chiseled. Perfectly framed.

He also thought of her shaving it off if they were married. That bothered him, seeing how lovely it was. He would much prefer to stroke it and enjoy its beauty. If they did make a connection, maybe he could convince her to secretly tuck it under a wig. Why he even thought that, he could hardly guess.

A long ivory-colored hair ribbon trickled down over each of her shoulders. It matched the color of her blouse. The ends hung like streamers, extensions of the ribbon that was tied to encase her half bun at the back of her head. Adam caught sight of the sculpted hair pinned tightly at the back as she turned toward her father. The hairdo was meticulous in appearance, curl upon curl. Adam realized it had likely been made just for him. She half turned once more, and Adam watched her lips as she spoke to her father.

"Please, come sit down, *Tata*, and you too, Mr. Goldfarb."

"Please, everyone, call me Adam."

Bina Gvirzman added in, "Fine then, Adam. Come sit. Teme has prepared some beautiful treats. We'll sit and get to know each other a bit, and then we'll head into the dining room for dinner."

The subtlety was not lost on Adam. The lady of the house was letting him know that Teme had skills in the kitchen. Well, two for two so far. She's pretty and she's adept in the culinary department. Adam already felt the visit would not be in vain. The Gvirzmans' daughter seemed lovely.

Delighted with the royal treatment and especially with the wonderful accents in their English pronunciations, Adam hesitantly admitted to himself that he also needed to make an impression. He needed to put his best foot forward. *Converse in their first language.*

In perfect Yiddish, Adam conveyed that he would be more than happy to switch to Yiddish for their sake. "Surely it is easier than your speaking English."

Aaron replied for everyone. "Yes, thank you. We only use English and French when absolutely necessary, so we're not as proficient as when we speak in Yiddish or Flemish. Actually, it will be a relief to stop using English." The elder Gvirzman gave a hearty laugh. He felt compelled to add,

"Of course, Hebrew is another matter, entirely. We are all quite proficient in the language of our people."

Adam took note of the less than subtle hint in what would likely be an evening filled with them. OK, so Teme was proficient with Hebrew besides every other language that had just been listed. The back and forth went on for a solid half hour before Aaron, as head of the household, felt it was time to move things along.

"Come, everyone. It is time to enjoy *Shabbos* with a good meal."

Adam watched Teme as she stood to leave. He could see that she was slender despite her modest outfit. Her ivory blouse was trimmed at the collar with very pretty lace, which, he would find out later, she had made with her own two hands. The sleeves of her blouse were gathered at the shoulders, and they puffed out like balloons on her arms before gathering once more at two cuffed wrists. A charcoal-gray pencil skirt hugged her hips as it reached down to rest at her ankles. As Adam drank in the shapely figure, he suddenly heard a voice in his head that seemed to come from nowhere.

"Cover those elbows and knees because somehow just one inch higher on the hems and sex is in order."

Here's your proof right here, Danny. She's covered from head to toe, and still I'm thinking of Teme in a way I probably shouldn't be. You bet, one inch higher and thoughts of sex will get even worse! Yet, in a far corner of his mind, Adam was toying with logic that was not his own. Logic that was arguing on Danny's behalf. *Whatever Teme does, no matter what she says, it is not her responsibility to protect you from yourself. That's your job. Step up and take responsibility for your shortcomings. Don't put the onus on Teme.*

Adam finished the silent conversation abruptly. *Sorry, Danny. You have no place here.* His thoughts of Teme were interested and, at this early phase, hopeful about finally making a match with someone. He wanted, no, needed to push all thoughts of Daniella far away where they couldn't mess with his mind. He wanted to make his family proud, and a match with Teme would be his golden ticket.

Teme was notably graceful. Adam couldn't help but notice the swish and sway of her hips as she circled the table, placing a small challah roll onto each person's bread plate. Her movements were so perfectly feminine. Little sparks of chemistry ignited in his loins, and this time, they flared for an acceptable girl. Little sparks that had nothing to do with substance. Little sparks that had everything to do with lust, sprinkled with the knowledge that this was acceptable to his family and community.

Adam couldn't even tell the difference between lust and love because he had never been instructed in human emotion. Sadly for him, Teme was equally naive. Hasidism emphasized God and devotion to the Almighty's holiness and laws. It was completely cocooned from anything that would detract from that obligation.

In an effort to distract himself, Adam began to look around and take note of his surroundings. The Gvirzman household seemed like a step back in time. Had he not known it was December of 1984, he could have easily believed it was 1884. The dining room furniture was made of deep, dark wood with intricate scrollwork visible on the breakfront and chair backs. A chandelier with candleholders resided over the table's center. Perhaps when it was not the Sabbath, the family lit candles instead of using the overhead lighting that was recessed into the tops of the sidewalls. More likely, they used both during the weekdays in an effort to bring in light.

It was always dismal and dreary in Antwerp. Rain was the predominant weather pattern, and it was classically dark most of the time. They surely needed light to bring brightness into the smoldering grayness of the dining room. Yes, they probably did use both the candles and lights during the weekdays. Even so, now, when it was the Sabbath and candles were strictly forbidden, the recessed lights could barely dominate the room. Their light gave a pale glow that evoked the charm of yesteryear.

Adam glanced down at his plate. A thread of gold bordered the rim of the fine china. The thin line burst out in a delicate pattern every two inches or so as it arced around the plate. The flatware was also gold, ornate, and heavy in the hand. Everything seemed to cry out *Old World*, but that was the way Adam liked it. It felt comfortable and safe. Tradition. Everything, traditional. For him, this was definitely home away from home. Everything he knew and loved, like a warm, snug blanket around him.

Once Teme sat down, the expected Friday evening prayers began. Aaron Gvirzman sang loudly and proudly on behalf of everyone at the table. He recited *Eshet Chayil* as he gazed over at his wife. She sat silently as he spoke it to her. Adam watched and wondered at the possibility that although he praised his woman of valor, Aaron Gvirzman might not have one in his wife at all. Maybe she was difficult or demanding. Maybe she wasn't generous or any of the things that the recitation from Proverbs declared. He doubted it. If Teme was the product of her mother's upbringing, or even her grandmother's, all three of the generations of women at the table were shining examples of an *eshet chayil*.

Adam heard Daniella's voice in his head once again. She hadn't actually said the words, but based on what Adam knew of her, she might likely think them. There she was, arguing that the praising of woman was a token gesture because deep down, men knew they'd taken so much else away from the females in society. Best to recite a portion of Proverbs that celebrates a woman for her ability to cook, make clothing, and run a household without becoming idle. That especially praises her understanding of the need to make her husband look good in the eyes of the rest of the community, of her need to support him to the utmost.

It was driving him crazy that he seemed to be more and more attracted to a style of thinking that differed completely from what he had been taught. Even so, Adam wondered if perhaps Daniella understood beyond the words and grasped their deeper meaning. *Why am I questioning this? Why do I even feel any unrest about this?* At this very early juncture, Adam did not understand that his own thoughts were actually at the helm. His subconscious was merely utilizing Daniella as the tool for his imagery.

In any case, Adam wanted his own woman of valor. He could be happy with a traditional wife who could easily deliver the status quo of Orthodoxy. Why shouldn't a man have a wife who doted on him? Yet, through no fault of his own, the voice of another Jewish woman was speaking in his mind here and now, when he didn't want to hear her in his head at all. She was an intrusion that seemed to arrive every time Adam was confronted by a traditional scenario.

Even so, Teme and he began to exchange quick glances between courses and during the ensuing discussions as the evening progressed. Conversation flowed at the dinner table, but it mostly took place between Aaron and Adam. The women had their own exchanges, but they were hushed in tonality. Clearly, they were making an effort not to overshadow the important exchanges between the two men.

The women, for the most part, remained occupied with serving up dishes and making sure the men were comfortable and well fed. On a very subconscious level, Adam made note of the fact that the women did not really participate in their serious discussions at all. He would have loved to engage Teme in a debate of some kind.

Instead, Adam had to be satisfied with the simplistic back and forth that occurred between him and Teme, who was delightful and charming throughout.

"Would you like another glass of wine, Mr. Goldfarb?"

"Please, and call me Adam."

Teme looked to her father for approval. Aaron Gvirzman nodded in turn, indicating she could oblige the request. It seemed as if the nod indicated that he had duly noted that she was putting her best foot forward and that he wanted her to continue. He gave her a second nod complete with a quick wink of the eye to let her know she was doing just fine.

"Here, let me serve that to you, Adam." Teme reached for his glass.

This was all in the hopes of creating a *shiddach*, so the mannerly behaviors persisted. Everyone had put his or her best foot forward. Adam was enjoying it all simply because it was all so...perfect. Yet, the fact remained that another woman occupied his thoughts in a quiet corner of his mind. He really couldn't get Daniella's presence to leave the occupied space, and in fact, she had lingered there since day one. She was consuming his thinking enough that, then and there, the notion he had been idly clinging to for several weeks came very much alive. Now, through no fault but his own, a dangerous idea was gelling like an amoebic blob invading his brain.

For his own sake, for his own peace of mind, he would make absolutely sure that his Judaism was thee Judaism. That he was not misguided or closed minded, as Daniella had implied on their last date. He wished very much that he could forget her, but one Daniella Sobler had plagued his mind from the moment of their angry good-bye.

Part of him was truly interested in her point of view, and she had made him question things for the first time in a very long time. It had been three months since they went their separate ways, and still he found that she was always creeping into his thoughts. Enough so that Adam had made more than several secretive trips to the local library, all in an effort to become more worldly.

He kept up with the repeated trips because one book would lead him to another. History and science were of particular interest to him. There was so much he didn't know. So much he never learned. The world was a fascinating place. People, more so. In gathering the information, he quickly learned that he was living the phrase "stuck between a rock and a hard place," and he didn't know which way to move between them. He was squeezed in and not sure which way he needed to turn to dig himself out of the hole he had created.

Daniella seemed to be constantly challenging him to consider that his Judaism could be observed in an entirely different way from the one he knew all too well. More than that. That the outside world was not the horrific monster he had always been led to believe it was. Adam was starting to understand that he had always had questions about his observances and that the information he was gathering was providing answers.

Daniella was not the cause. She was just the vehicle that drove the questions to the forefront of his brain. Adam couldn't even admit at this early phase that, as with all things in life, *Hashem* probably put her on his path for that very reason. Consciously, he still believed her to be a test sent by God. A way to try to trip him up. He was attracted to Daniella, and that made things even worse.

He wondered if, after three months, she even thought of him or wondered the same thing herself. Maybe she'd had second thoughts about being a *hazzan*. For a reason he could not explain, being with Teme in the Gvirzman home made him want to spend time with Daniella as well. He imagined himself a magnet standing in the middle of two opposite poles, unsure of which way to lean. The image made him chuckle softly. *Hey, I know about that now. Magnetism and the two poles on the earth.*

Adam took a peek at Teme. *Hashem, please help me.*

As if in answer to his plea, Teme's coy style caught Adam's fancy once more when she ladled a bowl of tomato soup for him. She made a small yet provocative comment as she leaned over to drop the soup into the waiting bowl.

"Everything was made from scratch. I like to make sure my cooking is pleasing."

Without sitting to enjoy the soup herself, Teme returned to the kitchen to retrieve more goods. She waited in there for several minutes, working busily all the while. Adam could clearly hear the metallic noises of serving spoons against dishes behind the swinging doors that separated the kitchen from the dining room.

Teme laid out several varieties of cold salads as appetizers. A platter of elongated endive-like leafy greens and a platter of breaded chicken cutlets that looked herbed to perfection was presented next. Teme must have seen the way Adam stared at the strange white leaved steaming vegetables.

"It's called Witloof. Have you never seen it before?"

"Actually no, I haven't."

Bina Gvirzman was about to interject a comment of her own but Bubbe Yedida caught her attention by grabbing her hand underneath the table. Better to have Teme continue the conversation and keep the young man engaged.

Teme continued. "It's called white leaf because of the color but it is actually a relative of chicory root. We eat it a lot in Belgium. The Dutch and the Germans have their variety of it too, so I'm told."

"Well, if you eat it often, it must be delicious." Adam smiled at Teme as she served him his food. He had a fleeting thought of another woman serving him, in a restaurant to be exact, and the smile he had directed toward Teme became wider. Yet Adam made no connection between his thoughts and the gesture. By the time the Belgian chocolate mousse was placed in front of Adam for dessert, he was metaphorically floating in cuisine heaven. He had forgotten about Daniella altogether.

It was clear that Teme had prepared the delicious meal and had done so especially for Adam. Admittedly, he was pleased. It felt nice to be treated like a king. The meal was a message that a prospective bride could cook. Who wouldn't want a wife who could cook? However brief, he existed in a content bubble of belief that his future was encased in a woman named Teme. At least, it lasted until his flight home.

In seat 7A of flight 2055 nonstop to London, a restless Adam squirmed and shifted positions regularly as he thought about Daniella and Teme. He had so much on his mind regarding the two. Here he met someone whom he could build a future with, and he still could not get another woman off his mind. What a mess he had on his hands!

He had prayed for a woman who could become his wife, and it was as if *Hashem* had decided, after hearing his queries, to test his resolve by providing two. Two that he found quite attractive. Not just two, but two extreme opposites. Surely, it had to be a test. Yes, it was a test. Two appealing women, each attractive in her own way.

Adam furrowed his brow. *What if I don't pass?*

Adam checked out his clothes as he gazed in the mirror of the men's room at Heathrow. He still looked the part of a young college kid, having changed his outfit after he checked in at the airport back in Belgium. The diamonds he'd purchased while in Antwerp were tucked neatly into his backpack, which presently rested under the sink in front of him. There had to be at least a million's worth in his small sack, but he looked so much the part of a university chump, he wasn't worried in the least. He checked himself in the mirror once more as he washed his hands in the bathroom sink.

His attire of crewneck sweater, blue jeans, and parka, complete with ski tag attached to the zipper, made clear to everyone that only college supplies rested inside his knapsack. All traces of his suit, black woolen coat, hat, and more were neatly folded and by now resting quietly inside the next flight's hull. He wouldn't don those clothes until safe at the airport back home.

It may have well been the college-kid image that pushed the final envelope for Adam that day. After a nap on the plane, he began to think about his dilemma in earnest. He looked at the clothes he was wearing and the lifestyle they represented. He realized something that up until that point he hadn't been aware of at all. And it was so simple. He was confused about who he was and what he wanted to be.

Maybe that was the reason Daniella had entered his life. *Hashem* was providing a way for him to explore the bigger world. To find out exactly who he really was on the road to his own destiny in life. Just as his outfit allowed him an opportunity to shed his Orthodox skin and free him to exist as someone else entirely, well...Adam wanted his mind to be freed in the same way.

The potential to live outside the confines of his tightly knit community was tangible. It was there for the taking, and the impetus was presented in several dates with a modern Jewish girl. He had taken a bite of the apple just as Adam had in the Bible, and he still remembered the taste after three months. He was still inquisitive, and he was still attracted to the mainstream girl called Danny.

He was in a different world with her. Well, her world, actually, because it certainly wasn't his. A big, juicy apple that was shiny and red. He desired it. In reality, he had for some time. No, a long time, actually. He had wanted to explore the other side as far back as he could remember. He had just never consciously verbalized the notion before.

To make matters worse, he really liked Danny. Really, genuinely liked her. Chemistry sparked with her, and he'd be lying if he didn't admit that to himself. A secretive spark that was different from the sparks he felt for Teme. And with no experience, he could not decipher that one was based in love and the other lust.

Being with Daniella had given him a chance to shed his skin, so to speak. It had given him a taste of life outside his community. He was intrigued by the thoughts she expressed, and he felt a certain level of excitement in being with her. She was a woman who was not constrained by her beliefs; rather, she embraced them in a new and different way, and he liked that.

He realized he would never be fully happy until he proved to himself one way or another what it was he really wanted for himself. What he wanted for his future. Danny was forbidden fruit. Teme was fruit too, and in her case, she epitomized the nectar necessary to pollinate the flower called marriage.

Sadly for Adam, his resolve to explore both worlds of Judaism left out the fact that he had already fallen hard for Daniella. He did not recognize the feeling for what it was. He based his decision to test the waters in opposite oceans simply on his confusion. His only thoughts centered on what was best for him.

Adam was so inexperienced at the game of life and, certainly, at the nuances present between men and women that he didn't even realize that he had already created a monster. The monster was in the form of geometry. The dreaded triangle. Not any simple triangle. The worst of all possible triangles. The love triangle. Even sadder, neither Daniella or Teme—or even Benny, for that matter—knew they were about to become the points that joined the shape together while Adam busily drew it.

Daniella and Teme

"I don't believe my eyes. Look who it is. Please, come in from the cold."

Benny was beyond flabbergasted that Adam had the courage to walk through his doors after three solid months of no contact with Danny. It must have taken a lot of courage to enter, knowing the possibility of seeing someone he formerly socialized with was suddenly very real. Benny was impressed and curious all at the same time. Lucky for the young man, Daniella wasn't on duty that evening. *No chance of a scene of any kind, thank goodness.*

"Hello, Benny. It's so nice to see you again."

Adam walked up to the register and put his hand out for a shake. Benny accepted. After all, he had no personal grudge against the young man. Not really. Just a bit of anger, perhaps, but no more.

Benny turned to look to his side.

"Adam, this is my partner, Nate. You remember him, yes?"

"Yes, of course I remember him. Nice to see you again, Nate." Adam put out his hand once more.

"Nice to see you too, Adam."

"Well, come have a seat." Benny directed Adam toward a table. As the two began to walk, he added, "Danny is off duty tonight."

"Actually, that's a relief. I was praying she wouldn't be here. I really came here to talk to you."

"Me? Really? That seems a bit strange." Benny looked into Adam's eyes and realized the young man was being truthful. Benny concluded with, "Well, OK, then."

Benny turned to Nate as he walked further away, raising the volume of his voice to ensure that Nate heard him. "Nate, mind the fort. Thirty at least. Seems I'll be talking for a while."

Benny looked back at Adam. "Come on, Adam. This way. We'll have some tea and cookies, and you can tell me what's on your mind."

Once the wares had been set down, the two men were free to speak privately. The restaurant was not overly busy, lending itself to a peaceful backdrop.

"What's on your mind, Adam?"

"Benny, I've done a lot of soul searching these past three months, and I realized that a big part of me missed Danny…terribly."

Adam's mouth curled up in a nervous smirk as he stole a glance at Benny. He didn't want eye contact, only a brief peek to gauge Benny's reaction. Adam looked downward as he continued.

"Maybe, just maybe, I could make something work. I don't know her parents, and I don't even know how to contact her home. This was the only place we shared together.

Every time we made a plan, it was to meet here, and then we'd just meet here again. The only place I was phoning was here, on the days I knew I could reach her. You're the only one I can turn to, to find out if I can see her again."

Adam made no mention of Teme. No mention that he needed to explore life on the other side so he could decide once and for all what it was he wanted. As far as Adam was concerned, he did not need to divulge his personal affairs, only his desire to connect with Danny so he could enjoy her company.

Adam watched Benny take a careful sip of his tea, and he could tell that Benny was contemplating his answer. In those quiet seconds, Adam thought about how he had handled his parents when he had returned from Belgium.

He indicated that Teme was indeed a lovely girl but that he wanted to make more trips to Antwerp before fully committing to anything. Besides, he also wanted to see how Teme would react to the fact that he could be in Antwerp only so often. He was a businessman who traveled. How would she feel about that?

"Let's test it out for a while and see how Teme handles things," he had said.

Tsivia had looked at Nachum and said to him, "It would be good to see if she has the patience and wisdom to tolerate Adam's line of work."

Nachum agreed but only so much. "I'll accept that rationale for a while, but don't drag things out, Adam... understand? Her own father is in the business. She knows all about the travel. If you're interested, and because this is a long-distance relationship, it wouldn't be fair to keep the family on a string. And it would make us look bad."

Adam had agreed. "Just give me a little bit of time. That's all I ask."

Adam refocused and looked at Benny who was definitely concentrating on the matter at hand. He hoped Benny's response would allow him to spend time with Danny while in the United States and with Teme during trips to Antwerp. He did his best to appear sincere about the whole matter with Daniella so that Benny would be his champion.

Benny, being none the wiser about the situation, sounded like a hopeful cheerleader when he replied. "Adam, I can feel Danny out and see if she would consider a second try but not before I get some things straight with you. You know, a lot has happened in the months you've been away.

"First of all, she just applied to the seminary last month. She's serious about being a cantor. If you plan to try to make things work with Danny, you have to accept that she is not nor ever will be Orthodox in her thinking. Knowing she wants to be a cantor, she may well become—now what is that catchword? Ah, yes! She'd become Conservadox. But that would be it. Are you really ready and willing to try to make it work with her? Are you ready to try life outside the fold?"

Adam replied with a nod of his head, but no words came out of his mouth.

Apparently taking the nod to mean a sincere yes, Benny continued. "Even more, assuming you won't want either your parents or hers involved until absolutely necessary, it means I'm the parent at the moment. Right?"

Benny didn't wait for an answer. "Do you understand she is like a daughter to me? I'm going to have my eye on you."

Adam nodded once more.

"Last, I'd like to give you a little test, so to speak. I want to give you one last chance to back out before you dive in. I'll be right back."

Benny got up from his seat and headed toward the back of the restaurant. He returned with a cassette tape in his hands.

"You know, Adam, God really does work in mysterious ways. Not one week ago, Danny gave this to me. She told me it was a gift. She recorded the pieces that she plans to use in the audition part of her application. She said it would be a wonderful memory, my special souvenir to look back on when she is Cantor Sobler. A memento just for me.

"Here you are." Benny held out the cassette for Adam to take. He resumed his speech.

"OK, if you are so sure you want to try to establish a relationship with her, you have to accept that she chants prayer aloud and sings to the world, men and women alike. That she plans to be a *hazzan*. I can't help but think this is your way to prove your sincerity. Here, take it. Go somewhere and listen to her sing. If you can handle her public singing and, more importantly, her ambition, it's a good sign."

Adam reached out for the cassette, his fingers trembling slightly.

"When you've finished listening, come back and talk to me about what you heard. Return the tape to me and share your thoughts. I'll decide then and there if I'll tell Danny you're interested once more."

*A*dam had booked a thirty-minute time slot in the listening booth at the public library, located in the northernmost tip of the county. As far as his neighborhood was concerned, the northern end of Epson County was half a world away. A foreign land that they were forbidden to travel to. They didn't drive there, shop there, or, heaven forbid, live there. That separation ensured that Adam could listen to the cassette without ridicule from neighbors.

He couldn't help but notice the wide-eyed stares when he walked through the library doors. Everyone seemed to be drawn to the *yarmulke* atop his head and the *tzitzit* hanging from under his shirt. He was, no doubt about it, an oddity in a town known for being not only the oldest in the area but also uber-patriotic. No matter. His library card was valid anywhere in Epson County, and he needed to take advantage of the fact that he could listen in peace, far away from the prying eyes of those in his own neighborhood.

He could almost hear his mother's pleading and, worse, his father's wrath as he pondered the possibility of them finding out he had a library card.

"Adam, it's a can of worms you're opening up. There is so much in print that provokes sin. Books that put bad ideas into people's heads. You're asking for trouble. You're to give me that card right now. I'm going to cut it up."

Those would surely be his father's words, and his mother would stand by his side and nod in agreement.

Once inside the listening booth, Adam made himself comfortable and loaded the cassette player. He placed the headset over his ears and adjusted the volume as he heard Daniella's voice say, "Benny, this is for you. I hope you enjoy listening to my audition pieces. The first is *Kol Nidre*. The second is the *Hashivenu*, which I know is usually chanted as part of the Torah service by the whole congregation, but I had a personal reason for wanting to perform the prayer as a solo song. The last is an art song. I picked "Habanera" from Bizet's *Carmen*. A bit risqué, I'm sure, but I do need to be able to show my range of skills. Here we go!"

Adam pressed the stop button down. He needed a moment to strengthen his resolve. He needed to gather his bravado and forge ahead. He was about to listen to a woman sing, and not only sing but, of all things, to start with the *Kol Nidre*. She said it was her first piece, which meant he would be hearing it the moment his finger pressed the start button.

The prayer was practically the cornerstone of *Yom Kippur*, the Day of Atonement. It was the declaration that any vows or promises, oaths or obligations made in the year past could be annulled, absolved, forgiven, and made completely void. More so, it was understood by Jews everywhere that when one made the declaration, one could do so in the presence of sinners and to declare the important statement alongside them. The hope was that every person could gain atonement.

The prayer was essential because it was human nature to be rash in making promises that one could not keep or carry out. In the end, all people were sinners of one sort or another. Who was wholly righteous?

The prayer provided an opportunity to begin the solemn day by acknowledging that very fact. It was a stepping stone to betterment as a person. It was a chance to start anew for the year ahead. Most important, it was a direct conversation with God. Each congregant poured out his remorse through the voice of the *hazzan*, which in this case was the voice of Daniella.

How many times had Adam heard the beautifully haunting melody? How many times had a rich, deep, masculine voice sung it out for all to hear? Would the world come crashing down on Adam as he sat in the booth? He would be listening to it when it was not Yom *Kippur*. Was that a sin? Would he add a woman's voice propelling the words into his ears to his own list of sins before the next *Yom Kippur*? Adam pressed the start button.

A rich, velvety smooth mezzo-soprano voice entered Adam's ear canals, invoking exactly what it was meant to. Inner reflection. Inner contemplation. With eyes closed, Adam found that within no time, the inflection of sincerity, the invoking of piety took him in.

The solemnity of prayer. He heard emotion. Even without seeing her, he knew Daniella was feeling every single phrase with all her heart. He had no thoughts of sex or of any aspect of feminine allure. His brain was drenched with soulful, heartfelt prayer. He recognized, too, that Danny was fully committed to the task of conveying those very qualities to the listener as the sound penetrated his own brain.

Adam was eager to continue listening. He wanted to prove to himself that any form of singing Danny did, he could handle. As he listened to the *Hashivenu*, it became apparent to him that Daniella had a God-given talent. Her voice was angelic.

She excelled at invoking emotion and pensive thinking through prayer merely using the sounds she was able to create. Not reminding himself that this was just a recording, that at least he did not see her when he listened, Adam believed he could take on the challenge of spending time with Daniella. He stopped the recording to dwell on his conclusion further. Confidence took a stronghold, and he was sure that the third piece would be equally easy to listen to.

As the words of "Habanera" rang in his ears, Adam could hear the teasing quality of Daniella's voice. No, that was the wrong word. He could hear the challenge. He knew enough to know that *l'amour* meant love in the French language, but he was far from fluent. What was she saying? Why was she challenging in her tone while singing about the subject of love? Was he crazy to think she was actually challenging him? How could that even be possible? She'd had no idea he would be listening to the recording. So why the teasing tone of voice?

Was God punishing him with *Kol Isha*? Hadn't he been told countless times that if a person sinned against the Hasidic way of life, God's punishment would be immediate? God was torturing him now by proving that Daniella's voice was in essence sexual. He pressed the stop button and thought about what Daniella would have to say about that.

He could do no more than conclude that she was doing her best to invoke emotion in a nonreligious context because that was what the song seemed to require. If indeed it was about love, she had to imply that with her tone. Surely, that was the only purpose in her provocative melody.

He had to know what the words meant so he could prove himself correct. He popped out the cassette, put it in his pocket, and headed off into the library to find out about the piece. It took him a while, but eventually he found the information he needed about Bizet's *Carmen* and the well-known "Habanera."

The translation of the song astounded him. Indeed, it was about love, about its elusiveness and the challenge of the game of love that occurs between people. It was exactly what Daniella invoked with her tone. He was impressed. Especially since he, as the listener, felt challenged.

Since their first meetings, he had felt challenged not only by a possible game of love but by her opinions of everything he himself stood for. Somehow, listening to the song had invoked that even further. Hadn't she challenged him at their last meeting? Hadn't that been the case before they went their separate ways? Hadn't she been bent on proving how wrong he was to believe that it was sinful to pray alongside women? She had challenged him about anything and everything that had to do with his Orthodoxy. *I am so confused. Which way should I turn, and who is the right woman to pursue?*

Adam felt compelled to delve further into his private hellish dilemma. He returned to the main area of the library and asked the librarian to recommend some books that dealt with male and female relationships.

"Books that start with the basics, please."

Adam sat for almost two hours before he closed the last of the two books the librarian had retrieved for him. Simple books that explained flirting and the basic norms that could be expected in teenage and young adult socialization.

His frustration now seemed insurmountable. Among his own community and the men he looked up to, not a one had explained any of the subtleties he had just read about. And according to what he read, the personal struggles he was dealing with regarding Teme and Daniella were perfectly normal. Why hadn't he been taught any of this?

He had to figure himself out. He had to see both women so he could know once and for all what he needed to do. Surely he could figure out what he wanted out of life if he had more time with each of them. He'd keep reading up on it too. He'd get guidance from books instead of people. Perhaps he was not being fair to the women involved, but it was what he required to make himself less torn.

It was beyond difficult to feel pulled in a new direction while holding steadfast to the comfort of traditions. Daniella was forbidden fruit, and Teme was temptation in the guise of stability. His plan would hopefully solve his dilemma.

He gave little thought to his selfish motives. No thought to the fact that once Adam made his final decision, going one way or the other, one of the two women would be deeply hurt. His own journey needed to take precedence over theirs.

Adam concluded it was not in his nature to treat any woman poorly, totally contradicting the fact that he was giving neither woman a fair chance. He was convinced he could handle the situation he was about to create. He didn't even realize he would be adding insult to injury simply because of his inexperience with women. Sadly, he remained oblivious to the fact that a man shouldn't string a woman along just for the sake of testing the waters.

Adam could only focus on the fact that this planned experiment was about him. This was about his test. He needed time to figure himself out. One of the two women was his future. Of that, he was sure. He had to find out which. He would take the journey and leave the rest to the good Lord above.

"So, you're returning the cassette to me. What did you decide?"

"Benny, thank you for letting me borrow it. I did listen to it, you know."

"Yes, but what did you decide?"

"That she has a magnificent voice and I didn't fall apart listening to it. I heard exactly what she wanted to convey. There was prayer and introspective thinking in the first two pieces and a challenge in the third."

"All true, Adam, but you're still evading my question."

Adam sighed and looked into Benny's eyes. "I decided that I want to see, know, and try to understand what life is like for Daniella. I want to try my best to function in her Judaic world. I'd like to see what life is like on the other side. Can you talk with her, Benny?"

Benny found it very hard to determine the level of sincerity in Adam's words, but at least he could hear the determination. Once again, he naively thought about the possibility of a match for his darling Danny. *How awesome would it be if she had the approval and caring of an Orthodox Jew? It would mean he really loved her. That despite everything, he supported her Judaic efforts. And after all, doesn't she deserve a strong and committed love?*

"OK, Adam, I'll tell her everything you just told me. We'll see what she thinks, and we'll take it from there. Give me your number, and I'll phone you either way."

"I can't give you my phone number. I've always called from a phone booth when I've phoned here. My folks can't know I have regular contact with you or anyone else outside the fold. I'd be ridiculed, I'm sure. I could call you every other day and check in. Would that be OK?"

For the time being, Benny decided to accept the solution Adam presented.

After ten days, Benny got a call at the restaurant and spoke with Adam on the phone to convey a positive response from Daniella. She had been taking time to think it over. She chose to give it another try. Benny made sure to express the heart of the matter.

"However, Adam, she told me that since she can't have you over to her home just yet, for the same reason you can't have her in yours, she wanted to find a neutral way to meet again. She hoped she could think of something. When I heard that, it gave me an idea, and I've already run it by her.

"You two are Ashkenazic. I'm Sephardic. It occurred to me that maybe a good way to start would be to have both of you over to my home for a *Shabbat* dinner. Show both of you how the other half lives. That sort of thing.

"As far as the *kashruth*, I'm as strict as I am at the restaurant, and frankly, I'd be very insulted if you questioned my knowledge of it. You'd just have to trust me that I keep a kosher home and accept the invitation to eat in my home.

"In any case, it would be a way for both of you to reconnect and do so on common ground, namely the Sabbath. My family will be with me, so you two won't be alone, either. You won't be forced into trying to make conversation with each other if it gets awkward for you both. There'd be other people to talk with. What do you think?"

Adam had no idea what excuse he'd dream up to tell his folks he'd be away during *Shabbos*, but he'd think of something. Something to do with the business and the need to travel just prior to *Shabbos*. The lie would be the first of many, but he really wanted to experience a Greek *Shabbat* as well as see his darling Danny again.

"Thank you for the invitation, Benny. I think it's a great idea, but what about a place to stay? I won't travel during *Shabbos*. Also, is there a *shul* I can go to?"

"No worries, Adam. I'll put you up for *Shabbat*. There is a synagogue that is a walkable distance from my home, and it's Modern Orthodox, so no worries there either."

There was no mention about Daniella's transportation to the Kalabokas house or the fact that she would leave at the end of the evening, meaning she would be driving home. Let Adam judge each event as it occurred. When he spoke with Rose, Benny would just make sure she was willing to add two more settings to the table.

Benny was residing in his naive bubble, believing that somehow, someway, common ground would lessen the stark differences between two Jews from very different backgrounds. Daniella had long ago become one of his favorite people, but Adam was already working his way into Benny's heart. The fact that Adam was extending an olive branch to such an extent, even if the impetus was a pretty girl, showed a willingness to try a different way of life. Benny liked that very much. And the young man was respectful. Benny liked that even more.

The good Lord should forgive him for thinking such a thing, but the fact of the matter was that many of the super-religious were condescending when they dealt with their less observant fellow Jews. It was nice to have a connection with Adam rather than judgmental condemnation. It reminded Benny that there was good and bad in all groups, and certainly, he should not judge an entire group by the misconduct of some of its members.

When Benny hung up the phone, he shook his head in resignation. The fact remained that there were many groups of Jews that would work tirelessly to pull the two youngsters apart. Of that he was sure. The two would have to be very strong in heart and mind to overcome the blocking stones. Monoliths, actually.

Benny reflected on the thought some more. Funny, there was always a quiet understanding between him and every single one of the Jewish customers at the Daily. No matter the year, no matter the personality, no matter the reason for the customer to walk through his diner doors. They had a connection, that unspoken bond they shared simply because they were all Jews. That concrete knowledge of needing to stick together in order to stay strong. A shared heritage—a common ancient language and a common set of rules and regulations, born from Torah and Talmud—simply because they were all Jews.

Jews could go anywhere in the world and still connect with other Jews because of that quiet understanding. They could even participate in a synagogue service anywhere in the world, no matter that they didn't speak the native language. As a Greek American, Benny could travel to France, Mexico, or Japan and walk through the synagogue doors to participate in a service. Hebrew was the language of the Jew, a beautiful silken thread that wove every single one of them together. Unspoken connection. Always, connection.

The prayer service was a thread too. It followed the same flow throughout the world. *Shacharit* service for the morning. *Mincha* service for the afternoon. *Maariv* service for the evening. Never changing. Always rock steady. Benny could even tell the time of day and, more so, the day of the week, merely by the melody in use when he walked through the sanctuary doors. Every last Jew connected, creating a community of brethren for all time. God's chosen people.

The County housed the superreligious in closeted towns within its domain. It was also home to Jews who chose to be less observant, including those who were egalitarian in their practices—mainstream Jews who were willing to interact with the rest of the community and take part in the outside world. These two polar-opposite Jewish worlds were unbending in their view of the other. Benny shook his head. *Talk about clash of the titans!*

It wasn't Jew against Jew literally. No one was duking it out on the streets or spewing hate for fellow Jews like some crier in front of a town hall...at least as far as Benny knew. It was simply a matter of each not being able to accept the other's level of observance or inter-pretation of Jewish law, Torah, or Talmud.

As a result, each side chose to have nothing to do with the other. Jews were completely alienated from their own kin. So sad. So very sad. Benny couldn't help but reflect on his own past at that moment. Hadn't the Holocaust taught them anything? What was wrong with these people? In the end, weren't they all Jews?

The Hasidim that reside in the area come from different sects. Aren't they always at odds with each other as to how to interpret the laws of Judaism? And that's within the same branch of Judaism, for gosh sakes. This rabbi said that. That rabbi said this. This is forbidden. That is forbidden. It's all nuts!

If that wasn't bad enough, there were the ultra-Orthodox, the Traditional Orthodox, the Modern Orthodox, the Conservadox, the Conservatives, the Reformed, and the extremely creative Reconstructionists, who were the latest in Judaism. The list could go on. Add to that their cultural backgrounds. Greek, Italian, Russian, North African, South African, Indian, Japanese. Even Chinese, for crying out loud! So many Jews worldwide, and all so different. All of them arguing that their way was better than another. Especially those of European descent. All of them hard pressed to admit the other was just as much the Jew as they were.

It made Benny crazy and angry all at the same time. As he thought back to his own yesteryear, he acknowl-edged the bottom line. In the end, they were all Jews no matter what they said or did. The rest of the world never let them forget that. Hadn't the Holocaust proved that? He was determined to diminish the barriers no matter how high the sects built them. Benny smiled. *Enough of that. Let's just hope for the best. Rose will certainly help the process along with her great cooking skills.*

Benny knew he was a lucky guy. Even though Rose was American born, the fact remained that his wife was of Greek ancestry. He just got a break that way. He wanted to believe that he would have pursued her no matter what, but even he admitted it comforted him to know their backgrounds were the same.

The link between them was there, and it was solid. Commonality in the way they practiced and the traditions handed down to them from their ancestors. It made for ease of living as a couple. Rose savored the heritage and its traditions as much as he. *Well, all right, then. This will be a challenge no matter how you look at it. Let the matchmaking begin.*

The noise level in the Kalabokas home was no different from that in the Goldfarb home. A certain hurried excitement prevailed when a family was preparing for the Sabbath meal. A hubbub of activity laced with the cacophony of giggles from grandchildren. Without a doubt, these were the prevailing sounds in the active space of a Friday night in any observant Jew's home. Adam watched the hustle and bustle with a smile on his face. He understood the hurried paces. *Well, so far, this is very familiar.*

The sun had not set yet, but time was of the essence, so everyone was moving at a fast clip. They expected Daniella any moment, and an eagerness pervaded the air. It was something tangible, something he could relate to. Something he felt right and comfortable about. Something he loved to be a part of…preparations for welcoming the Sabbath.

"Are you sure you don't need me to do anything, Mrs. Kalabokas?" Adam spoke loudly enough for Rose to hear him from her place in the kitchen.

She walked into the living room to give her answer. "Nonsense! Just sit, relax. Go sit down." Rose shooed Adam away. She pointed as she added, "Sit there. It's a comfortable sofa. And please, call me Rose."

Well, that's two for two. My mother also refuses to let me in the kitchen.

As Rose turned to get back to her duties, she paused. Then she turned back once more so she could readdress Adam.

"Actually, why don't you answer the door when Daniella arrives? That would be a big help."

Adam saw through the casual remark. Matchmaking was at hand, but in a real way, Adam was grateful. Answering the door would help break the ice and allow for a private moment before he and Daniella joined everyone else. Indeed, the bell rang not two minutes after his exchange with Rose, and there was a moment of intimacy the moment he opened the door. He could feel it, and somehow he knew that Daniella felt it too. All he could do was smile. Happily for him, Daniella reciprocated.

"Danny, it is so very good to see you again. I'm so happy you agreed to this." As he made his remark, Adam couldn't help but take notice of how lovely she looked. *Did she do that for me, or is that how she dresses for Shabbat?* She had on a floral skirt that flowed around her knees, and it billowed ever so slightly when she stepped inside. A bright salmon-pink shell with a thin, matching cardigan completed her outfit. She had done up the top two buttons of the cardigan so that it would stay put. The sleeves fell just below the elbows, and Adam couldn't help but wonder once more if she chose the outfit for his sake or if it was how she always dressed for *Shabbat*. Off-white shoes graced her feet, and to Adam's thinking, they were reminiscent of the ballet slippers he had seen in an ad long ago when sneaking a peek at a library magazine.

Her hair was pinned up into a soft twist, and he could smell a faint aroma of roses emanating from her as she walked past him into the entryway. With all his heart, he wished he could reach out and give her a big hug. Instead, he shut the door. Daniella turned around to face him.

"Adam, it's so good to see you again too. I think it's good that we can start over in such a meaningful way, sharing *Shabbos* together. *Shabbat Shalom*, Adam." Daniella gave his arm a quick squeeze as she smiled. Adam thought he could feel the tenderness it conveyed.

What he couldn't feel was that in Daniella's case it was all an act. Her greeting intimated a certain level of comfort. In reality, she was completely void of trust in Adam. She was wary of his intentions as well as the purpose for the entire get-together.

Benny's voice cut through the conversation. "Ah, there you are. Welcome and blessings on you both for sharing *Shabbat* together with my family. Rose will be lighting the candles in just a few more minutes."

By the time everyone reached the dining room table, the sun had long set, and the darkness of the skies indicated that the Sabbath had entered in full regalia. The candles glowed brightly atop the shelf that formed the sill of the dining room bay window. Their melted tops indicated that the Sabbath was all that mattered. Happiness pervaded the room. The tangible emotion was joy at welcoming the most savored of all Jewish holidays.

The little ones were seated at a special table of their own, which was adjacent to the larger table for the adults. The adults touted it as the children's own private dining area, but its real purpose was to keep them from invading the sacred space that housed the adult prayer as well as grown-up conversation.

With all three of Benny's daughters and two sons-in-law present, Benny was wise enough to have gotten through all the introductions prior to seating everyone. It meant nothing would interfere with the business of formally welcoming the Sabbath. At that moment, the only concern was prayer. Delicious food would follow. Time together with loved ones would be the icing on the cake.

Adam and Daniella sat to the left and right of Benny. It meant they could see each other from across the table. Benny was seated at the head. Rose sat at the other end. Everyone else was somewhere in-between. A beautiful table had been set, and again, Adam could not help but note the similarities between this gathering and those of his own family. Wine goblets were present for all. There were two beautiful twisted breads not unlike his own family's Ashkenazic challah bread. There was an ornate washing bowl with matching pitcher. It rested on its mount waiting for the blessing of washing the hands.

Benny had pulled Adam aside earlier in the evening and explained that everyone in his house prayed together, and the women actively so. "We have our own traditions that I am sure will be unlike the Ashkenazic ones you are familiar with. Things will be the same in their way, but I'm sure everything will be very different for you, Adam. Just la-la if you're so inclined, but certainly do join in if you can pick up a melody quickly."

Benny apparently decided he needed to add in one more comment.

"You can't insult my family by standing up and leaving the table because my daughters are singing *Shalom Aleichem*. They do so in beautiful harmony, and they know how much I love to hear them. You understand that, Adam? Through my years here in the United States of America, I've become very egalitarian minded. I've left many, many old notions behind. I believe with all my heart that my wife and daughters are committed to the task at hand and therefore have the right to pray as loudly and heartily as I do. In this case, Danny too. I can't wait for her to chant the blessing over the wine. I'm very proud of them all."

"I understand completely, Benny. Believe me, I thought it over, and I'm here because I really want to be here. Everything is different, and I recognize that. I'm willing to sit and witness *Shabbat* in your home."

The singing of *Shalom Aleichem* began the evening. Benny's three daughters sang in perfect harmony. Everyone smiled during the song. The melody was different from the one Adam was used to, but that was of no consequence because he knew all the words. He looked at Daniella. Daniella looked at him. Her unspoken message seemed to say, "Deal with it."

He looked at the Kalabokas girls, each with a joyful smile of her own. He thought about the words that welcomed the angels. He looked at the happy smile planted across Benny's face. He was obviously proud of the women he had raised. Adam chose to leave the moment untouched, free of any thoughts on his part, and he listened quietly.

Benny blessed his children, and then his children blessed their own children. All the proper readings and *brachot* were recited and in the proper order. Everything was the same yet so different. Rituals in their proper order. Welcoming the Sabbath with one's heart. Pride in one's Jewishness. And still, nothing was the same at all.

Melodic tunes and heartfelt prayer prevailed in a new and exciting way. Even Daniella, who, like him, did not know the Kalabokases' rituals, was busy clapping and trying her best to join in. It was unlike any style Adam had ever seen or heard. Everyone was participating.

It was a far cry from his own experience. For Adam, the singing of Hasidic men around a huge dining table, joyful at the presence of *Shabbat* as they sang a *niggun*, was his own comfort blanket. Admittedly, experiencing the spirit and excitement around those tables as they hummed the wordless tunes was like drinking a sweet liquor. It warmed the bones and brought comfort.

Adam looked around the table and saw happiness on the many faces, and enlightened moods too. Despite the communal prayer, husbands were not reaching for wives or wives for husbands. No one was insulted by the presence of the other. Everyone was clearly enjoying the Sabbath for its own sake. Each fully committed to establishing the beauty of *Shabbat*. And that aspect of commitment to the Sabbath was exactly the same as in his own home.

During the evening meal, conversations abounded. Back and forth, one to another. It wasn't hard for Adam to deduce that he was witnessing love, family, and even community in the small world of the dining room. In essence, it was once again the same as in his own home. Certainly no less wonderful. Adam was with brethren. Jews, just like him. That blatant fact couldn't be denied. They simply did things differently.

He wondered why so many in his own community insisted that the "outside" Jews were not real Jews at all. Here they were, an entire family of these so called outside Jews, enjoying the entrance of *Shabbat* into their lives and obviously relishing it. Adam looked around the table and felt a sense of contentment. *Remember the Sabbath day, to keep it holy. How could Hashem not be happy about this?* For the first time Adam thought, *Let Hashem judge the motivation behind an act and not the lowly mortal eyes in the sockets of men. Different doesn't necessarily mean wrong. It just means different.*

The foods at the table only added to the Sabbath delight. Adam was eating foods quite different from those of his ancestral Romanian upbringing. Unique flavors that he had not experienced before. Even the simpler foods, like potatoes and asparagus, were herbed to perfection.

He thoroughly enjoyed a faso soup (bean soup), keftikas (meat-and-leek patties with tomato sauce), patates spiros (braised potatoes), and avgolemono sauce (chicken-and-lemon-flavored sauce) over his asparagus, to name a few. He couldn't even repeat most of the names if he tried. The foods kept coming one after the other. Lamb was the highlight and specialty of the evening.

A moment of identical customs did occur during dessert, and it brought a huge smile to Adam's face. Tea was served in a glass. It reminded him of his own *Bubbe's* tradition. Adam smiled as he thought about her sipping the hot liquid after taking a bite of a sugar cube. She would insist it was the only way to enjoy hot tea. The traditions parted company, however, when a delightful baklava was served for dessert.

Adam couldn't help but lean forward across the table, bend his head in an effort to lower his voice, and softly ask Daniella a question about the food.

"Danny, have you ever eaten dishes like this before?"

"Actually, yes. Benny has his Greek heritage day the first Thursday of every month, remember? He serves up Greek food all day long. He even has some musicians in the restaurant during the dinner hours so he can set a mood. I've worked on those days, and they're wonderful, Adam. Absolutely wonderful! Makes me want to be Greek."

Adam saw his opportunity and didn't waste a single moment in nabbing it. "Well, lucky me. Next week has the first Thursday in it. I'd like to go to the Daily and experience more Greek culture. Will you be working then?"

"Actually, yes, I will be."

"Danny, can I ask for you to be my waitress?"

Adam spoke the question in the hopes that Daniella would register the unspoken one. He really wanted to start over. The question then remained—did she?

Daniella knew there was some type of spark between them. She felt it every time she was in his presence and it was no matter that they hadn't seen each other for months. If he was here to experience a *Shabbat* with her, didn't it mean that he wanted to give it another try? Maybe, just maybe, they could make a go of it. And didn't everyone deserve a second chance? He wouldn't have asked about her work schedule unless he was feeling something. She hoped she was correct in her summation.

She smiled at Adam, reached out, and rested her hand on top of his. He didn't pull away. She let the touch of her fingers indicate how she felt.

"Adam, I'd like that very much."

dam found it hard to put into words just how special he had felt during the past Friday at the Kalabokas house. The only words that kept coming to mind were *happy* and *free*. He would have loved to talk to his parents about the experience, but he could already hear his father's condemnation. Well, perhaps that was a strong word. He could already hear the fear in his father's voice.

His father would fear that, somehow, Adam would begin to observe in a way that the community would frown upon. He would caution his son not to return there for another Sabbath. Adam could already hear his mother deeming the events of the evening an incorrect observance. She would say they had not celebrated in the way they should, which of course was the Ashkenazic European way.

It was beginning to bother Adam more and more that his parents judged other traditions without full knowledge of those traditions. At the same time, he did not know how to resolve the feeling. It gnawed at him like some hungry beast, and he was not able to satiate it despite his best efforts. For the time being, it was easier to remain quiet about his goings-on.

Here he was now, having just finished a delicious Greek meal of huevos haminados (eggs cooked in onion-skin broth), sole agristada (sole with egg-lemon sauce), and leek-and-potato patties that looked just like *latkes*. Danny was his waitress, providing smiles galore and quips to make him laugh as he enjoyed his meal. It made him happy. Plain and simple, happy.

He liked that when she served him food, she had more to say than that she had cooked it herself. However unfair that might seem in regards to Teme, it was the plain and simple truth. Teme did not comment on the local politics—or much of anything, for that matter—unless it was about household duties and obligations.

Musicians gathered in the back corner of the restaurant and began to play. To Adam's surprise, some of the patrons got up to dance. They began to serpentine around the tables as Benny led the way. Women held the hands of men, and no one seemed to care. When they passed by Adam, Benny grabbed his hand and pulled him in.

Adam felt embarrassed but giddy at the same time. Most certainly, he was quite unsure of what to do. When they passed by the musicians, the music came to an end. Adam would have loved to sit back down, but the music resumed so quickly that he barely had time to catch his breath. The music had changed to a slower rhythm, and Benny began a dance of his own. He looked at Adam and signaled him to follow. The patrons cheered the two men on.

"Let's see if you can keep up, Adam."

The only thought going through Adam's head was that Benny's steps were not unlike a *depka* despite the slower music. Adam felt no trepidation about joining in. Deep down, he loved to dance, and after all, it was only Benny. No harm in dancing with another man. *Pretend you're dancing with* Tata *or* Feter. *Ignore the fact that the eyes of men and women are on you.* Adam gave it a try and found he could mimic Benny's steps. Soon enough, he was dancing comfortably alongside Benny, ignoring the fact that women were standing on the outskirts with no *mechitzah* in place. It was the first time that Adam had danced in full view of the opposite sex, ever.

The physical manifestation of his feelings came in the form of *ruach*, that ability to feel unabashed joy and spirit, inspired by communal music. It was a familiar feeling. He'd experienced it many times when dancing with the men in his community. Did he even care that this time the women were right there clapping and moving to the music? When had he last showed spirited joy in the midst of women and men together? Never, he thought. And in that brief moment, there was sadness in the joy he called dancing.

This is perfectly fine. Where are the lightning bolts? There are none. Hashem *is not going to strike me down. There is only joy. Enjoyment of life. I'm as light as a feather.*

In a remote corner of his mind, Adam realized this was probably one of the many reasons why people from his neighborhood didn't patronize the restaurant. It may be kosher and have proper certification, but it encouraged behavior that was unacceptable in the eyes of his community. Dancing could lead to lewdness, after all.

Adam danced alongside Benny and smiled at Daniella, who was standing off to the side. She was clapping and moving to the beat with some of the other women.

The chemical sparks flew through the air between the two youngsters. Benny reached out for Daniella and signaled her to join in because of his own sense that something was happening between the two. He had his own determination to strengthen those sparks any way he could. Daniella took hold of Benny's hand without signaling to Adam that he should take her free one. The last thing she wanted to do was overwhelm him. It was nothing less than utter shock and amazement when Adam reached for her hand himself and gave it a fond rub with his thumb. She was now sandwiched between the two men, a link in the chain that formed the dance circle. Others quickly latched on.

They danced and twirled about. Happy patrons one and all, sated and enjoying great music. The passersby on the street could look through the glass windows and witness the fun and enjoyment inside. The dance circle became so large that all the patrons were touching shoulder to shoulder in the small space. Sparks flew even higher. The emotion was living and breathing between Daniella and Adam. It was virtually palpable.

Adam began to dance in place, his movements not unlike those of a Hasid feeling complete jubilation. Holding arms up, snapping fingers, swaying like a curling ribbon in the breeze. This was the music of the Greek Jew, but its spirit was relatable. And if the music felt good to the soul, wouldn't other Jewish customs be equally delightful?

Adam decided then and there that he would learn about Jews around the world. He'd borrow books and read about their customs, traditions, and values. He'd continue to look for the common ground that surely must exist among them all. He would try hard to forget that here in the good old United States, the land of the free, he was isolated from the bigger world, existing in one that was unique unto itself. It was a big world out there, and he wanted to explore it.

As Adam continued his dance, Benny moved over to Daniella and spoke in her ear.

"Go home early, Danny. We'll clean up just fine without you."

She gave Benny a big hug and said, "Thank you."

When the music finished, Daniella gestured to Adam to step away from the crowd and sit on one of the bar-stools at the counter.

"Goodness, Adam, catch your breath. You were really having a time of it over there!"

"That was fun, Danny. It's been a long time since I had fun like that."

"Well, I can't guarantee fun, but I can at least offer some conversation. Would you think it too forward of me to ask if we could continue our evening together for a while longer? I'd like to ask you a few things, Adam."

"Danny, it's more than OK. It's great. I'm having such a good time. I don't want this to end. We'll go for a walk, how's that? We can make some plans to see each other again. That is, if that's all right with you?"

"One thing at a time, Adam. What's OK for right now is going for a walk."

Adam walked with Daniella around the shopping plaza that was a half mile from the restaurant. They talked about the weather and the Greek night experience.

They acknowledged the friend they both had in Benny and the luck they had in having a second start as friends. Adam suggested they walk to the highway overpass on the opposite side of the restaurant.

"We can watch the cars zoom by, and we can talk some more."

They stood peering out at the headlights rushing by, and Adam spoke from the heart.

"Danny, I think we're both honest enough to admit there is some type of chemistry between us. I can hardly believe it when I say that, but there is, isn't there?"

"Before I answer that, where exactly are you going with that statement? You know I want to be a *hazzan*, and nothing, Adam—nothing—is going to change that."

"I know, I know. All I can say is that with you, I feel free. I'm free in a way I can't be otherwise. I can let a different Adam exist when I'm with you, and it feels so good to let my guard down."

"You know, Adam, *Hashem* didn't make religion as we know it today; mankind did. All those rules and regulations you live by were created after the fact. After Torah. All *Hashem* wants us to do is to praise and connect to the source that is the Almighty, and to love each other, and to take care of the good earth that was given to us. Even you can't deny that."

"No, I can't. You're quoting Hasidism."

"Not Hasidism, Adam. Judaism."

Daniella continued. "I have to believe that *Hashem* will know the sincerity of both our devotion no matter how we express it. What kind of almighty being are we talking about if we say it judges based on how we did something and not why we did something? Pettiness is a human quality, not a Godly one."

Deep down in his subconscious, Adam knew she was right, but his conscious self was still processing, learning, and figuring it all out. Sadly, it was also doubting and second guessing. Yet the only way to know things for sure was to see it all through for its own sake. To experience it all so he could reach some kind of conclusion.

"Well, if I'm on a journey, which it seems I am, I'd be happy if you'd go on it with me. I'd love for you to be my tour guide as I travel down an unexplored road."

Adam's mop of flowing curls shimmered in the light that came from the highway lamps attached to the overpass. The distraction was overwhelming for Daniella and she momentarily drifted into a bubble of thought.

Who would have believed it? I'm deeply attracted to this Orthodox man. I want to know him better. I like the idea of being his tour guide. Maybe we could grow together as a couple and overcome whatever obstacles come our way. There has to be a middle ground. There just has to be.

"Adam, I suppose I'm willing to give it another try. Everyone deserves a second chance, after all."

Daniella stopped to think for a moment.

"What about our parents? My parents will be very upset that I'm interested in someone who is so *frum*. I can hear it now...'Danny, are you crazy? He'll put so many restrictions on you; he'll take away your dreams. You'll be wearing clothes that cover you from head to toe, and your head will be covered with a *schmata* of some sort. Even worse than a head scarf, a wig, *vey is mir*, because your hair would be shaved. That's what a marriage to him would get you!' And believe you me, Adam, that would only be the beginning of their rant."

Adam laughed and joined in. "Adam, are you crazy? She's trying to be a man. Wanting to be a female *hazzan*…whoever heard of such a thing? That she even has the *chutzpah* to sing in the presence of men…it's a *shonde*. A real shame, I tell you."

They both laughed at their antics. It was a small bit of levity to ease the weighty seriousness of their dilemma.

"Danny, may I…." Adam stopped his sentence and reached out to embrace Daniella in a kiss. His lack of experience didn't matter, either. Some things were instinctual. The emotions impassioned their kiss even more.

A swirl of thoughts circled in Adam's brain. *Dearest God, so this is what heaven is like…I pray the darkness here in the street makes me no more than a silhouette…I'd be mortified if someone recognized me…Who would be here, anyway?… Daniella, don't stop kissing me; this is wonderful.* On and on it went, but in essence, the kiss lasted a mere fifteen seconds of the night hour. Realizing that neither should out-step the self imposed boundaries, they pulled away from each other at the same time. Adam, however, made his feelings clear.

"I like you so much, Danny. So very much. I'm just afraid. I'm not even sure what to do. What do we do, now?"

"You tell me, Adam."

"I guess we see each other as best we can and don't bother telling our parents until such time we might really have to or even want to. Is that what we do?" Adam didn't wait for an answer. "It's not really lying, is it? It's more like not bringing something to their attention because it would bring them worry and distress. Pick the lesser of two evils. Isn't that the Jewish way?"

Rationalization, perhaps, but Adam was desperate to find an acceptable answer. By the time they got back to the restaurant and their respective cars, they had decided that they would meet at places far enough away that their parents would remain unaware of their relationship for the time being. Perhaps they'd grab a cup of coffee or a sandwich. Maybe they'd walk through parks. Maybe, for the first time in his life, Adam would take in a movie at a theater somewhere out of town or listen to a concert.

They would do this whenever Adam was available, and Daniella would have to accept that he traveled for business. She'd have to accept the fact that she could only see him from time to time, which of course would mean when he was in the States. And wouldn't it be worth it? Each of them had a goal in place. What better way to see if their chemistry could trump their issues.

Daniella gave Adam a slip of paper with a telephone number on it.

"My parents installed a second phone line a couple of years ago because they didn't like how much phone time my siblings and I were taking up on the house line. They thought it would free up the main line for what they felt were more important calls than teenage chitchat. My parents never pick it up since they know it's one of our friends calling. And my siblings, well, if for some reason they're at home and pick up, they won't hassle me about who's calling. They would just say something like, 'Danny, there's some guy on the phone for you.'"

Daniella was still unsure about the matter, knowing there was a small chance that her parents would listen in somehow. She'd have to be very careful when she talked with Adam on the phone. To her thinking, though, at this point in time it would be worth the effort to give it a try. She did, however, need to articulate one concern.

"Thinking about it, maybe we should come up with some type of code that means I need to hang up."

In the two weeks ahead, Adam was actually able to spend many days at Daniella's side. It seemed their time together was occurring with an emotional relish that both were trying hard not to accept. Both loved to participate in the back-and-forth debates that were fast becoming second nature in their relationship. Daniella challenged Adam constantly, and he adored every single moment of it.

Adam began to view himself as feeling alive for the very first time. Oddly, he also felt at peace. Whether walking in the park or sipping coffee, the two could talk for hours about all sorts of things. They could connect in a way that was new and different for both of them. It, was akin to a *haver,* a study partner, just of a different sort. A good one at that too. Perhaps they were not learning Talmud, but certainly, debating life as a Jew and the ways Jews should live.

Adam had begun to spend many evenings at the restaurant. He would arrive about fifteen minutes before the end of Daniella's shift and wait for her in the back booth they considered their own. He never gave himself away, because he dressed in the least possible Hasidic way, whatever that meant. He considered it a top priority to blend in and be a nobody.

Whenever Benny was on duty, he would bring tea and cookies to the table and chat with Adam while he waited for Daniella. It happened often enough that Benny officially pronounced Adam as the next of his daily diners.

"It's great to see you here so often, eating, enjoying, and feeling at home. You've become a daily diner! Well, in your case, I know that's not really possible with your travels and all, so maybe not quite daily, but it's wonderful just the same."

Adam couldn't agree more. When he was with Daniella—or even at the Daily, for that matter—he felt released from the chains that bound him to his strict lifestyle. His time there was a distinct removal from his regimented life. Yet the remote voices in the farthest corner of his head continued to chide him. The guilt was strong. Everything he was doing and trying was unacceptable. If he were found out, he would lose everything that meant anything to him.

Adam pictured his mother weeping uncontrollably because Adam had shamed his father by attending his first movie with Daniella. Worse, he had held her hand in the darkness and rubbed its soft skin with his own fingers. No, even worse than that. The movie had left him with questions about cowboys, who they were and what their lifestyle was all about. Their romantic masculinity had made him kiss Daniella in a mimicking way.

The gnawing guilt became especially palpable when Adam brought Daniella to a kosher restaurant they agreed to meet at in the east end of the city. It was in the *frum* neighborhood that the rest of the world referred to as the Black Hats territory. They ate at a restaurant that rested on a street corner considered to be the very outskirts of that particular neighborhood, a mere short bus ride from the school Daniella attended, yet a world far away. Adam had wanted to make it easy for her to meet quickly after her classes that morning, and it was, for the most part, conveniently located.

"Why bother returning up to the county? I'll come into the city and wait till your classes are finished. We'll meet up at the restaurant and have a nice lunch there."

Daniella was loaded down with a tote full of books on one shoulder and handbag on the other as she arrived. She also arrived wearing blue jeans. Her modest top, which covered her arms, did nothing to detract from the fact that she was wearing pants. Adam took one look at her and worried about criticism from those in the restaurant. Daniella seemed perfectly comfortable in the restaurant, but Adam kept looking around, acting as if the eyes of the world were upon him.

"You don't feel awkward, do you, Danny?" Adam tried to seem nonchalant.

"I'm OK. These folks just know I'm not from around here, and that's why they're looking at me. Besides, look at how I'm dressed compared to you. What Hasidic woman wears jeans? It would be no different if an observant Jew came into the Daily, Adam. Everyone is just surprised."

"Are you sure? Looks like folks are staring."

Daniella could practically hear the people in her head. They were lecturing her. They knew a less observant Jew when they saw one. They could tell she was not one of them. She was a curiosity and, worse, a bad influence. They were silently questioning Adam. *What are you doing with someone like her?*

"Danny, let's leave here. Let's just order sandwiches to go, some hot coffee too. Let's find a nice park somewhere."

Daniella didn't say a thing in response. Adam was clueless to the fact that inside her mind, she was feeling mad. In reality, there was a frustration for them both but for different reasons. Adam was not ashamed of her, personally. No, that was definitely not the case. It was simply that he was taught that a girl like her was shameful. For Daniella, it was anger at being judged unfairly.

Daniella would have loved to shout out, "We're just two people enjoying each other's company. What right do you strangers have to make us feel guilty?" She wanted to, but she didn't. Instead, she skewed the event completely by keeping the conversation light and nonspecific once they settled themselves outdoors.

It was an even bigger disappointment when, later that day, Adam announced his travel plans. He did so as they lay down on the grass side by side in order to peer at the sky and play the childish game of seeing shapes in the afternoon clouds.

"Danny, I won't be able to see you for about two to three weeks, maybe even a month. I have to make a trip to Belgium for the business."

As Adam continued to stare up into the clouds, he assured her how much he would miss her company and how much his time with her was special. He said that discussions with her were always so interesting, enough so that he could hardly wait to return for the next one. Adam turned to his side and propped himself up on one arm.

"Danny, I love our time together. I hope you believe me when I say that. When I return, I will get in touch with you right away. It's a promise."

Being completely unaware of a woman named Teme, Daniella could do no more than believe every word Adam said and acknowledge that, indeed, they were becoming very good friends, and perhaps even more. It was getting harder all the time for her to resist Adam's boyish charms. She hoped he'd get romantic again and that his actions would indicate his seriousness. She wanted to try to reach the next level. She gave no thought to the possibility that she was merely a vehicle, a conduit, if you will, to the bigger world that was always out of Adam's reach.

"I love our time together too, Adam. Our discussions, our insights, our connection. You're such a wonderful person."

Adam heard the sincerity and saw the affection etched into the peridot eyes that stared directly into his. Piercing eyes, pulling him in, and there was no turning back. He had been dreaming of kissing her again, ever since he mimicked the kiss of the cowboy from the movie and the beckoning call was consuming him.

In the fleeting seconds, Adam didn't look around to see who might be watching. He leaned in to kiss Daniella. He kissed her gently at first, intending to pull away quickly. The mere touching of lip against lip made Adam want more. His attraction to Daniella was not to be denied. Despite his overall lack of experience, he kissed her heartily and artfully. Instinct took over, and fervent desire settled into his open mouth. Passion found residence between the two pairs of lips. Butterflies fluttered down throats into two stomachs.

Adam couldn't help himself. He stroked her hair, gently pushing it away from her eyes. He kissed her more deeply. The sensation building in his gut was driving him on, and he could feel his *yetzer harah* creeping in and wanting more. His *yetzer harah* laughed all the while as he pulled Daniella into his arms for more. It took every last ounce of strength to pull away from the kiss he had created. He smiled at her warmly, giving no indication that at that very moment, thoughts were whirling through his head, upsetting him terribly. Thoughts otherwise known as his conscience.

He had kissed her because he wanted to but also because he could. Daniella did not follow the laws of *negiah* because she did not buy into the possibility that even the slightest touch would necessarily lead to sinful intimacy. In his world, a man never touched a woman, ever. In his world, only one's wife would be handled in such an intimate way, and even then, certainly not in public. Somehow, he doubted that the men and women he knew would kiss like that anyway or even know how to.

In her world, touching happened all the time. It came in the form of handshakes, a rub on the arm to express understanding, or even a brush of the hand to move a stray hair off the face of another as he had just done to her. In her world, it didn't mean that sex was the inevitable outcome. For Adam, however, it was crystal clear that the touch meant his feelings were brewing stronger than he dared to admit.

He rationalized that Daniella had the Conservative version of *tzeinus*. She was modest, and humbly so, but in a less extreme way than the Orthodox women who observed *tzeinus*. Much like the women in his Orthodox community, she didn't dress in revealing clothing. Daniella did, however, wear blue jeans, and sometimes her sleeves rose above the elbows or her skirts were slightly higher than her knees. In his world, the reality was that Daniella didn't observe *tzeinus* at all. It was a grave sin for a woman to wear a pair of pants, period, end of sentence.

She wore very modest jewelry, same as her Orthodox counterparts, but was freer with makeup. The cosmetics didn't make her look cheap, though. They certainly didn't make her look as if she was asking for it. Adam had learned that phrase in one of their many discussions about modesty. In fact, she had a very natural look about her. She was a pretty, *shayne maidel*. A pleasant, attractive girl.

She just needed a quick change of clothes to make her appear more Orthodox. Adam found it offensive that if Daniella were to change her appearance, somehow miraculously and suddenly, his aunts, grandmothers, and mother would all commend him for finding such a beauty. The fact that she didn't dress that way somehow made her evil. It made her the wrong kind. What did that mean, anyway?

At one point during one of their more serious conversations, Daniella had even shared that she believed in saving herself for the man that would be her husband. No different from in his own community. Yet the fact that she kissed him meant she'd be willing to kiss any boy she was interested in, and that made her no good. Adam was playing a mind game with himself, trying to prove that there were enough similarities that one could commend Daniella's virtuosity in light of the fact that they kissed.

The difference was in the fact that she was willing to kiss and hug a man to test the waters. And that kiss! No matter that there was still some level of modesty in her overall thoughts about romance. Adam was thinking in a way that was far from innocent. His conscientious self came trampling through and finally took hold.

No matter that she was less observant. He had great respect for her, enough so that, as much as he might like to, he would push her no further. He would not take advantage of her leniency. *Just because you want her, that doesn't mean you should take advantage of her. Be a mentch, Adam. She's not that kind of girl.* Adam let go of her completely.

"Adam, that was *so* nice," Daniella practically purred.

With all her heart, Daniella believed that this was the next step in their growing relationship; that Adam was willing to exist in a new and different world. She was eager for and excited about future possibilities. Could it be? Were they really on their way to a more solid relationship? They could talk about anything, so it seemed, and they were constantly honing the fine art of fair debate. Now, that kiss. Daniella wanted more.

Daniella was whirling ideas of Conservadoxy in her mind. A middle ground that they could obtain so both could be happy. She was a kosher kid and observant within the context of the modern world. That was a step in the right direction. Maybe Adam could eventually come around to the idea of her wanting to be a *hazzan*. She pondered the possibilities as she acknowledged a new and exciting thought. She had a feeling she was falling in love with Adam Goldfarb.

Adam had just sealed a deal with one of the most respected diamond dealers in Antwerp. A great sale to say the least. The traditional handshake had been made and words of *mazel u'bracha* had been happily expressed. Luck and blessings. Not only for this deal but for so much in life. Each man had been content with his business savvy.

Adam was leaving the major trading area off of Pelikaanstraat and heading toward the Belgelei to the attached apartment units that housed the Gvirzman family and others. Those apartments had an Old World smell, but Adam summated it with Old World charm. In any case, he was used to it by now, along with the dreary gray days and the frequent rains.

All things aside, Adam felt very much alive and at home despite being so far away from his own home. The diamond business practically sang to him, and the Gvirzman family made him feel as if he was already a member of their family. They were actually quite kind to him, learned for sure, and mostly, they were a family much like his own.

Each time he came for a visit, they behaved more and more as if he had already become their son-in-law. Warm, caring, and ever mindful of seeing to his needs, each did his or her part to make him want to seal the deal, and soon. He liked each individual member of the Gvirzman family too. Even staunch *Bubbe* Yedida. And Teme, well, she was easy on the eyes. That made coming to their home especially pleasurable.

Each time Adam traveled to Belgium and visited with the family, Teme's demure behavior struck a chord. Her delicate features practically beckoned him, and it seemed she was prettier each time he saw her. She also proved herself to be knowledgeable in the traditional sense. That was certainly a feather in her Hasidic cap! The home cooking wasn't anything to sneeze at either.

Adam had made very clear to his parents that he was interested in Teme before he had left for this particular trip. Unbeknownst to him, they had been in touch with the Gvirzmans the moment Adam left the driveway. The wheels were in motion, and all had decided that Teme's *Bubbe* Yedida would supervise and oversee the young couple through an entire relationship, all the way to the *chuppah*. They were scheming, plain and simple.

The wedding canopy was most certainly the goal of both families, and they would do anything necessary to make it all work. If all went well, the Goldfarbs would travel to Belgium in the near future, ready to make nuptial plans. It wasn't a formal *shiddach* just yet, but instinct dictated that it would be soon. Best to let the youngsters have this one visit before pushing for the finality of marriage planning. With Adam's trip schedule, both families understood that a *shiddach* would take longer than usual.

It had been decided that on this particular trip, Adam would take Teme out socially. A date during his last afternoon in Belgium, which he made a point to keep open and available on his trip calendar. The suggestion had been made prior to his leaving the United States, and it had been thought about for days after his arrival. It took clever scheming on the part of all involved, and that included Teme. The date would leave both with a yearning to have more time together. If Adam had his date with Teme just before leaving, the two would miss each other as a result. Teme would look forward to Adam's return. Adam would be eager to see Teme once more.

That afternoon had finally arrived. Adam had accepted the suggestion readily because he, too, was eager to move things along. The date would give him the time he needed to become closer to Teme, or at least get to know her better. His time with her was especially limited, since, unlike Daniella, Teme would be closely guarded and not free to socialize with him in private areas.

He knew that he'd make a good impression on Teme if he showed how much he knew his way around her city. He could show how much he knew about its history and culture. Women liked a smart man, or so he had been told. He had learned about the area before his first trip to Belgium. As a buyer of diamonds, he needed to know the inner workings of a city that was considered the major hub for Hasidic dealers. As a result, he could make her afternoon interesting. He was sure of it. Adam had everything planned in his mind.

Bubbe Yedida had made mint tea and babka rich with swirls of chocolate intimately laced throughout the luscious coffee cake. It was for the youngsters to enjoy, but of course, that meant everyone who was at home at the time would partake of it. The baking was Yedida's own bit of scheming. It created a segue, since she next suggested they needed to walk off the calories. A silly segue, at that, since the date had already been planned. Bina feigned ignorance as well. She stopped her sipping and blurted out, "Excellent idea." Her tone clearly implied some type of hidden agenda.

Yedida gave her a look firm enough that Bina, face flushed, resumed sipping to hide her supposed error. Teme just sat looking hopeful. Adam, inexperienced with women, was oblivious to the subtle messages all around him. He noted nothing more than his own nerves.

He and Teme went walking alongside De Keyserlei. The riverside was busy enough to provide a bit of distraction when silence fell between them. Teme listened as Adam shared his knowledge of the city. She seemed focused, almost as if she were processing every one of his words. Adam equated her look with one of attention, and it pleased him greatly. He continued his informative speech as she stole occasional glances into the window shops.

Adam thought she was listening, evident by the fact that she was giving the occasional nod of her head to show agreement. In reality, she was dreaming about which pieces of furniture she found attractive in the store windows. She was deciding what type of furniture suited the couple best. After all, Adam was knowledgeable and had a lucrative career, which meant he'd be good husband material.

For the most part, the date was like the other first dates Adam had arranged in the past. He got to know a young lady by easing into light conversation, and that was a good start. It would take a bit of time to get into more serious matters. Adam already knew some basic things about Teme. She was confident (evident by the way she seemed to know what she wanted for her future). She was socially charming and gracious. She could cook up a fantastic meal. Most important, her Old World Judaism was precious to her.

Each had a newspaper cylinder filled with potato fries in hand. It provided a convenient excuse for both to refrain from speaking time to time and just look at each other as they placed handfuls of fries in their mouths. Each of them politely masticated and thought separate thoughts.

Adam could not deny the physical attraction. Teme was a beautiful girl. When she smiled at him, he noted it once more. Sadly for him, he could not possibly know that after Teme's study of his features, she surmised the likelihood of adorable children and nothing more. With nothing better to do, each stuffed another handful of fries into their mouth.

They had walked down to the Schelde earlier, and Adam had shared what he knew about the port's history. He was well informed about the area, and that was a good thing. Even if he had done some quick homework in a last-minute effort to learn about the port, Teme remained impressed that he had taken the time to be knowledgeable. Who didn't want an intelligent man for a husband? And his cuteness, well, that was a bonus.

Adam had taken her to Stadspark as well. They had sat near the little lake and finally begun to talk about what they wanted in life. It had become clear, and quickly at that, that Adam was cut from the same fabric as she. They were both Ashkenazi. His Romanian heritage was extremely similar to her Central European upbringing, and that meant a strong connection in the eyes of both their communities.

Adam spoke about wanting a large family, which made Teme especially happy. Since World War II, Jewish families were smaller in number throughout Europe, and she was determined to change that and increase the Jewish population. *Hashem* should will it, she wanted a veritable truckload of kids.

All in all, Adam was proving to be great marriage material and, generally, a good catch. He made a living. He wanted a family. He was traditional. He was handsome. Teme would do her utmost to keep her best foot forward. Best for Adam to see her superior qualities so he would take the bait. Adam was what she wanted. After this afternoon, she was sure of it. To have a home and children of her own would be the ultimate feather in her cap. To have it with Adam would be a superior feather at that.

Adam was quietly reflecting on his situation. During his prior visits to Belgium, he never took notice of how much Teme's father doted on her. He'd heard Teme's father call her *prinzesin* but had assumed he did so because she was the youngest and had only brothers for siblings. Now he realized that Aaron Gvirzman thought the world of his lovely daughter and, in his way, put her on a pedestal. The thought was a bit jarring, but Adam decided he was being silly to worry over it. In fact, he rationalized that it was especially nice to see the behavior because, admittedly, many Hasidic families favored sons over daughters.

With four brothers ahead of her, it would have been far more likely that Teme would have been ignored. A female afterthought that needed tending to from time to time. Adam would soon come to know that Aaron Gvirzman took the stance that if he found his daughter a man as worthy as his own sons, she'd be more than a princess. She'd be a queen.

Perhaps the senior Gvirzman wanted to make sure his only daughter did not feel left out or insignificant because the brothers had more obligations than she. The reality was that she was most likely being gussied up for a future husband. Teme needed to look good for the sake of her father's honor. People needed to know that Aaron Gvirzman raised a daughter who was an expert with children, cooking, and cleaning. That was surely why Aaron Gvirzman gave Teme the nickname *Prinzesin* when she was a child. A way to let her know she was perfection.

Adam could not have possibly known how correct his rambling thoughts were. Had he been a fly on the wall of the Gvirzman living room years ago, he would have been privy to a statement Aaron Gvirzman had made to Teme that proved Adam's summation was spot on.

"Temele, *prinzesin,* my *shayne malkele.* You are more than a princess. You are a beautiful queen among Jewish women. I'm very proud of this. No longer a little girl, my child. You have truly grown into a beautiful, proper

Jewish woman. A queen among women. You will make the perfect wife and raise sons that will make us proud."

Deep down Adam knew, even at this early juncture, that Teme had been trained to expect a certain way of life without question. With Teme putting her best foot forward, he could see no more than the fact that she had championed the art of becoming exactly what she was taught to be.

He could also see that Teme was eye catching and gracefully feminine. She behaved like a proper Jewish woman at all times. She was acceptable. She was what his family dreamed of and wanted for him. He knew how eager his parents were to finally marry him off. In fact, for both families, it would mean the joy of marrying off the last and youngest of their children. Adam briefly recalled his mother's dreamy hopefulness of having the community dance around her and bless her for giving away her youngest.

As they headed back toward the apartments, kids whooshed by on bicycles, townsfolk stepped out to wash sidewalks, and dull-colored buildings peered out from every corner, reminding them both that this was life in Antwerp. Adam knew he could be happy in Antwerp, despite its regular dreariness, simply because the heart of his beloved diamond industry resided there.

Yes, it was truly the heart. Its blood vessels were the roads and highways traveled to get there. Airplanes zoomed overhead to follow imaginary airways in the sky so they, too, could arrive in the city that was the diamond heart. This was comfort. This felt like home. He could feel content here. His most precious diamond of all, a marriage to seal the deal.

Adam had ensured Teme's safe arrival at home. He checked that all his belongings were packed and that he was truly ready to depart the Gvirzman home. He said all the necessary thank-yous, even adding a comment about looking forward to returning. With suitcase in hand, Adam walked to the car he had rented. He was on his way to the Netherlands. He stole one last glance at the building he had just left, reached for his keys and opened his car door. From his vantage point, he could see nothing more than bricks and glass windows. He could not see the three ladies sitting together in the Gvirzman living room.

A giggling, joyous Teme sat with Bina Gvirzman and *Bubbe* Yedida. In the quiet of the family living room, Teme was free to speak openly with her mother and grandmother. Things were looking very good. Very good, indeed. The Goldfarbs should be updated immediately. Plans for the future should begin. She was sure Adam would seek a marriage. She could feel it in her bones.

Teme was grateful that fate had sent Adam across an ocean to be by her side. She was ready and willing to tolerate his travels just so things could get underway. More than anything, she was ready and willing to finalize a *shiddach*.

In another place entirely, Adam was driving his rental car, headed toward Amsterdam. He had some minor business to engage in before returning to the United States—a delivery to a new dealer who would sell diamonds to the local jewelers in Amsterdam.

He drove along mindlessly, at least in terms of the road. Thoughts of his day with Teme kept coming through. They were pleasant enough, yet, as is common among all young men, the tendency to let thoughts of one woman prevail led to thoughts of another. Adam found himself once again thinking about Daniella. She represented everything that his community considered wrong for him, and yet he cared about her just the same. He felt connected to her just the same. A link he could not yet identify as the segue to the life he should be leading. To the life God really had in mind for him.

With no formal *shiddach* yet solidified, Adam still had a bit of time to think it all through. He wanted to see Daniella again and make absolutely certain he was making the right decision about his life. A big world waited out there. There was a different way to live, and he had been given a taste of it. A very yummy taste. He was attracted to it for reasons he could not possibly explain except to say that he was free to be the person he wanted to be, every time he experienced it.

He would make the most of his time in the United States and decide once and for all if he was supposed to turn left or right at the tremendous fork in the path of his life. He wondered why he, of all people, faced such a choice. Why *Hashem* practically plagued him with such a huge dilemma, he could hardly guess. What his true fate was, he truly didn't know.

He could be a Jew who followed the rules to a tee. Question nothing. Interpret and consider, but only within the context of following God's laws. Then again, he could be a Jew who interpreted and considered the rules in order to question them without fear of punishment. What a predicament! For the time being, he knew only that he was a Jew. The way in which he was meant to be a Jew was another thing entirely.

~

"Benny, Benny! Oh my gosh! I did it!"

Daniella came running through the front doors of the restaurant waving her acceptance letter. It was official. She would graduate from college in late May with her music education degree in hand, the teaching credentials she rightfully earned, and the bonus of beginning her studies to become a cantor come the fall. Could life get any better!

"That is so wonderful, Danny. Your parents must be so proud of you. I know I am!" Benny paused and spoke his next thought aloud.

"What do you think won them over? Your singing? Your commitment?"

"Well, I'll never be one hundred percent sure, but I do know two things I said that must have pushed the envelope."

Benny smiled at Daniella. Her joy was as clear as a sunny day, and Benny could tell she was eager to share her thoughts.

"Tell me...tell me what cleverness got my Danny into the program. No, wait! Come, let's sit in our special booth, and you'll tell me everything. Tea and cookies, Danny?"

Daniella smiled brightly. "Tea and cookies, Benny! A celebration!"

Once seated, comfortable, and ready to share, Daniella divulged her experience to her captive audience of one.

"Well, they told me that many candidates come to them with beautiful voices but seem to be missing something from deep inside themselves. Others have mediocre voices yet shine from within their soul. They asked me what made me think I was special. Why I believed I belonged there. They wanted to know why they should consider me as a future student.

"I relayed one of my student-teaching experiences that I had shortly after I began to mull over the idea of applying to cantorial school. I told the audition committee that while I was teaching solfège to the children, using a simple melodic run of notes, one of the children blurted out, 'Hey, that's the *Hashivenu* prayer we say at my synagogue.' Well, all I could think to myself was that of all things I could put together with musical notes, how interesting it was that I came up with a Hebrew prayer. Like it was destiny speaking to me and letting me know that the prayer was innate within me, and somehow subconsciously, it came out through my hand gestures."

"That's beautiful, Danny, but what is solfège?"

"Oh, I'm sorry, Benny. Did you ever see the movie *Close Encounters of the Third Kind*? They used it in the film.

It's a set of hand signals, and each represents a note on the scale. It makes it fun and easy to teach children music that way. Watch."

Daniella put her hand up for Benny to see and moved it in the same way one would sign the letters of the alphabet to a nonhearing person. Each symbol was a note. Daniella's melodic voice rang out.

"Do-re-mi-fa-sol-la-ti-do."

"How marvelous! I could never figure out what they were doing in that movie...with their hands, I mean. I always thought it was some kind of new system they made up between themselves and the aliens. An agreed-upon language, since they couldn't speak each other's language. Music, of course! That would be a universal language. Seems like you spoke it with the audition committee."

Benny laughed at his insightfulness.

"But, Danny, you said two things may have won them over. What was the other?"

"I told them that I had a commitment on one particular Friday night that I couldn't get out of. It involved a good friend, and I felt I couldn't let her down. The entire time, though, all I kept thinking was, I wish I was at *shul* and celebrating the Sabbath. I felt frustrated that I was denied welcoming in *Shabbat*."

Daniella became pensive and reached out for Benny.

"Benny, I have more I'd like to share."

Benny could see that weighty thoughts had taken hold of Daniella. She needed to talk. She needed guidance. He was honored that, through the passing of time, she'd come to think of him as a mentor of sorts. Someone who could advise her from a less subjective viewpoint than a parent might. Of course he'd lend an ear. He spoke that thought aloud.

"Of course we can talk more. Let me tell Nate to man the fort for a while longer."

When Benny was seated once again, Daniella brought up the two concerns that were now forefront in her mind.

"Benny, this means I can only work here full time until the end of summer. Once the program begins, I'll be living on campus. The whole experience means being able to stay at the school all the time and interact with my fellow students in a dorm."

"That's not a problem, Danny. Whenever you're around, on a break or something like that, if you want to come in and work, you'll work. If not, then you'll come in as a daily diner. You're always welcome. Simple as that. I'll miss you, and I'll be losing a great waitress, but look at what I'll be gaining…the right to say I know a female cantor!"

Benny reached out over the table and gave Daniella's hand a reassuring squeeze.

"Anything else troubling you?"

Daniella let out an exasperated sigh.

"Actually, yes." She paused only for the briefest of moments.

"Adam will be arriving back in the United States soon. How do I tell him and find a way to move forward with him? Benny, I think I'm falling in love with him. How do I let him know?"

Daniella paused once more, looked skyward to gather her thoughts, and then resumed gazing at Benny. Her eyes were welling up. A veritable signal to Benny that she spoke the truth.

"And then there's my parents. How do I tell them about Adam?"

For Benny, the two questions conjured up angry thoughts. Thoughts about how Jews make each other miserable. Thoughts about creating differences where there should be none. In fact, thoughts that irked him to the core. Those supposed differences created walls. Nothing more. Walls that were so firm and strong it would take nothing less than a bulldozer of the heavenly kind to break them down. *Energy wasted on piffle. In the end, we're all Jews.*

Benny remained convinced that Jews should be a united force, forever showing the rest of the world they were here to stay. Respectful of each other's differences because it was more important to prevail. One powerful unit, a Rock of Gibraltar. The conviction was soldered into his brain. A unit so strong that no one in the world could ever destroy Jews again. Wasn't it always the groups with dissension in the ranks that splintered and thus became fragile? Couldn't Jews see that? Benny could do no more than momentarily push his anger aside. He answered the question honestly.

"Danny, the ultra-Orthodox and even some Modern Orthodox frown upon us and say we're not real Jews at all. We've lost our way. We in turn think they're fanatical and outdated. We think they give the rest of us Jews a bad name. We resent that they make it hard for the rest of us because they refuse to connect with the public. It's a terrible and vicious cycle. So tragic. So sad."

Benny shook his head with regret. He patted Daniella's hand with affection, hoping she could sense the care and concern departing his fingertips. He allowed his hand to remain atop the back of hers as he continued.

"All you can do, my dear, is be honest with your parents and be honest with Adam. Tell each how you feel and then pray, Danny."

Benny clutched Daniella's hand, affectionately embracing it. He looked directly at her. He spoke from the heart.

"I'm here for you no matter what. I support your dreams and your right to love someone. I will never condemn the fact that you want to praise God through your voice. And I certainly will not cause you grief for caring about an observant Jew. Love is love, Danny."

Benny was a father figure, friend, and teacher rolled into one. He was actually akin to a best friend or confidante. How lucky Daniella was to know him. To work for him. To experience his culture and wisdom.

As the two sat and silently acknowledged what they shared between them, each came to his or her own summation. Daniella knew Benny was right. Benny knew that what he said was right. Each was thinking how wonderful it would be to prove the Jewish world wrong. Benny could see that certain look on Daniella's face. With a strange mix of fear and trepidation laced into endless hope, Benny decided to urge Daniella to forge ahead.

"Just do it, Danny. Tell your parents about Adam. Tell Adam about your acceptance into the school and the way you feel about him. The rest, I'm afraid, you'll have to leave to God."

Leaving it to God seemed more frightening than any dilemma Daniella could conjure up. Leaving it to God meant having faith. To even muster up faith and really believe from within that one could rely on it was among the greatest of human challenges. A grand test to push one through life and bring one to understand its purpose.

It was simply a matter of Daniella accepting the challenge.

Knowing there was nothing left but to make that choice or not, Daniella responded, "Wish me luck, Benny."

Daniella wanted to discuss her thoughts and ideas with her folks just as Benny had suggested, but nonetheless, she was scared. Much as she loved them, she knew that when she let the cat out of the bag, her parents, and especially her mother, would be hell-bent on getting Adam to think, act, and dress like a mainstream Jew. The mere hint from Daniella's mouth that Adam seemed to be on shaky ground in that regard, that often he hinted at concerns he had about his own life, would cause her mother's wheels to turn. She'd figure out ways to help him see the light of day.

It was a double blessing that Benny had the idea to invite Daniella for coffee at the Kalabokas home, in order to give her a chance to talk about it some more. He suggested she could even practice her words on him and Rose. Perhaps they could shed some insight on the matter. Besides, she would hear the opinions of a woman who was not her mother and who, therefore, was far less subjective. She could even get some input from Rose's mother, who Daniella had been told was visiting for a week. It would be interesting to get the added opinions of a prior generation.

This would be an opportunity to share thoughts about Adam without parental ridicule. It would be far better to sit and talk with Benny and Rose first and solidify what she wanted to convey to her parents. Benny was such a good egg, and he had a wonderful way of being supportive without being critical. Rose seemed equally so.

"I'm looking forward to talking with you outside the restaurant, Benny." Realizing the implied insult she had woven into the words, Daniella added, "Gosh! I didn't mean to imply anything about the Daily. It's great to talk here too. It's just that in your home, things will be more private."

"I understood what you meant. The visit will do us all good. Oh, and Rose's mother will be visiting as well. If you'd like, she'll read your coffee grounds for you as a special treat. She loves to get a chance to practice her art now and then. You're a good excuse to do so."

"People still do that? And, wait, don't people do that with tea leaves?"

"Rose's grandmother learned to read coffee grounds from her own mother way back in the day. She, in turn, taught the art of reading the grounds to Rose's mother. Rose herself was so spooked by how accurate the readings could be, she committed to not learning the art at all. I think my three girls have all shown an interest in doing it, but sadly, it's only my mother-in-law who still does it."

"Sure, why not? It would be fun." Daniella smiled as she spoke, but her expression quickly became serious.

She paused, refocused on the matter at hand, and then spoke further.

"I may want to talk to you about some other things as well."

Benny heard the subtle tone in her voice that indicated she needed to express worrisome thoughts.

"Will it bother you that Rose and her mother are there at all? Did you want to speak privately?"

"No, it won't bother me at all. It's not a matter of being private. I just have some ideas, and I'd like a more objective audience to express them to."

Several days had passed since that conversation. Now, Benny and Daniella were seated in his living room. As in most private homes in that particular area of the county, the living room was adjacent to the kitchen yet far enough away from it that some semblance of privacy could be maintained. With a wall dividing the two rooms, the illusion of privacy was enhanced even further, and one could at least pretend not to be overhearing the secret comments crossing the barrier between.

Rose and her mother were currently preparing Greek coffee and a tray filled with baklava and special cookies that harbored a trace of licorice flavoring. The family loved the subtle taste of ouzo laced into their cookie dough and it was a staple in the Kalabokas household. The clinging and clanging the two women created, helped drown out the living room conversation. Despite that, the smells were beckoning across the threshold that divided the two rooms. Daniella did her best to ignore her senses as she began to speak.

"So, Benny, I want to talk about Adam for a bit. I've been doing a lot of thinking and—" Daniella paused. "Benny, I think I'm falling in love with him. Crazy, huh?"

Benny reached out and gave Daniella yet another reassuring pat on the hand. The kind that simply said, "Continue. I'm here, and I'm listening."

"You've seen him in the restaurant many a time, so I have to assume you, too, have a sense of who he is as a person. I mean, beyond all the polite *hellos* and *how are yous*. There's a forward-thinking and somewhat liberal person buried in there underneath it all, don't you think? Don't you get a sense that he's searching or something?"

Benny said nothing.

"I can't help but feel that he cares for me too, even though he hasn't said so yet. I mean with actual love words. He does tell me I'm a special friend, and he does rub my hands once in a while."

Daniella was not about to divulge that they had also kissed more than once. For some reason, it was too embarrassing to admit.

"We're supposed to meet in two days. Stroll in the park and enjoy the afternoon. That sort of thing. I think he is going to tell me that he wants to try to make things work. There was something in his voice that sounded so nervous, almost frightened, when he called me. I have to assume it's fear of moving forward.

"Anyway, I've been thinking. Compromise just has to be possible. We only need to sit down and figure it all out. And isn't so much in place already? We both keep kosher. We both celebrate the holidays. We both know much about Jewish history. Soon, I'll know so much more as I begin to learn about Torah and Talmud at the seminary. And couldn't I become a cantor and just accept the fact that in his family's home, I'll have to leave it all to the men? They can pretend all they want that I'm not a bona fide cantor. Does it really hurt me in the long run? I guess I'm trying to say that, knowing how difficult it would be for Adam to function in a Conservative way when around his family, wouldn't it be fair for me to function more Orthodox when the need arose?"

Benny raised the level of his voice as he uttered a bit of sardonic response. "Oh, how kind of you, Danny... are you in a bubble all of a sudden? You're talking about Hasids! Do you honestly think they'll make that kind of compromise? A woman in a man's role?"

Benny's tone turned fatherly.

"Sweetheart, do you understand that to them, even the fact that you wear pants is grievous? A terrible sin. Woman and men are not supposed to wear each other's clothing. It gives the illusion of wanting to pretend to be the other sex or some such nonsense.

"And do you know what *tiflut* is? I learned about it from an Orthodox man once. It's the notion that if you do teach women advanced Torah or Talmud or whatever, you're also sinning. Women tend to be light headed, whatever that means. Somehow they will inadvertently trivialize the intricacies of God's commandments. They think only men have a higher ability to understand what God demands of us.

"What right does anyone have to take from you who and what you are? Are you ashamed of being a cantor in front of someone else's eyes simply because they don't like that you are? That you would actually pretend you're not one, for their sake? I hate to be so down on you this way, but isn't it akin to saying you can't be the kind of Jew you want to be? Isn't it a way of denying who you are, simply for the sakc of another's interpretation of what a Jew is?"

Benny looked at Daniella to await her answer.

She knew he was right, but she wasn't ready to fully admit it.

"That's how you see it, Benny? Don't you see compromise as a solution?"

"Compromise is a solution, Danny. But only if it is between two people who are willing to create it. It's only between you and Adam. Once you two come to your own conclusions, no one else's opinions should matter. No one else should dictate your life to the two of you. The moment you allow other's opinions to matter, compromise isn't happening at all."

"I don't want our parents to suffer hurt at our expense, Benny. And believe me, our parents will be hurting inside. Adam loves his. I love mine."

"I understand, really I do…and you're right. They'll be hurt. But…"

Benny paused long enough to gather his thoughts. "Here, let me tell you a quick story so I can explain better.

"I had a customer a long while back now. Fell in love with a woman who had two teenage children, and he certainly hadn't expected to fall in love. It just sort of happened. He was crazy about her. He married her, and that was despite the fact that his parents were dead set against him 'inheriting' two children."

Benny's tone laced the word *inherited* with venom.

"He came into the restaurant one day, looking quite forlorn. He sat down on one of the barstools by the counter and ordered coffee and a doughnut. And then he just sat there. Sat there and stared off, looking as if the weight of the world was on his shoulders. I couldn't help but go over and introduce myself. I asked him if he wanted to talk.

"He told me that he had taken his wife over to his parents' for lunch. The kids were in school, and it was just the four of them. His mother had the audacity to make a comment about the children being an unexpected burden on her son. It actually made his new bride cry."

Daniella was absorbed in the story. "What happened, Benny?"

"He told his mother to apologize. That, in turn, embarrassed his mother enough that she refused to do so. So, he simply got up from the table, retrieved his wife's jacket as well as his own, and announced that they were leaving. He didn't say another word to his mother.

"You know, Danny, the mother could have begged him not to go. She could have apologized. The father could have said something as well. Instead, they allowed pride and what they considered proper protocol to get in the way. Even worse, they allowed their opinion over something so truly unimportant to create a rift where there didn't have to be one."

"Benny, somehow I feel the parallel coming on. How did your conversation with him end?"

"So there he sat, telling me that his wife was full of pride that day. That she commended him for standing up for her. That she felt honored that he made no excuses for the fact that she was married once before and a mother to some other man's children. Yet he was plagued with the pain of knowing he had gone against his mother's wishes."

Benny continued so he could reach the point of his story.

"Here's the thing, Danny. We can worry that we hurt someone's feelings, but we can't and shouldn't give any credence to comments made simply because a person wants things to go their own way."

Benny looked Daniella squarely in the eye and gave her shoulder a tight squeeze.

"That mother said her comments in order to be hurtful. She said them because she wanted her son to marry a single girl. She said them because she was being selfish. She gave no thought to her son's happiness and contentment with his new bride and stepchildren. Or to the fact that he was truly happy with his new family. But mostly, Danny, mostly she said it because that was what she was expected to say. The dictates of society were behind her vicious comments."

"OK, Benny. I get it. So you're trying to tell me that I shouldn't compromise the person I actually am."

"You or Adam, Daniella. If he loves you, if he wants a relationship with you to get serious, he needs to be proud of the fact that part of you, part of who you will be in the future, will be a *hazzan*. That you may even be endowed with the title of *hazzanut* sometime in the near future. Neither of you should pretend that you're not who you are."

Benny could only hope that things would work out for the two of them. He liked them both, and their battle was a tough one. Mind you, he didn't know Adam nearly as well as he knew Danny, yet every time Adam visited the restaurant, he was respectful and easygoing, and he seemed to try so hard to be worldly. And that was despite being such a cloistered young man.

Sadly, Benny realized that, outside the confines of the restaurant, he really didn't know his customers, and certainly not Adam, all that well. He didn't know any of Adam's inner or deepest thoughts or convictions. He only knew Danny's. His biggest fear of all…that Adam would not be strong enough to fight the whims of his communal upbringing.

Benny and Daniella talked some more but only briefly before Rose and her mother came into the dining room with their wares. Rose placed her tray down and declared, "Time for a bit of brew and dessert. Come on in here, you two."

The presentation was lovely to look at. A large oval platter housed concentric rows of baked delights. A steaming urn and delicate cups with matching saucers were at the ready. The Greek coffee smell was consuming the air, begging for attention. The brew was intensely strong, but the flavor provided a great counter to the sweetness of the desserts.

American coffee was so unlike its Mediterranean counterpart. The Greek brew was heady enough that it needed to be sipped in slow increments. Eventually, Daniella emptied her cup of the bold and bitter fluid. When she took her last sip, Rose's mother instructed her to leave the cup untouched.

Rose's mother walked over to Daniella and asked to trade places with her. She then sat down in the now empty chair while Daniella stood off to her side. She gently pulled the cup and saucer in front of her. She stared inside and sat pensively as she gathered her thoughts.

Gazing into the muddy residue, Rose's mother saw a great hurt was about to befall the young lady. Based on the conversation she had just overheard, she surmised it may well have to do with the young man that had been spoken of. The grounds were never specific that way. It was always a matter of taking one's best guess based on known information. And she had just learned that there was a troubled romance.

She didn't have the heart to tell the young girl that she saw heartache and broken romance. Better to tell her only the good she saw in the muddy reflection. Indeed, she did see something grand as well. She would focus on that.

"You're a lucky young lady. I see a great future ahead for you. A lifelong marriage and four children. A good, strong career that will last you a lifetime. You will be doing something you love. Music, I see lots of music. I see children around you because of music."

Daniella smiled brightly. She thought of the fact that a cantor had to tutor many, many children throughout a career. To train them to be a *Bar* or *Bat Mitzvah* or to chant a portion of a service. And her own children...the muddy sludge showed her own children? It could only mean that perhaps some way, somehow, she and Adam would work it all out.

She would talk to Adam, and then, assuming all went well, she would tell her parents how she felt. She would find a way to assure them that she was strong enough to overcome any obstacle. She would assure them that she could do so and that they would not lose a daughter to the Orthodox community. Hopefully, God would remember that she was going on faith.

s fate would have it, Marcia Sobler already knew about Adam. She admitted her knowledge of him the moment Daniella made her confession.

"Your father and I are well aware that you've been interested in this Adam person. In fact, we've known about him for almost two weeks. Believe you me, I've been wanting to ask you about him from the get-go, but your father said we should wait and see if you'd bring him up yourself."

Marcia gave her daughter a glowering stare.

"Obviously, with you mentioning him now, well…" Her voice trailed off as she crossed her arms over her chest, waiting for her daughter's answer.

"How did you know, Mom?"

"I'll tell you, but then please talk to me about exactly what is going on here."

Marcia explained to Daniella that she had found out because of Vonnie and because of her monthly meetings for Women's League at the restaurant.

"The meeting at the Daily went well, and we were so busy yapping about the program we planned that Vonnie inadvertently left her planner at the booth. She didn't realize she had done so until two hours after we left. Naturally, she returned to retrieve it. Nate was at the counter, and he already had the planner in hand when he saw her come through the door."

Marcia paused for dramatic effect. Let her daughter sweat it out a bit. She was still irked by her daughter's choice not to tell her about this Adam fellow. This was a way to give a tiny bit of payback, no matter how small. A bit of motherly umbrage for being left in the dark.

"When Vonnie turned to leave, she saw you sitting with an Orthodox young man in the corner booth. Very clever, Danny, waiting until you knew we'd be out of there, but you forgot that half the people we know go into the Daily. It was simply a matter of time before you would have been discovered."

Oddly, Marcia Sobler was more indignant about the embarrassment of hearing about her own child from someone else than about the matter itself. When it came to actual romance of any kind, she felt it was her mother-given right to know things first. She would always be her daughter's champion once she knew.

"I do wish you would have told me about him yourself. It was embarrassing to hear it from Vonnie. Especially when she described the way the two of you were looking at each other. She was shocked, and she called me the moment she got home, going on about why I didn't tell her that you were seeing someone. Do you know how foolish I felt that I didn't even know what young man she was talking about? I had to pretend it was no big deal and that I knew about it all along."

Marcia paused one last time.

"Don't ever do that to me again, Daniella."

"I'm so sorry, Mom." Suddenly, Daniella began to cry.

Marcia instinctively switched back to caring-mother mode as she stood with open arms to hug her daughter.

"Daniella, what is going on?"

It was time for Daniella to come clean. Better that her parents had some idea about Adam and how she had met him. How she was feeling about him.

"Maybe you should ask Dad to come downstairs. It's probably better if I talk to both of you. I know you usually talk to Dad on my behalf pretty much every time something comes up, but I'd like to do the talking myself this time. No disrespect intended, Mom. I'd like Dad to hear it straight from my mouth and not secondhand from you."

When Ira and Marcia were sitting comfortably at the kitchen table, Daniella began her explanations from the very beginning. In a nutshell, it came down to one simple fact. She was very much attracted to Adam. Despite their religious differences, which Daniella tried very hard to trivialize, she was extremely interested in a romance. Wisely, Daniella left out the comment that she felt as if she were already falling in love.

What she did mention was what she knew to be the important fact. Adam would not be able to dissuade her from her dream of being a *hazzan*, and he would not turn her into a *frum* individual. Best to make sure her parents understand from the get-go that that would never change.

"No dark clothing that hangs around my knees for me, thank you very much. No opaque tights in the middle of summer. I get hot just thinking about it. No shaving off my hair that I love so much. Certainly, no being told I can't do things because I'm a woman." Daniella paused. "Please, believe me when I assure you that I will not become *frum*."

Ira Sobler looked at his daughter. He gave Marcia a light squeeze at the base of her elbow to assure her. He spoke for them both.

"We believe you, honey. Seriously, though, how do you expect this to work?"

Daniella answered honestly.

"Adam seems to be having some type of inner struggle. There is definitely a part of him that would like to loosen the reins and step outside the confines of his upbringing. I can't explain how I know that. I just do. I can see it and feel it even though he hasn't said as much. It seems to be there every time we talk. All I can do is hope he stays interested and, mostly, that he is brave enough to deal with whatever is going on inside his head."

"Can we meet this Adam?" Marcia Sobler asked.

"I'll let him know that you finally know about him and are asking to meet him. That's the best I can do for now."

"Well, your father and I still have mixed feelings about this, but like he said, we believe you. I guess we're willing to give it a try. We are, aren't we, Ira?"

"I suppose so. I'll be honest though. I think both your mother and I are still taking this with a grain of salt. I'm not even sure we like the idea at all."

Daniella looked back at her mother, who was giving her a look that indicated she was already on Daniella's team. That she would let Ira say his piece but would do whatever she could to protect Daniella's hopes.

Daniella was grateful that, as always, she could rely on her mother's strength and courage when things got rough. She looked back to her father and made a comment of her own.

"Don't go prejudging, Dad. If you do get to meet him, please be fair."

Not even one week later, when Daniella told Adam that her parents knew of him, did the fateful day come when Adam agreed to stop over at the Sobler home and meet and greet Daniella's parents. His only problem was his travel schedule.

"Danny, please make sure that your parents understand that I'm not sending a snobbish message. You know, reluctance to step into their home or anything ridiculous like that. Please make sure they're aware that it is a terrible combination of travel and of finding a way to visit without letting on to my own parents."

"My parents will understand, but I think they'd want your parents to know."

"I'm not in the same position as you, Danny. My parents will be mortified if they find out I'm seeing a less than *frum* Jewish girl. You know, I actually know of someone who did just that. In fact, he married her. He married a perfectly nice Modern Orthodox girl.

"One step shy of disowning him, his family never goes to his home to visit. They only go to his parents' when there are supposed to be family get-togethers. His parents refuse to step into his home. It puts a huge stress on them both, I'm sure. And each time they do go to their home, his parents continually try to get them to come back to the community.

"But here's the sad part, Danny. When I asked after his family and he gave me this explanation as to their lack of visits, he said it was because his home wasn't kosher enough or observant enough for them. He, a man who all his life knew how to handle those requirements. Suddenly, it's not good enough anymore.

"He has children that his parents don't even see that much. Their sworn oath is to keep it that way unless visiting with the children means a chance to educate them and free them from what they view to be sinful living. You know what that's an alias for? Utilizing public facilities like the library and community center or going to a movie or a concert. Their only relief was that at least he married a Jewish girl who is close in practice to what is expected of her."

Adam paused in an effort to attain delicacy in his phrasing of the next sentence.

"Then he added that they clarified that she really wasn't a true Jew because there was a time when she wasn't even Modern Orthodox. Her origins were far less observant, it seems. They've offered to help her finish the journey and be a complete Jewish woman."

Deep down inside, the story was fodder for Adam. It was yet another example of things about his Hasidic life that bothered him. More and more, the narrow-mindedness of the Hasidic viewpoint troubled him. The more he became involved in the bigger world, the less he wanted to remain in the shelter of the one he'd always known. Yet he buried those thoughts deep down inside his being. The rest of him was still attached to his family, his community, his career, and the brainwashing belief that the Hasidic way was the only way. He shared none of that with Daniella. Instead he responded with a general fact.

"I don't know if I'm ready to deal with my parents in that way. Much as I hate to admit it, I think they'd say something similar. The icing on the cake, Danny…that acquaintance of mine, he told me that, ultimately, he'd have to break ties with them if they kept it up. Know what? They'll do it to him first. Believe me…they'll cut him off first."

Daniella's response was a look of hurt. Or was she insulted or sad? Adam couldn't tell. Daniella looked as if she was about to respond, but Adam continued to speak before she could utter a single word.

"Danny, it isn't a matter of being brave and just dealing with it. It's a matter of my willingness to accept that if I move ahead, I'll possibly lose everyone and everything that means the world to me. Not just my parents. My siblings, Danny. My nieces and nephews. My friends. Pretty much everyone. A shunning, Daniella. An honest-to-goodness shunning."

Daniella sighed the heavy words, "I understand, Adam."

She never even bothered to tell him she had been accepted into the cantorial program in the city. Baby steps. One thing at a time.

Adam took Daniella's hand in his. He gave it a loving squeeze, the kind that a husband would give to a wife.

The message seemed clear. "Be patient with me. You mean something to me. Trust me." Wasn't that what it was saying?

The unspoken message held one that was even more evident, no matter that it, too, seemed hidden. The one that Adam and Daniella both continued to deny in their own way. One telegraph pole linked to another. Message received. Chemical spark. Spark of the divine. Souls, eager to connect. Wanting to connect. Praying to connect.

"I'll figure something out. Just give me time, Danny."

*A*dam had been tossing and turning all night. He'd had five, no, six outings with Daniella since their conversation. Little get-togethers squeezed into his schedule before he left for overseas. Each snuck into a secret life that Adam was living. Each better than the last. Each bringing a feeling akin to being at home. Comfortable.

He and Danny connected on so many levels that even he was surprised by how well they got along. They were friends, pals. Worse, he was starting to realize... no, wait, that wasn't the right word. He was starting to admit to himself that the basis for a lasting relationship with a woman really was strengthened by the fact that they were friends first.

He had heard that once from a non-Jewish customer who was busting at the seams over his newfound love, a woman who had been the best friend he could have asked for when he was growing up. A woman whom he recently rekindled his friendship with, having bumped into her in a store. She was more than a good friend. She was confidant, lover, and most definitely, the women he could picture raising his children. And the words that stuck with Adam the most…"I feel freer with her than I have ever felt in my entire life. She's the part of me that was missing."

Adam hadn't learned to think that way. For him it was about growing together in a relationship called marriage. He'd been told countless times that he'd meet a woman who would spark his interest enough that he would want to grow in the relationship together with her. Wasn't that another way of saying he would meet a woman he hardly knew yet somehow would instinctually know he could have a decent life with? Did that even really work? What about his own parents? Didn't they seem more like a partnership, in terms of running the household and family, and far less a completion of each other?

Adam was confusing himself. He'd seen countless couples in the neighborhood who seemed to be well suited to each other. He'd go as far as to say that there was genuine love between them. A kindness and softness. A caring that was evident to everyone. Besides, there were other cultures in the world that did matchmaking in the exact same way as his own community. Some couples did not even meet until their wedding day. Didn't the system work?

Daniella knew so much about the stories and even the lessons of Torah. Hadn't she said she had years of Hebrew School under her belt? Such a strange name the Conservative movement called their Jewish education. The students obviously learned far more than Hebrew when they attended their classes. It was evident that the Conservative movement was doing its job to a fairly decent extent. Adam couldn't deny it. Daniella could hold her own when they talked about all things Jewish.

When she mentioned that her family put up a *sukkah* every year to celebrate *Sukkot*, the feast of Booths, it solidified for him that non-Orthodox didn't necessarily mean a Jew who forgot it all. In fact, Adam was not sure why he had been told that about mainstream Jews. If it were so, they would pay no mind to the holidays. Certainly, they wouldn't bother to put up a *sukkah*. There were things that were definitely important to the Conservatives. Adam was realizing just how unfair it was to clump every outside Jew into one single group of nonbelievers.

Daniella had said that the Soblers put up a *sukkah* every year. They knew they were obligated as Jews to do so. Well, it was the same with his family. The Soblers kept a kosher home, just like his own family. Daniella had said that too.

The only difference was they did so within the context of the modern world. Daniella said it was proof positive that one could remain a Jew and be part of secular society. Adam recalled one very biting comment that Daniella had expressed at the beginning of their socializing together.

"How naive to believe that an entire planet filled with people, each coming to God in his or her own way, is in reality one big test for a small Jewish community that hides like an ostrich. If we are all failing as miserably as you say and God is furious with us, why are we still here, unpunished?"

Adam was quite impressed by the bravery Daniella showed back then. She had shown no fear of talking to a man the way she did. As time moved on from that initial interaction, Adam had gathered more and more tidbits like that from her. They urged him to find out even more. He became eager to learn. His teachers were books and now movies as well. The more he began to question the notion that there was one die-hard way to observe Judaism, the more he was determined to find an answer.

Daniella was bringing to light ideas and notions that Adam had always had but had buried deep in his thoughts as far back as he could remember. He just had never allowed them to surface before. Although difficult to admit, the notion that Daniella's Judaism was just as valid as his kept lurking dangerously in the back of his mind. More so, that he was attracted to her version of practice.

She had shared that every year her family had an open house during *Sukkot* and invited others to come and fulfill the commandment to dwell in the little hut. *Remember that your ancestors were forced to dwell in the desert for forty years. Remember how fragile their dwelling places were. In an instant, their little huts could have been blown away in the desert wind. No shelter. No comforting security surrounding them. That is symbolic of how life can be: as fragile as this hut. Remember to be grateful for the bounty that Hashem has given you in life, whether it be simple or grandiose. It can be gone in the blink of an eye.* Adam hadn't said those words to Daniella. She had said them to him.

It meant she understood. It meant that the holiday had meaning for her and that she believed in what she said. Yet even those were not the words that had struck him to the core. The ones that did, had come when she said to Adam, "I am *Sukkah*, Adam…I am *Sukkah*."

Adam had looked at her with wonderment even though he had an inkling as to what she meant by her statement.

"Tell me, Danny. Tell me why you are *Sukkah*."

"*Sukkah* represents me. I am fragile inside, Adam. I can easily sin, forget what is important in life, and turn away from *Hashem*. I have to be strong and steady against all that this world throws my way.

"Just like a *sukkah* struggles against nature, I have to continually do my best to not allow the rest of the world to knock me down or destroy me. Even things like the rain that ruins the *sukkah* or the winds that cause it to sway are symbolic of those things that could deter me from staying strong and being the best Jew I can be."

"Danny, that's lovely."

The imagery Daniella painted in his mind, the notion that a person could be *Sukkah*, gave Adam so much food for thought, he could barely digest it. He wanted to, though, because he needed to savor the sweetness of her words. For the very first time, Adam admitted that the notion of being a good Jew, whatever that really was, had far more to do with the feelings inside the soul rather than the dictates of the religion. The soul that instinctively knew what was good and right.

He wished more than anything that he could sit in the Sobler *sukkah* and celebrate under the stars with them. He wanted to take part in their discussions and relish the common belief system that in essence they shared, without the confines of conformity that were so prevalent in his own neighborhood. He couldn't, though, because he

was still afraid. He still gave heed to the prevailing surface thoughts. It was all a test that *Hashem* put forth to
test each and every Hasid. That the outside world was a
devil that tried to lure.

He could not come up with a single decent reason
as to why he wouldn't be home with his family during
Sukkot. That he would actually state he had plans to celebrate elsewhere was ludicrous. The only place he would
celebrate was in his own family's *sukkah* or that of his
neighbors and friends. He was not prepared to lie to
his parents about the matter, either. The holiday would
come and go, leaving him to do no more than imagine
celebrating it in a conservative way.

He and Daniella formed a strange combination,
when it came to matters such as this. It was one of connectedness and Judaic belief, never mind the chemistry
between them. Even so and despite it, they were continual polar opposites. Knowing this and still harboring
fear, Adam was pushed to test his own parents on the following evening. He did it in the best way he knew how,
during conversation at the dinner table.

"I wanted to tell you about someone I know from
the business who works in California from time to time."
*Hashem, please forgive me for that small lie. I'm trying to pro-
tect Danny by what I'm about to say.*

"Anyway, this colleague of mine heard about a young
woman who is causing a ruckus in the Conservative Jewish community in San Francisco because she wants to
become a *hazzan*. Seems he does business with some man
who attends a Conservative *shul* out there, where this is
all happening. The man told him about one of the female
congregants…the one that wants to become a *hazzan*."

Adam paused. "I was wondering what your thoughts were about that."

Tsivia Goldfarb provided no more than a subdued chortle. She rose from her seat and said, "Maybe I'll go and make us a plate of *nosh* since dinner is over."

Adam had caught the look in his mother's eyes, and more than anything he wanted to ask her if the look was because she wanted to agree or disagree with the idea of women doing anything beyond cooking the next meal or cleaning the drapes. He didn't want to get her in any sort of trouble with his father for daring to ask such a question, so he left her to her presumed task. At least she was in earshot and could listen in.

Nachum Goldfarb answered in a practical and well thought out way, but not before producing a snide harrumph.

"Son, men are obligated by law to observe and perform *mitzvot*. It's our sacred duty. You know that women aren't obligated in the same way. They have obligations, but they're different than ours. Running a household or raising children takes so much of their time and energy. They were designed by *Hashem* to perform those sacred duties. It's understood they can't fulfill the *mitzvot*."

He leaned in further to his son and whispered softly. "You know that women can be a bit light-headed at times. Emotional, for sure. They're not capable of the higher thinking we men are. Through no fault of their own, women would trivialize every aspect of prayer and devotion because of those very qualities."

Realizing he hadn't quite addressed the question well enough, he continued. "If a woman started to take on the duties that traditionally belong to men, wouldn't she in essence be taking away his opportunity to fulfill his mandatory obligations? His obligations. Not hers. She doesn't have any that are mandatory except when it comes to the family, Adam. You know that."

Nachum clarified his comment. "A woman standing on the *bimah*, *davening* the morning prayers, the afternoon or evening prayers, well, wouldn't she have taken away the man's place? And isn't he, and not her, obligated to say those prayers? Wouldn't it be a sin, then, that she took that away from him?

"Forget prayer. What if she's pretty? What if she lulls a man into thoughts of her in a forbidden way? She'd do that the moment he could hear her soft voice or see her lovely face, perhaps even her comely figure. It's no place for a woman, ever."

Adam could hardly believe that when he answered, he practically quoted Daniella. He answered with something that Daniella herself had expressed when they had revisited their long-ago discussion about women's prayer.

"*Tata*, may I pose a question?"

"Of course."

"If a man is obligated, regardless, then how could a women *davening* take his obligation from him? Would the man stand there and cross his arms like a child would, pouting and saying, 'You took my prayers from me?' Of course he wouldn't. He is obligated no matter who is praying around him or where they are praying. Also, if she is finished raising children and, in essence, has far less to do in her home as a result, wouldn't she be able to devote her time to those obligations?"

Nachum considered the question, rubbed his chin, and shook his head in contemplation. He explained further.

"You're not understanding, Adam. It is an enormous task for a man to shut off what is going on around him. Everything is a distraction. She would blatantly be placing *Kol Isha* on the ears of every man in the synagogue. How many of the men would still focus on the prayers? You tell me how many men would still be pious at that moment?"

Nachum Goldfarb leaned in to be secretive once more. He apparently didn't want to offend his wife, who was standing at the far end of the kitchen placing herring slices on plates.

"There's the bigger issue too. *Tiflut* would be at the helm."

"*Tata*, is *Hashem* concerned with the fact that Mama might be praying right next to you or rather that the two of you have come before him in prayer?"

Tsivia Goldfarb had been listening in all along. The decision now was whether or not to butt in. Her motherly instincts were already holding up red flags, one after the other, and she feared for her son. He was expressing some dangerous notions.

"Adam, where is this coming from? Since when do you ask your father such crazy questions like that? And what kind of girl would this be?" Tsivia answered her own question.

"I'll tell you. Seems to me that young lady is a woman who wants it all. That's a woman who gives no thought to the fact that she is stealing a man's obligations right from under his nose. That's a woman who wants to be a man. Better still, that's a woman who thinks she's entitled to those things that clearly belong to men. It's *chutzpadik*, if you ask me."

"Mama, you sound so convinced. You couldn't see someone like that having good motivation in her heart?"

A very concealed part of Tsivia could see it. At least, the good motivation part. An intention to try to connect with *Hashem*. Something like that could be forgiven. However, it was crucial to do what was good and right, and what was necessary to be a good Jewess. That was what mattered in the eyes of the Lord. She had been taught that from day one. She prepared to respond, but Adam posed a second question.

"What if she were sitting at your *Shabbat* table, as a guest in your home, and wanted to pray with everyone?"

"What? So she'll sit and tell your father, 'No need to say the *Shabbat* prayers, Mr. Goldfarb. I'll do that for you!' Wouldn't that be just ducky! In his own home. His castle. If anything, she'd better be respectful of whose house she is in and remain silent."

She paused for barely a moment. "Now that's a good Jewish woman! One who understands how important a father's role is as head of the household."

"What if she was a member of your own family, though? What if she felt that way inside but was afraid to tell you? What if, perhaps, she was a daughter-in-law that married in?"

Tsivia went from worried to frightened. She couldn't help but think to herself, *Men may think we can't see hidden meanings. Hah! Then why are you sitting there, Nachum, thinking this is just interesting discussion? Why can't you see that our son is asking so much more right now?* Tsivia wanted to be sure to answer vaguely. She didn't want her son to feel the wrath of his father.

"Adam, you should pity the poor girl. You should pity the man who is her father. You should feel sorry for any man who would be married to such a girl. Such an issue to have on their hands."

Tsivia Goldfarb allowed her features to make clear to Adam she was becoming perturbed. That she wondered if Adam was trying to tell them both something.

Adam answered the unspoken question currently plastered on his mother's face by directing his answer to both of his parents. He tried to sound as if the whole thing didn't matter to him.

"Of course, I'm not trying to tell either of you something. I'm just making conversation about such a curious matter."

"Well then, I can guarantee you, no one in our family would ever be that disrespectful," Nachum stated assuredly.

Tsivia gave Adam another peculiar look. Worry appeared in her facial creases, laced with concern and even a bit of anger. Adam wondered if his mother already suspected something and wanted to give him fair warning. Could that possibly be?

As if in answer, she added to Nachum's sentiment. "And none of my children would ever hurt us by marrying someone like that. My children all know how much their father loves them. How much I love them."

She looked Adam in the eyes when she spoke of her own love. She finished with, "It is very important to keep the righteousness of our family in good standing in the community."

For extra measure she added, "Jews who think that way are not authentic Jews. They have forgotten the laws and traditions and are trying to create some new kind of Judaism. They'll destroy our whole way of life if we let them."

Adam knew in his heart that his mother merely based her answer on the way that she herself had been raised. Unlike him, she did not read outside books, had never seen a television show or a movie. He wanted to correct his mother and tell her that she was talking about Ashkenazic interpretation of the laws and traditions, an interpretation found in one small community, namely theirs.

He wanted to remind her that their way of life literally handed down traditions from the heart of Europe. Those traditions just so happened to work their way over to America. He wanted to tell her that *authentic* was hardly the correct word to use. What about the Jews in Africa, Asia, and even Australia? He laughed to himself, realizing that Daniella's influence on him was becoming stronger and stronger all the time.

Nachum Goldfarb who had been listening intently, decided the conversation needed to be ended. He looked at Adam and decided to bring a bit of levity and joy to the weighty conversation. He did so by making a definitive point and warning of his own.

"How wonderful that you have met Teme and don't have to deal with such difficult issues. We're very blessed that you are such a good and observant son. Of course you are, Adam. How are things going with Teme, anyway? You know, we'd like to move along with a *shiddach*. Are we ready for that, Adam?"

Tsivia Goldfarb looked at her son with hopeful eyes. She and her other female relatives had spoken many a time about the joy of sitting in a chair and receiving blessings from all who danced around her. Too many times now, she reminded Adam that to marry off one's last child was the golden dream.

How frustrating that of all the topics that could be chosen, Nachum Goldfarb had chosen Teme and a request to make the match complete. This was all so hopeless. Adam had received the answer he had expected and dreaded, but still, he wasn't quite ready to commit to Teme. How he wished his father had chosen a different way to steer the conversation.

"*Tata*, I like Teme just fine. I get along quite well with her family, and she'd be perfect for me in so many ways. I just want a little bit more time."

"Adam, you've had enough time already! Why are you being so hesitant?"

Adam could hear the angry tone in his father's words. How could he defuse the ticking time bomb that was his family's eagerness to marry him off?

His father spoke once more, with an ultimatum that Adam was not ready for.

"Adam, you have another trip to Antwerp coming up next week, yes? A long one too, so you told me. It's been more than enough time to get to know Teme. You've been there two times over the last two months. You've been spending quality time with the whole family. Overall, you've had enough of getting to know them and seeing how you feel about it all. It's time for an official decision.

"I expect you to return from this next trip with a decision made, and I expect it to be positive. A long-distance *shiddach* will take a good amount of time, and we need to get the ball rolling. You'll disgrace our good name if you *shlep* this out any longer. You understand me?"

"Understood."

With a heavy heart, Adam left the conversation realizing it didn't matter that he was unsure about what he wanted. It didn't matter that he knew he felt more than a simple attraction to Daniella. It didn't matter that he had questions that he wanted to explore further and in more depth. It only mattered that there were expectations. It only mattered that Teme was considered a good match. The wrath of his father and the standing of his good name in the community frightened Adam enough that he would not stand up to the man he loved.

The coming trip was going to be a long one, just as his father said. Three weeks, to be exact. And everyone in the Gvirzman and Goldfarb families had been anticipating that this would be the final visit before an official *shiddach*. *Bubbe* Yedida had seen to it that the two were as happy as two peas in a pod, content and snug in their perfect world during his prior two stays at the Gvirzman home. Hadn't she arranged for outings for the two youngsters that assured they would have nothing less than connection after connection as they got to know each other? Both families were on a mission. A united front to get what they all wanted.

Adam would be seeing Daniella tomorrow. One last outing with her before the trip to Antwerp took place. He wouldn't say anything to her just yet about the whole matter. In fact, he'd call her and tell her that he'd stop by her home to pick her up. That would mean meeting Daniella's parents. It would leave Daniella thinking that all was right with the world…at least for the time being. It would make her happy that he met her folks. He wanted to make her happy even though he knew that ultimately he would be hurting her.

Once again in his naive bubble, he thought Daniella would focus more on the kindness of his willingness to meet her parents and not on the possibility that it would be the one and only time he met them. The last thing he wanted to do was hurt her. Surely she would see that.

He made a conscious effort to ignore how cruel he was being in the long run. In essence, he knew he would hurt Daniella deeply, simply because a woman named Teme existed. Instead, he chose to remain hopeful that he could find some way to manage the situation he had put himself into and desperately wanted to stay in. Maybe Daniella would be willing to remain his friend in the United States. They could visit whenever he was in town, and he would still be able to enjoy time with her.

Adam's conscience said otherwise. It was asking Adam how he could deny the fact that he had fallen for Daniella, and hard. Painfully hard. That he was already deeply in love with Daniella.

*T*he doorbell rang. Marcia looked at her husband. A nervous smile blossomed across her lips.

"Here we go, Ira."

The Soblers gave their daughter a moment to open the front door before they entered the foyer themselves. Standing in the front hallway area, they waited for the formal introductions to occur.

"Mom, Dad, this is Adam Goldfarb. Adam, I'd like to introduce my parents, Marcia and Ira Sobler."

Marcia and Ira both noted that the young man was not dressed in typical black and white. He had on a pair of blue jeans, of all things, and his shirt was light-blue plaid. He wore a lightweight indigo sweater over his shirt, which seemed to complete the appearance of preppy collegiate. His *tzitzit* hung at his sides, peeking out from under his sweater, providing one of only two indicators that the Soblers were not being duped. A black crocheted *yarmulke* graced the young man's head. His appearance was bizarre simply because it made it hard to

believe he was a black hat. He looked like a college-aged
Modern Orthodox man, frumpy hair and all.

Marcia supposed he wore the clothes he used for
travel. Daniella had shared a lot of information about his
work transporting diamonds, so she already knew that
Adam owned separate wardrobes. She found it more
than interesting that he was willing to dress the way he
did for this particular occasion. Did it mean he was willing to step into their world in an effort to make their
daughter more comfortable? Did he do it simply for the
sake of a good impression? She would have loved to ask.
Of course, she wouldn't.

In its own way, though, the notion earned brownie
points in the back of Marcia's mind. And being none
the wiser, Marcia thought it was the first in what would
hopefully be many other indicators that he was leaning
toward a more open lifestyle.

Adam and Ira reached out to each other in order to
shake hands. Their grasps were simultaneously firm and
strong, a fact that was noted by each of them. They were
sending an unspoken message between themselves, saying, "I accept you."

Indeed, both of them felt it between their fingers
and looked at the other with a quiet understanding. Marcia looked at the young man and didn't reach out for
him at all. Naturally, she assumed he would not want to
have contact with her, which in itself was silly because
Daniella had mentioned that he'd held her hand once or
twice. Then again, Marcia was someone else's wife. She
was a Jewish woman. She wanted to be respectful of his
belief. She gave Adam her best smile and acknowledged
him with a nod. Seeing this, Adam didn't press her for

a handshake. However, he was admittedly impressed that the Soblers knew about the rules and regulations of Orthodoxy.

"It is very nice to meet both of you. Daniella speaks of you often."

"Likewise, Adam. My husband and I have heard so much about you. Please, won't you come in and sit for a while?" Marcia swept her arm outward toward the den.

Marcia wanted him to stay awhile. He'd just gained more brownie points with his friendly manner and his kindly smile. *I can see why Danny finds him charming.* Certainly, she wanted to see more of the reasons that he had impressed Daniella to the extent he did. She wanted a bit of interview time so she could try to get to know him better.

Unfortunately, fate would have it otherwise. Today's date was a matinee three towns over. Driving time needed to be taken into account. They would have no real time to spare for a possible cross examination. Certainly, Adam and Daniella weren't ready for that, anyway. Besides, there would be no point. Today was the day that Adam planned to come clean about Teme.

"Thank you for the offer, but I'm taking Danny to see a movie. We need to leave right away if we want to make it on time."

"Well, OK, then. Have a good time, and we hope to see you again, Adam."

Marcia had indicated they were free to go by the inflection in her words, but disappointment resided in her head. Ira reached out one last time for a good-bye handshake, which Adam gladly accepted.

As he and Daniella stepped outside, Adam turned and added, "It was truly nice to meet you."

After closing the door, Marcia peered through the middle windowpane, which was at eye level and atop the front door panel. Pushing the sheer curtain aside, she took a quick peek at the young couple. Two smiling faces were looking at each other, already engaged in conversation as they walked down the front path. She let the fabric go and turned to her husband.

"Did he say *movie*? Since when do the Hasidim go to movies? Tells me a lot right there. What do you think, Ira?"

"Seems like a decent fellow. Time will tell."

Marcia gave a more involved summation, one that was typical of a woman's intuitive thinking.

"I don't like that we had an entire meet and greet in our hallway entrance. I almost feel like it was done on purpose. Did you notice that he referred to her as Danny? Means he has merited the honor of using her nickname. You know that Daniella only lets certain people call her Danny. Tells me she feels strongly about him. Who would have thought? Our Danny, of all people!"

Marcia thought about it further.

"He was so friendly. Did you notice that?"

"Yes, I did."

"And the way he dressed!"

"Maybe he's Modern Orthodox now?"

"I don't think so, Ira. Daniella said he was a Hasid. I hate to be stereotypical, and about our own people, no less, but he still has that aura despite his clothes."

"That aura?" Ira laughed while asking his question.

"Ira, come on, you know what I mean. He's going to a movie, Ira. A movie!"

"You sure you're not acting shocked simply because you know where he hails from?"

"No, I'm not! And even if he is Modern Orthodox and not Hasidic any longer, doesn't that still make him *frum*? We were always hoping and praying that the children would meet nice Jews to date and, hopefully, marry. God was listening and gave us exactly what we asked for. We can't even complain about it!"

Marcia changed the sound of her voice. "No, God, you heard me wrong. I didn't mean a Traditional Orthodox man when I was saying all those prayers! You misunderstood me." She continued with, "If this gets serious, Ira, we'll be explaining ourselves to our friends over and over."

Marcia paused and reached out to her husband.

"I hope and pray that Danny is true to herself. I don't want to end up like the Rothenbergs. You remember them? Selma is always telling us how her daughter became so *frum* after meeting that man named Moishe. She ended up marrying him, and Selma feels like she lost a daughter. Everything Selma does now is not observant enough or kosher enough for her own daughter. Her own flesh and blood! And her daughter has the audacity to tell her so! It's like a slap in the face, I tell you!"

This was about Marcia's own daughter, and that made it scary. She didn't want to be like the Rothenbergs. She wanted it to be OK and prayed it would all work out for everyone's sake. She could see that Daniella really enjoyed the young man, and she wanted her daughter to be happy. She actually hoped there was a good outcome waiting ahead. For now, she would be sure to let Daniella know that so far, was at least for now, so good.

Marcia had no doubt that the youngsters were reflecting on the meeting as well. She loved that expression about being a fly on the wall and wished that she were privy to the conversation she was sure they were having. She pulled the curtain on the small pane aside once more. She could see the car in the distance, nearing the end of the street. Daniella's head was turned towards Adam. Indeed, conversation was occurring. Marcia could only wonder what they might be saying.

"Your parents seem very nice, Danny, and also accepting."

Adam smiled at Daniella and spoke aloud the thought that was whirling in his mind. "The fruit doesn't fall far from the tree. I have to assume they are great people because of the daughter they have raised."

"Adam, that is so sweet." Daniella laughed as she continued. "Yeah, I am pretty decent, aren't I?"

"Yes, you are, Danny. I think you're wonderful."

Adam stole a quick glance at her but was grateful that he needed to keep his eyes on the road. This was getting harder and harder all the time, and he knew that on the imaginary highway that was his own road in life, he was getting extremely close to the crossroads. And life goes on, doesn't it? You can't just stand there and refuse to progress on the road of life destined to be yours. You have to turn when it throws you a curve. He'd have to turn, because his own imaginary crossroads was all too real. *Give me strength, Hashem. I am so drawn to this girl.*

"You're wonderful too, Adam."

Daniella paused for just a moment before divulging her own hopeful wish. "Do you think I'll be able to meet your parents?"

Torturous as the question was, plaguing him because he already knew the truth, Adam was able to squelch the wince that was his automatic response. Instead, he answered as vaguely as he possibly could.

"I don't know, Danny. They are great people too, but they are traditionalists. What more can I say?"

There was no way that Adam would hurt her by telling her she was completely unacceptable and would remain so unless she became as observant as the other women in his community. Likewise, she would have to let go of the idea that she had the right to become a *hazzan*. There was no way that he would admit that deep down, he already knew a future with Danny was highly unlikely. He could not bear to admit that this was most likely their last official date together.

The matinee came and went, but not without further testimony to Adam's wants and struggles. He had reached out for her hand as they watched the movie. He had rubbed the top of it once or twice with his thumb. He quietly reveled in the softness he felt. He gave no thought to what he was doing or why Daniella had allowed it. He thought only about the fact that he had the good fortune to have found a Jewess who made him feel alive. One who challenged him and cornered him into mulling things over before drawing conclusions. One who made his heart beat a bit faster every time he looked at her. One who made him feel...complete.

"Adam, how wonderful to have you in our home again." Aaron Gvirzman gave Adam a friendly pat on the back as he indicated that Adam should go into the spare bedroom to unload his belongings.

"Please, put your things down and make yourself at home. Teme will be back shortly. My wife and mother have prepared a little tea and some things to *nosh* on. We'll all sit and talk for a while."

When Teme walked through the door and entered the living room to greet her family and Adam, the only thing Adam seemed to be able to notice was the fullness of her hips as she walked his way. There was a poutiness to her lips despite her smile, and Adam found it alluring, making him wonder what it might be like to kiss them. Teme's crystal eyes lined in their kohl lashes stared coyly and beckoned in their own way. A perfect package.

Admittedly, Adam was very curious about what lay underneath the wrappings of her clothing. She was so shapely and trim. He felt a raw chemistry about her that, unfortunately, he did not recognize as simple lust.

The feeling was so intense and strong that Adam could do no more than chalk it up to his *yetzer harah*, a silent confirmation that everyone was right about the desire to sin. He wanted to touch her hair and feel the curve of her hips resting in his palms. She was easy on the eyes. The conservative clothes she wore held a mystery within. His feelings were so strong that they overshadowed the more important things, such as how well he would be able to connect with Teme about the matter everyone called life.

Adam resided in a blind spot. He couldn't discern lust from love. He couldn't move on in his mind to weightier things, like issues that would affect them both. How to run a household; how to raise a child. How to stay fulfilled in each other's eyes. He could only think about consummating…mating.

Teme asked him if she could bring out the head covering she had been working on. She explained that she had been asked to make it for a family that was preparing their own daughter's bridal trousseau. It would be the head covering the future bride would use for lighting the Sabbath candles.

Teme's mother eagerly piped in. "Yes, yes. Do show Adam what you have been working on."

Yedida, Aaron, and Bina sat like kids in a candy store, eager for the goods to show themselves. Eager for Adam to witness the treat that was their daughter and granddaughter's talent. Teme scooted down the hall as fast as her legs could take her there and came back only moments later with several items in her hand.

The talent that resided comfortably in Teme's nimble fingers was self evident. Adam thought Teme was holding a piece of an angel's wing. The lace work was so intricate, so delicate, that Adam could only imagine it fell from heaven. The workmanship displayed the purity that one would hope every woman could convey as she wore the headpiece and lit the candles on *Shabbat*.

Teme had also brought out a second work that was still in progress. It was an effort on her part to prove how involved her craft really was. She wanted him to see that her talent was, in fact, awesome. Even her family sat with grins plastered on their faces over the simple fact that Teme was so artistically adept. Her talent would enhance home and family. All people needed beautiful things to grace their home, didn't they? Adam just had to be impressed and amazed. Who wouldn't be?

"This is the actual paper pattern I need to follow," Teme said. "See how I mounted it onto this padded board? Sort of shaped like a pillow, just firmer. The revolving cylinder in the middle holds the pattern nice and tight for me. Then I put the pins in through different points in the pattern…all these pins you see here. That's called pricking because it perforates the paper at specific points."

Teme realized she was about to get too technical, but she wanted to show how knowledgeable she was about her craft, so she added in one more comment.

"This is called torchon edging with half-stitch scallops in the design. Once I finish the piece, I'll sew it onto a plain-white apron along its edge. I'll do the same on the pockets of the apron. It's the apron the bride will use on *Shabbat* or maybe the High Holidays. She will look beautiful wearing it!"

Adam looked down on the little pillow that had been placed on his lap. Twenty-four tiny bobbins hung down from it. Each one of the wooden pegs was holding wound thread at the top and a weight at the bottom. The weighted ends were shaped like teardrops. On the other end of the pillow, the finished lace edging was hanging over the edge, proudly showing itself for all to see and admire. Inside the circumference of the pillow board, the cylinder filled with pins and thread rested safely inside a nook built into the pillow itself. The thread twisted one way or another as it lay over the paper pattern inside it. The paper that was waiting patiently to be copied.

"Teme, this work is beautiful. It's such perfection. What do you call this?" Adam delicately picked up and stroked the finished piece falling from the pillow board onto his knees.

"Thank you, Adam. It's called bobbin lacing. It's what I'm best at, but I can also tat, do hairpin lacing, filet netting, and really, anything that requires fine thread and needle." Teme was beaming.

Adam had confirmation about something he already learned about Teme. She was precise and meticulous in everything she did. The way she helped in the apartment her family called home; the way she helped observe the Sabbath. Even the bobbin work resting on his lap was testimony to the fact she possessed those qualities. Wouldn't she run a precise Jewish home, then?

Adam failed to admit to himself that it was quite likely that if she was that way with some things, she would be that way with everything. Teme was determined to perpetuate the Jewish lifestyle she felt was paramount to being blessed. To being good. In her defense, she didn't know any better. In fact, it was the only thing she really did know. Teme knew nothing of relationships or what they needed to thrive. She knew everything about the importance of being an eventual mother and homemaker.

All efforts to downplay the fact that Teme would expect no less than a meticulously run marriage, steeped in every bit of tradition and observance, were not only continued by Adam but by everyone in the Gvirzman living room. Teme was proof that her parents raised a woman who knew that men didn't want a woman who outstepped her bounds. They had long ago made a grandiose assumption that any man would like it if she kept quiet and ran the household.

As for Teme herself, well, she just wanted the perfect husband. Like a master artist, she was brushing Adam into the perfect picture she had painted for herself, secretly sweeping the brush a stroke at a time. It completely obscured the fact that, once those initial layers of paint were gone, there would be little substance underneath for either of them. There would be no common goals and no common opinions or ideologies to keep the painted glue from weakening.

When the two were strolling outside later that day, Teme told Adam about who she was named for and what she felt she owed to her two great-great-aunts. It only added to the picture she had painted for Adam. Namely, that she was a properly motivated young woman. Motivated to be a good Jew for both their sakes. Motivated in order to perpetuate the Judaism that had been stolen right out from under her family during the Nazi era.

Adam could do no more than believe that she was perfect in every way as she stared at him with those ice crystal eyes. Those ice crystals were so stunning that Adam often felt as if he were being pulled right into them. Between them and the honey-colored hair dripping down around her shoulders, Adam thought he would burst inside. Lust had taken a strong foothold, as, sadly, had their families' matchmaking.

She is perfection in every way. She is what I know and what I am accustomed to. She is what will make my family happy and content. She is the key to making two families and, actually, two entire communities happy. Two Jews who, together, will be a strong and committed couple.

The situation had lost sight of one extremely important thing. How many times had Judaism purported that the eyes were the windows to the soul? That if one looked deeply enough into them, one could actually hear their words, the unspoken truths that lay hidden but could be revealed if one looked hard enough.

Teme's eyes were the color of ice. Ice is cold and hard. You can't budge it. Had Adam looked deeper, he would have seen Teme's determination to perpetuate what she thought was the only true way to live. Adam completely missed the fact that, in cold hard truth, he and Teme had nothing in common. Especially in light of the fact that he would continue to question his Judaism, despite his best efforts, and ultimately want out of Hasidism. By the time the quick stroll was completed, Adam had stated those things that Teme hoped he would. That she was the best possible match for him, and they needed to move forward.

Adam had conveniently pushed all his feelings for Daniella to the far recesses of his mind. Every detail, all the way down to the color of Daniella's eyes. He would try to forget that she was unafraid to express the right to be different. That she loved humanity for its own sake and not because anyone dictated to her exactly how to live life or who to be. *Lock it up. Lock it all up now, Adam.* His parents would win. The Gvirzmans would win. He was not brave enough to leave his community or his way of life. He would lose everything he'd ever known if he did.

At a pivotal moment, a moment when he needed Daniella's convictions to strike a chord in his heart, Adam made the wrong choice. Like a thousand fools before him, he mistakenly presumed that the voices of reason all around him were the ones that conveyed God's wishes and even the truth. When, in fact, God was not saying anything at all.

Just as before, Adam found himself bogged down by weighty thoughts as his plane flew back to the United States. The thoughts, however, were far more detrimental than any Adam had ever had in his life. He scarcely even knew how to deal with them. He certainly had no clue what to do with the mess he had made.

He had left the Gvirzman home completely mesmerized by the perfection that was Teme. He had indicated to her parents and grandmother that he would like to proceed with the arrangements to make a *shiddach*. He had let them know in the careful way he had chosen his words that they should speak to his parents, knowing he was about to return home.

Now, he was sitting on the plane wondering how he would explain it all to Daniella. She didn't even know that Teme existed. Once things got underway, he would be in Antwerp frequently, and quite likely, he would hardly see Daniella at all. Maybe not see her ever. There was even a chance that he would remain in Antwerp, at least initially. Once he was wed to Teme, his life would change forever.

Adam felt nauseated just thinking about it. He was about to look like a total *schmuck* in the eyes of someone he had become extremely fond of, someone he wanted to be close to. No matter that he continually planned out what to say. Adam knew he would become lessened in Daniella's eyes. He leaned back onto the plane seat and closed his eyelids. He was sure he was going to be sick.

By the time Adam arrived home, enough hours had passed that he was able to allow cold logic to set in. He turned the key in the back door lock while preparing for the momentous announcement he was about to make. As he stepped over the threshold, he shouted out, "Mama, *Tata*, I'm here."

His parents came rushing out from the kitchen overly eager to greet him. It was the dead giveaway that, somehow, his grand announcement had been stolen right out from under him. A part of him was furious about the matter, but a bigger part of him was relieved that he didn't need to be the one to share the news.

"Adam, the Gvirzmans called while you were in flight. My little *yingele*, all grown up and ready to marry. My little boy, now such a wonderful grown man! I'm so happy!" Tsivia Goldfarb was practically beaming as she clasped her hands together.

"*Mazel tov*, son. I'm very happy for you," Nachum Goldfarb added in as he reached for a hearty handshake.

Caught up in the momentary enthusiasm, Adam shared his parents' excitement as they went into the living room to sit and talk about it all. The overall and prevailing decision was that Adam and Teme had already spent enough time getting to know one another. They had already built the foundation for a relationship.

Time was of the essence because of the strenuous combination of traveling back and forth and trying to plan a wedding. It would take several months, but Tsivia and Nachum had been through it before with their other children. There was a more pressing reason to get the task accomplished. The longer it dragged out, the greater the risk the two would succumb to sin.

It never occurred to members of the Hasidic world that the rule to never touch was so strictly adhered to, that sinning, although thought of often, was probably the last thing either partner had in mind. The youngsters simply didn't know how to kiss, how to make love, or even how babies were made.

They had no instruction because it would have been immodest to delve into any of it. Even the young women, more often than not, didn't have a clue as to what menstruation was. They'd freak out and run to their mothers, upset with all the blood pouring out from between their legs. Many mothers gave the answer they themselves had heard years before. Learn to deal with it. They never reviewed or discussed any of the mechanics of biology, or psychology, for that matter.

Adam went to his room at the back of the house that night, realizing his life was finally at the fork in the road that he had been dreading for weeks on end. Actually, he had already passed it. He would be leaving the comforts of his little room. He would be living halfway around the world for months at a time. He would be leaving the free and unrestrained Adam, the one who was enjoying the bigger world, far, far behind. Actually, he would have to forget that Adam altogether. In fact, he was going to leave that Adam stranded on his imaginary road.

It was almost as if two Adams had existed and had been driving on the road of life together, side by side in the same car. Mirrored twins, yet fraternal ones at that, for each was his own person. The free and unrestrained Adam on the one side, the traditional Adam on the other. The traditional one was also the driver. Now, the more worldly Adam was being pushed out of the car and off the road. Dropped by the more sensible Adam, who knew better.

Adam reflected on the fact that Teme and he were the golden standard all Hasidic families strove for. Didn't everyone want to be the golden standard? His mother had let him know that Teme would be the envy of many girls who had hoped to make a match with him. He in turn would be the envy of young men hoping for a bride as beautiful as Teme.

He thought about how lovely Teme was to look at and knew he'd have no trouble in the attraction department. He wondered what it would be like to kiss her. *Hashem, please let her not be a cold fish.* So, too, for the first time, Adam acknowledged that in the time they'd been together, he really hadn't been able to tell if Teme was attracted to him physically. He hadn't seen the signs, but then again, Teme would never behave in the same way that Daniella had when they were together.

Teme was so adept at the laws of *negiah* and of *tzeinus* that she offered no indication in her body language, save for the occasional tip of her head so as not to gaze in his eyes or the lowering of her eyelids to briefly cover and then expose the beautiful orbs within.

Their discussions were all based on planning what their future home might be like. They'd had no in-depth discussions about life in general, why they lived it or how the world affected them. Things Adam loved to mull over and contemplate with Daniella until he was talked out. Things he discussed in depth with Daniella. *Danny, my Danny. A mentch in her own right. Mentchlich enough that she'll understand I'm between a rock and a hard place. At least, I hope so.*

Naively, Adam thought that once he told Daniella about Teme and about how limited his time would be in the States, she would still be willing to lend an ear and be a good friend. That she would be her wonderful self and support his endeavors as he muddled along through his life. Not a mistress, *Hashem* should forbid it. He would never do such a thing or expect such a thing from Daniella. He just meant a really good friend.

He'd introduce her to Teme, and when they were in the States, they'd all visit. Maybe she'd even give him helpful advice about Teme. She would remain his pal and spend time with him whenever possible so they could continue their wonderful discussions and debates. And somehow, somehow he would be able to push his own attraction for Daniella aside. Adam's naive, foolish thoughts were all part of his secret desire to have his cake and to eat it too.

In all those hopeless and naive thoughts, Adam never once acknowledged that perhaps Daniella herself was far more than a friend to him. That the very fact that he thought about her so often or the fact that they connected on so many of life's issues indicated that he cared for her deeply. It never occurred to him that theirs was the real basis for a lasting relationship. That in spite of their different viewpoints about Judaism, they meshed like a husband and wife should. That without recognizing it yet, he was, in actuality, deeply in love with Daniella.

Adam called her the very next day and arranged to spend an afternoon in one of his favorite parks. This would likely be their last time together for a long while, so he wanted to make the day as pleasant and as memorable as possible. They would hike around the little lake at the park's center and then follow one of the foot trails by the lake's edge. He'd be sure to take the trail that had the huge rocks and trickling waterfall. It would be a good place to sit and tell her about Teme.

He'd incorporate his perfectly rehearsed lines into the classic conversation males knew the world over. The one that began with, "I don't want to hurt you." The one that made an intelligent man look pathetically stupid because, indeed, the rehearsed lines would hurt the woman on the receiving end. Those painful lines that, without saying it, stated quite clearly, "I love you…really I do. But I think I love her more."

They drove to the state park just as planned. They followed the trail that encircled the lake and delighted in the pleasurable mix of sunshine, a gentle breeze, and superb conversation. Adam gave no indication of what was to come. Daniella smiled brilliantly, acknowledging the perfection of the day as well as her good fortune in meeting such a wonderful man.

As they sat on the big rocks that outlined the lake's shore, they marveled over nature's scenery, commenting on the colors of the trees and on the birds that were chirping their joyful tunes. It was nature at its finest in a peaceful place meant just for them. Peaceful because Adam had given no indication of what was to come.

He suggested they walk over to the big oak that stood a few feet away. There, they could rest against the trunk and talk some more. Adam let Daniella sit down first, her back firmly rooted against the rough bark. He slid himself down so that he could lay his head on Daniella's lap. He looked up into the peridot eyes he adored and reached to stroke her fallen hair further away from them so that their brilliance could catch the sunlight.

"Danny, I..." Adam hardly knew what to say, and for a reason far beyond his conscious grasp, he no longer wanted to say anything. Traces of raw distress began to envelope his features as he gazed up at Daniella.

"Adam, are you all right? You look almost, well, pained."

"Danny, please kiss me."

"What?"

"Please, Danny. Just kiss me."

Adam turned himself so that he was lying right next to Daniella. Two lovers on their sides, facing each other, ready to declare their love.

Daniella cupped Adam's head from behind. Her fingers wove into his curls, and she felt their softness caress her fingertips. She kissed his lips gently and smiled as she gazed into his eyes. There was love in that look and it was conveyed to Adam. It urged him on. One last test. One last test to decide it all.

"Kiss me harder, Danny."

Adam took Daniella into his arms. For that one moment, he let himself forget who he was. He focused on no more than the woman in front of him. He pulled her into his arms as tightly as he could.

Daniella succumbed to the urgency. She literally melted into Adam, practically limp as she responded to the kiss he placed on her lips. Passion and heat ignited together, and the chemistry between them caused sparks, same as always. She twirled Adam's curls and caressed his neck all at the same time. Adam's brain registered every single one of the unspoken messages she was sending through her fingertips. The messages were clear as they ran through Adam's mind. If Daniella could have heard them, she would have had the comfort of knowing she was loved. *This woman really loves me. Heaven help me, she really loves me. I'm in love with her too. Dearest God in heaven, I'm in love with her too. Hashem, help me.*

Daniella could feel Adam's erection right through his pants, and she hardly knew what to do. She wanted so desperately to advance their romance. She wanted to be with Adam forever. But what did he want? How should she even respond to this? This was a religious man—a man who would be conflicted. Daniella decided to follow Adam's cues, believing they would lead to a pre-ordained heavenly outcome that would lean in her favor. The conclusion was devoid of the fact that Adam was lost in his own private hell.

Adam began to respond automatically. He kissed her repeatedly, moving his lips down, deep in the nape of her neck. All the while, he was pressing himself further and further into her flesh. The rubbing sensation was too much for him to bear, and Adam had an orgasm then and there. His moans traveled into Daniella's ear, their reason quite clear.

Adam broke the kiss, realizing what had happened. He was beyond embarrassed, and he hoped and prayed that Daniella would not ridicule him for such blatant behavior. Instead, she rested her head directly under his chin, fitting into the perfect nook that waited there to receive her. She could not see the red in his blushing face or the distress in his eyes.

In the quiet darkness that formed inside Adam's neck and chest, Daniella said nothing more than, "It's all right,

Adam. It could happen to any man, I assure you." She wanted to make absolutely sure he could trust her to keep silent, keep this newfound secret. "I won't tell a soul...promise."

Daniella was well aware of the fact that some men had an orgasm immediately, and it was not because of her own personal experience. It was because her mother was very thorough when teaching Daniella the facts of life. The lessons had included how a man would be very embarrassed about such lack of control. She hoped her words helped. She retrieved some Kleenex from her pocket and handed them to Adam.

"I always carry these because of my allergies. Here, try to wedge it into your pants somehow. I'll stand up and turn my back."

However awkward the situation was or what Adam's intentions for the day were, all was momentarily forgotten as the two did their best to remedy the situation. Once Adam was somewhat cleaned up, he looked at Daniella as if he were a dog that didn't understand language.

"How do you know it happens to men?"

"My mother told me years ago. You know, back when she was preparing me for relationships and what happens between men and women."

"Your mother speaks to you about things like this?"

"Of course she does, Adam. Doesn't every mother want her child to have a loving relationship? Understanding of the opposite sex helps strengthen the bonds in a relationship. My mother didn't want me to be afraid of any of the things that might happen to men or women. She wanted me to know that everything sexual has its reason."

This was yet another confusing fact that Adam would now have to contemplate. He'd pocket the information in his imaginary file cabinet that was his religious dilemma and bring it out from time to time to mull over and reconsider. In his world, no one spoke about anything sexual, ever. He couldn't help but wonder if Hasidic couples who married even had a single clue about why their bodies worked as they did. The mechanics behind the wonderment. The biology of it all. Biology was science. Science was not God. It took the holiness of God's acts and declared it as its own. Science was off limits.

Adam could only utter a naive comment. "It feels so good."

"I would think so. Wouldn't *Hashem* ensure procreation by seeing to it that it felt really good? Now that's what I call superior thinking!"

Daniella laughed as she contemplated her own summation. She gestured that both of them should stand up so Adam could clean himself off further. She handed him more tissues. She turned and walked a short distance, just enough to give Adam some semblance of privacy.

Adam was able to wipe himself and wedge a spare Kleenex into his pants. He placed the used tissues in his front pocket so he could dispose of them later.

"Danny, you can turn around now."

Daniella walked back to Adam, and the two looked at each other.

"I feel like such an idiot."

"No, really, Adam. It's OK." Daniella laughed. "I guess I should take it as a compliment."

"Oh!" Adam thought about that as he uttered the ex-
clamation. "Yeah, I suppose so." He looked at Daniella
with trepidation. "Danny, come here."

Adam took Daniella in his arms once more. Their
height difference was enough that Adam could rest his
chin atop her head. His nose drew in the scent of her
hair as she remained hidden in the nook they had created together. Daniella had used Clairol Herbal Essence
shampoo that day, a scent she loved because the smell
was akin to the smell of a spring garden. She heard Adam
take in a big sniff. He pulled her in further.

"Danny, you smell so wonderful."

She thought it was all about the scent. In reality,
Adam was using the remark to help prepare himself to
divulge that this was actually the end.

The nightmare was front and center. It was alive and
rearing its vicious ugliness for Adam to acknowledge. He
was in love with a woman who he knew for a fact would
be unacceptable to his family. The fact that she affected
him the way she just had practically sealed it. It registered then and there that it had been a losing battle all
along, and he'd lost it long ago.

He would have to move on. Adam knew if he chose
to be with her, his family would not eat in the home they
created, nor in the home of the Soblers. They might not
even attend the wedding, stating that the only acceptable
rabbi was their own. Of course, their own rabbi wouldn't
perform the ceremony either. Daniella was not a complete
Jewish girl and would not merit the privilege of his family's
rabbi seeing to their bliss. In essence, everything was moot.

His family would practically hate Daniella and everything she stood for. They would harbor constant

disapproval and even disdain for Daniella's choices and beliefs, especially her decision to become a *hazzan*. In time, the result would be that his beloved mother and father, his siblings, and every friend he ever had would shut him out. The thought of losing family and friends frightened him. It was a demon he didn't want to face.

For the first time, Adam registered a specific conviction and completely understood that it harbored something even baser than the silent statement he was currently making in his mind. It was so simple, yet it contained so much depth, that he could do no more than feel grateful to *Hashem* that he finally understood it at all.

Everything his family would say or do through the years, if he married someone like Daniella, would be emotional abuse at its most vicious level. It would be no different from the husbands who tell their wives repeatedly that they're stupid, inefficient, worthless. Only in this case, it would be his own family continually urging Daniella to reconsider and do what was right.

To have his own parents, siblings, and entire community, for that matter, constantly belittling Daniella's role as a *hazzan—Please, Hashem, please let her dreams be reality—* would be emotional abuse, plain and simple. *Hashem forbid that she would fall victim to abuse like that. Isn't that what happens to people? To have one's role, ability, or right to exist in a certain way get shot down repeatedly, day in and day out. Doesn't that make them succumb to the abuse? Doesn't one start to believe it or have self-doubts?* Didn't he know for a fact that the one or two people who did leave the fold to marry outside were virtually shunned because of their ways? And what about the hapless soul whose family was so disgusted with the choice that they uttered the dreaded words, "You're dead to me?"

Despite the fact that it was utterly wrong to make any person feel that way, Adam found the thought of losing his connection to his family and community so painfully frightening that he couldn't bear it for even a moment. Sadly, he didn't even recognize that he himself was also a victim. He was too weak at heart and too confused. As a result, at this young juncture in his life, he made the wrong choice. He'd already concluded he could not live life without the family and friends he had known since the day he was born. He was sure he could not survive his parents' turning their backs on him.

If Adam chose to live in Daniella's world, even he would fall victim to the abuses every time he would try to come and visit in the neighborhood. They would all do their absolute best to get him to be a *ba'al teshuvah* and return to the ways of the community. They would urge him to repent in his heart for having left in the first place and for committing the sin of straying into the outside world. Berate him for allowing his wife to behave in such unacceptable ways.

Even worse, his colleagues in the diamond district would think less of him. If he left the fold of Orthodoxy, they would ask what else he was capable of doing. Maybe his dedication to the diamond industry would be permanently tainted because his colleagues would think less of him, and that in turn would mar every business exchange he tried to make. A life with Daniella held enormous ramifications.

To help give his decision more conviction, he thought, *Maybe, just maybe, Hasidism really is the true way, and I'm being blinded by Daniella's trappings, just like I've been taught is the case. I've fallen prey to the evils of the outside world.*

Adam had a fleeting thought about King Edward of England. He had recently read about him in the bookstore near the Daily Diner. Danny had taken him there so she could pick up some books. He had perused the history section while he waited for her to shop and had read the jacket cover of a book he had randomly pulled from the shelf. It had happened to be about the king.

Hadn't the king abdicated for love? Hadn't the political upheaval, the long-term effect on the monarchy, and so much more grossly affected his nation as a result? Hadn't he and his eventual wife, Wallis Simpson, suffered a similar emotional abuse as a result? Wouldn't it be the same for him? Wouldn't it be better to let Daniella live her life, and happily at that, unfettered by his family's personal desires?

It was all a convenient excuse. Adam was afraid, plain and simple. He was young, inexperienced, and just plain scared. It made him angry that he couldn't rise above the feelings of fear. He was perturbed, too, that people could make happiness a commodity rather than a God-given right. Yet the extreme level of rage could not push Adam to the other side and make him willing to deal with it. Adam's thoughts petrified much in the same way a thousand year old leaf fossil would. Stuck in a state of being that was unable to change.

"Adam, are you sniffing my hair, or..." Daniella's next words were encased in confusion. "Is something wrong?"

Adam pushed Daniella away from him. He lifted her chin upward, forcing her to look up into his eyes. A thin wall of water was visible in each socket.

"Adam?"

"Danny, I have to tell you something."

Daniella could do no more than stand there in silence and prepare for what he had to say. She already knew it was bad.

"Danny, as you can imagine, my family has been pushing at me for some time to settle down and get married. Since I'm the youngest, that's especially so."

For the briefest of moments, Daniella let herself think foolishly. Somehow, he was going to tell her that he would make her his choice. Could it be? She felt that hope manifest itself like a shot of queasiness in the deepest part of her gut.

The thought was fleeting, however. If it were so, logic dictated that Adam would not be so somber. If it were so, Adam would be dancing for joy over the very fact that somehow he had made his parents understand about her. She forced herself to look directly into his eyes. Eyes that were becoming further weighted with a glossiness, as if he were trying to put distance between his thoughts and what he saw in front of him.

"I don't want to hurt you, Danny." Adam paused to garner strength.

Daniella took a step back. Adam put both arms out to stop her from stepping further away. He held her in place.

"There is a woman in Antwerp that my family has introduced me to and hopes to make a *shiddach* with.

I've met with her several times while in Antwerp." Adam could get no further.

Daniella loosened herself from his grip and began to take steps backward as she asked, "Are you telling me that you've been seeing someone else every time you've traveled?"

Adam read the body language perfectly, yet he could only recite the classic line used by countless men the world over.

"Danny, please...let me explain."

Daniella roared out her rebuttal. "Explain? Explain what, Adam? That you've been seeing another woman and didn't tell me?"

She got right to the point. "Do you love her, Adam? Do you want to be with her?"

Adam made things even worse with his answer.

"She is everything that would make my family happy."

"Oh my God! Did you hear what you just said?" Daniella looked upward in an effort to stop her own tears, but they began to fall despite her attempt.

"Hooray for them, Adam. Hooray that your family is happy. What about you? Is she everything that would make you happy?"

Daniella stood stiff as a board, waiting for an answer. Stupidly, Adam was too honest when he gave it.

"Admittedly, I'm not sure about love at this point, Danny, but I have to believe it is a possibility at some point in the future. I know she is traditional in every sense of the word, and when we talk about things, she is quite clear that she would live a lifestyle equal to mine."

Adam kept to himself the fact that she was pleasing to look at.

"That tells me nothing, Adam. Do you love her? Does she make your blood boil with passion? Does she make you believe you can do anything? Does she understand you in a way that others can't?"

Adam was hard pressed to come up with an answer. He really didn't have one. Teme and he didn't know each other that way yet. True, Teme didn't affect him in the same way that Daniella did, but with no basis for comparison, Adam didn't know what the differences indicated. He didn't have the freedom to even find out. He and Teme wouldn't come to know each other in that way until they were married. He was actually lucky that he even got to know Teme at all. Some folks met days before they married.

The silence made things clear. Defeat had become the victor. Daniella was the loser. All hopes for romance were lost.

"Oh my God, you plan on going through with a *shiddach*! You're not even brave enough to tell your family about me or to say you'd like to give us a try. You didn't even tell your family about me."

"Danny, I…"

Daniella backed away even further. For the first time ever, she used foul language in Adam's presence. It was the only way to express the depth of her rage.

"You used me. You son of a bitch, you used me." Daniella made a grunting sound brimming with disgust. "How could you?"

She paused to catch her breath.

"What was I? Some sort of reprieve for you? A little fling before you got on with the rest of your life? What were you planning to do, Adam? Take it as far as you could go before dumping me? Make me your practice round?"

Daniella's language became even more heated. "Push it to the limits. How far can I get with Danny? Kiss her. Caress her. Maybe if I'm really lucky, she'll let me touch her." She paused only long enough to catch her next breath. She decided to be cruel.

"Poor baby, so inexperienced he can't even control an erection."

Adam remained silent. Daniella just continued.

"How dare you, Adam! How dare you! I'm good enough to satisfy your *yetzer harah* but not good enough to be your wife? You bastard!"

Adam stood frozen in place. He could not get through to Daniella in her present state. A part of him also viewed every word that came out of her mouth as rightful punishment.

"Well, guess what, Adam! You made me fall in love with you. I'm in love with you, damn it. I'm in love with you."

Daniella cried in great heaving sobs that made it hard to catch her breath. Her body shook with despair. She continued to speak, but the words were short and choppy, coming between great gasps of air and vain attempts to control her breathing. Her body trembled with the weight of each sigh.

"You're the one who lets me be who I am deep inside. You are, Adam. You're the one who makes me feel like I can do anything! Oh my God, how could you? I loved you, Adam. I loved you. Damn it, I love you."

Daniella sank to her knees, paying no mind to the bramble and dust that scratched at the taut flesh under her stockinged legs. Her head sank into her waiting hands and the tears flowed. Adam stepped over to her and put his hand on her shoulder in a vain attempt to provide comfort. She shrugged it off as hard as she could.

"Leave me be, Adam. Go away."

"I can't leave you here, Danny. How would you get home? Come on, come with me, and maybe we can talk about this on the way back."

Adam reached out his hand to help Daniella stand. She sensed it there despite the fact that her eyes were hidden in her hands. She looked up and made sure that Adam could see the venom they harbored.

"Talk about it? Are you suddenly insane? There's nothing to discuss or talk about. You're planning a *shiddach*, for gosh sakes." Daniella softened her tone as she stood and continued. "There's just a simple question, Adam. Do you love me?"

This was a crossroads of a different kind. Adam could let the question be or give Daniella a small piece of relief. He decided to go with the latter. He would answer the question to let Daniella know what his true feelings for her were. He would try to help her understand that this way was best.

"Yes, Danny, I love you." Adam paused and repeated himself, whispering in a heartfelt tone, "I love you, Danny, but…"

Daniella stopped him before he could get one word further into his sentence.

"No buts, Adam. You either love me enough or you don't."

He wanted to say, "But I want you to become a *hazzan*, and that means I do love you enough."

How could he possibly make her understand that he did love her and wanted her to attain her dreams and aspirations? That being married to him would make the life she wanted impossible. That his love was great enough, he was willing to let her remain in her world so she could thrive and bring all her dreams to fruition.

In his case, he had chosen to prove to himself that he might have been wrong all along. That Hasidism was what was true and real, just as he had been taught, and he needed it. That Daniella was his test. Did any of that even matter? Was it ever really about him?

Now, he finally understood the heart of the matter. In seconds, God's plan had become clear. It wasn't even about his system of belief. He simply needed to let Daniella become what she was meant to be. His lifestyle would only burden her. God was telling him to let Daniella reach her dreams. And although he couldn't articulate why, Adam knew in that moment that God planned for her to succeed.

He remained silent. Better to let her think he didn't love her enough and thereby allow her to move on. She already thought that, anyway. His silence was the final nail, driven in deep, sealing their fate. He would accept it all as rightful punishment for hurting her.

"Heaven help me. You don't, do you?"

Daniella began to back away. Adam spoke to her retreating figure.

"Danny, please, let me try to explain better," as the space widened between them. He reached out to try to grab her hand. Daniella turned and began to run.

As the distance between them widened even further, the only sound she could hear was the crackling of branches under her feet. Her running creating a sound symbolic of the breaking in two of souls that seemed to be one. Great hearty branches yet fragile under the surface, needing nothing more than a jolt to break them apart. Snap! Completely broken.

Her ears registered a whispered word that would haunt her for years to come. It rustled through the trees, carried along on the breeze. It said, *beshert*. It was practically a dull drone in the increasing distance. It was the last word she heard from his mouth. Fated. Fated one.

Daniella would never know if he was implying that it was *beshert* that their relationship should end this way or that she was his true *beshert* but this ending would be better for her sake. And truly, there was a difference between the two. The latter would mean that, regardless of what happened in their lives, they would be each other's fated soul mate, destined to live with unending heartache because they could not be together. The half that would make the other whole. Destined to remain apart for reasons only *Hashem* was privy to.

Adam waited five minutes before leaving the trail himself. He wanted Daniella to have some sense of dignity. To feel that, somehow, she had championed the situation and maintained the upper hand. He could at least give her that. Besides, he needed the time to muster up his own resolve.

Leaving the quiet space of the woods, Adam walked into reality. He felt a clear indication that the dread was now a thing of the past and that he needed to move on. The stain in his pants was dry and no longer visible. No proof of sin remained. No proof that his feelings mattered or that they even existed in the first place.

Naively, he hoped that as the parking lot came into view, he'd see her there, standing and waiting by his car. He was her means of transportation. She needed to get home. He hoped she would come to her senses enough to wait for the ride and the chance to really talk everything through. When the vehicle came directly into his line of vision, he saw that she was nowhere to be found.

He sat in his car for some time, hoping to see her. It was evident that she was gone, but as to where, he could hardly guess. When his watch proved that a total of twenty-five minutes had passed, Adam began to panic. He didn't know what to do. He prayed she was safe and begged *Hashem* to ensure she returned home unharmed.

As if in answer to his prayers, Daniella's father, Ira, drove up from the main road and entered the parking lot. Adam recognized him and knew that it was time to leave. He backed out and drove down to the far end of the lot so that Ira Sobler would not see him. If Daniella had called her father to come and pick her up, and since Mr. Sobler knew that the two of them had a date today, well, he already must know something was wrong. Adam was already the bad guy. He drove over to the exit gate as soon as he saw the Sobler wagon drive down the main entrance row.

A majestically old-fashioned stone building stood adjacent to the parking lot. It housed the main administrative offices in addition to the main ranger station. The facility stood like a watchdog, lined with state-park police cars guarding its periphery. Daniella had been standing in the upstairs office, peering out from the massive glass window under the center arch of the building, watching the scene below. She had been watching from the moment Adam entered his car until the moment he evaded her father. A part of her was filled with sorrow for the hapless Adam who was completely lost as to what to do next.

Daniella had entered the building, climbed the steps to the upstairs offices, and muttered a quick prayer that she would be allowed to use a phone. After assuring the secretary that her call was local, she had received permission. Goodness knew what she would have done if the answer had been no. She didn't have enough money for the bus, and she certainly would not have gone down to ask Adam for a ride.

She hated that her father had to come so far. More so, that she had been curt on the phone.

"I need a ride...No, I don't want to explain right now...He's just gone, Dad, OK?"

It had taken Ira Sobler almost thirty minutes to reach the state park. Daniella had long stopped crying by the time he arrived, but an eerie silence had replaced her tears, and that was what greeted Ira when he came through the administration building's doors. Daniella had made a point to come down the stairwell to greet him at the door. She didn't want a scene.

Daniella spoke a single comment before they departed.

"Please, Dad, don't ask me a single question. I just can't handle it now."

Ira obliged the request, and they drove home in silence. When they walked through the front door, Marcia stood there waiting. Daniella stepped in and looked at both her parents. They were patiently waiting, hoping that she would at least divulge some small piece of information. Looking at them both, Daniella's eyes began brimming with tears.

Daniella moved over to the steps. Her initial and natural reaction was to avoid the pain of the situation. She hesitated on the first step, took in a deep breath to gain some resolve, and spoke as her back was turned. She owed at least something to her parents.

"I was falling in love with him. Every day, I was falling in love with him."

Marcia lovingly replied, "What does that mean, honey?"

Daniella was already standing on the third step when she turned to answer the question. Better to get it out now. Better to be over and done with it. It would hurt no matter when she told her parents.

"He told me there was someone else. He told me that a *shiddach* was in the making. I can't see him for even a single moment more, then, can I?" Daniella turned and began to climb the stairwell.

Marcia looked at Ira, and they both knew to be quiet. They already understood that Daniella had done what was necessary and right. It only mattered that their beloved Danny was hurting. Best to stay silent. Best to let the hurt prevail and be over and done with in its own time. To see a daughter suffering, and deeply at that, was torturous enough. A foolish comment would do no more than overwhelm Daniella altogether.

Daniella took two more steps up, hand gripping the rail tightly to lend her support. She paused on the fifth step and turned toward her parents once more.

"I want to be in my room for a while."

Ira smiled and said, "Take all the time you need, sweetheart."

Marcia added, "We're here if you need us, Danny. You know we love you. If you want to talk, just come and get us."

In her head, Marcia was saying so much more. She was silently infuriated and extremely disappointed that her daughter had been turned aside like yesterday's news. Crazy as it seemed, she had liked her initial impression of Adam and had hoped that perhaps the two could have had something. How could he turn away the charming, smart, kind-hearted person that was her daughter? Marcia wanted to give him a piece of her mind.

She ached for Daniella. That her daughter's hopes were crushed, never mind that the pain came from an Orthodox man. Hurt from a man was simply hurt from a man. Men could be so stupid. What was wrong with them? Such idiots, and always at the worst times!

When Daniella shut the door to her room, closing out the world in essence, she shut out a chapter of her life. The story was over, a sad story with no winners, and she, a central character. She wanted to forget the tale. She would find the strength to get over her hurt and move on. She would find a way to fall out of love with Adam.

Does time heals all wounds? In this particular case, the plastic surgery known as life did little to repair the hurt inside as the days changed to weeks, and then to months. Despite the passing of time, several years in fact, the deepness of the wound festered under a Band-Aid of smiles and happy moments. In essence, the wound was covered by life, but the pain underneath remained.

Cantor Sobler

*F*ive years had come and gone. Daniella had finished her cantorial studies ready to take on the world and share her skills. Graduation day inferred the title of *hazzan*, and a very new Cantor Sobler graciously received the diploma of *hazzanut*.

As fate would have it, the role of women in the Conservative movement of Judaism went through a colossal paradigm shift during the 1980s and even the early 90s. Especially in terms of the roles of rabbi and cantor and a woman's ability to even become one in the first place.

Daniella had begun her program in 1985, but by 1987, two women had already received the diploma of *hazzanut*. It was a huge change from 1952, when women were allowed to received cantorial and Jewish music degrees but only men could receive the honor of *hazzanut*.

When those first two women received their esteemed diplomas, the Cantors Assembly voiced disapproval and barred membership in their then-exclusive organization. The assembly voted down membership for

women yet again in 1988, 1989, and 1990. Miraculously, in December of 1990 the winds of fortune changed.
By 1991, a vote of twenty-nine to one allowed women to
be full-fledged members in the Cantors Assembly.

It was vitally important for cantors to have access to
such a hardy networking group. It kept them in touch
with each other as well as the continual changes and rul-
ings in the Judaic world of prayer. And, of course, the
same held true in regards to Jewish music.

For Daniella, it was a blessing that she graduated
in the very same year that those winds of change came
blowing through. Like many other female colleagues,
she joined the assembly the moment she could. As a re-
ward, she garnered a great deal of information, ideas,
and innovations from her colleagues. In terms of her career, Daniella felt quite sated.

Maybe God was giving her special attention to re-
cover from the hurt. Not only had Daniella's dream
come true, but she attained employment immediately
upon graduating. That was a rarity among new cantors. It
took time to find a good fit between a synagogue and the
cantorial style said synagogue had in mind. She was one
of the lucky ones. She even had a romance or two along
the way. Destiny was at the helm, and it guided her well
before her diploma was even placed in her hand.

Daniella unofficially began her search for a job as a
cantor when she was in her fifth and last year as a student.
She obtained student placement a drivable distance from
Epson County. That she found employment at all was in
itself a blessing. Very few students were that fortunate.

It was only a bit of dumb luck that kept her at the
same synagogue after she graduated. Mostly, the gift of

her voice, which was now better trained and far more refined, earned her the spot. The pleasant sound she created with it was the impetus for a bona fide contract and a request to continue with the house of worship as their liturgical leader.

This new, egalitarian Conservative synagogue had been constructed two years before she graduated. It rested in the heart of a neighboring suburb that was just over the border from Epson County and actually, in the next state. It was a mere forty-minute car ride from home and also from the Daily Diner she knew and loved so much.

The synagogue was in need of a cantor, being that the congregation was so young, and the student placement was a blessing. It allowed them to remain budget conscious as they solidified their standing in the community. Daniella would earn a meager salary, and her beautiful voice would attract members. Most new congregations were not that lucky.

To their surprise, they were able to establish roots quickly. Many Jews in the area had been looking for a modern synagogue that kept up with the times, let women participate, and somehow through it all maintained a strong sense of tradition. As the membership grew and came to love Daniella, they offered her a job as full-time cantor with a three-year contract to start.

Although Daniella wouldn't know it for a long time, she would remain at that synagogue for many, many years. She would become their beloved cantor, and she would be a very big part of the reason that the rafters filled regularly, especially during the High Holiday season. Life was good to her, and *Hashem* bestowed many blessings. Eventually, she became engaged to a man she had met through a friend.

Benny would have been wise to leave things be at that point, but once more, he rocked the boat in an effort to set things right for his darling Danny. After five and a half years of emotional quiet, he tipped the boat just enough to upset the delicate balance of her happiness. He did the last thing on earth that anyone expected he would do.

It was the summer of 1991. Benny was doing no more than laughing at his customer's joke when who should come walking through the doors of his restaurant but one Adam Goldfarb.

It might have been five and a half years, but Benny recognized him immediately. The curlicue mop top was unmistakable. The gentle shuffle to the walk and the reluctant smile, even the pensive look were all features that Benny had committed to memory. The only thing that seemed slightly different was Adam's style of dress. If anything, it seemed less religious. Benny saw the *tzitzit*, and Adam wore the black *kippah* bobby-pinned to his head, but the shirt and pants were very modern. Besides, Adam's feet were covered by sandals.

Adam tried to catch Benny's eye and wave a hello, but Benny turned his gaze back to his customer. He didn't want to deal with Adam's presence at all. *You're the bastard that broke my Danny's heart.*

Benny knew all about it. Daniella had called in sick for three days in a row after the fateful breakup. When she finally mustered the strength to come in to work, she told Benny about everything…everything! She dragged her feet and moped for days on end, trying in vain to be her efficient self. For the first time, Benny had thought of her as a lousy waitress. Benny's anger over what Adam had done to cause it all lay deep in his memory banks.

Nate was conveniently standing next to Benny at the counter when Adam came through the doors on that July evening. Benny didn't even bat an eyelash as he asked Nate to seat the patron who had just walked in. Nate, however, was apparently so surprised that he couldn't help but make a comment.

"Benny, isn't that Adam Goldfarb?"

"Nate, please, just do it."

Benny didn't greet Adam that night, or the next, or even the next after that. It was completely against his nature to be so rude, but he was hurting inside. He could have asked Adam to leave, but that had never happened in the history of the restaurant. Not once since the day it had opened. The last thing Benny or Nate needed was for word to get around that the management of the Daily Diner had booted out an Orthodox person. Shouts of bias would surely ring through the county.

Curiosity took hold at that point. On the fourth night, Adam had once again become a daily diner at the Daily Diner. Why he kept coming in, Benny could hardly guess. He noted how forlorn Adam looked. He noticed that Adam kept asking to be seated at the booth he used to sit in when he first met Daniella. Benny even noticed that he kept ordering salami and eggs with a cream soda, same as he had with Danny on that first night.

It was on that fourth night that Benny let the *mentch* inside of him prevail. He would do the right thing and break the silence he had originally vowed to keep. A good businessman didn't let personal matters affect

him. He would greet and be friendly toward his customer. Adam's repeat visits were putting money into
Benny's pocket, and that fact alone required that he be a
good host. Benny was feeling very nervous when he approached Adam at the booth.

"Hello, Adam. May I sit down?"

Adam rose and stood at the side of the booth as he
reached out to shake Benny's hand. Benny accepted graciously. Adam shook it wildly.

"Benny, I'm so glad you came over. So very glad. I
could tell you didn't want to bother with me, so this
means so much...so much."

Adam kept shaking and speaking all at the same time.
"It is so nice to see you again, Benny, so very nice. Yes,
please join me. I would love so much to have the chance
to talk with you."

As they sat down, Benny asked a general question
simply because he didn't know what else to say. He
wanted to ask a million questions. He wanted to put it
straight to Adam: *How could you hurt Danny the way you
did? You pulled the rug right out from under her.*

"How have you been, Adam?"

"Benny, do you have some time to sit and listen?
You're truly the only one here in the county I can talk
to."

Hadn't Benny heard those words once before, long
ago? Didn't he learn his lesson the last time? Benny
was too intrigued by the fact that the request was
coming from the other half of the equation, so he took
the bait.

"Sure, let me get Nate to mind the restaurant. We can sit in the back room, because if we stay out here, customers are bound to interrupt us to say their hellos to me. Go ahead into the back room. I'll meet you there. I see you finished eating. I'll bring us some tea and cookies."

As Adam watched Benny walk into the empty room with a tray of tea and cookies, he couldn't help but smile at the character that was Benny Kalabokas. Daniella had told Adam long ago that if Benny brought you tea and cookies, he was on your side. You mattered to him. He was there for you, whether as pal or friend. Adam hoped the latter would be the case.

The depth of sorrow pouring out from Adam, fell onto the listening ears of Benny. Benny would have surely received an A+ for being a good listener. Adam had made clear his reasons for leaving Daniella, and Benny actually understood them, enough so that he eventually made a verbal slip. One mistake that inadvertently divulged a piece of information that should have remained unspoken.

When it occurred it was mostly because Benny couldn't help himself. Part of him wanted to slip because, deep down, he felt that Daniella's fiancé was not the man she should be marrying. There was something about that guy. Benny didn't quite know what. A nice enough man, but Benny always thought he seemed to be on another page. He was scripting his life with Daniella, always two pages ahead of the action, yet not consulting Daniella about any of it.

Despite anything that may have happened, Adam and Daniella had the chemistry that two people should have in order to nurture a relationship. A chemistry that Benny couldn't see between Norman and Daniella. That special something that he couldn't put into words. Benny wanted to bring it back. However subconscious, it was a desire that had remained through the years.

Benny simply wanted people to be free to live their lives, happy and at peace, and certainly without the rest of the world butting in. He gave the information to Adam for that very reason. He gave it because of everything Adam had shared. He gave it because he wanted the two to be a couple. He gave it after hearing the next comment come out of Adam's mouth.

"Benny, I know it might be hard to believe, but mostly, I left Danny because I wanted her to succeed as a cantor. If I continued on with her, my family and my neighborhood would have made her miserable. It was far better for her not to have to deal with that."

It may have been 1991, but Epson County still housed several traditional communities of Jews that were Modern Orthodox, Traditional Orthodox, Hasidic, or a garden variety of Judaism that no one was sure of except for the fact that it was an observant one. Every one of those groups would have given her grief. What caught his attention however, was that Adam said the word *mostly*.

"What do you mean, *mostly?*"

He was surprised when Adam was forthcoming with his answer.

"The other reason, and probably the bigger one, was that I was a coward. I was too afraid to leave my Hasidic life for good.

"Even worse, Benny, I foolishly allowed my *yetzer harah* to control my life when I was dating Danny. It's really true what they say about it. It's just pure evil. It makes you not think straight. It takes away all good reasoning. In my case, it pushed me in the wrong direction."

Adam was amazingly blunt as he continued.

"It made me feel so attracted to Teme, and I believed that was reason enough to create a good marriage with her."

In an effort to clarify the comment, Adam added, "She looks like someone plucked her off of a cameo pin. Ivory skin, soft complexion, ice-colored eyes, curves in all the right places, and hair that drips like honey."

He snorted with derision. "That was before she started shaving it off and wearing that ridiculous wig."

The comment caused a momentary shift in his thinking. He was suddenly living through a memory as he sat with Benny. He was making a mental note of a conversation he'd had long ago with Teme.

"Teme, your hair is so beautiful. I would love so much to be able to stroke it, play with it, brush it. I wish you would grow it in and leave it there. It would be our little secret."

"No, it wouldn't, Adam. I'd go out to the market or to visit the family, and somehow they'd know. Even if it were under a hat or a scarf. My parents would talk about my immodesty. The neighbors would tell them of my immodesty. My parents would give us both grief but especially me."

"Teme, don't you see that you look just as beautiful in your wig? You attract the attention of men all the time. It doesn't matter what you have on your head. They almost can't help themselves. You're extremely beautiful to look at."

"All the more reason to cover up. I don't want anyone pointing fingers saying anything bad about me."

"Aren't they the ones sinning, then? They'd be gossiping."

Teme couldn't see it that way. The only thing the conversation had done for her was make her start to wear frumpier clothing. Even the healthful glow in her face became dulled and uncared for because she decided that using a bit of blush was vain.

Adam let the memory go and returned to the conversation at hand.

"Once you get past the fact that Teme is such a pretty package, you get your brain wrapped around a cold, hard fact. That a cameo is hard material. It's not flexible. Teme is a cameo, Benny. A pretty shell with a hardness that you can't bend. She is too afraid to do anything that would offend or upset anyone. We argue all the time now. She makes my life miserable with her constant worries about what the community might think. I can't even connect with her in personal conversation. The moment she hears me verbalize a controversial thought, I'm chastised. All it has done for me is make me admit I don't belong there. I probably never belonged there.

"And you won't believe what the tipping point was. Funny how, with all the deep thoughts, questions, and concerns I've had all these years, it took a simple matter to push my conviction into a solid space. The tipping point was the rumors that have started in the Lubavitch community that Schneerson is the messiah."

"Yes, I've heard those myself. Word gets around, so I guess it got to you too, even overseas?"

"Benny, I realized that it's idol worship, plain and simple. A direct slap in the face of the Almighty himself. A direct disregard for the commandment: Thou shalt have no other Gods before me. These people are taking a human being and insisting he is some quasi-deity. A direct link to God. I am convinced the fervor will only grow. And what will the people do when he dies like any other mortal? What will they do when they realize that the world didn't change during or after his lifetime? He's not exactly in the best of health, and he's old. I finally realized that we Hasidim are in a bubble, just like everyone says we are. I want to get out of it."

"What are you trying to say, Adam?"

"I'm saying I'm miserable. I'm saying I hate my marriage. I'm saying I made the worst mistake of my life when I said good-bye to Danny. I'm saying I no longer want to be *frum*. I'm saying that I've grown up, finally. I'm saying I'm no longer afraid."

"So what do you plan to do? Divorce Teme and go crawling back to Danny?" Benny took pause, realizing how cheeky his tone sounded. "I'm so sorry, Adam. That was completely uncalled for."

"No apology necessary. My heart wants to do that. I want a divorce. I want to get down on my knees and beg Danny to believe I've always loved her and I want to live in her world. I want her to know why I left her to her dreams." Adam drew in a deep sigh and exhaled it deliberately.

"I'm willing to give up my entire way of life for hers. I can't even begin to tell you the influence she has had on me...that I question so much, so often, and too often." Adam laughed before he continued. "That I've wondered all these years if our way really is the 'right' way." He made quote marks in the air when he said the word *right*.

"I question everything, every time something is celebrated or discussed in the house. It has irritated Teme to the point of pure disgust. She resents my wanting to be an independent thinker. How ironic. That was all Danny ever wanted."

Adam sighed and spoke his new truth. "I know that the world won't come crashing down around me. The Almighty is not sending down the bolts of lightning I've been taught to fear." He paused so he could word his next thoughts as correctly as possible.

"I've come to realize I really do relish the fact that her Conservative way of life allows a person to question without feeling like they've committed some grave sin by doing so. Don't get me wrong, Benny. I see merit in observance. If a Hasid is truly committed to the teachings, the rituals, the expression of faith as dictated by our community, he or she should be respected for their faith. Perhaps even honored or blessed. I have to believe, though, there is a middle ground for people like me. Some strange blend between the Orthodox and Conservative viewpoint that would give me those same feelings of commitment."

Adam didn't share that he had been meeting with a Conservative rabbi every time he was in the States over the last two years. That he found ways to excuse himself from his parents' home once the initial visits with family and friends were over. He'd invented bogus stories about needing to check out some diamonds in the city or head over to a department store at the other end of the county just so he could meet in secret with a Conservative rabbi. What was the point in telling Benny about it? Benny only needed to know the outcome. Adam was ready to take some bold steps and change his way of life.

"My friends and family are getting tired of my constant questioning, and I can tell that they don't hold me in as high an esteem as they used to. I know it's because of the questions I ask. I can see the look of shock and even a bit of disgust in their eyes. Almost like they think I'm not quite as good a Jew as I used to be. My own parents have started lecturing me to clean up my act because rumors are circulating."

"Why do I feel like it sounds as if there is more?"

"Because there is, Benny. *Hashem*, help me, there is. I have a wonderful boy, age two and a half. But, Benny, Teme is pregnant with our second."

"So what do you plan to do, and why are you here?"

"I'm here because this place was my only real joy. This place was where I felt alive. This place brought me the one I believe is my true *beshert*. I know that, now. I can sit here and almost feel her. I can sit here and remember her. I made a decision that every time I visit the States, I will come here to the Daily and as often as possible. Just to have some small piece of comfort."

Adam made a lighthearted pun. "Even if that means I'll be coming here *daily* when I'm in the States. I just want to feel some happiness. As to what I plan to do, that is a tough one, Benny. I have to really think things through, and I suppose much of it depends on the questions I'm about to ask you."

Adam hesitated so he could garner some strength.

"Benny, please, I beg of you, let me know about Danny. Is she married? Is she available? Is she *Hazzan* Sobler?"

"She's engaged, Adam, and very recently so, I might add. Maybe three or four weeks at the most. I suppose the guy is decent enough. I don't really like him. She is indeed Cantor Sobler and is so well loved by her congregation that I'm sure she'll be at her post for a long time to come." Benny looked at Adam and smiled. "I'm sure that's no surprise to you. Between her personality and that amazing voice that comes out of her mouth, well…"

"Is she close by? Is she marrying soon?"

"Fate was on her side. Of all the places she could have possibly been hired, she is employed locally, even though it's one state over. How's that for crazy luck? She's a cantor at Beth David. I've attended services with my wife, Rose, a few times now just so we could listen to her chant. It's beautiful, Adam! I tell you, beautiful!"

If Benny had known that Adam would pocket the information with the intention of going to Beth David, he would have certainly kept the information to himself. He would protect his "adopted" fourth daughter in every way possible, and that included protecting her from being hurt by one Adam Goldfarb for a second time. The fact remained that Benny, didn't.

"As to a wedding date, well, she hasn't told me of one so I have to assume there isn't one just yet. Last time she stopped by, she mentioned that she was going to start looking at wedding venues. That was about it."

The Master of the Universe was the puppeteer. The ministering angels, the stagehands. No mere mortal should ever believe he or she can finish the work that has been crafted in the heavens above. Even Benny's strange subconscious notion of comparing Danny to his deceased mother and have her come out winning fell into this category. People, including Benny, are not meant to know what is beyond their grasp. If they did, they would never learn a single thing about life or why we are meant to live it. They would have nothing to strive for, accomplish, or most important, learn. It is the wise soul that allows life to unfold so one can learn from it. It is the wise soul that remembers that planet Earth is just one big classroom.

dam could hardly believe his good fortune, especially in light of the fact that his life was such a mess. Benny was kind, receptive, and willing to be a *mentch*. May *Hashem* bless him always. Benny had given him some peace of mind.

Adam could relish the fact that Daniella was a *hazzan*. His Danny. She had made it! She had shown the world she could accomplish her goal and live her dream. He knew she had her own congregation and they were pleased to have her there. Wasn't that the icing on the cake she had been baking all these years? Most important was the piece of information that had nothing to do with her career at all—that she was not yet married. There was still time. Time was of the essence, however, since Benny couldn't divulge a wedding date.

As he sat in the terminal preparing to head back to Antwerp, he thought about the impact that his conviction to leave his Orthodox way of life would have on just about everything. He believed with all his heart and soul that he could be a good Jew even away from the confines of his community. When he had consciously concluded such a notion, he could hardly guess. Probably, it had been festering for years. Growing like a cancer. Nonetheless, it was a fact as concrete as any he harbored in his brain and certainly as weighty as the fact that his decision would receive no support from family or friends. Certainly not from his wife.

It was a solemn Adam who settled into his assigned seat, and yet he was quietly happy. A certain sense of relief enveloped him in the space that was his window seat. Relief because he had consciously reached a decision. He stared out the tiny window and watched the sun glow over the distant horizon. God's sun. A piece of God set in the universe as yet another visible symbol that a great power guided us all.

Adam smiled at the setting orb. God was talking to him in his head. Telling him in his heart of hearts that he was being true and correct. He felt it as he mulled things over. Adam's God was a kind and loving God. He was no longer the demanding and vindictive God who would punish him for the slightest error. God was with him all the way down to laying a path directly at Adam's feet. He'd placed it there almost two years ago, now.

How many visits had he and Rabbi Simon had at that point? Adam had lost count. The rabbi had been the one person who miraculously arrived on Adam's path at precisely the right time. The one who had helped him think things through each time he visited the States during the past two years. The one who had guided him well before Adam mustered the courage to approach Benny. How he had even come across the rabbi was a strange miracle in itself.

During one of his visits to the States, Adam made a point to visit the Conservative movement's rabbinical and cantorial seminary in the city. For a reason he couldn't understand, he genuinely wanted to see it for himself and gain a better sense of the Conservative movement and, especially, the place where Daniella likely received her cantorial training. Merely a peek inside. Just a quick visit to quell his curiosity. He found it hard to admit that the ulterior motive was to see for himself the place that educated so many in the ideologies that attracted him.

He wanted to visit because a quick tour would provide an objective voice void of the scrutiny he always heard in the opinions of family and friends. As a youth, he had learned about Conservative Judaism only through the voice of Hasidism. As a young man, his own conclusions had been shaken to the core. Both experiences, no matter how well meant, were subjective in nature. A visit would be a good thing. It would provide an outside voice, merely stating fact.

Adam had made an inquiry of a passerby heading into the seminary as he stood outside the school's front entrance that day. He laughed just thinking about it. He'd had absolutely no idea that he was addressing one of the seminary's professors. Not only a professor but a rabbi.

The rabbi was dressed as the stereotypical professor. Khaki pants, easy cotton shirt knotted at the top by a colorful bow tie. Lightweight sports jacket and loafer shoes to finish the look. Folks from Adam's neck of the woods would not think for even a single moment that they were addressing a rabbi. The man looked more like a college student than any rabbi Adam had ever known. A brightly colored *kippah* clipped to the man's head and a clean-shaven face skewed the rabbinical image altogether.

"Excuse me, would you be able to tell me if visitors are allowed into the seminary?"

"Well, that depends on several things." The rabbi put his hand out for a shake. "I'm Rabbi Simon. Is there something I can help you with?"

Adam accepted the gracious handshake. "My name is Adam Goldfarb."

Adam was already thinking how many in his community would insist that this man who called himself rabbi was not a rabbi at all, simply because he had not studied or obtained the title in the Orthodox way.

The rabbi continued. "I'm one of the professors here. Did you want to visit, or do you have a group you'd like to bring here?"

Adam didn't quite know why, but he felt an aura of safety about the rabbi, and it was instantaneous and strong. Maybe it was the fact that the rabbi didn't flinch even once over the fact that a Hasid was asking for a tour. The rabbi's sincere smile only added to the strength of Adam's summation. It made Adam decide to be honest with the rabbi from the get-go.

"I'm quite the Orthodox Jew." Adam laughed and continued. "You probably figured that out already. Anyway, I come from a very cloistered community, and now I continue to live in another one in Antwerp. I'm curious about the bigger world of Jews."

Adam remembered that he wondered if the rabbi might have been thinking something like: *An Orthodox Jew who feels limited by his community. He's on a personal mission of some kind. It's not just curiosity.* Adam surmised that because of the strange look on the rabbi's face when Adam had told him he was curious. Nonetheless, the rabbi had remained silent, and Adam had continued.

"I was wondering if somehow I could learn more about the Conservative movement. I'm very curious about it."

Adam concluded he was not there by accident. *Hashem* had seen to it that they should meet. As if in answer to the very thought, the rabbi asked the question that became the pivotal moment in Adam's life.

"Adam, do you have some time now?"

"Yes, I do."

"Come with me. I'd like to show you something."

Adam was shown, or rather given a tour of, the extensive library, one of the crowned jewels of the seminary. Adam couldn't help but notice it was filled with an enormous collection of literature, reference books, Talmudic interpretation texts, Torah commentary, history books, and so much more. The biggest jolt, however, came when he realized it contained people he would never have expected to be there.

He saw far more than rabbinic or cantorial students sitting in the library. Men, women, young adults, and older adults, some of whom were definitely not students, were all busy using the library. Yet the most surprising of all were several men in the classic black clothing, complete with black hat and *pais* curls peeking out from under their rims. Hasids. There were Hasids using the library.

Adam was amazed they were even present in the knowledge-filled space. He counted five of them skimming through books, taking notes, and obviously studying. They distracted him enough that he only half paid attention as the rabbi began to tour the library for Adam's benefit, pointing out the extensive volumes of knowledge housed within.

The rabbi gave Adam a moment to take in the scene before him, which was the enormity of Jewish literature available to the community. Adam however, focused on the Hasids.

"Do you get Hasidic visitors often?"

"There are no differences between us, Adam. We're all Jews. We all agree that Torah lies at the heart of our beliefs. We all affirm that there is one ultimate being, an essence so great we can't even comprehend it. An essence that guides us and the entire universe, and we call it *Hashem* because we hardly know what to call it at all.

"These men are here because our seminary possesses resourceful books that contain a wealth of Judaism in the pages inside. Deep down, these men are well aware of the validity of these books. However, there are barriers the moment they step back outside onto the street. Barriers put up by each of us because of differences in the way we interpret the contents of these books. Come. Let's step outside the library so we can talk."

The rabbi led the way and settled himself against a wall by the back stairwell. Adam stood next to him, waiting to hear what the rabbi would say next.

"Have you ever read *The Butter Battle Book*, by Dr. Seuss? No, I suppose you haven't. I bought it for my grandson in 1984, shortly after it was published. Great book. The concept was akin to *Gulliver's Travels*."

The rabbi glanced at Adam. "You probably haven't read that one either. Well, in a nutshell, the butter battle is about two sides preparing for out-and-out war, simply because they have a different method of buttering their toast. The butter and toast are butter and toast. They'll be eaten no matter what. Only the method used to butter the toast is different. In Gulliver's case, he watches war being waged over which side of an egg to crack. Never mind that the egg was still an egg and would be eaten regardless.

"The beauty of Judaism is its permission, if you will, to let a Jew question everything. Conservatives take that to heart, Adam, same as you, I'm sure. You must have had study groups where issues were discussed and contemplated. We Jews understand that questioning leads to greater truths. Judaism is Judaism. It's only the interpretations that have separated us. How can one group invalidate the way another group expresses its belief? Now that's a question for discussion!"

Adam responded, "Even I know that the arguments over interpretations or even expectations are over the top at times." Adam was thinking about the many times he'd heard stories about one Hasidic sect disliking another over a seemingly simple matter. Perhaps their own butter-and-toast issue. Even worse, he recollected stories, for example, of a home being set on fire because so-and-so didn't attend prayers at one *shul* and had the audacity to go to another. Or that some *schmendrik* got beaten up for not handling his divorce correctly. He'd heard the stories from hushed voices afraid to speak the truth. Afraid to admit that they were no better or worse than their Jewish and non-Jewish neighbors. Daniella got into his head at that moment. He could hear her clear as a bell pealing through the rabbi's next words. It was almost as if two people were speaking at the same time because he heard her as the rabbi spoke. He remembered what she said.

"Adam, did you know there is a flyer at the post office with a photo and it is of a Hasidic man? Know why it is there? To warn the public that he has been showing up at public parks and exposing himself to the children. We're all human. We all have our faults. In no way is that man better than me." The Rabbi's words were hauntingly similar to the long ago words of Daniella, in the conclusion they were meant to bring about.

"There's good and bad in every group, Adam. Every single one. We're all human. The ultra-Orthodox have an underbelly, just like any other community. There should be no notion of *holier than thou*. I don't know exactly what you thought to find within these walls, but simply put, all of us here are Jews trying to understand God's law and how to apply it in life."

Adam interrupted. "There is, though, isn't there? I mean, that notion of *holier than thou*."

All his life Adam had been taught that the outside Jews were basically condemned, and it was through their own doing. They didn't follow the laws correctly, and they allowed themselves to be influenced by the *goyim* around them. He had grown up with the conviction that only the way his community lived their Jewish lives pleased God. Only they understood what it meant to connect properly with God. For the first time, at least on a conscious level, Adam admitted that the notion bothered and embarrassed him.

Rabbi Simon answered honestly. "There are times when I'm in conversation with an Orthodox individual and I sense certain things are being implied in their words. That they believe that God is pleased simply because they are more rigid in their observance than I. That God is not happy with me because I'm not on the same path as they are."

Rabbi Simon took pause. He looked at Adam and placed his right hand on Adam's bicep, giving it a gentle squeeze.

"But here's the thing, Adam. As far as I'm concerned, I am on the right path. My journey is leading me directly to *Hashem*. No one can tell me otherwise."

The rabbi had spoken his piece. At the time, Adam was a perfect stranger, curious and also friendly, and yet, the rabbi took the opportunity to share opinions that weren't necessarily asked for. Adam was sure that somehow, that sharing was the purpose of the strange meeting in the first place. That it was all meant to be. As if the rabbi had read his mind, he continued their conversation with a question that was more like an invitation.

"So what is it exactly that has brought you here today, Adam? What are you looking for?"

Adam thought about his answer, and it came bursting out from his mouth as if he could no longer control his lips. Almost as if he had been holding it back for the longest time and was grateful to set it free.

"I'm no longer happy with my way of life. I had a taste of the bigger world for many years, and I can no longer ignore it. Enough so, that I've been secretly learning about other forms of Judaism from books whenever I've been away from my home. I want to understand what it

is about Conservative Judaism that seems to draw me
in. I want to make an informed decision for myself. I
thought coming here would help somehow."

Rabbi Simon had responded with an offer that came
as a surprise to Adam. After all, and not to be punny,
the rabbi didn't know him from Adam back at the time.
Adam laughed to himself realizing just how funny that
thought really was.

Adam assumed it was simply because the man was
a rabbi. A teacher. Any opportunity to bring enlightenment to a fellow human being, Jew or not, was part and
parcel of being a clergyman.

"I could meet with you from time to time if you'd
like. We could talk about the heart and soul of Conservative Judaism and about what you have studied. And then,
you'd be able to make an informed decision about it, just
as you said."

Adam shifted in his airplane seat. His meetings with
Rabbi Simon had been eye-opening, to say the least. At
times, he'd even felt as if Daniella were speaking through
the rabbi's mouth. So much of what the rabbi shared was
in keeping with comments Daniella had made when she
explained her way of life to him. So very much. It meant
not only that Daniella's comments were true but that she
was quite learned about the Conservative movement.

Yet those meetings with Rabbi Simon revealed so
much more. Mostly, that all the teachings in Conservative Judaism were neck and neck with his own. The
prayer services were practically identical. *Shacharit* in
the morning, *Mincha* in the afternoon, *Maariv* in the evening. Nothing was left out. The Torah and *Haftarah* readings, or any other additional readings, for that matter,

were all done in the correct order, in the correct way, on the correct days and the correct weeks. Again, nothing was left out.

All the holidays were remembered and observed. All of them, all the way down to the required fasts throughout the year. *Kashruth* was maintained, and the Conservative movement was stringent enough to go through the meticulous cleaning ritual before Passover that rid homes and businesses of *chametz* and its many varieties of leavening. Same as his own community did.

Rabbi Simon was one among many who sold the *chametz* for the week of Passover so that no Jew would own any, a small yet very significant Judaic requirement that was not overlooked or changed in any way. In essence, the components of both forms of Judaism were all the same. So what was it that made Conservative Judaism different enough that his own community found it unappealing and wrong?

Adam shifted in his plane seat yet again. He grimaced as he turned, not because of any physical discomfort but because of what he knew to be the heart and soul of the matter—fear of the bigger world. The outside. The big, looming evil that was the rest of planet Earth. The component that could cause change. His community lived a backward life stuck in centuries-old notions. They obviously feared that modernity would steal their way of life right out from underneath them.

All people were petrified of change. His people were no exception. Change meant loss of power. Change meant new rules. In the case of his own community, change would also include empowering women, and that, in turn, would diminish the power and control of the men. Adam no longer believed that men were wiser, more insightful, or more capable than women. He laughed thinking about whether any of the men had ever heard of Margaret Thatcher or Golda Meir. What did they have to say about those women?

Rabbi Simon had suggested to Adam that he read about the history of Hasidism in books that were outside his own community. Objective texts that were merely factual. His assignment, to see if anything differed from what he himself had been taught. Nothing did. The books were indeed factual, and nothing new under the sun had come to light from the words written across their pages. Well, perhaps Adam did take note of one thing: nowhere in the texts was there a condemnation of the movement. No one pointed out that Hasidism was simply the wrong way to be a Jew.

After many visits with Rabbi Simon, reading text together, reviewing Talmudic law, and discussing it, Adam forever changed his convictions. He had become one among a very small minority of Orthodox men who believed that *Halacha* did not exclude women from ritual or observance practices. If one studied Jewish law thoroughly and interpreted it without bias, one would be able to admit that women could do so much more than they were allowed. In no way would it diminish his own obligations or prevent him from being the best Jew he could possibly be. More so, that one could live a good and holy Orthodox life and do so in the greater modern society. Overall, that he in particular, could be a good Jew outside of the Hasidic world.

Perhaps Adam could have leaned toward Modern Orthodoxy. They, too, were grounded in the bigger world. Had he never met Daniella, that would have been the likely outcome for him. He would have reached similar conclusions and sought out the lifestyle that would support his convictions. He was sure of it. With no Daniella in his life, he would have eventually sought the only other group that would have understood him. He did have a Daniella, though, and she had a life he admired.

Rabbi Simon had told Adam about a Rabbi Roth who came up with a clever metaphor regarding *Halacha*. One was to imagine a chessboard with a game in progress. In terms of the Orthodox communities, a glass dome had been placed on top of the game shortly after the *Shulchan Arukh* in the sixteenth century. The game remained untouched and had never been continued.

The Conservative movement took the dome off and continued the game, moving the pieces as necessary to keep the game vibrant and, of course, to keep their side winning. The Reform movement not only took the dome off but decided to change the playing pieces and rules as well. And in all of this, the underlying guidance to the game, the major rule to play it, was the question that frustrated all the Jewish players the most. Where did God's hand end in all this and the human hand begin?

Adam smiled and cuddled up into his jacket, which he had been using as a blanket. Danny, his clever Danny. Hadn't she shared a similar metaphor, and hadn't she done so long before she entered the seminary? Which of course meant she had already been smart and insightful about her Judaism. Adam recalled his picnic with her outside of her university campus grounds, sandwiches at the ready and discussion strong as always. She had likely been inspired by the Jewish history class that she had taken that day.

"Adam, you know, as I see it, Judaism is like an LP."

"What in heaven's name can that possibly mean?"

"Well, the record album is Judaism. You put the record on and then, oh no, one of those awful skips. It plays over and over and over."

"Meaning..."

"Meaning the Orthodox are stuck, just like the skip. The same rules over and over, and they refuse to change them."

"Really? Interesting. So what would you say for the Conservative and Reform?"

"The Conservative give the needle a nudge so the song can continue and you can find out how it will progress."

"And the Reform?"

Daniella laughed. "They're so disgusted with the skip, they change the record altogether!"

Adam was already thinking about the clever metaphor when Daniella added in something that, looking back on it now, had likely been the seed that was planted in his own mind. The one that started it all.

"Adam, no disrespect to any of the Traditional Orthodox or Hasidic communities, but..."

Adam had given her an encouraging look so she would be brave enough to be honest when she spoke.

"I can't help but feel that in your world the notion of questioning constantly is indeed there, yet, if it deters from the rules at the heart of the community, it is chastised, punished, belittled. To me, it seems you can

question, but you have to question in the way they tell
you to question. And if you're a woman, don't question
what they tell you at all. Accept it as your station in life,
and that's the end of it. I'm grateful every day for being
able to question and to watch the Conservative movement make changes and move with the times. To constantly work at being good Jews but to be part of society
as well."

Daniella took a moment to pause and collect her
thoughts. She continued. "To be an interactive part of
humanity and help make it better. What good is it to be
apart from the rest of the world? To shut yourself out?
To hide like an ostrich? If the neighborhood is bombed,
aren't we both destroyed? Well, that's drastic, but you
know what I'm trying to say."

"I do, Danny. But aren't there those in the Conservative movement that also prevent you from doing things?
Aren't there men who are against women *davening* the
prayers alongside them, leading a service in their presence, or reading from a Torah scroll? Basically, aren't
there traditionalists in the Conservative movement?"

"I'd say it's back to the LP, Adam. The Conservative
movement has its naysayers, but the bottom line is they
are at least discussing all these things regularly. They're
trying to look into the future. In fact, change is already
underway. Mark my words, Adam. The day will come,
and soon, when women will be cantors and rabbis, and
halachically speaking, the movement will be able to show
that there is no reason to forbid it."

And wasn't Danny right? His Danny, a cantor now. A
cantor contracted with a specific synagogue that already

loved and adored her. A cantor who had been educated over five years to get it and get it right. How could anyone look at her and instantly denounce her years of Judaic study as invalid? How could anyone say the degree she had earned, and rightfully so, was invalid?

Adam cringed at the thought of anyone doing that to Danny, but then, as he looked out at the night sky through the airplane window, his features softened. The window provided just enough of an angle that he could see the stars. A radiant smile took over. The conclusion had finally been reached. *I'm a Conservative-minded individual trapped in an old-fashioned Orthodox world. I need to change my life, and time is of the essence because my Danny is engaged. I want to be on life's path with Danny,* Hashem. *She is my* beshert, *and you tried to tell me. I just didn't listen. Forgive me for not listening. Come what way,* Hashem, *I will deal with whatever you throw my way. Just give me strength. I'll need strength to close the doors on my current life. Especially in terms of my son. But I don't love Teme. I don't want to be with Teme. She makes my soul very sad. I know you know the depth of sorrow my marriage brings to my heart and mind. Arguments every day. Sleeping on separate beds even when we shouldn't be. You know this. So help me,* Hashem.

Adam could have gone on and on with his prayer. It would be to no avail. God already knew the heart of the matter. Adam could do no more than hope that his wishes would come true.

As the plane began its descent, Adam tried to mentally prepare for what lay ahead. He'd be asking for a divorce. Imminent rage and disgrace would follow.

Imminent shunning. Imminent pain. At least he'd start with something only slightly less difficult. He'd start by asking for forgiveness from Danny. He'd start by asking for a life with her. He'd start by embracing a whole new way of life. He'd start by being reborn.

dam hoped he'd be able to make his crazy scheme work. *Hashem* should forgive him for all the lies he had spoken in the last few weeks. Summer was coming to an end. The High Holidays were fast approaching, and lying was the last thing anyone wanted to be doing when the goal was to become a better person in the year to come. Yet, instead of reflecting on his sinfulness and begging for forgiveness, here he was, actually adding to his list of sins.

He hadn't planned to be in the United States during the holiday season, but now that he knew where to locate Daniella, he was a man on a mission. He needed to lie in order to spare his family as much hurt and shame as he possibly could. Surely *Hashem* would take that into consideration when determining the year ahead for him.

He had let Teme know that, much to his surprise, he would be in the United States after *Rosh Hashanah* passed. An unexpected potential buyer had come under his radar, a buyer too good to pass up. Adam even came

up with a fake name. He also made clear that he could
not return home immediately after finishing the business. It would be too close to the onset of *Yom Kippur*
when he finished all the business exchanges.

Yes, a potential new customer, he had said. Too good
to pass up, he had said. Too far away from his parents'
home, he had implied. No matter how he tried, he
would not be able to be with Teme or the family on *Yom
Kippur*. And because of this unexpected trip, he'd have to
wait until after *Simchat Torah* to return home to Belgium.
A complete and total pack of lies.

"I assure you, Teme, I'll fly home as soon as I can. I'll
find a good family that can host me for *Yom Kippur*. I'll
be in *shul* all day, fasting and observing, just like a good
Jew should be. I'll see to it that I locate the Orthodox
community closest to where I'm staying and get myself
there before sunset of *Erev Yom Kippur*. I'll be sure to arrive hours before sundown of the holiday's onset. Don't
worry about me being unable to observe such important
days."

Convincing Teme was easy. She cared only that Adam
did what was right. She probably wouldn't even miss
him at all. And even though he didn't love Teme, that
simple fact irked him to the core. Well, he'd have the last
laugh, wouldn't he? Once he took this first step, once he
was sure that Danny would be receptive to him reenter-
ing her life, divorcing Teme would come next. Adam felt
terrible for thinking such a mean thought, but he would
not turn back on his decision.

He did want to be as fair as possible. Adam had already concluded that, even if Daniella didn't want him
around, he would go through with the divorce. He just

wanted out. He wanted a different life. He wanted to be, well, he wanted to be Adam.

Convincing his family about his need to travel during the High Holiday season was a bit more difficult than dealing with Teme. Especially when it came to his mother.

"Adam, I don't understand. You'll be only hours away. You said so yourself. What? Maybe six, seven? You can't tell this new customer of yours that you need to end things early so you can get home for religious reasons? You know you could easily drive here or take the train."

"Mama, I know, I know. It's just that this client isn't Jewish. It would be different if he were. Then, of course, we wouldn't have scheduled anything. But this is a potential new client that is an important one. If I can start business with him, it will be a personal financial boon for me. I don't know how long it will take to close the deal, so I may not be finished on time. I'd never make it on time. Better to stay put and observe *Yom Kippur* close by to his business. Even you would agree that is the proper thing to do. Not to take a chance. The business is on the far end of the city. Just imagine me driving and what if the traffic delays me? Suddenly, the sun is going down. I'm out of time."

Adam wanted to reassure his mother. "I'll find a good Orthodox *shul* close to the business. I'm sure I can because we're talking a major city."

Adam wanted to make sure his mother was completely sated. He decided to add in more fodder.

"I'll tell you what, Mama...after I break my fast, I'll get a good night's rest and drive straight home to you right after breakfast the next morning. I'll stay through *Sukkot, Hoshan'ah Rabbah, Shemini Atzeret,* and *Simchat To- rah.* I'll be with you and *Tata.* Teme will understand. In fact, she'll be relieved that I'm with you. She would be very upset if I chose to fly home any time during the holiday week. She feels very strongly when it comes to observance; you know that. She would be pleased that I'm with you."

Knowing that his mother would likely keep insisting and also that she'd point out that arrangements could be made to stay with a Hasidic family somewhere in the city, Adam made sure to say something that would get his mother to stop her arguing.

"I am a grown man. I am a married grown man. I don't need to be told what to do. I am well aware of my obligations during the High Holidays. Please don't treat me like a child."

What a tangled web Adam wove. In reality, he had no deal to make at all. He would even lie to everyone after the holidays, saying that the deal fell through. He'd feign regret and say he'd rather not talk about it. He had already thought up some vague comments in case the family pushed him for information. What he hadn't figured into his little web was the possibility that his mother or father would inquire of Tzvi why the business would do such a thing. That reality would come biting at his heels like a vicious dog at one of the lowest points of Adam's life.

Presently, he was resting quietly on his hotel bed in one of the lesser known hotel chains, which happened to be a twenty-minute walk from Daniella's synagogue. His parents would be heartbroken if they knew he was less than 40 minutes or so from their home. But he was solid in his conviction to experience one of the holiest of days through the eyes of Conservative Jews. The only day that was any holier was *Shabbat*. The holiest day of all was when *Yom Kippur* fell on *Shabbat*. It was a blessing that at least that was not the case this year. Adam would be free to leave the moment he could.

Adam had eaten heartily and well, in order to gear up for the fast that was now only hours away. He selected a proper suit and would dress in it soon. He'd be sure to tuck his *pais* curls gently behind his ears and replace his black hat with a white *yarmulke*. Adam reached over to the bed and checked his *tallis* bag to make sure the *yarmulke* was there. His holy cloth rested inside, as did the paper ticket needed to enter Daniella's synagogue. He removed the ticket from his bag and stood up to place it into the breast pocket of his suit.

It would be *Erev Yom Kippur* soon, and he would be spending the next twenty-four hours in *shul*. More precisely, in Daniella's *shul*. How lucky he was to be able to attend services there at all. Adam sat down on the corner chair of his hotel room and recalled the conversation he'd had with the synagogue's receptionist.

"Hello. This is Adam Goldfarb calling. Is it possible for a noncongregant to purchase a ticket for *Yom Kippur?*"

"Let me put you on hold, and I'll find out for you."

Adam had remembered that most Conservative synagogues had individuals pay for tickets at the High Holiday season. Daniella had explained the reason to him long ago when they spoke about anything and everything. With nothing better to do as he waited for the receptionist to get back on the line, Adam started thinking about that conversation.

"Adam, I'm hoping and praying that I can pull more people into *shul* by sharing the excitement, joy, and connectedness that communal prayer offers. Unfortunately, I'm the first to admit that the Conservative branch is lacking in one particular area, and I'll even admit, it is because we function in the secular world.

"Just like there are Christians who only go to church on Christmas and Easter, we have Jews who only come to synagogue on *Rosh Hashanah* and *Yom Kippur*. Since we don't do weekly collections like churches do, it is our golden opportunity to receive funding by charging for a ticket to get in. And believe you me, synagogues everywhere are packed during the High Holidays. No matter how unobservant, no matter how many times they break the Sabbath or eat *traif*, they all come. Especially on *Yom Kippur*. The tickets go like hot cakes and we run out of them quickly."

"Hello, are you still there?"

"Yes, I'm still here."

"Luck is with you, Mister Goldfarb. We have two open seats left. They are way in the back, but they are available. Everything else has been assigned. Also, since you mentioned you're not a congregant, you'd have to pay a different fee than our members."

"That's fine. I'm happy to pay the fee. I'm just glad to know you have a ticket available. What would be the best way to get the ticket?"

Adam had arranged with the secretary to hold the ticket at the synagogue until the following Thursday. He did so after some friendly chit chat with her revealed that both the cantor and rabbi would not be in on that Thursday afternoon or herself for that matter. Adam wanted it that way and so, feigned needing to pick up the ticket at that time. Another lie, pretending it was the only time he was available to do so. The secretary was very helpful.

"The bookkeeper will be here, however. She'll be in the office and I'll leave your ticket with her. You can hand her the payment."

Adam was looking at the ticket now, realizing he would be in a completely different environment. His *Yom Kippur* experience would be unlike any he'd ever had. He would be in a sea of Jews, men and women alike. Would he even feel a sense of the holiday at all? He certainly hoped so. He was eager to prove that the experience of celebrating with Conservative Jews would further solidify the recent convictions in his heart.

He began dressing for the start of the holiday. It was a thirty-minute walk in total to Beth David, and he didn't want to be late for the service. He quickly checked his *tallis* bag one last time after suiting up, and then he peeked into the hotel mirror. A pair of worn-out white canvas sneakers graced the otherwise dapper image. He wore the old foot coverings as a symbolic gesture to prove to God that he could forego the vanity of leather at such an introspective time.

Adam would do his utmost to stay unnoticeable in the sea of people that would descend on the synagogue. He would come and go quietly. He would see to it that Daniella couldn't place his face in the crowd. He would be an anonymous soul who came to make peace with God. He'd keep his head down and peer into his prayer book.

Adam knew that many synagogues opened the walls that rested between sanctuary and social hall. They needed to do so simply to accommodate the large numbers of worshipers who gathered during the High Holidays. Sitting at the back of such a massive space would help ensure his anonymity. Surely, like most *hazzans*, Daniella would be too busy to peruse the crowd and look for people. She would need to focus on her role. She would focus only on bringing heartfelt prayer and, hopefully, consolation to the masses. Adam could do no more than eagerly await the consolation that she could bring him as well.

"*G'mar chatimah tovah.*"

The rabbi began the holiday with the formal greeting uttered by Jews everywhere on *Yom Kippur*. He was stating that everyone should be sealed for a good year. His perfect accent literally rolled the phlegm-like *ch* sound from the back of his throat and out of his mouth, expressing the heartfelt sentiment to one and all as he smiled down on the crowd. For some reason, it made Adam recall that Daniella had said she had taught her young students how to make the perfect *ch* sound by giving them a musical connection. She had simply taught them to say the name Bach, as in the composer.

The seated congregants were perfectly silent as the rabbi offered the traditional greeting. Adam was taken by the insightful comments the rabbi offered next. He noted that Daniella, was facing the ark, ready to *daven* at a moment's notice. Even so, that her eyes were looking at the rabbi, while she listened to him. She was probably anticipating her cue to begin.

"As Cantor Sobler chants the *Kol Nidre* prayer, I not only ask that you reflect on the traditional meaning of the words but I'd like you to consider the following: in English, *Yom Kippur* is referred to as the Day of Atonement. This year, let us not think on the word *atonement* as atonement. Let us break up the word so that it is pronounced at-one-ment." The rabbi paused. "At-one-ment. Not only with ourselves but with *Adonai*, our God. To be whole in our mind and heart. To be one unit, one soul that can reconnect and start anew. May the words of the *Kol Nidre* prayer bring that sense of one-ness to each of you."

The Torah scrolls were removed from the ark, and individual members of the synagogue held them as Daniella began the chant that Adam had heard year after year and once, long ago, from her recording. This time, however, he heard a voice that was trained and experienced. One that had knowledge leading the way. Adam looked upward, closed his eyes, and absorbed every word. This holiday, he would feel at-one-ment, just as the rabbi suggested. He would feel it through Daniella.

A sea of people swallowed up Adam to the point where he truly was just another face in the crowd. Second to last row, fifth seat in. Far away from the main sanctuary doors. Far away from the *bimah* where Daniella stood. She was continually facing away from the congregation, looking toward the Torah ark as she enveloped herself in her own sense of connection. Adam assumed a similar scenario would occur the next day, *Yom Kippur* Day, and so he would still be able to remain anonymous. He couldn't have been more wrong.

Adam, being Orthodox, did not realize that Conservative Jews were not hard pressed to be in *shul* at the start of services. He was more than shocked when he arrived on time for the start of services on *Yom Kippur* Day, just to witness that only a small crowd was in attendance. He did not realize that congregants would slowly and steadily trickle in as the hours passed. He knew that if he sat in his assigned seat, he'd stick out like a sore thumb.

Lucky for him, the synagogue had an overhead sound system that allowed the service to be heard in certain parts of the building. Adam located a small room with a sign on it that read, *Minyan* Room. The group of ten people required to have communal prayer usually had a smaller sanctuary designated to them somewhere in a synagogue's building. Adam knew, then, that the room where the daily prayers were recited would likely have a speaker. He turned the knob, grateful that the door was not locked. He sat in the dark room for an hour and a half before the voices of many trailed through the speakers overhead. Adam realized it meant the sanctuary had finally filled up.

He moved into the main sanctuary shortly before the Torah service began, once again hidden and unrecognizable. He was sure of it. To his thinking, the sea of congregants swallowed him up. Surely, he would be able to hide himself in the sea of people as the processional for the Torah brought Daniella and the rabbi, as well as the Torah carriers, by his area of seats.

Adam kept his head bent low as Daniella passed by. She was busily shaking the hands of congregants, greeting them, wishing them a good year ahead. As she neared him, Adam reached down to the seat in front of him to retrieve his *tallis* bag, which rested on the seat rack and turned his back away from the passing processional. He was certain he would go unnoticed by her. Daniella, the rabbi, and the Torahs all passed without issue.

Adam sighed with relief as he watched the first Torah being placed on the reading table positioned on the *bimah*. It meant he had not been seen. Now, he could look forward to the Torah reading as well as the sermon the rabbi would give once the readings were completed. He had loved the comments the rabbi had made last night, and he hoped for a repeat of inspiring speech.

It was obvious that the rabbi chose Daniella's chanting as the focal point of his sermon for that year. He was clear in pointing out just how much Hebrew prayer connected an entire congregation. How it brought about community and connection to the Almighty. The words penetrated Adam's brain in bits and pieces because he was busy trying to absorb every single one that the rabbi uttered.

"*Nusach* basically means *certain way*. You, the congregant, can hear a *nusach* melodically chanted by Cantor Sobler and know exactly what day of the week it is or what time of day it is. Certainly, then, you are aware that it is *Yom Kippur* when you hear the melodic chants designated for today. And why does our cantor chant prayer? Why do any of us chant prayer? Why do we as a congregation sing our prayers rather than recite them verbally? It is because for us, prayer is liturgical poetry. Singing it, rather than just speaking it, brings us *kavanah*. It brings us the intent and spiritual purpose.

"And what is the intent of our prayer? To feel the prayer with our soul. To connect everyone to another. To bring us together as a family known as the Jewish people.

To have a collective voice of praise as a community. One big, booming voice lifting up toward the heavens, praising the creator of the universe.

"So what is Cantor Sobler's role, not only everyday but, especially, today? It is to help every single one of you, myself included, to fulfill the intent of prayer. In the same way that Cantor Sobler starts us off with a *niggun*, a simple wordless melody to get us into the spirit of *Shabbat* each week, so, too, must she help us feel the spirit of *Yom Kippur* today.

"Last night, Cantor Sobler chanted *Kol Nidre*, bringing the solemnity of the prayer, the very emotion of it, to us as a people. When she chants *Avinu Malkeynu*, "Our Father, Our King," you can hear and have some understanding of…the knowing, the awesomeness of that which we call God. Close your eyes now and listen to the intent in her chanting the *Hineni* prayer. Listen as she chants on your behalf, asking God to accept her as the messenger for you, all of you, the people of this congregation."

A hush fell over the room. It was so quiet, that even the slightest sigh from a congregant's lips would have been heard. Adam noticed that, indeed, a number of people had closed their eyes. He closed his too. The prayer was one of his favorites. Humbly asking for strength and guidance, a cantor chanted it as the "voice" of the sinners. Their agent, as it were. He was about to listen to it through a female voice. He could hardly believe he was there and, more so, that he felt worthy to be there. He was sure that *Hashem* was present and listening too.

Adam's soul went to a special place as the prayer stirred his heart. His face lifted upward, and he could feel the holiness that Daniella's voice invoked. She was praying on his behalf. A beaming smile crossed Adam's cheeks as he listened. He was hearing purity.

He thought about the sins of his own community. Too many to count. We're all human, after all. Certainly, they were guilty of invalidating the purity of Daniella's prayer because she had the audacity to chant in front of men. For the first time, Adam really understood that holiness was not about following the rules. Rules that were dictated, memorized, and barely questioned. It was about intent, just as the rabbi said. It was and always should be about intent. Daniella intended to bring worship to the forefront.

It was about *Hashem* being very aware of what came from the soul within, heartfelt and remorseful. It wasn't about countless individuals doing things because they had to. Because the law dictated such. Because they thought it gave them automatic righteousness. Mechanical rote. Surely, *Hashem* knew how much the *Hineni* meant to Daniella. Her heart was in every word.

The Lord always speaks to us in the strangest of ways and at the most peculiar times. For Adam, *Hashem* spoke at that very moment. All the dark conclusions that had been resting in the deepest recesses of his thoughts came charging to the forefront. Now, they were convictions. Now, they were facts that he understood and accepted completely. Now, they gave him courage.

His heart was not in his marriage, much as he loved his young son. His heart was not even bound up in the rote of his Orthodoxy. It was only bound to the beliefs in his soul. The beliefs he now realized could flourish whether or not he resided in an Orthodox community. His soul was a Jewish soul. That was all that mattered.

On *Yom Kippur* Day, when fate is sealed, Adam's had surely come to light.

He'd take it very slow, and by no means did he plan to become nonobservant. He loved his Judaism and the belief system it rendered. He loved to observe the traditions and rituals. His realization only meant that he felt happier when he was part of the bigger world. He would ask Teme for a divorce, come what may. He'd accept that his own community would likely shun him as a result. That he'd possibly lose his child in the process. He'd accept whatever *Hashem* had in store.

Well, the Almighty, blessed be the name, was certainly paying attention that day. Three things happened in succession as a result of the fate that the Lord had sealed into the Book of Life for Adam Goldfarb. The first being that, despite Adam's effort to remain undetected, he had forgotten that most rabbis and cantors look out on the congregation over and over in their own secreted way for very specific reasons.

They gauged the attention spans of the congregants, the numbers that remained, and even the temperaments of the individuals in the room. For those reasons alone, it was natural that Daniella had taken notice of the man who sat hunched over, obviously hiding himself from the processional. When the processional had been bombarded by hands jutting out to shake the clergy or kiss a Torah scroll with a *talis* fringe or prayer book, people wanting to be sure it was noted that they came to services that day, he had been noticed.

Daniella had glanced at the swirling curls and certain curve of the shoulders that she remembered as Adam's when she had passed by. Could it be? It was beyond

bothersome that such a thing was happening just before she had to recite the *Hineni* prayer, a sacred text
that required the utmost focus. She would have to work
overtime to block out her wondering, at least until that
prayer ended.

One could practically hear Daniella's sigh of relief
when the prayer was relegated to the past. She had taken
a quick glance toward the section where she thought she
had spied him. She timed her little peek for just before
she would chant the *Musaf* service, the afternoon portion of prayer. Mere seconds, just to see if her hunch
was right. It was all she could do to keep herself calm as
she stole that glance, wondering what *Hashem* could have
possibly fated for her, showing her Adam on *Yom Kippur*
of all days. Adam had continued to keep his head down as
much as possible, and somehow it was concluded that it
meant Adam didn't want her to notice him at all.

Adam had slipped out at some point close to the end
of the afternoon portion. When Daniella went to her office to lie down for the small break between that portion
and the late-afternoon Torah reading and *Mincha* service,
he was nowhere to be found. She rested her head on her
office recliner and could do no more than wonder why
God had placed Adam in her synagogue.

She saw him again during *Ne'ilah*, as *Yom Kippur* was
coming to a close, but she was too tired and hungry at that
point to let herself dwell on his attendance. She thought
mostly about food to break her fast and a chance to get
off her feet and relax. She probably should try to find
him when services were officially over. Doing so would
give her an opportunity to find out what it all meant, but
honestly, she didn't want to know. On the day when life

was renewed, God showed her the man who broke her heart. What kind of year had God slated for her? Adam had left as soon as the final *shofar* blast sounded. He was nowhere to be found at the holiday's end.

The second event that followed *Hashem's* plan for Adam occurred the next morning. He drove to his family home only to be told the dreadful news that Teme had miscarried on the morning of *Yom Kippur* Eve. The holiday had begun by the time she had settled in her hospital bed, but she was safe and sound and awaiting his return to Belgium. He would have been told sooner, save for the fact that the time difference meant that his own family did not find out until *Yom Kippur* was over in the States. Belgium had already said its good-byes to *Yom Kippur*, but the holiday was still progressing on the eastern seaboard. The Gvirzmans had no choice but to wait and call as soon as the holiday passed in the West. Not sure of how to locate Adam, they knew he'd be at the Goldfarb home when *Yom Kippur* ended, since that was what Adam had told them.

Upon hearing the news, Adam knew he'd have to wait to express his desire for a divorce. Teme had to heal and be well enough to accept the way he felt. No matter how much he did not love her, he would not hurt the mother of his child in such a mean-spirited way. When the time was right, he would make no mention of Daniella; rather, he would only reflect on the fact that he was not happy with the marriage.

The third event in the succession centered on Daniella. Adam could only have found her location if Benny had told him. Daniella needed to find out for sure. She had planned to drive over to Epson County on the weekend after the last of the holidays concluded. The planned trip was in order to spend the day with her parents to begin discussing wedding plans. Her true motivation however, was so that she could excuse herself for a while, stating she wanted to visit Benny. Feign a desire to surprise him when in reality she wanted a private visit to find out why, after years of absence, Adam had suddenly reentered her life.

In all this, Daniella completely ignored the butterflies she had felt when she gazed at Adam sitting in her congregation. She ignored the fact that she had registered how handsome he was. She even ignored the fact that, for those few precious seconds, her fiancé hadn't existed at all, and neither, for that matter, had the entire room of congregants. Worse, even *Yom Kippur* had fallen from existence for an eternity of seconds. After years of resting in the secret hiding place in Daniella's heart, Adam Goldfarb still mattered. After all the time that had passed, the notion of love still came to the surface, eager to swim.

"Oh my goodness, Danny! What a surprise! It's so good to see you! Are you here for a bite to eat? Come, I'll seat you."

"Hi, Benny. Actually, I'm not here to eat. I want to talk with you. I need to discuss something. Can you spare some time?"

"For you, always. Nate, come on over here. Look who's here!" Benny kept his tone lighthearted, but he surmised he was in some kind of trouble.

"Nice to see you again," Nate responded, and he smiled as he walked toward the register counter.

"Nate, watch the front, if you don't mind. I'll be in the back for about fifteen minutes, let's say. I'm going to talk a bit with Daniella." Benny paused, noting that Daniella had a serious expression on her face. He felt he had to add, "Is this a tea and cookies session?"

"I guess it is."

Benny felt badly when he heard who had showed up at Daniella's synagogue. Adam's presence there, and during

the holiday, no less, was the last thing Benny had expected. Obviously, the visit had been a result of his chat with
Adam. Benny was hoping that Daniella would forgive him.

"Please, forgive me, Danny. I can only be honest and
tell you that the information just kind of slipped out. If
you only saw how miserable he looked. It was pathetic,
I'm telling you! He was coming into the restaurant repeatedly. That in itself already made me think things were
not quite right for him.

"You know, I love having daily diners, but for the first
time in my life, I was actually praying he'd stop coming
in daily. He was bringing me and even the customers
down with his forlorn look and his sad, faraway eyes. He
was literally here every day, every single time he was doing his business in the city."

Benny looked straight into Daniella's eyes before
emphasizing his next point.

"Even worse, Danny." Benny paused ever so slightly.
"He ordered salami and eggs with a cream soda every
time he was here and always asked for your old booth. I
know why, too, but before I divulge that, I want to say to
you that if you think about what I just said, even you can
come to the correct conclusion."

Frustration no longer etched Daniella's face. Sorrow was now the clear conqueror of her features, and to
Benny's surprise, she began to cry.

"Danny, honey, what's the matter?"

"Oh, Benny, this makes everything such a mess."

"What do you mean?" Benny reached out to give Daniella's hand a consoling pat as it lay atop the booth table.

"Benny, I've never stopped loving Adam. My gosh, I
can't believe I'm saying that out loud. I thought I moved

on. I really did. I was so sure I was happy. Seeing Adam, sitting there, praying, and I swear to you, he had a look on his face that seemed as if some great knowledge was gifted to him, well..." Daniella paused and appeared to struggle with her thoughts.

"Lately, I had been questioning if my fiancé was really the right person for me. I like Norman just fine, but...well...I had already started to wonder if I was settling in some way simply because I was twenty-seven and wanted to get on with starting a family. I have been praying constantly for guidance and for a sign of some kind so I would know whether or not to move ahead with a marriage. Seeing Adam, all I could do was acknowledge the flip-flops my gut was doing, and my heart felt like it was skipping beats. Hoping and praying he was there because he was the sign. That he was the answer to my prayers. On *Yom Kippur*, Benny. On *Yom Kippur*!

"Hearing what you said about him coming into the restaurant, and the fact that he was at my synagogue, tells me he's pining for what we once had. He came like a message. Wasn't that God's way of telling me that my fiancé really isn't the right person? And you're the reason he came into my world and turned it upside down. God was directing you too." Daniella started crying all over again.

"Benny, I don't know what I'm supposed to do. What am I supposed to do?"

"You're not supposed to do anything, Danny."

Benny chose not to focus on the fact that he had completely turned the rocked boat upside down. He merely focused on the moment and the need to bring it to a close. He tried to articulate his conclusion in the best way possible.

"Only a fool would try to make concrete decisions about their life at such a time. All you need to do right now is think about how you feel about this present situation. That's all. Sort your feelings, like good eggs from bad ones. That sort of thing. You know, I have to believe that God will help you figure it all out. Trust in that. You of all people should be able to trust in that. It just takes time."

Daniella sat so silently that Benny became a bit unnerved. He wondered what she might have going through her head and wished he could make her divulge it. He hoped he hadn't offended her somehow. Much as it pained him, he opted to honor the silence she seemed to demand. Why make things worse with unnecessary words? He waited patiently until she was ready to speak once more.

"Benny, I have a favor to ask."

"Anything, Danny. Anything, sweetheart. You know you're still like a daughter to me."

"Well then, Benny, just like you let your grown daughters live their own lives with their husbands, let me live mine by my own direction. I'm twenty-seven and a successful cantor. I'm on my own path. Let me do it on my own. If Adam comes in here, don't give him any more information, OK? Let him do his own legwork in the same way I'm asking you to let me do mine."

Benny was flabbergasted. In so many words, Daniella was telling him to stay out of her affairs. After all they'd been through and shared together, she was turning down future help or support he might want to give. Help that would have come from a good place, with good intentions. Didn't she realize just how much she—and Adam, for that matter—meant to him? In his heart, well, they had a place there. He felt love for the two in a way that was actually hard for him to express.

Benny just didn't understand. He could not recognize his own twisted reasoning as to why he was so determined for Daniella to succeed in life and in love. All his feelings for Daniella arose because of a subconscious comparison with his mother. Somehow, he placed Adam in the role of his father just to complete his psychological game. It would be a long while before he understood that, in this particular case, his desire to help was truly an interference. A gross interference.

Hurt or not, he'd honor her request because he cared for her very much. If Adam came through the doors of the restaurant yet again, going through his routine yet again, Benny would excuse himself one way or another. Otherwise, the temptation would be too great. Benny felt a strong desire to see two people who loved each other best the world and come out winning. The urge was so compelling that he could only prevent himself from running interference by hiding in the back. In time, he hoped and prayed that Adam would take the hint and stop coming to the restaurant so often.

"*C*antor Sobler, there's that same gentleman on line two asking to speak with you. Shall I put him through?" The synagogue receptionist sounded matter of fact. How could she possibly know that Daniella already knew Adam? To the receptionist, he was simply the pesky man who kept calling and asking to speak with the cantor. The receptionist looked up at Daniella, who had entered the office just after Adam had been placed on hold. The red flashing light blinked urgently as it indicated Adam's presence on the second phone line. The receptionist stared as she waited for an answer.

Daniella swallowed hard, feeling as if her heart had dropped into her stomach. This was Adam's third call that day. The last two attempts had been cut short by the simple comment that the cantor was not available. Daniella had instructed the receptionist to tell him that. Daniella feigned being busy at work in her office. Too busy to take a call. *I'm too afraid to speak with you.*

Breathing a heavy but quiet sigh and gaining composure, Daniella said, "Ask him to please hold a minute, Adele. I suppose he must have something urgent on his mind, and I guess I've been rude not to take the call. I'll take it down in my office."

Daniella made the short walk to her work space and closed the office door. She wanted to continue to refuse the call but knew that would seem suspicious. After years, Adam was still putting her between a rock and a hard place, damn him. She sat down at her desk, took in one last breath, and picked up the receiver.

"Hello, Adam."

"Danny…" The way Adam sighed out her name was more than she could handle. It invoked feelings. That made her angry.

"Why are you calling, Adam?"

"Please, Danny. Can I come and talk to you in person to explain why? Please don't make me talk over the phone. It's so impersonal, and you deserve so much more than words through a telephone line."

Daniella would have liked to say that she did deserve more, and long ago at that, but the simple truth was that deep down she wanted to see Adam again. She wanted to hear from his own mouth why, after six years, he was contacting her now.

"Against my better judgment, I suppose so."

A day had passed. There she was, having just been notified by Adele that her appointment had arrived. Daniella's hand held tight to the intercom receiver as her nerves churned in her gut. She imagined what might be happening on the other end of the line. Was Adele wondering about the handsome man in her office who was most definitely not one of their congregants? Adele spoke, interrupting Daniella's thoughts.

"Or would it be preferable to have him wait until you come out to get him, Cantor Sobler?"

Daniella could hear the befuddled tone intertwined in the question. She concluded that the receptionist was feeling quite surprised that a seemingly *frum* male was coming to see Cantor Sobler, a female *hazzan*. Adam likely had *tzitzit* hanging at his sides or some other dead giveaway that he was observant.

Daniella opted to have Adam sent to her. She couldn't let on that she wanted her first moment with Adam to be as private as possible, no matter that the desire was completely wrong. When Daniella hung up the phone, she stood up quickly to primp as she straightened out her skirt. She grabbed her handbag and furiously searched for her compact mirror. Her eager hand ferreted out the looking glass, and she took a quick but studied glance. She threw the mirror into her desk drawer just as she heard the rap of knuckles against the door.

Sparks were instantaneous even before the door was opened.

The moment Adam stepped over the door's threshold, he begged Daniella in a soft voice, "Please, Danny. Please. Close the door so, for the briefest of moments, I can greet you in the way I have been dreaming of for weeks on end. I promise you can open the door after just one hug hello."

Mr. *Frum* breaking a cardinal rule, and immediately. A man and a woman should not be in a room alone together, ever. And this would be the sin of all sins—a married man asking a woman to close the door and see him in private. Against her better judgment, Daniella complied.

She wanted to be in his arms. Against all logic, she wanted Adam to hold her. To both their surprise, when the door closed, they immediately rushed into the other. They held tight, frozen in time.

Daniella had the sense that Adam was smelling her hair. Had he recognized the earthy scent of years before? Maybe he wanted to kiss her desperately. A part of Daniella wanted him to abandon every single notion of what was considered manly and cry huge tears as he begged for forgiveness. Daniella wanted him to want her, to the point of desperation.

Daniella could feel his body shaking as if he was trying to compose himself. A complete role reversal of the heart-wrenching scene of years ago. He was a helpless babe who in silence was begging for reassurance. She couldn't help but begin to feel overwhelmed by emotion. It was all she could do to keep her water-filled eyes from dropping tears.

They both had roles they knew they needed to play. In an effort to keep some semblance of authority over the situation, Daniella sat down behind her desk and motioned for Adam to sit on the other side in one of the two available chairs. Her gesture afforded her a few moments to refocus on her hurt and anger.

"Why, Adam? Why are you here?"

"I'm here to correct the worst mistake of my life."

"What is that supposed to mean?" Daniella's voice sounded taut.

"It means I am willing to do whatever it takes to be with you again."

"Are you married, Adam?"

Adam paused and replied guiltily, "Yes." He hesitated before adding, "And I have a young son."

"How dare you!" Daniella stood and pressed her fists onto her desk for physical support. "Get out."

Adam didn't budge. He merely looked at Daniella with pleading eyes. She, in turn, felt compelled to continue.

"Knowing how you left me! Knowing what your presence here is doing to me! Knowing you left me in love with you! You, a married man, coming to me and saying that. What are you doing? Are you asking me to be your mistress here in the States? Is that what you're doing, Adam?"

"No, no. Danny, you don't understand. Please, sit down and let me explain."

The engagement ring on Daniella's finger flashed a beam of sunlight from the outside window. It was a reminder that she was planning a wedding. Adam had taken notice of it. It was a sober reminder of what their present situation was. Was there still a chance that she would accept his explanation?

"I'll give you five minutes, Adam."

Daniella sat back down but on the edge of her chair. Neither said a word when the five minutes became an entire hour. Adam poured out his heart to Daniella, freely sharing how the pressures of his family and community had cornered him into the worst decision of his life.

"I was a coward, Daniella. Somewhere deep down I knew that I was happier in your world and wanted to be with you. I could *be* when I was in your world. *Hashem* should forgive me, I was just scared. Does that make sense?"

It did make sense in a strange sort of way. Enough that Daniella was willing to listen to whatever else Adam had to say. Maybe after six years Adam would right his wrong. Daniella remained silent. Adam apparently took the silence as a cue to continue.

"I suppose you'll never believe me, but my other reason was so that you could become a *hazzan*. I wanted you to be unfettered by the harassment my family and friends were sure to give you."

Adam smiled at Daniella. "I loved you that much, Danny."

He continued. "If I brought you to my family, they would have made you feel horrible for even dreaming of becoming a cantor. I couldn't do that to you. I couldn't bring that kind of pain to you. Even back then, I wanted you to succeed. Deep down, I wanted my Danny to be a *hazzan*."

Somehow, he had just managed to diminish the hurt by a fraction. Somehow, the message of love behind the actions he took was beginning to take the upper hand. Daniella did her utmost to stay in control. She didn't want to let the admission soften her anger.

Adam continued and got to the heart of the matter. "I'm asking Teme for a divorce."

So her name is Teme. It was all Daniella could do to appear unfazed.

"And what is it exactly that brought you here to tell me you want a divorce?"

"I'm asking you to be patient, even though you've been put off for too many years already. I'm asking you to forgive the worst mistake of my life and trust me when I say that I want to spend the rest of my life making it up to you. I want you to believe me when I say I'm leaving my old life behind. I'm saying to you that the moment I am free and clear, I want to marry you."

How strange life can be. Daniella wanted to jump up and down simply because Adam Goldfarb wanted to marry her. Yet she could do no more than reflect on a belief she had embraced since her teens. Simply put, life was a test. One big, gigantic test that God had designed to see if people would pass or fail. It was the segue to everything that came next in a person's afterlife. It was *Hashem's* way of seeing whether or not someone made the grade. It was the learning tool to make a person as holy as possible so that person could merit the next life. Well, what in heaven's name was this, then? Was she supposed to drop everything and just swoon with joy over the fact that now Adam wanted to marry her? Did the Almighty want her to jump up and down or berate Adam for such foolishness?

How many times had Daniella recited the Prayer for Peace with her congregants, reminding herself and everyone that we came into the world for three reasons: to praise the Almighty, to take care of the precious Earth that was given to us, and simply to love. It was all about love. Love of God. Love of people. Love of life. Certainly, then, love of your fated soul mate. Was that person actually Adam and not Norman?

Hashem put the choice to her. She could stay with someone ready and willing to marry her, give her children, and provide a good Jewish home. Someone who seemed to love her. Someone who insisted she was the perfect fit in the picture he painted of his future. Daniella looked down at her engagement ring.

But wasn't that the choice Adam had made years ago and regretted? Didn't Teme fit into the picture his family had painted, yet Teme was, in essence, a bad fit. In her heart of hearts, Daniella knew she needed to return the ring. She had already decided the marriage would be a mistake, and that had been well before Adam reentered her life. She was already secretly working up the courage to find the necessary words to break her engagement. Adam was simply the impetus that pushed the notion to the forefront of her brain.

In her heart, hadn't she always thought that Adam was her *beshert*, no matter that he was Orthodox and had been brought up so differently than she? Even long ago, hadn't she determined that she was willing to travel an incredibly difficult path in order to be with him? Hadn't she conjured up ways she would deal with the naysayers and mean-spirited notions of both communities?

"Adam, I need time to digest all of this. You can't just waltz into a person's life and think things will change simply because you want them to. You're hoping for a relationship with me?" Daniella trailed off for effect. "Earn it."

There was no way whatsoever that she would let him off the hook then and there. In fact, the moment she uttered the thought aloud, she thought to herself, *Wait a minute. Am I crazy? He can't seriously believe that he can just change this with the snap of a finger. That I'll come crawling back. Let him squirm a bit. Let him wonder. Let him prove his sincerity.*

"Daniella, I want to tell you to take all the time you need, but selfishly, I'm thinking ahead. I don't want you being in your midthirties before we could even marry or start a family together. I want to be with you the moment my divorce is final. If I say I'll be back in the States again five weeks from now, is that enough time?"

"Adam, it will be enough time for you to try to contact me and see if I respond. That's the best you'll get."

"You realize, Danny, that regardless, I'm going to go through with this divorce. Even if you tell me in five weeks that you're staying engaged and will marry, I will go through with it, and I will spend the rest of my life loving you and praying for your happiness.

"I will still live outside of my community here in the States. I will not go looking for a wife either. I'll accept the loneliness and isolation because all I want is you. I'll accept it as rightful punishment for having messed up so badly with you. I will love you till the day I die."

Never in her life had Daniella heard anyone express love for her in such depth. Appreciation of what she was to or for another soul. Even her fiancé had never put it quite that way. To describe the sudden epiphany as overwhelming was an understatement. Somehow, though, a bit of clear thinking crept through.

"Adam...your young son..."

"I'll likely lose custody of him. Once I make my choices known, I'll likely be forbidden to see him, as well, or allowed to see him only on rare occasion if I'm lucky."

"Why?"

"Because I'll be poison to him. I'd put bad ideas into his head and pull him away from the sanctity of the communities holy lives. As he grows, they'll convince him that I've turned my back on Judaism."

Something about that statement clinched it. Adam was even willing to accept the possible loss of a child. He was truly saying he wanted to choose a life with her, and Daniella believed every word. Despite the passing years, she still knew him. She knew he was 100 percent sincere. Certainly, if he was ready and willing to deal with custody issues, he must be dead serious. Wouldn't he need her love and support? Secretly, it was already there. Actually, it had never left. Still, she wanted to be wise about it all, and she was determined to make him work for the privilege of getting her back.

"The fact that you're here, saying this to me…" Daniella's sentence drifted off.

"Are you saying you forgive me, Danny?"

"Adam, I'm not saying anything for the time being. My greatest wish was always that you would love me."

Daniella choked a bit on her words but somehow muddled through the rest of her speech. "You hurt me deeply, but you're back and telling me that I'm all you ever really wanted. I need to really believe it. You need to make me believe it."

Adam leaned forward. His words came out in a whisper.

"I love you, Danny. I've always loved you."

Adam stood up from his chair as he continued.

"I know you need to believe it. I'll spend every day of the rest of my life making you believe."

"And if I take you back, you understand how miserable this will become? Are you ready to be spoon-fed misery?"

"Believe me, I understand. There will be people that will virtually hate me, hate us. They'll accuse you of breaking up my marriage. They'll accuse me of being a womanizer. I'm sure there will be people who will mock us because they'll hate what we represent. There will be people who will feign friendship and polite behavior because they'll be curious about us. I could go on with the list.

"An Orthodox man, hopefully, married to a Conservative female *hazzan*. Really, though, is it any different than when a Palestinian has married an Israeli? Or when a black person marries a white one or a Jew marries a Catholic. Is it? And despite it all, don't those couples persevere? Somehow, they persevere. I have to believe that they do so because *Hashem* wills it. Doesn't that seem to be the only explanation?

"I believe with all my heart that together we're mature enough to handle it all. We were both young and I was so foolish when we first met. Now, we've both grown. I hope to use the next five weeks to get my divorce underway. To make sure that both the Gvirzman and Goldfarb families understand my conviction to get it done."

The bar called raw emotion served Daniella a round of tears. It was useless to hold them back. She knew Adam was truthful. She could see that he wasn't playing a pathetic game, and that made it all so difficult. They were now two adults working overtime to constrain their feelings and desire to reach out to the other.

When Daniella finally walked Adam toward the front door of the synagogue, she had pink and swollen eyelids. The meeting between the two individuals had been intense, a fact that would be obvious to anyone who saw them. The teary eyes were immediately noticed by Adele as Daniella passed by the office door.

When Daniella turned around after watching Adam depart, she couldn't help but notice Adele's lips pressing tightly together on what would be the first of many faces that harbored intense curiosity. The receptionist was obviously suppressing a question to the nth degree, and Daniella knew she had to nip it in the bud then and there.

"Adele, you'll know soon enough, only not today... OK? He's a man going through a serious personal struggle." Daniella hated that she took a truth and presented it as a lie.

Daniella walked away before any further conversation could ensue. She did so knowing the gossip mill would start churning and there was nothing she could do to halt the production line. In the weeks ahead, she would receive mail at the synagogue, occasional phone calls, and even flowers. The letters with no return address. The calls from a different made-up name each time but the voice always the same. The flowers with no card attached. All the while, Daniella knew the source. All the while, Daniella was becoming a believer.

dam was presently on board his flight back to Belgium. He had *davened Mincha* and *Maariv* in the aisle as soon as it was permissible to stand. He didn't do so because of the pressure of feeling that if he didn't, God would be angry and strike down the plane. It was more about a private moment with the Lord to say thanks. Deciding that with all the time changes, it was best to recite both the afternoon and evening prayers, Adam, for the most part, was feeling very good and very connected.

He no longer cared about the fact that Daniella had the prestigious title of *Hazzan* Sobler. In fact, he was proud of her because of it. He would have shouted it out to the passengers if he hadn't thought they'd think him loony. She had always known so much about Judaism in general, and certainly she must know so much more now. And didn't he want a wife who was knowledgeable that way? He wondered why he had ever let his family convince him that it was a sin for a woman to want to connect to God in such a public way.

In fairness, Teme was learned too. Adam supposed that the difference resided in the application of said knowledge. Teme used it almost as if it were a weapon. In her efforts to keep the family true to Judaism, she chided and lectured those who veered from the accepted notions. She took the fun out of Judaism.

Daniella, on the other hand, used it as a learning tool that would excite others. She encouraged that excitement through song and involvement during services. He imagined her at the piano, encouraging boys and girls to join in on the fun. In Teme's world even something as simple as clapping hands and singing with the men during a joyous moment at the dinner table was considered reprehensible. How many times had Teme gotten up and removed herself from the room when the male guests in their home sang rousing choruses? She said it was not her place to be there with them. Worse, how many times had she looked at him as if he'd grown a third eye when he had suggested the possibility of her singing in mixed company?

Adam leaned back in his airplane seat to let his mind replay a loathsome scene he'd had with Teme. The scene would surely sour the bile in his gut, furthering his motivation to be courageous and ask for the divorce. He visualized his living room, with him standing in it. Teme was coming in from the room down the hall.

"Adam, I expect you to help our guests feel at home and especially to let them see that we are a family of good Jews, meticulous in every way, all the way down to our *kashruth*. I don't want them questioning anything."

"Teme, why would I try to make someone not feel at home? What could possibly motivate me to do such a thing? And why would I want to make a guest question the validity of how my household is run?"

"You have this bad habit of speaking your mind, Adam. Worse, in the name of discussion, you end up asking questions that to me, to my parents, to just about everyone, do no more than make it sound like you yourself question your Judaism."

"Doesn't questioning bring enlightenment? Isn't that how we learn and grow?"

Teme had a bad habit of changing the direction of a conversation the moment she started to feel cornered. There was never any ownership on her part. Adam surmised she did so simply because she was so steeped in what she had been taught. For all purposes, she was brainwashed. She simply didn't know anything beyond her own upbringing's concept of what being a Jewish woman meant.

"Adam, you have no idea how stupid you sound when you question the basics like keeping kosher, keeping the Sabbath, or even what I, your wife, should and shouldn't be doing in the household. Almost like you don't know anything. No husband of mine is going to embarrass me in front of guests with nonsensical discussion."

"Would you prefer that I let you do the talking?"

"What? So people will think my husband has no mind? Why can't you be more like my father?"

On and on it went. Stupid, foolish answers from Teme's mouth that had no bearing on anything. Adam had left that petty argument, and others like it, feeling exhausted and defeated. Teme never budged in her thinking. She never found enlightenment or movement into a different and more understanding plane. Almost as if she was stuck where she was. Adam laughed briefly. *She's the skip in the record that Daniella told me about. Teme plays her song over and over with no desire to finish the song that is her life.*

The one-sided discussions were only part of the emotional and mental anguish. Sadly, it trickled all the way down to the bedroom. Teme focused solely on her duty in the bedroom and not on the love that should be behind it all. It was clear to Adam that no true love for him resided in her heart. Maybe a fondness, perhaps. Certainly no more.

That broke his own heart in turn. If she did love him, surely she would intimate it with her hands, with her mouth, or even in a sound that might escape her lips and fall against his ear. That he could be stupid enough to think a pretty outside meant an automatic understanding of lovemaking or of life, well...

Teme would lie in their bed stiff as a corpse. He'd even caught her clutching her fists at her sides as he pumped away maddeningly. How many times did he just focus on finishing? How many times did his heart ache because all the stories he'd heard of pleasing one's wife, loving her, and being in such a holy place with her at that special moment, at one with God, didn't apply to him at all?

Worst of all, how many times did he conjure up Daniella's face when he made love to Teme? How many times in the middle of the sex act did he wonder what it would be like with Daniella? *Hashem* should forgive him. How many times did he recall her hands threading through his curls? And how many times did he imagine finishing the sex act with Daniella and stroking her hair in turn, brushing it away from her face as a way to say, "I love you?"

Didn't he always feel relief during the two weeks of reprieve he got each month? Those two weeks when Adam knew he did not have to be physical with Teme. He actually looked forward to that time. Teme's menses would occupy at least one week, and the other would comprise her period of *niddah*. Adam counted on those seven additional days to help him gear up once again for the torture of trying to love a person who didn't seem to love him in the way he had always hoped to be loved.

He dreaded those days when she returned from the *mikvah*, announcing that her ritual bath was completed and they needed to make children. She didn't come home lustful and wanting. She had a look of dread that silently said, "I know we need to make a family, so let's get this over with." What husband could enjoy making love to his wife while his eyes witnessed body language that said the entire act was distasteful?

One of the things that angered him the most was that she always insisted that sexual behavior was sinful. Touching for exploration...sinful. Kissing body parts... sinful. Sex should be swept under the rug so it could be hidden and forgotten. He was deeply angered that she had learned such a falsehood. He had come to believe that love encompassed all, even sexuality. It was holy, not sinful. It was a pleasure that God gave as a gift to humans. He could hear their last argument in his head.

"Teme, everyone who is in attendance at the *mikvah* knows you are coming home to have sex. How, then, is that hidden?"

"It's quietly understood. It's our duty as wives."

"So it's not hidden! The attendant knows. The ladies that might be there know. How is that any different than immodesty? She's standing there knowing you are coming home to me and I'm going to have intercourse with you."

"Adam, we don't talk about going home and having sex. It's totally improper to do so."

"Teme, would it really be so wrong for you to touch me so you can arouse me?"

Adam threw the comment out from left field. He was trying to catch her with her guard down so she would speak more from her heart and less from her head.

"Adam, that's disgusting. Why would you talk to me this way? I'm a good Jewish woman, and to act like an animal in order to make children is horrible."

Adam knew that she simply didn't know anything beyond what she had been taught since childhood. He knew that since their love was not strong enough, or rather was nonexistent, he would not be able to make her see things differently. That made the decision of asking Teme for a divorce an easy one. The reality of it, however, would be a disaster in the making.

Adam didn't want to keep rehearsing how the conversation might go, but it was as if he were compelled to do just that. Years of pent-up frustration came to a head and filled his mind in the quiet hours of the plane ride. He supposed it would help to prepare him for what would greet him once he landed in Belgium. He kept playing scenarios in his head and trying to gauge their outcomes. He reminded himself that there were many times in life when one needs to experience a living nightmare in order to wake up to the beauty of life on a new morning. He prayed for strength.

When Adam turned the key to the door, no wife ran to greet him. There was no son, either, but that was simply because it was very early in the morning and his little one was fast asleep. Flights to Europe always had Adam landing at the crack of dawn and returning to the house when the sun was first rising.

Adam could hear Teme clunking away in the kitchen. Quite likely, with the time of day being what it was, she was preparing some breakfast. She was dutiful that way because, as she herself told Adam, "A good wife will make sure her husband's needs are met in the proper order and at the proper time." Adam put his bag down in the hall and walked into the kitchen. Not surprisingly, it was not a hug or a kiss or any other kind gesture that greeted him. It was merely a half smile as Teme whisked away furiously, one hand on her pot handle and the other whirling round and round.

"Glad you're finally home, Adam. Three weeks straight this time. It's really tough not having my husband here, let alone a father for Shmuel." Teme paused and looked up from her preparations. She paused again, almost as if she actually contemplated showing some tenderness. A kiss on the cheek to say hello or an affectionate rub on the arm, asking if the flight was OK. Adam could see the struggle choreographing its dance across her features, and for the briefest moment, he was hopeful. He waited for words of, "Welcome home, I missed you," but ultimately, she chose her usual route.

"You're always away, Adam. It's just not fair."

"Teme, I'm in the diamond business. You knew how it would be from years of watching your father's own experiences."

"You're talking about my father. You're my husband, and that makes it different."

Adam thought but didn't say, *If it's different, you'd show me how much you missed me. You'd put that whisk down, make me feel welcomed to be home, and spend some quality time with me. You'd talk to me, for goodness' sake, and without a lecture.*

Apparently oblivious to anything Adam might be feeling, Teme continued her little speech.

"If I didn't know any better, I'd say your trips to the States have gotten longer and longer. People are starting to ask me why you're gone more than you're home. And I don't know what to tell them." She paused again and snickered.

"I know what they're implying. That you don't want to be here. Your diamonds are more precious to you than our family or our life here. I really resent the position you keep putting me in, Adam."

Teme used a mocking tone and changed the pitch of her voice. "*Why isn't he here for Shabbat, Teme? Why wasn't he here on the High Holidays? Couldn't he have made other arrangements? Who doesn't come home for the High Holidays? Who, Adam? Can you tell me that?*"

She changed her tone once more as she echoed the summation she had received from her mother after her miscarriage. "*He's displeased God so much that you, my poor Teme, had to suffer for it by losing the baby.*" Teme frowned at Adam. "It's so embarrassing, and you don't seem to care that it is."

Adam hadn't been sure how he'd ask for the divorce, but Teme had just made it easy. It was always about her. It was always about the community. It was never about them as a holy couple. With his son asleep, he also had the upper hand because she wouldn't raise her voice to a screaming level. Heaven forbid that Shmuel be disturbed or, better yet, that she let her son hear any discourse between them. Time was of the essence, then, and it was clear that the time was now.

"Teme, I want a divorce."

Teme looked at Adam as if she suddenly didn't understand the language coming out of his mouth. She dropped her whisk onto the counter and replied, "What?"

"You heard me. I want a divorce. I don't love you, and you certainly don't love me. You're not happy, and frankly, I'm miserable. I have no pleasure in being married to you."

Teme could have begged. She could have cried. Teme sought justification.

"What do you mean, I'm not happy? Look at our beautiful apartment. It's filled with everything a family could want. We have a beautiful son who is hopefully the beginning of many more to come. Then our beautiful home would be filled with the sounds of children. I'm respected. I've become a true *Eshet Chayil*, a true woman of valor. I'm a content *balabusta,* running my home efficiently and like clockwork."

"Yes, Teme, you're exactly what you've always wanted to be, but what about me?"

"What about you, Adam?"

"Where am I in the little speech you just gave?"

"You're the father of my child. You're the provider who has afforded me these wonderful things. You're my husband."

"Do you love me, Teme, or do you love me for what I bring you?"

And there it was. The same song and dance Teme did whenever she felt cornered or became aware that she had been caught in some type of truth that she herself recognized but wouldn't admit. She redirected the conversation.

"Adam, everything I learned from my parents, my schooling, my whole way of life about what is good and right, that's what I have now. You gave that to me."

Adam laughed derisively. "Oh, and that's love?"

Teme couldn't believe she had just heard that question come out of Adam's mouth. In her world, it *was* love. That Adam could ask such a foolish question was ridiculous. If one fulfilled the obligations demanded of that person, then in essence, one was fulfilled. Teme was fulfilled. She was fulfilled because she was a good Jewess. She did what her community expected of her. She did what her family had raised her to do, and most important, she did what God expected of her. It was what she herself wanted to do and yearned for.

If one was content, then one was experiencing love. Perhaps not the silly notion of romantic love. She didn't have the need for such piffle. She knew that God didn't either. God expected so much more. To Teme's way of thinking, she was attaining a far more important love. Love of God. Pleasing God. Doing what was right in God's eyes. She had no hesitation in answering.

"Of course it is. You're the one who doesn't know what real love is all about. If you did, you'd stop questioning what *Hashem* asks of us and just do it."

Teme needed to drive her point further. "How many times have I had to redirect you because you say or do something that questions the very foundation of who and what we are? You do that in front of family and friends. You do that in front of our son, for goodness' sake. He's learning every day, and make no mistake that he'll learn to do that from you. That's just what I need! A son who won't be a good, observant Jew because his father is making him believe he has the right to question his very foundation."

Yet another conversation was going around in circles, never budging from the spot where it began. Never advancing to any level of higher understanding or even a simple compromise. Adam decided to be direct.

"Teme, you have never known what is in my heart because you have chosen from day one not to reside there. If you did, you'd know how much I love my Judaism... love it! Do you hear me? And how much I want to do what is right in God's eyes. It's God's job to see into my soul and decide my merit. Not yours. You have no right to imply that I am not a good person simply because I don't think like you do about our Judaism. I need to be my own kind of Jew, and I can't, being married to you. I need to be divorced from you!"

Teme was adept at picking up the unspoken subtleties when words came out of her husband's mouth. She knew his body language. She knew his style when speaking. She could see beyond the simply stated fact and hear a completely different sentence in her head. In great part, it was the driving force behind many of the hurtful things she said to him. Adam had a mind of his own and it frightened her. Now however, there was another fear that crept into her mind.

"Is there another woman?"

Adam wasn't guilty of adultery, so there was no shame in giving an answer. It never occurred to him that his answer would give Teme fuel for fodder. That she would take his simple words and use them against him to achieve the best possible circumstance in a divorce.

"There was one once, long ago, before we were married. This isn't about her…" Adam trailed off.

Like Pharaoh's heart, Teme's was being hardened to the point where justice was begging for the upper hand but doing so in the form of revenge.

"You're hoping she'll be a part of your life. You want to be free of me so you can pursue this woman. I can see it in your eyes. Who is this miserable woman who has done this to my marriage?"

"No one has done anything to your marriage, Teme. Our marriage was wrong from the get-go. Besides, you couldn't possibly know her. She's from my long-ago past. My very long-ago past. And this is not about her, anyway. It's about you, Teme. It's about the fact that you have not made me feel complete or content since day one. You're the reason I want a divorce."

"You're a miserable excuse for a man, Adam."

Adam was a kind man. He could be direct and not shoot verbal daggers as Teme was doing. Nonetheless, she had just crossed a line. She tended to be mean when she was afraid. If she couldn't come out on top, at least she could be hurtful. That was her style. It was her way to make Adam feel as miserable as she. The cornered animal striking out to hurt. The comment was as demeaning as she apparently hoped, and Adam was more than incensed by the cruelty of Teme's words. This time, however, he would surprise her with a comeback. This time, he would put her in her place.

"And you, Teme, are a beautiful package, but when you open the box, it's empty. Completely and totally empty. You fool everyone into thinking you are a precious gift when in fact you're just an empty shell. You're as shallow as they come. You have no substance or worth in any single sentence you utter because everything you say is just rote. No mind of your own. You do only what you've been taught to do."

Even Adam was keenly aware of the extreme cruelty of his words. He softened a bit in an effort to lessen the pain of his verbal onslaught. He didn't want to stoop to her level by continuing to rant with accusatory statements.

"If only you'd realize how wonderful you'd feel if you allowed yourself to be filled with what really matters in life, and I don't mean following all the rules. The potential for a whole new Teme to emerge would come stumbling through."

"I am filled with what really matters. My good home matters. My good name matters. My good manners matter. Your silly notion of what Judaism is or could be for us is what's ruined this marriage. That and some pathetic woman from your yesteryear. And to allow thoughts of her to creep into your brain to the point of making you leave…"

Teme was a cornered bird protecting her nest and her little one inside. She was pecking away at the brutal beast attempting to destroy her very existence.

"Your notions, your ideas, they're a poison. It's like they are a cake you've been baking, and now asking for a divorce is the icing. What is that phrase? You're adding insult to injury. You are prepared to completely destroy my reputation by making me a divorced woman. Don't you realize what you are doing to us? Don't you realize how a divorce will disgrace my family's good name? Adam, how can you be so heartless?"

"Teme, do you hear yourself? Not once have you begged me, 'Adam, don't go. I love you.' It's always about the community for you. It's always about the rules."

"Get out of my house, Adam. Pack your bags and get out. It's you who has made life miserable. You and not me. You've questioned a perfect world and done your best to point out its imperfections. I won't have you ruining my good home any longer."

Adam simply turned and left the kitchen, which only served to irk Teme further. She needed to come out winning. He was destroying her life and pulling it right out from under her, almost as if he pulled an imaginary rug from under her feet. She needed to see that she had hurt Adam to the core. She let the words spill out of her mouth without any hesitation.

"Don't you dare wake Shmuel. Let him sleep in peace. Besides, he hardly sees you anyway, with all that constant travel. He hardly knows you're even his father."

Teme made a vicious snort. "He'll hardly miss you at all, Adam. In fact, he'll probably not even know who you are once you're gone. And don't doubt it, Adam. He'll be mine and not yours! I'll see to it! I'll keep him protected from your evil thoughts. Thoughts that would only doom him as well. Everyone will back me on that too. I'll see to it."

Adam would not give Teme the satisfaction of seeing that she had struck a chord. She would not see the wince of pain that halted his steps for the briefest of moments or the anguish in his eyes. His son. His innocent, precious son. In Adam's fantasy world, he envisioned teaching his son to be a good soul not only in God's eyes but to an entire world.

Adam's reality was a wife who would have scrutinized each lesson Adam taught in the home. Even worse, she would have corrected what he taught to his children, insisting that his lesson would not find favor with their rabbi or the community. With all his heart, Adam knew he had already lost his son. The moment word got out that he wanted a divorce, Teme would see to it that he suffered the consequences of his decision.

How many times had Adam heard the horror stories of husbands who would not give their wife the proper Jewish divorce document called a *get*? Who were vindictive, and as a result, religiously speaking the woman remained married even if she was civilly divorced. She'd be a hapless soul unable to find a new provider to take care of her and her children. She'd be unable to work, too, because she had spent years as a housewife and lacked any other skills.

Well, what about when the shoe was on the other foot? Teme would victimize him and punish him in the best way she knew how, simply for having the audacity to divorce her and ruin the status of her family and the reputation they had in the community. She'd agree to the divorce just for the pleasure of punishing him via their son. The rest of the world would know her plight and dote on her so she could forge ahead.

Adam knew it was far worse than that. The community would protect her and little Shmuel because they were faithful members of the fold. She might be the venom that started the poisoning, but everyone else in Adam's Hasidic world would add to it without any consideration. They would all conclude that he was so tainted by the outside world that he was a complete danger to their way of life.

Adam packed a small suitcase and peered into Shmuel's room before walking back toward the kitchen. He stood in the doorway for what seemed like an eternity and allowed tears to streak his cheeks. His precious son. His beautiful young man who was already showing signs of a mop-top curlicue head of hair and a smile that could melt a frozen heart. He wanted to kiss his son but knew that if he touched Shmuel, he'd lose all control.

It took all his strength to walk back to the kitchen, suitcase in hand. He knew Teme could see he was crying. She was crying too. He put the suitcase down on the floor and spoke in one last attempt to change the inevitable. It was his duty as a husband to at least try.

"Please, Teme, won't you consider trying to be more open about things? Maybe come with me and live a whole new life. We could share custody of Shmuel, and you'd be able to start anew as a single woman without the bonds of this place holding you back."

Adam could see it in her body movement. The briefest of moments when she actually considered what he said. It was almost as if she was struggling to get something out from within herself. It left as quickly as it came, and she merely said, "You know where the door is, Adam. You don't belong here."

The nightmare had begun, and it would be a long time before Adam awoke.

The synagogue ladies had come in for their monthly meeting. Benny watched them in the same way he usually did but noticed that this time, the meeting was short. They were discussing a personal matter in lieu of planning synagogue functions. At least that seemed to be the case. He looked at Marcia Sobler. She appeared agitated, and her tone conveyed annoyance. Her comments were loud enough that Benny could catch snippets of each curt sentence. He surmised that somehow it all had something to do with Daniella and Adam.

Benny wanted to try to catch at least a few full sentences. He walked by the table several times, feigning concern for other patrons in the restaurant. It was all he could do to appear unfazed by the goings-on in the booth, because the gathered information overwhelmed him. It seemed to equally overwhelm Marcia Sobler's friends, who were listening intently to every word Marcia shared. Daniella had broken her engagement.

Daniella was planning to get back together with that Hasidic man from years ago. She was serious about him and was planning marriage.

Benny could have won an Academy Award, and likely for best actor, when the group came to the register to pay for their meal. He was completely stone faced and quiet, asking no more than if everything had been OK with their dinners. He made a point not to look Marcia in the eyes.

Benny had kept all of Daniella's secrets intact from the moment she began to share them in confidence. All those years, and never once did a comment from Benny let Marcia know he was privy to her family's personal life. It made perfect sense that she would continue to remain unaware of that fact as long as Benny kept his cool.

As far as Benny's patrons were concerned, he was a nice man who was a good boss and, in his own way, a good friend to many. Certainly he couldn't possibly know of their lives outside the glass doors of the establishment. So it would be of no consequence to speak about personal affairs at the Daily when in the confines of a booth. Besides, didn't everyone do that? Didn't all people share gossip when they dined together? Marcia Sobler never would have thought that Benny knew anything about Daniella's personal life at all.

It was all Benny could do to stay calm. Thoughts were reeling inside Benny's head. Had she really broken her engagement? Was she really pursuing Adam? For now at least, he would have to keep his concerns to himself. As fate would have it, he would not hear from Daniella for several days. He feigned complete ignorance of the matter and did his best to sound shocked as she shared her story.

He certainly wouldn't let Daniella know that her mother was yapping her frustrations to her friends, sharing personal family matters in the form of idle gossip. The last thing Daniella needed was further hurt. Benny continued to listen, but ultimately, his feigning turned to true surprise as she divulged the reason behind her call.

"Benny, Adam has shared his news with his parents. They are so angered and frustrated by his decision that they are refusing to let him stay in the house. Well, I think Adam's mother might have relented if only his father... well, there is just no reasoning with either of them, presently. They're committed to the idea that if they go along with Adam, they will look lessened in the eyes of their community both at home and abroad."

"Danny, that's so sad. A parent turning their back." Benny drifted into his memories for a moment, remembering his parents' doting and constancy. He had relied on their love to keep him safe. The thought served to anger him further. "Shame on them. So what will Adam do? Where will he go?"

"Well, that's why I'm calling. Benny..." Daniella paused, apparently to muster courage.

"This is all very ironic, because I know I've asked you to let Adam and me figure things out for ourselves and I'm about to do the opposite."

"Go ahead, Danny."

"You've been more than a friend to me through the years. You've been like a favorite uncle or a beloved grandfather. Take your pick. The sentiment's the same. You're practically my guardian angel."

"Danny, that makes me very happy to hear. What is it you're looking for from me?"

"I have a huge favor to ask."

"What is it?"

"Adam is in a hotel at the moment. He can only afford that for so long before the tab will get too expensive. Can he stop by the Daily and maybe, just maybe, you'll let him use the spare office in the back as a place to sleep? He won't mind that it's filled with storage boxes. He really only needs a bed."

"And when he needs a shower? Or when the staff needs to dig out a box of toilet-paper rolls at eleven o'clock at night? What then, Danny?"

"I know, I know. It's just that you're the only safe haven I know of at the moment. My parents will eventually come around; I just know they will. But this is too raw for them right now. They need time to adjust, and that means no married Orthodox man in their house trying to get a divorce and get their daughter as well.

"And you know I can't have him here at my apartment. Not while he's still married. Even when he's not married, it can't happen. Not until he's married to me. Never mind that it's wrong in our own minds. His wife would use it as further proof that he's gone off the deep end. That he's a danger because he's turning his back on everything that is moral and sane."

Benny once again entered his yesteryear bubble. Visions of his mother and father being pulled apart from each other passed through his mind. He had no clue how they had met their end. And even though he didn't witness the actual event, he could feel the pain of the scene that he had painted for himself. His mother screaming and begging with her arms out toward her beloved husband; his father's eyes speaking volumes to her as each was pulled in a different direction.

Benny couldn't even understand why events surrounding Daniella's life seemed to do this to him from time to time. She was from another generation and certainly another time. Perhaps at some point he'd figure out why she brought him to thoughts of his mother, beyond the fact that she had a similar look. For now, the concern was and should be for Daniella and even Adam. That was all that mattered. Benny decided to let his thoughts go, and he concluded that Daniella had to come out winning no matter what. He'd do whatever he could to help ensure her happiness.

Benny was already thinking about the spare rooms in his home. No children lived in them. His girls were grown and on their own. Each of their rooms was a guest room now. Rose would understand. He'd make clear that they were simply acting as a boarding house. He'd downplay the possibility of personal involvement in the youngsters' matters or the fact that it might put Rose and him in a peculiar situation. They were, after all, providing shelter to a Hasidic runaway.

"Tell Adam to stop by Thursday afternoon, and I'll talk to him. We'll take it from there. See how it goes. Better that you aren't some sort of middleman relaying messages back and forth between us, Danny. Better that I talk to him myself."

"Benny, *Hashem* should bless you for the countless times you've been kind. I don't know what to say."

"Don't say anything, Danny. Let's see how this all works out first."

It was two days later when Adam walked through the restaurant doors. Benny could see the sorrowful look on his face and the stress etched into his unsmiling cheeks. It broke his heart.

"I'd like to say how excited I am to see you, but instead I'm going to ask, are you OK, Adam?"

"Hi, Benny. Nice to see you again."

Adam attempted a half smile and reached out to shake hands. He continued to speak as the grasp was cinched tight.

"I'm just tired, Benny, that's all. Tired and overwhelmed."

"Well, young man, you know the drill. Tea and cookies in the back room, and you can tell me what's on your mind."

"Are you sure you don't mind?"

"If I did, I would never have invited you in the first place."

"*Hashem* bless you, Benny, and protect your good name. That you would do this…"

Benny put his hand up in the classic halt position. "Adam, please, let it go, and let's just sit and talk."

Benny would never get into the reasons he would do this, or any other thing, for that matter. He did things simply because they needed to be done. For him, this was about justice. Justice for Jews everywhere. Two Jews were in love and wanted to live life together in happiness and without fear. The world should leave them alone.

As Adam shared the details of his divorce situation and his family's reaction to it, Benny became more and more incensed. There was no question now. Adam would stay in his home and get his life in order so that he could be with Daniella. Benny would do his best to take a backseat and let time and patience steer the two lives. It would mean that the Soblers would now come to learn that he was involved in Daniella's life. He'd have to accept that too, come what may.

"We'll expect you tomorrow before sunset. You'll share a quiet *Shabbat* with us. What you do after *Shabbat*...well, what will you do, Adam? You implied that your fellow diamond dealers may not hold you in the same esteem, and not because of the divorce as much as your decision to live outside the Orthodox communities."

"I have some ideas and, in particular, want to speak with a gentleman in the city that has spoken to me about opening a jewelry store in Epson County. Each time I stop in with diamonds, he brings it up. Almost as if he's hinting that he'd like someone like me to manage his new store. It's a huge compliment, really. And if it's really so, I mean, that he has this in mind, well, I think I'd be good at running a jewelry business. I certainly know the products."

"Are you implying that you'll give up all the travel?"

"Benny, I love the diamond business, don't get me wrong. I just don't think it would be a good idea to be in Antwerp making deals and knowing that Teme's father could appear at any moment. The animosity is already setting in. It will only get worse over time. I've shamed him by implying that his daughter makes me feel miserable. And something else, Benny. Something I didn't even realize until now...I looked forward to the travel so I could get away from her."

"Adam, such a mess."

"It won't be any worse than what it's always been."

"Don't be so sure. You're going to need all the help you can get. Is there anyone else you can turn to?"

"Not really. No, that's not right. I think my sister Aviva will be a bit more understanding than everyone else. I'm pretty sure she'll keep some contact with me, or at least try to. She'll certainly be pressured by everyone else to not contact me at all. I do plan to contact Rabbi Simon at the seminary. He was kind to me these past two years, sitting and talking with me about issues that virtually weighted my shoulders. I'm sure he'd be willing to chat again, especially if I need the support."

"So tell me, Adam. Has this even started? What's involved here, and how long will it take you to be divorced?"

"Believe you me, it's started."

With that, Adam shared how complicated the divorce process was. He had to abide not only by Jewish law but by Belgian law as well. He would not be considered divorced in the eyes of his fellow Jews unless the proper documentation was prepared, reviewed, and carried out in the correct manner. Even if the Belgium divorce went through first, he'd be considered married as long as the Jewish divorce remained undone.

At least the rabbis involved in the process were more concerned about the exactness of their work in creating a kosher *get* than about their personal feelings regarding the matter. In reality, their personal feelings were not favorable at all. If Adam's concerns had centered merely on displeasure with Teme, they would have been more accepting. Adam's decision to stray from the fold distressed the rabbinical court who presided over the matter, especially in light of the fact that he and Teme had a young son to educate in the ways of Hasidism.

As Benny listened to the details, he gave an occasional tsk-tsk or shake of the head. What God hath brought together, let no man put asunder. Hadn't he heard a phrase that went something like that? Probably in some movie or TV program that had a wedding scene in it. Maybe in a scene about a church wedding. In any case, it was obvious that every religion took marriage to heart. A sacred union falling apart was nothing less than a heartbreaker.

Well, that was all well and good if the marriage held at least one person who was in love with the other. This case involved two people who didn't love each other at all. People could be married in seconds, but divorce… divorce extended suffering for the sake of keeping marriage in the lofty realm that was supposed to be holy. Nonsense as far as Benny was concerned. If the people didn't love each other, well…

Notions of God having created the institution of marriage in the first place weren't exactly true either. At least Benny thought that to be the case. He remembered learning how the concept of marriage had developed… now when was it? Back in the Middle Ages or some such time back then. He seemed to recall society had created it for the sake of maintaining property rights or something like that. Prior to that, marriage had been a simple matter of agreeing to cohabitate.

Benny shook his head as if chiding himself for getting the facts wrong. Even in biblical times, a ring had been the token of betrothal. The Bible was very clear that couples were husband and wife after a ring exchange or property exchange. In essence, then, that was marriage.

In fact, the mere idea of two people in a partnership throughout their lives was the very pinnacle of holiness, and Benny knew he was dead wrong to think otherwise.

Adam had finished talking and indicated he was ready to leave. As he shook Benny's hand and said his repeated thank yous, Benny's thoughts drifted elsewhere. He thought about his Rose. His wonderful, loving, adorable Rose. Such a treasure. Such a good wife. The loving thoughts made Benny feel somewhat angry toward Adam as he stood and shook hands with him. He even made a disgusted grimace as he watched the retreating figure.

What had Adam been thinking back then? He went into his marriage with eyes open. He could have been brave and pursued Daniella from the get-go, but he didn't. He chose the destiny he currently resided in, so he had no one to blame but himself! Benny thought about it some more, and then his thoughts softened.

He was being incredibly unfair, and he knew it. Wasn't it just last week that he had overheard that youngster in the restaurant? The one who'd had the audacity to say that he was embarrassed to be a Jew sometimes because Jews allowed themselves to be herded like cattle to their doom by the Nazis.

Benny had overheard the boy say it to his friends as he passed their booth. Such an ignorant comment, and from the mouth of a Jew, no less! It didn't matter to Benny that the kid was likely no more than fifteen. Benny couldn't control himself as he butted in on the conversation.

"When you have brutal forces all about you, cornering you into decisions you don't want to make, literally stripping you of your humanity and holding a gun to your head, ready to pull the trigger at any moment, what then? They insist you do everything they say or be shot on the spot. Those people were brave, young man. Brave, you hear me? Every last one of them. Brave for trying their best to carry on in the face of evil. You should be ashamed of yourself.

"Try to imagine just for one moment that you're sitting here and some soldier comes barging into the restaurant, sees you, and grabs you by the collar. He drags you out and says you're a worthless excuse for a human being. To amuse himself he shoots you in the leg and then insists you try to walk. All he does is laugh while you suffer. You know who should be embarrassed? Every last person who let it go on and on! Every nation that ignored the plight of others.

"You know what? You should go home. Go home and learn your history."

Benny had walked away infuriated, leaving a truly embarrassed young man in the booth. His friends, equally quiet. Benny had thought to himself that day, *Sure, go home and tell your mother and father how I yelled at you. Tell them what I said. Believe you me, they'll tell you I'm right.*

Benny would never in his wildest dreams equate anything the Jewish people did with the behavior of a Nazi. But wasn't it true that Adam, too, had been pressured in a way he didn't know how to deal with? Under the circumstances, hadn't Adam taken what he thought was the best course?

Benny raised his hand to his forehead and gave it a light slap. He was crazy for thinking anything about Nazis at all or comparing them with anything decent in life.

Nazis are a portion of hell. Pure evil defecated onto life by a madman. Nothing more than shit. Defecated shit...Dear God, forgive me. Forgive me for even trying to compare them with anything in life. Why did he always do that? Why couldn't he control those thoughts when they surfaced?

Benny came out front to let Nate know he'd be staying in the back for a while. He wanted time alone to think about everything Adam had shared, and in a more thoughtful and productive way than focusing on pigs who called themselves people. He wanted to review the situation and think about the ramifications. He'd do so over his lunch, in peace and quiet, and in darkness.

"Nate, I'm going to hang in the back for a while. A late lunch break. OK with you?"

"No problem, Benny. It's quiet at the moment. Go enjoy your lunch."

Benny sat in the stillness of the darkened back room, biting off bits of sandwich in his half-dazed state. He replayed his conversation with Adam in the quiet of his mind and shook his head over the complicated matters involved. It was bad enough to seek divorce in the civil world. To have to attain it twice...

For what was likely the thousandth time, Benny became irate with the human race. Humans that weren't human at all. Humans that made life more complicated than necessary and certainly more painful. Humans that could dish it out but couldn't take it. What was it with people? Why would people begin to think for even a moment that their way was the only right way?

Benny had always felt that Messiah wasn't some glorious being heralded in by the prophet Elijah. For Benny, Messiah was people. Every single one of us in the human race. Once we all understood, once we acted the way humans should act, the concept of Messiah would already be in place. That would be when God would create a messianic age. Then and no sooner.

Well, it would take one person at a time on the road to get there. Benny would be one of those people. He would be brave and do what was right. God had brought the two youngsters back together. God was talking, saying they were meant to be a couple. Benny, on the other hand, was listening. He would obey the Almighty. He would let the good Lord puppeteer him in whatever way was needed.

Hashem. My rock in whom there is no flaw.

ccording to Jewish law, there are very precise requirements for a kosher *get*. It must be written by a *sofer* who has received explicit instruction regarding the document's preparation. This expert scribe inks the document into twelve lines of Aramaic lettering. Twelve happens to be the numerical value of the word *get*, and it has been a long-standing tradition to continue using Aramaic language for the text. The phrasing is not unlike that of a civil divorce document. Two kosher witnesses, meaning they must be fit and proper in the eyes of the Jewish court, will sign underneath the twelve written lines.

The document must be freshly penned. It can't be predated. It must have no blank spaces and no erasures. The presiding *Beth Din*, which is the traditional Jewish court of law, must accept its physical appearance. The rabbis who sit on this esteemed court are considered experts in divorce matters. Every one of them is a man.

Benny didn't know much about the process until Adam shared the information, and he was certainly unsure if Sephardic tradition followed suit in their own divorce proceedings. He was greatly relieved, however, to learn that at least the Ashkenazim give both the man and woman the right to consent to the divorce even though it's not mandated.

Adam told Benny that if the husband refused consent, *heter meah rabbanim* would come into play. It would be as if one hundred rabbis confronted the man, urging him to give the wife the divorce and doing whatever seemed necessary to get him to comply. Benny could just imagine the hapless woman, possibly abused, dealing with an alcoholic husband, or goodness knows what, praying to be released from the vindictiveness of her husband's refusal if such were the case.

In Teme's case, the shoe was practically on the other foot. Adam was more than willing to sign divorce papers as soon as possible. Teme milked the drama, already playing the hapless victim, brutalized by her husband's need to be less observant. His misguided ways were shaming her and her son. That was what she had told her family. His refusal to relent and become ultra-Orthodox without question were affecting the entire community. In reality, Teme was cleverly designing a mountain out of a mole hill because she was deeply hurt.

Adam had told Benny he had no doubt that she'd be remarried in no time after the divorce. He was sure she would find a very *frum* man so she could continue to prove that Adam's waywardness was sinful and a danger to their son. She'd remarry because of her conviction that marriage was her destiny as a woman.

As to little Shmuel, Adam would have to leave custody to her. Teme was arguing that somehow Adam's views and ideas would taint the thinking of their son's young mind. Everyone in the community, whether family or not, was already convinced of the idea that this was so and that Shmuel needed protection from straying. There was already talk of needing to supervise visits if Adam insisted on seeing Shmuel, because God forbid, Adam would put the wrong ideas into his head. The boy was only two, practically a baby, but he'd start to learn soon enough. If Adam was insistent, Teme would see to it that Shmuel was hidden away, and Adam's attempts would be in vain.

It broke Adam's heart, and the pain would last a lifetime, but it was better that he left Shmuel to the community and to his mother. It would insure that, at least on some level, he and Teme would maintain *shalom bayit*, peace in the home. And in a real way, hadn't he already lost his son? He was gone so often that heaven only knew what food for thought Teme fed Shmuel whenever he was away.

It amazed Benny that, despite the intricacies of a divorce settlement, a simple piece of paper could change one's marital status. It took minutes to make a marriage, and despite any years of turmoil to get the divorce, once the paper was written and handed over, within seconds a person could be single once more. All from the mere exchange of paper. Astounding!

The simple act of the husband giving the divorce document to his wife in the presence of the *Beth Din* would finalize the Jewish divorce. Once that occurred, the document would be cut by the supervising rabbi and kept in the *Beth Din's* files. Because they needed to abide by civil divorce laws as well, the *Beth Din* would keep the pieces until the civil divorce was finalized. Once proof of that was obtained, each partner would receive his or her piece of the *get*. This would indicate that the *get* was not only given but accepted. Both individuals would be free to remarry.

Benny thought to himself about how wonderful it would be if Adam and Daniella could marry as soon as they had the *get* in hand. The process was straightforward and quick as long as both parties consented, and that would be the case for Teme and Adam. It was the civil divorce that would muck up the process for his two youngsters.

Belgium had specific laws regarding divorce, same as any other country. There were two types, by either specific grounds or mutual agreement, and neither way adhered to Jewish law. Since divorce changed the status of each individual, it was considered a matter of public order, and therefore, divorce must be declared by a judicial decision outside the context of religion.

Belgium courts often used the grounds of physical and mental cruelty, and custody of the children often went to the mother. This was an egg in Teme's basket. She would claim emotional stress. She would claim that Adam's divergence from traditional thinking had strained the marriage to the brink of extinction.

The bottom line, however, was that they mutually agreed. And according to the law, they met the requirements for their divorce. They were both at least twenty years old, and their marriage contract was at least two years old before the filing of the petition.

Adam told Benny that the only area that might be murky was that they needed to have a de facto separation of at least two years. The two years seemed like an eternity to Adam. He had hired a lawyer in the hopes of proving that his many weeks of travel time could apply to this requirement. It would lessen the time frame involved in his wait to be with Daniella.

All so complicated. All so sad. This was the first time Benny knew of anyone going through a divorce. He thought of Rose and of how content they were. He thought of the partnership they had in raising their girls together. They had waged no wars and made no efforts to control each other. And Benny knew the reason why. Theirs was a marriage based in love. Plain and simple.

Adam had told Benny that he'd loved Daniella from day one. He had just been scared. For Benny, it meant that their marriage would have the right basis. It only needed a chance. Benny got up from the table, empty sandwich plate in one hand, glass in the other, fully committed to the idea of being God's angel here on earth.

A future mother and father together, to raise children in love, happiness, and most important, peace. Benny smiled as he stood in the dark of the back room. He, a momentary angel. He, helping God to create a future generation of Jews. God working in a very mysterious way but still speaking clearly to Benny.

Baruch atah Adonai, shomayah tefilla. Blessed is God, who listens to prayer.

"Adam, I'm trying to appeal to your sensibility." Aaron Gvirzman had requested a meeting with his son-in-law in a last-ditch effort to fix the shameful situation that had developed between his daughter and the young man before him. His son-in-law was a loose cannon, ready to explode at a moment's notice. Surely, there had to be some semblance of a chance that one could reason with him. The elder Gvirzman continued.

"I want to help you, Adam."

"I understand you're trying to help me, but nothing you can say will change any of the facts. I want a divorce. I am completely unhappy. I'm miserable."

"I'll have Bina talk with Teme. People can change. Bina will help Teme. You'll see."

Aaron Gvirzman still thought he wanted to help his son-in-law. He was hoping to cure his son-in-law, although of what, he couldn't be sure. He felt pity in his heart for the wandering soul who was so obviously lost. His daughter came first, though. Always, she would come first. He would do nothing less than fight for the integrity of his daughter, even at the cost of hardening his heart toward Adam. At that moment, Aaron Gvirzman was hardly aware of the thought that shot through Adam's mind.

You can't bring life to a dead twig. "It's not just about Teme. It's about our whole way of life as a couple. I feel like I'm suffocating."

"What, suffocating? We're the chosen ones, Adam. We have the joy of the Almighty in everything we do, every moment of our lives. You and Teme can fulfill *Hashem's* will together. How is that suffocating? I don't understand."

How could Adam explain? Certainly, he could not offend his father-in-law by implying that Teme sucked the life out of every obligation they had as Jews. That she never tried to think for herself, whether from her heart or her mind. That she was unable to consider that life held endless possibilities. That she exhibited no tenderness for Adam, never offered a loving touch as a mere thank you for being a good husband. That she was no more than a pretty package that he viewed as an empty box inside.

The heart of the matter, the very worst of things, was that her only concern was perfection. Teme cared only for being correct in the eyes of her little world. She insisted upon carrying out every Jewish law to the nth degree. She saw no room for questioning, ever. For Adam, that was no way to live.

The reality was that they were just two very different types of people. Two people who never should have

married in the first place. Adam had built up resent-
ment...that everyone was so busy trying to marry off
children, no one took the time to really consider the
wants and needs of the people involved. Whether she
admitted it or not, Teme, too, was unfulfilled.

How could he make his father-in-law understand that
for him, it was like being a robot that just did what it was
told? He could no longer live in the rigid context of his
upbringing. How could he explain that true happiness as a
Jew did not come from living life in what he now believed
was the lifestyle of a quasi-cult? At least not for him.

Adam knew that many of his fellow Hasids were
happy and content in the lives they had. More so, that
they were kind, loving, and mindful of others, and that
included their own spouses. That none of them would
ever equate their lifestyle with cultish fanaticism. The
problem wasn't even about any Hasids as individuals.
Each of them should be judged on his or her own merit.
No, it was simply about Adam. Adam needed to break
free from the mold. He needed to expand like loosened
gelatin when it's tapped out of the confined space of the
mold that once held it.

"Teme and I have different views on everything. It's
a big world out there. You know that. You've traveled far
and wide, same as me. Teme is cloistered and accepts her
communal world as the only world. She has said as much
to me. She says everyone else is wrong about everything.
How can she possibly know that without ever having experienced the bigger world?"

"She's a proud Jew, and I'm proud of her for being
so. She knows the outside world will destroy her in a
heartbeat."

"Because she was taught that, not because it's true! Look, I know you are proud of her, and I also know that she should be happy in her Judaism with someone who feels the same as she, but that's not me! It's just not me. I'm a proud Jew that happens to question everything about Hasidism."

Adam decided to throw imaginary lighter fluid onto the smoking embers. He needed the elder Gvirzman to really understand this was serious and it was happening. And at this point, Adam had nothing to lose.

"Maybe it's not such a sin to let women have equal rights. Why can't women have clerical roles? Why can't they pray publicly in the presence of men? Why do they have to keep their heads covered with wigs and hats when they still look just as lovely? Why don't the same rules apply to men?

"Maybe it's not such a sin to interact with non-Jews on a regular basis. Maybe we can learn to be better Jews by caring for our neighbors beyond those who live down the street from us. Why do we think we're above the laws that apply to the towns we live in? How can we be so elitist?

"Even the mundane things pique my curiosity. Electricity, for example. Isn't the current always there? Isn't using electricity merely the act of pushing a lever up or down, almost as if I stuck my hand in the line of the current and that temporarily stopped the flow of the electricity? So, why do we forbid the use of electricity on the Sabbath? I'm not the one kindling any kind of flame, creating the electricity myself. It exists there all the time.

"These are only a few of the questions I have and struggle with every day. I want to explore them. Every time I try to, Teme or someone in this community or my community back in the States tries to talk me out of it. They do no more than insist that I'm treading in dangerous waters and that the community is God's example of what is expected and right. That God will strike me down if I leave.

"And all of you threaten me with excommunication and how sad I'd be if I had none of you to depend on or to turn to. All of you have the nerve to assume that God himself is angry with me for thinking these things. Who are you, to make such a judgment? Who are you to presume for even one moment that you know God's will?"

Adam finished with the blasphemous thought that had plagued his mind for weeks.

"I've been reading about many so-called fringe groups. The remote Mormons with many wives and the restrictiveness of their lives in their hidden communities, far away from the public eye. The Amish who, like us, live a lifestyle that is from another century. The traditional Amish who are not in keeping with modern times at all. No electricity or phones. There are other groups too. Each clear that they don't intend to coexist with outsiders. They are no different than us Hasidim when it comes to being remote or being behind the times. Each one of them as elitist as us. Each one insisting that God will strike them down if they don't follow the rules."

"Those groups are different, Adam. *Hashem* didn't choose them."

The snobbery of the statement incensed Adam.

"So, you're chosen. You are the one who is absolutely one hundred percent bona fide what God is looking for and wants from us."

"I am one of the chosen people. That is all I will say."
Adam softened his stance just a bit.

"I actually feel the truth of being chosen. I really do. But can't I be an example to the world and its nations through Torah, or even Talmud, for that matter, and not necessarily in the Hasidic way?"

Adam paused in order to give Aaron Gvirzman a chance to consider the question. Despite the effort, the elder gentleman remained silent. Adam decided to continue.

"Isn't it a waste that we're supposed to be a light unto the nations but we keep said light hidden among ourselves? All these groups I mentioned are cultish in their own ways. Well, guess what? We're actually cultish too. We live in a bubble. I don't even know that our way of life is even psychologically healthy. We're part of a big world that we shut ourselves out from. I've been well traveled enough that I can say it's beautiful out there. I realize that now. I can still be a good Jew and exist in it all at the same time."

Sympathy for Adam was snuffed out in the very instant that Adam finished his comments. For Aaron Gvirzman, the only concern was about the safety of his daughter and grandson. Safety from what was surely a man gone mad. Besides, it had just occurred to the elder man that divorcing Teme was not about discussions over the validity of Hasidism. It was about the fact that his son-in-law was ready to destroy a family, a marriage, an entire community.

"There is nothing left to say then, Adam, except that this meeting is over. Whatever your motives, your thoughts, your ideas, it is clear to me that you are indeed the danger my daughter has said you've become. To imply our way of life might be wrong, even worse, sick, is blasphemous."

Aaron Gvirzman shook a scolding finger at his son-in-law. His brow furrowed with anger.

"You've been tainted, I know. I know all about your trips to that seminary. To that restaurant. To that woman who dares to call herself *hazzan*."

The statement could only mean that Aaron Gvirzman had some type of network in the States. Spying, if you will. And wasn't that a sin, too? Wasn't it a fact, then, that Adam's father-in-law was guilty of bad behavior? Why couldn't the man see that?

Before Adam could even utter a response, Aaron Gvirzman continued with his rant.

"Your teachings would be a danger to my grandson and my daughter. They would bring nothing more than perpetual misery to our home and community. May the Almighty forgive you. You're a disgrace to our community. How could I have misjudged you so severely? If only I'd seen hints of this before we ever agreed to a *shiddach*."

With that, Aaron Gvirzman stood and, without handshake or kind gesture, walked away from Adam, who sat and watched the angry shoulders support the shaking head. Adam could hear the muttered words under Aaron's breath as the distance grew. "My daughter. How could he do this to her? To the family? A waste of a man. He should rot in hell."

Adam winced hearing that last desire. Pandora's box had been opened, and the consequences were now presenting themselves. It would take all of Adam's strength to believe he was not wrong for feeling the way he did.

That he was entitled to the feelings and that God knew what was in his heart and soul.

Adam could see a light at the end of the tunnel of his dark thoughts, but he could also see all the darkness he would have to navigate in order to get through to the other side. For now, he existed in the darkness. That meant the choices were up to him. He could think of the journey as sinking into the abyss, as falling down into the endless pit that was the end of life. Or he could remind himself repeatedly that the darkness was actually the beginning of his birth. The canal that would help him be reborn. It led to the light. A new life he should have been born into in the first place.

dam continued to sit alone and think about phrases that fit the scene he'd just had with his father-in-law. The blind leading the blind. The persecuted becoming the persecutor. The pot calling the kettle black. All those phrases had been created to imply that one was doing exactly what one was accusing the other person of.

His father-in-law's knowledge of the intricacies of Adam's life meant the man had been spying, and everyone who helped him out was equally guilty. Guilty for seeking out information that would be used to malign another human being. That was not the Jewish way. How could his father-in-law justify his own sinful behavior?

Adam knew, sure as he knew anything, that his father-in-law would wield the information he garnered like a knife meant to cut Adam to shreds. Adam stood and decided to return to his hotel near the airport. He'd be returning to the States soon, so he might as well start the journey here and now. He was more than ready and certainly willing to begin the transition to jewelry-store owner. The slow and steady process would take several months, but he was determined to persevere.

Marrying Daniella would come in turn, but for the time being, he'd make it a point to see her whenever he could. Besides, in terms of the Belgium courts, it would be in his favor that he was an absent father who left for the States and preferred to reside there. That he was a married man who was visiting another woman. Adam's lawyer had already indicated that it would push things along. That in all likelihood, it would speed up the divorce process by several months.

As he walked along, Adam's emotional pain set in. *How does one reconcile abandoning their son? Is it wrong to put personal happiness above a bad marriage? Is God angry with me? Have I lost my way?* His questions formed a whirlpool. They were spinning round and round, but somehow, another truth set in. A truth that was cold and hard. *We have the same exact humanity in our holy community that they have everywhere else. Alcoholism, sexual abuse, emotional abuse, infidelity, you name it. We only pretend it isn't there. There is no proof that one way of life is better than another. I will never accept that I can't be a good Jew unless I accept the rules without question. I am a good Jew that loves God with all my heart and all my soul. Surely God is aware of the fact. Any man who presumes to know God's will should be shaking in his boots as he figures out what he will say to the Lord when asked why he, a mere mortal, insisted he knew what God was seeking from each of us.*

The meeting with Aaron Gvirzman would be the last time he saw his father-in-law or any of the Gvirzman clan. His only remaining interaction would be with

Teme, and that would be on the fateful day that they were officially divorced. Adam resigned himself to the fact. He shouted out into the air, "I butter my toast on the underside. What do you think of that?"

He laughed after having done so. He had read *The Butter Battle Book* by Dr. Seuss after Rabbi Simon had mentioned it…so long ago now. The book applied to so many conflicts in life that were just, well, ridiculous. Sadly, the story was now his own. Hasids versus mainstream Jews. That's how Adam saw it. Jews bickering over nonsense and refusing to budge from their convictions.

Back at his hotel room, he double-checked that his belongings were packed and ready to go before checking out of his hotel. Out of habit, he had changed into his college-aged attire even though he was not college aged anymore or even traveling with diamonds. He looked into his suitcase one last time before closing the lid on his black garments. He had a strange notion of closing a casket.

What he would do with all his black clothes, he couldn't even begin to guess. More so, his distinct black hat that made clear he was religious. Maybe he'd donate it to a clothing drive or some such charity. He'd ask Daniella for help in figuring out how to buy a new wardrobe for himself. He was eager to wear what was in style. He'd pick bold colors too. Yet another symbol of his new life.

The courage was there, but the fear was too. Adam boarded his plane that day, unsure of what was on the other side. He only knew that he wanted to get there.

dam had finished his work for the day, reviewing paperwork at the jewelry store and learning about inventory, promotional sales, and holiday specials. In preparation to open up the county store, he had even learned about the expected caliber of customer.

It would be some time still. Perhaps a few more weeks before the doors to the new establishment were officially opened. No matter. He was certainly busy enough. Yet, in spite of that, Adam was feeling down about the abrupt changes brought on by his personal desires. He needed a chance to talk about his new life and to figure out how to adjust to the drastic changes his choices were bringing him.

On a whim, he called Rabbi Simon at the seminary. He thought it would be nice to talk and catch up. Actually, Adam was looking for moral support, and he remembered that Rabbi Simon had been pleasant and especially kind in discussing Adam's concerns. The rabbi agreed to meet with him once more, and soon at that. Before he knew it, Adam was sitting in the familiar office and look-ing into the eyes of someone he considered a friend.

"Rabbi Simon, I'm so glad we could talk again."

Rabbi Simon responded with a hearty handshake as he replied, "My pleasure, Adam. It's nice to see you after all this time. What brings you here today?"

Adam sat himself down and proceeded to walk the rabbi through his life, beginning with his initial inquiries about Conservative Judaism years before.

"I shared my curiosity with you back then, but I al-ways left one particular thing out."

For the first time, Adam told the rabbi details about Daniella. And so, for the first time, he outlined the im-petus for their meetings long ago, beyond the fact that he had been searching for answers.

"Adam, let's remove Daniella from the equation. Pretend she doesn't exist. Would you feel the same about leaving your community then?"

Adam thought long and hard before answering, and the rabbi afforded him the silence that permeated the room.

"Honestly, I don't know. I wouldn't have known any better or different if I'd never met her, would I?" Adam paused to reflect on his answer further.

"I suppose that's not really true. With all the travel I did and the exposure to so many places that were outside my community, it was bound to happen. I think I've al-ways felt like a square peg trying to fit into a round hole. Knowing Daniella just made it all more tangible.

"I have to believe, though, that Daniella was placed on my life's path for a reason. I don't think it was any ac-cident that I met her, or even Benny Kalabokas, for that matter. Besides, does it really matter? The bottom line is

I am happiest when I'm away from Antwerp and when I think about her."

Rabbi Simon knew many of the seminary's students past and present. In a place as small and quaint as the seminary, everyone either knew of or at least heard of everyone else. Certainly, Daniella's name rang a bell. The rabbi recalled that, several years back, she had been one of the first handful of women to receive the title of *hazzan* from the school. He didn't know her personally, though, and that was a blessing. It meant he could be objective when speaking with Adam.

Despite the revelation, Rabbi Simon couldn't help but wonder if the impetus for everything that the young man thought or felt was that Adam Goldfarb was in love with *Hazzan* Daniella Sobler. Then again, as Adam himself stated, did it really matter?

It occurred to the rabbi that the best tactic, the best way to be helpful, would be to give Adam food for thought and let him digest it on his own. Reach his own conclusions without any push from another person's point of view. Most likely, he only needed to hear a bit of general history.

"Adam, do you remember being here years ago? We met how many times? Three? Four? Maybe even five? Do you remember that we talked in very general terms? How I gave you background on the Conservative movement? You were pleasantly surprised by all the common ground between your level of belief and mine as a Conservative rabbi."

Adam nodded.

The rabbi continued. "For modern Jews, including Hasidim and the superreligious, the way we behave, pray, carry out our daily activities, and more has years and years of history behind it. That history brought us all to this point in time. Judaism was never based in faith only, except for one very important fact: our belief in one God.

"The only thing set in stone, and I don't mean to be punny, was the Ten Commandments. Everything else in Judaism was influenced throughout the millennia by the history occurring around it. Persian influences or Hellenistic changes, for example. There is much archeological evidence, even as far as India, proving not only a Jewish presence but that the way those people lived their lives was in keeping with the societies around them.

"In this world, many of the celebrations, harvests, or even rites of passage had influences from history and outside the context of Judaic faith. One need only look at the way certain sects of Hasids dress as the perfect example of that very fact. Dressing that way is not inherently Jewish or part and parcel of our faith. The clothing is simply the style of dress that was the fashion statement in the late eighteenth century in eastern Europe. Yet, nowadays, people assume it is the way a Jew dresses."

Adam sat quietly, absorbed in the history lesson.

"Anyway, back to the fact that, historically, Jews have been greatly influenced by the world around them. The influences were great enough that, ultimately, it led to a need for a more aristocratic leadership. A group to ensure the bloodlines of Jews remained pure. A body of experts to make the rules and regulations tighter and stricter. Ultimately, in time, the birth of Talmudic rabbis took place.

"Too many Jews were intermarrying in those ancient times. Too many were adopting the ways of their countrymen. Roman times are a perfect example of that. It was a natural progression that the goings-on during Roman times led to the need to tighten the reins. To cause Jews steeped in faith to work hard, and diligently at that, to preserve our way of life."

"All understood, Rabbi, and all very interesting. But where and how does this fit in with me?"

"Adam, you need only remember one thing. In terms of Jewish history, Hasidism and the Orthodox lifestyles of the modern-day Jew occurred so late in our Jewish history line that in no way can anyone claim to be leading the true, real, or only way to live a Jewish life. A person can only claim to know the best way to express their faith. It's that simple.

"The rules and regulations in your neighborhood are an interpretation based on Torah and Talmudic text. And one does not need to look far to see how the events and lifestyles occurring in eastern Europe in the late seventeen hundreds influenced the birth of Hasidism. That interpretation of our faith has lasted into the twentieth century essentially because of the influx of immigrants from Europe into America.

"In that regard, then, it is wrong, to my way of thinking, to insist that those lifestyles are the only way to be Jewish. That is my opinion, Adam. I suppose I'll end by saying it would be so wonderful if Jews could just respect each other and support each other rather than waste energy and effort on deciding who is and who is not a real Jew."

Adam had been raised from birth to accept and understand that he was among the chosen few to emulate the Almighty in this world and be a light unto the nations as a result. That it was his sacred duty to follow the laws of Judaism to the letter in order to find favor with God. That he served as an example for Jews outside the fold as to how they should be living their lives. That his way was the right way.

It had never occurred to him that his entire way of life was merely an interpretation from the teachings of a man who had lived at the end of the eighteenth century. A delightful soul called the *Baal Shem Tov* who began a whirlwind of controversy among the Jews of his day. And just as in so many other times in history, those around him either followed or shunned his ways. Other groups emerged, splintering off, each claiming they had a better understanding of the correct way to interpret the religion. Weren't there arguments to this very day among the different Hasidic groups? Litwak. Satmar. Lubavitch. Each with its own special take on things. Adam contemplated this enough that his brow began to furrow. His thoughts had gelled.

"Have I upset you, Adam? I hope not. I merely want you to understand that you need to figure out what Adam's interpretation of Judaism is. What is the lifestyle that will bring you closest to God? It's between you and God how you live life and feel that you are a good Jew."

"No, no. Not at all. I'm just thinking about what you said and realizing that I agree. I was just mentally admitting that it was always there, somewhere."

"Adam, you have to decide whether your Orthodox way of life suits you best or not. Do you want to be

Conservative? Reformed? Do you even believe in God? You have to think it through and follow your heart and mind."

The teacher in Rabbi Simon saw an opportunity to enlighten an interested listener.

"Adam, how many times have you heard that we in the Diaspora have to accept that we have lost ten of our twelve tribes? We're only able to trace the tribes of Cohen and Levi. Everyone else has been bunched into the group called Israelites. Yet we have Jewish groups throughout the continent of Africa. We have them in India, Spain, France, China, Canada, South America. Need I go on? So who's to say the remaining tribes are really lost at all? Maybe it's that we're everywhere and don't even realize it. Maybe all these groups are descended from those tribes, only we lost track of each other.

"Adam, there are Jews everywhere, living good Jewish lives according to their own customs and traditions. That is the only difference between them and us...the customs and the traditions. The faith is the same. The love of Torah is the same. The Talmud is the same. Every one of us is a Jew. You and I are Jews. It's only how we have chosen to interpret, create tradition, and customize our lives that might be different.

"My advice to you is to rediscover what is in your heart and soul. Search for the love of your Judaism that has always been there and find out what it means to you. Then go out into the world and fulfill your destiny. You have been angered at having a lifestyle dictated to you. Well, I don't want to sit here and dictate how you should feel. It's in your hands, Adam. Not mine. You are the owner and keeper of your soul. You are the one who hears it speaking deep inside of you."

That last phrase was the clincher for Adam. He had thought it all along but simply needed to hear it articulated outside of his own head.

"Thanks, Rabbi. Not only for allowing me some time today but for what you shared. Mostly, for not being judgmental. You are literally the first person who didn't dictate to me what I need to be doing."

Adam paused and lifted his eyes to make contact with the rabbi's as he spoke his next sentence.

"In my eyes, you really are a rabbi. A good rabbi."

It was a compliment, to be sure. It was based on the notion that in the eyes of the Orthodox and the Hasidim, Rabbi Simon was not a true rabbi. He had studied Torah and Talmud for years, become fluent in the history and language of the Jewish people, and observed the holidays faithfully, but he had done so under the wings of the Conservative movement. The fact that he had not achieved the title through Orthodox institutions provided the convenient excuse that his certification was not truly valid.

The few times Rabbi Simon had interacted with the Orthodox rabbis in the area, they were respectful enough. Kind and polite, actually, even eager to discuss and contemplate concerns with him. They made him feel at home and welcomed, yet he knew they did not consider him the real deal. That they felt a secret desire to influence him to think more like the Orthodox. He could have responded in a thousand different ways to Adam's awkward compliment, but he chose to answer with a simple truth.

"That's very kind, Adam. Rabbi or not, my advice is this...finish your divorce, marry the woman you love, be the Jew you know you are in your heart, and leave the rest to God."

enny sipped his coffee, waiting for Adam's arrival at the restaurant. It was evening time and things were quiet. He reflected on their past years and chuckled. Who would have thought in a million years that if anyone would become a daily diner, coming and going through the years, it would be Adam Goldfarb? A customer that hailed from the Hasidic section of the county. It was laughable.

Unlike today, the usual routine had been that Adam would stop in before leaving for the city during the early morning hours. He'd purchase eggs or challah french toast along with a cup of coffee and begin his commute to work in the early morning darkness. For some reason, Adam asked to meet for dinner on this day. He promised Benny that a full explanation for the request would come while they dined. With nothing better to do as he waited to share dinner, Benny reflected on the fact that Adam lived in his home.

Benny and Rose had insisted on housing Adam free of rent to help him save for his future as well as for his legal needs, which were still a thorn in Adam's side. Another motivation, however, had been the repeated failed attempts on Adam's part to convince his parents to let him move back into their house. They couldn't get past his change in style of dress or his shift in attitudes, no matter that *tzitzit* still hung down from under his shirt. He had strayed. He had turned his back.

Adam told Benny that his parents were ashamed that he had ended his marriage. Mortified that he had left a son overseas. Bewildered that he didn't want to be part of the community. Relieved that he hadn't ruined any younger sibling's chances for a good match since he himself was the baby of the family.

He brought shame and ridicule not only to them but to Uncle Tzvi as well. Poor Tzvi, he had been the one to tell Adam about the Daily Diner. It meant that he had been the one responsible for Adam's meeting Daniella.

One could be hopeful that perhaps someday things would change. That there would be a day when all of them might put their feelings aside long enough to let Adam know he still mattered. A day when blame throwing would end and reconciliation would begin. Benny was glad that Adam shared these thoughts and feelings. It helped him to understand better. It helped him to become a confidante for Adam.

Benny knew that going to the restaurant daily was Adam's way to ensure that he compensated Benny at least to some extent for the kindness Rose and he were showing by letting him live rent free. It meant that money still found its way into the Kalabokases' pockets. Money that

Adam was already earning as he trained to be a jewelry-store manager.

Benny also knew that Adam had spent the last week in Antwerp trying to settle the civil, legal divorce matters, and today was the day he had arrived back in the States. He had told Benny prior to his leaving that when he returned, he'd come for some dinner at the Daily before returning to the Kalabokas home to sleep. He'd probably want to talk about the trip and any progress he might have made. That he would not come for the usual breakfast at the restaurant.

It was odd, though. Knowing that Adam would have landed early in the morning and so that it should have been breakfast they would be sharing as they usually did, why the change to dinner? Benny had no qualms about pointing that out to Adam when they spoke. Benny wanted details. Adam had clarified that he was meeting with his new friend first, while he was still in the city but would wait until dinner to let Benny know what the meeting with his friend was all about.

Benny had heard about the new friend before. A young man who had also been a Hasid once. Benny liked that there was someone whom Adam could relate to, and he hoped that the two gained insight and support from each other. If that was what their meeting was all about, Benny was all for it.

Having this prior information, Benny reacted with nothing short of shock and surprise when a beaten and bruised Adam walked through the restaurant doors. The bruise under Adam's left eye looked painful and swollen.

"Adam, what in heaven's name happened to you?"

"I was beat up."

"Where did this happen? How did this happen?"

"Benny, I'm very tired, and I'm not very hungry, thanks to this." Adam pointed to his eye. "I would love some hot tea, though. Maybe just a cookie, too, and a chance to talk."

"Anything, Adam. Come. Come sit in the back."

The back room wasn't in use at the moment, so the room was nice and dark. It would help with the discomfort that Adam must surely be feeling in his eye socket. Benny continued.

"Tea and cookies, and I'll even keep the lights off. We can sit in the dark. I'm even going to grab you a bag of frozen peas from the back so you can put it over that eye. But please, Adam…when we're settled, please tell me what happened to you."

Benny wanted to listen to Adam's tale without a single interruption. He told Adam he felt that way but wondered if Adam wouldn't mind sharing how he met this new friend of his as well or even what that was all about. Benny thought that information might help him to understand the events of the day.

Apparently, the new friend was someone whom Adam had met with several times previously and then again just days before leaving for Antwerp. His name was Asher. Their connection had been instant. He was a young man who, like Adam, chose to leave Hasidism because he didn't buy into the edicts of his community.

Adam had been visiting at the seminary one particular day. He had an appointment with Rabbi Simon just to catch up and share news. When the appointment ended, Adam exited on to the main avenue in order to purchase a small salad. He intended to stave off hunger until he returned to the county. Asher spied Adam leaving the seminary, and apparently, the young man just knew. He followed Adam and approached him shortly after Adam sat down in the small eatery to partake of his meal.

"Pardon me. I know this is very forward of me, but I'm guessing you're someone who has chosen to leave the *frum* life behind."

Adam was curious. "What would make you say such a thing?"

"Your fringes are clearly visible, and even though you have curly hair, it's apparent you have a *pais* curl tucked behind each ear."

"And?"

"And Conservative Jewish men don't wear a *tallis* at all times, and they don't have *pais* curls either. So if you're walking out of the seminary like that, you must be Orthodox."

"Can't an Orthodox person visit a Conservative seminary?"

"Sure, but you're not dressed like an Orthodox person, are you? Blue jeans and a pullover sweater? C'mon! In fact, I'll bet that you're a Hasid. Well, I guess I should say ex-Hasid."

Adam told Benny that was when he took note of the fact that Asher was dressed similarly to him, fringes and all. There were soft wisps of hair curled behind each ear just long enough to wrap around the bottom of each ear lobe. Mostly, there was a strange look of understanding in the eyes. Indeed, moments later, the young man shared his own secret as he sat down at Adam's table.

"May I?" Asher never even waited for an answer. He pulled out the chair in front of him, sat, and looked Adam square in the eyes.

"I'm just like you. I left the Hasidic community two years ago, now. There's more of us too. We're out there, only nobody likes to talk about us, or even to us, for that matter."

A soft chuckle escaped the young man's lips, and he smiled as he continued.

"So we're kind of isolated, and it gets pretty lonely. I figured you could use a friend. Someone who would really understand."

The handshake came next, with a hearty, "My name's Asher. It's nice to meet you."

Things had progressed from there. Adam found out that an entire group of cast-off Hasids existed in the heart of the city. They had created their own little support group out of necessity and were six strong. Men and women both, who felt strangled by the upbringing they had been born into and who were seeking a different way of life.

After meeting alone twice, Asher suggested that Adam come and speak with the others who had created a new life for themselves. Hence, Adam had several evening get-togethers with people who really understood his hurt and frustration. Friendships were growing on solid ground. The notion that he and Daniella would eventually establish long-term friendships with many of them started to gel in his mind, and he thanked God repeatedly to be blessed with such good fortune.

"You don't understand how lucky I am to have you, Rose, and Daniella. Most deserters have no one to support them through a transition. The women in the group, they have it the worst. The only thing they were prepared for was to raise children and run a home. At least our little merry band of souls gives the women in the group a bit of support."

Adam shared that he had met with Asher that morning after leaving the airport and prior to coming up to the county. They planned to have a late breakfast together and meet with yet another new man who had just entered into the support group. A musketeer motto guided each of them: one for all, and all for one. They couldn't help but gain enlightenment each time they spoke to each other.

Adam rode the bus home, heart and mind committed to the idea that he was on the right path in his life. When he arrived at the depot a mere two miles from the restaurant, he walked to his parked car ready to indulge in a hearty meal at the Daily. It was early evening. All was quiet. No one had exited the bus at his stop except for himself and an older woman whose ride was already idling and ready to whisk her away. Indeed, in mere seconds, he was alone. The bus had long gone. And that was when it happened.

Adam was grabbed by two men, beefy and muscular. They smelled dirty. They felt greasy. Their tone was nasty. One of them even snarled with derision. But through the punches and kicks, it was what one of them uttered that affected Adam the most.

"Benny, he actually said to me, 'Maybe this will knock some sense into you, Jew boy.' How crazy is that? He didn't take my wallet or look for jewelry to pull off me. All they wanted to do was beat me up."

Adam hesitated briefly. He took in a long, sighing breath and continued. "I can't help but wonder if I was set up."

"What do you mean?"

Adam provided an answer. "Well, they could have been two guys who like to beat up Jews. You know, because we don't believe Jesus is God. Hoping it might make me rethink the idea because the alternative, according to them, is eternal damnation. Maybe that was the purpose of the comment about knocking sense into me. But I can't help but wonder…"

Adam paused again, sucking in more air so he could put bravado into the words that were hiding in his throat yet desperate to come out.

"What if my soon-to-be-ex-father-in-law or Teme or even someone from my old neighborhood arranged for that beating, and that's why that comment was made? An eleventh-hour attempt to frighten me into seeing the error of my ways."

"Oh, Adam, to say such a thing."

"I know. Believe me, I know. Only, my new friends have shown me articles, reports even. They took me to a police station once so I could see the photos of some Hasidic man that was arrested for sexual abuse."

"I don't follow."

"Benny, we're supposed to be a holy community. Yet, we have our good and bad, same as everyone else. We have beautiful souls who are kind, gentle, and caring. But we also have individuals who are drug users, alcoholics, rapists, and sexual predators. There are men who are fraudulent in business, dishonest in charity. I could go on. We're just the same like everyone else. It's only our isolationist attitude that keeps it well hidden.

"I never even knew any of that stuff until it was shown to me. In the end, we're just as human as everyone else. I can't even begin to tell you what I've learned from my little support group. Talk about eye-openers!"

"Adam, you're getting off track."

"Oh, sorry."

With that, Adam shared some personal revelations, explaining what he felt he now knew as a person who was standing on the outside, looking in on his former community.

"Maybe, just maybe, the notion of the means justifying the outcome is what happened to me. Maybe some twisted notion of knocking sense into me, to bring me back repentant, is what was at hand."

Adam continued in a mocking tone. "*It's a shame we had to hurt him, but Hashem will forgive us because we brought him back to righteousness.* Or maybe it was just plain spite. You hurt us, now we'll hurt you."

Adam was implying something heinous and his anger was the result. The anger could be heard as he continued.

"The beating couldn't happen in Belgium because I'd know without a doubt it was them. If it happened here in the good old US of A and outside of my neighborhood, well, then it could be anybody, couldn't it? A good way to keep their good name safe and intact. A good way to get them off the hook."

Benny could hear the agitation in the words that came out of Adam's mouth. The bottom line was it had been a senseless act of violence no matter who the perpetrator was. To beat up a defenseless person, to cause pain on purpose. Benny had to fight every urge from within. He had to make sure not to sink into the dark place in his own thoughts. Even so, he muttered under his breath, "Nazis."

Benny took a moment to consider what Adam implied. There was a growing frustration in the county regarding the superreligious communities. They were growing too quickly, and they were not mindful of zoning laws, fire-safety issues, or questions of what qualified as public versus private areas. Maybe it really could have been two men hell-bent on making a statement. Benny hated to think for even one moment that was the case. The bottom line was they'd never know. Benny decided to try to redirect the conversation.

"Whatever it was, Adam, it's over. Thank goodness you're all right, and God willing, it won't happen again."

"I'd like to call the police now that I'm here. I want a record of what happened. I want it noted somewhere. That way, if it happens to me again, well…"

"Yes, I suppose you're right. You can use my phone, Adam."

In the quiet of an otherwise lovely evening, Benny stared off and thought about the details Adam had shared. The fact that Adam was beaten was simply overwhelming. The mere idea of a Jew arranging to beat up a Jew sickened Benny to his very core.

Yet Benny's thoughts and feelings paled in comparison to the conclusions that Adam drew for himself after speaking with the police. For him, the beating was the symbolic gesture made by a divine hand in order to knock the old life right out of him.

When the beating was over and Adam lay on the ground, confused and bewildered, he had worked to make sense of his circumstance. Now, after speaking with law enforcement, the nail had been driven far into the casket. The lid, at that very moment, permanently sealed. A dead life lay inside. Adam realized that when he had stood up after the two men ran off, two things had happened in succession. First he had dusted off his clothes. Then had come the moment he had been waiting his whole lifetime for. He had been reborn.

*A*dam lay in the dark on the bed that Rose and Benny Kalabokas had so graciously supplied. He was unable to fall asleep courtesy of the countless wheels turning in his head. A simple police report had been filed and tucked away in what was likely a huge stack of other files at the station, each probably lacking the conclusions they rightfully deserved. It was of no consequence to Adam. He only cared that the report existed. It would be ammunition if the need should arise.

It wasn't the incident that plagued Adam as much as the other things he had heard that day. The university fellow that he and Asher had befriended…Menachem Baum, who was now in his last year of studies for a master's in philosophy (after having obtained a bachelor's in religious studies with a minor in philosophy), had blown Adam's mind with the wealth of information he shared.

Menachem had been absent from the Hasidic community for nine years total. Like Adam, he had struggled with leaving, and it had taken him years to muster up the courage. Now, years later, Menachem was a virtual professor able to share extensive knowledge with his new-found group of friends.

Menachem spoke of what he had learned about Hasidism and his own particular sect, from the perspective of outside research, of worldly scholars who studied many groups, their customs, and their traditions. In particular, from the professor at his university who was deemed an expert on the subject. A Dr. Joseph Greenberg. Everything that was learned, was counter to what had been ingrained in the Hasidic communities.

Adam had learned as a young boy that the Almighty and creation were eternally connected, and not just as a one-time deal when the creation occurred but on a regular basis. Every single day the connection was alive and well. It was maintained through faith. All Hasids never lost sight of this. Everyone else did.

He had learned that other Jews were drifters from traditional Judaism. Even the Karaites, although nowadays so few in number, were in the same category as "the others." Karaites didn't accept Talmud and only followed a literal translation of the Torah. So unless they converted to Judaism, they wouldn't be accepted as real Jews by any Hasidic sect. And the Reformed or the Conservatives, well, they were cults altogether. At least there was some hope for the Modern Orthodox. In the eyes of the Hasid, these former Jews were drifters who deserted the army, and they were all condemned. They were influenced by Western culture, which was shameful and reckless and on the fast track to eternal damnation. In essence, they, too, were *goyim*, the outside nations.

Adam had noted some of the notions drilled into his thinking as he grew up. Gentiles would kill Jews. The lesson of the Holocaust was that Jews needed to stay as isolated as possible. The Holocaust was punishment by God himself. Punishment for having the audacity to stray and believe they could break away from the rigid observances of the faith. Punishment for believing they could take it upon themselves to create an Israeli state. False Jews who were playing on the sympathies of the world to achieve the deed of creating the so-called Jewish nation.

It had even been drilled into his head at a young age that the community needed to avoid westernized texts because one should not indulge in anything that might put doubt in the mind. The notion of dinosaur bones was simply a test from *Hashem*. A test of faith. Working on the physical body was simply a waste of time. One only needed to strengthen the mind and the understanding of one's relationship with God.

Now, and for the first time, Adam learned what the outside world concluded about Hasidism. Beginning with the fact that outside Jews and even Gentiles all believed that the group that referred to all of them as cultish was, in fact, a cult itself. Hasids, Amish, Mormons, and similar groups were all seen as isolationists who were hell-bent on keeping the outside world far, far away.

Menachem said the growth in the movement didn't occur because the lifestyle was the correct way to live. It grew because of the high birth rate. Year after year, families were having five, six, seven, and more children. *Be fruitful and multiply* was the accepted command. Replace every Jew lost in the Holocaust. Babies kept the numbers high. Not deep faith, not religious obligations. Just lots of babies.

However, as a result, the movement found power in numbers. An entire community excelled at pressuring its members to conform in ways a small cluster of people never could. In that regard, the Hasidic community got its gold star. The communal aspect of the Hasidic life was very strong. Adam knew he would actually miss it.

Hasids wanted to make sure they remained different from the rest of the world. They made a point not to blend in. They maintained a one-size-fits-all mentality, and for the most part, it worked. Only a very small number of members, and oddly enough, usually males, questioned the teachings and opted to live outside the fold. For Adam, that statement was certainly true. He thought it was probably easier for men than women. Women were so severely restricted that leaving was sometimes impossible.

When Menachem divulged these facts, Adam found himself remembering Naomi Moskovitz. Menachem said the youngsters that left the fold were ill equipped to deal with the outside world. Did Naomi ever attain any skills other than those of housewife and mother? Did she ever have a chance to peek into another book? Even for the boys, studying Torah for hours each day and devoting only a small amount of time to secular studies left them all with no basic outside skills. Adam was lucky because he had literally been handed a career.

Being prevented from attending outside schools, none of them, and most certainly not the girls, got to attend a secular university. Girls were meant to be docile and modest in all things. They were supposed to feel the joy of submitting to their husband's will. Adam thought about Teme at that moment. She was the result of that sort of thinking. Adam knew he was lucky to be born a male.

Making matters even worse, English was their second language. Denied TV, movies, books for reading pleasure, socialization, or even basic interactions with the bigger world, every single one of them was ill equipped to function in everyday society. Eating a cheeseburger or going to a dance club was often the rebellious outcome. All because it was taboo.

Adam laughed thinking about Daniella all those years ago when he had first met her. He had been in his twenties yet hadn't even known how to kiss a girl! Only instinct had helped make his first attempt at kissing passable. And his education...his first conversations with Daniella had been by rote. He had spoken what he had learned. He had been embarrassed every time she seemed to best him in a conversation.

It was only when he began to make trips to the seminary and even some university libraries that he began to realize that in math, science, history, and English, he had the education of a sixth grader. Even in religious matters, he didn't have an understanding of the bigger world of Jews. Certainly, those Jews were not the demons they had been made out to be. One need only think about Rabbi Simon or Daniella, or Benny, for that matter. Adam had to face the fact that he was a grown man who knew about gems and about Torah but practically nothing about the world.

As Adam turned himself over once more, he let out a deliberate sigh, a sigh of resolve. He knew he no longer had a choice. Now that he knew the things he did, now that he himself was so much more educated, he was sure he had made the right decision. By the grace of the good Lord above, Adam had a loving guide to walk the walk and talk the talk with him. Together with Daniella, he would continue to move on and grow as a person. He'd live a good Jewish life in the way he wanted to and not the way he was told to. His divorce was just around the corner. It lay in the foreseeable future. A stone's throw away. He need only be strong.

The only remaining task was to try one last time to sit with his parents and help them understand. To convince them not to shut him out. They indicated a willingness to sit and talk with him, and under the circumstances, that was a special blessing. The odds, however, were so poor that Adam had wondered more than once if he should even bother to try.

Adam thought about one particular woman in his discussion circle. She was only twenty-five years old. She had been *frum* once but had dreamed of being a fashion designer since age thirteen. She would sneak peeks in magazines and finger fabrics between her hands while her mother shopped for material to sew clothes. She'd even lift the fabric to her nose at times, just to breathe in her dream.

She told the group that she secretly observed the sewn garments that hung on the shops' mannequins. They were usually dresses made from the latest patterns, which of course were based on the latest fashions. She'd close her eyes and try to commit the designs to memory. She'd imagine items of apparel that she herself would create for the masses. At home, however, when she helped her mother sew, she did exactly as her mother told her. Sew boring dresses with low hemlines and high necks, long sleeves and dull colors.

Yet, despite it all, it was not her desire to sew clothes with her name on the label that had her banished from her community. She told the circle of defectors that her own parents disowned her over the fact that she learned to drive a car. Her particular sect forbade women to drive. Adam could still hear her, clearly.

"Do you hear what I'm telling you people? My parents didn't disown me because I murdered or robbed a market. They cut me off, never to speak to me again, because I can drive a car! A car! A simple machine. The level of emotional pain and suffering is beyond anything you can possibly grasp or that I can possibly express to you."

Tears began to well up in her soft blue eyes when she spoke to the group that day. "I'm not a bad person. I'm not evil. I don't understand. The sorrow in my heart that my parents feel this way..." She trailed off and buried her face in her hands for a good cry.

All anyone else in the group could do was understand. They were all in some type of bizarre scenario that affected them the same way. Adam had different factors winding through his own situation, but his traveled road was certainly as treacherous as hers. Bending to the point that he could not see what might lie up ahead... just beyond the curve. The road cleverly hid the future and dared him to go for a drive.

For his own sake, for his own peace of mind, he'd have to make one last plea to his family. He had come to that conclusion after the support group meeting. And by some great miracle, he had finally convinced his parents to sit and talk with him and to do so without the rabbis in attendance. Adam knew it would be a slap in the face of God, and directly at that, if he turned the miraculous albeit reluctant willingness down.

"Just the three of us. Parents talking to a son. Son to his parents. The special bond we have undisturbed by outside voices giving their opinions to us."

That was how he had put it. It had been like twisting an arm to get his parents to agree. Twisting until he got them to scream out in pain, "OK, we'll do it, but let's get it over and done with."

His parents were not proud of his decisions. He was not the Adam they knew. The meeting would be a waste of time. A stranger was wasting their time. At least Adam could live his life knowing that he tried. At least God would see that he tried.

Adam punched his pillow with his fist. He turned. He punched his pillow again. It was the only way to express the rage he felt inside about his parents.

*A*dam, I still don't understand. You have a wife. You have a son. Yet you're saying good-bye as if it were nothing."

"Mama, that's not true. I realize how painful this is for everyone."

"Then why, Adam? Why?" Tsivia Goldfarb raised her hands as if begging for bread.

"Mama, we've been over this several times."

"Nachum, try to get some sense into the boy." Tsivia clutched her husband's arm fearfully.

"I'm a grown man, Mama."

Nachum would give it a try. "Son, Torah is truth. It's fact. It's indisputable. You have to live by its laws to have a righteous life." He could think of nothing else to say.

"Papa, you can live by Torah and yet be a part of the big world. It really is possible. And isn't it better to bring the joy of Torah to the greater Jewish community? Isn't it better to have them practice to the best of their current ability in the hopes that they'll seek more?"

"Hmmph!" Tsivia Goldfarb made the peculiar sound before emphasizing her own conclusions.

"I'll tell you what that is, Nachum. That's that woman that dares to call herself a *hazzan*. A *hazzan*! Yet she dresses in reds and oranges and shows her elbows and knees to the world. She's an immodest demon, that's what she is! She stole my son right out from under me! She's evil, I tell you."

Tsivia began to cry. She rested her face in her hands. "Adam, my Adam. I don't want to lose you."

"You don't have to, Mama. Where does it say you have to?"

Nachum was befuddled. He didn't know how to proceed. Never, never had this happened to his family or anyone he knew. Helpless as to what to do, he focused on his wife's outburst, turning the distraction into a scapegoat. "Tsivia, please, calm yourself. This is no time to be sentimental. And now Adam, please try harder to explain yourself."

Adam looked at his mother and father with sad eyes. "I feel like we are going around in circles. Do you really think *Hashem* despises all Jews except us? We're all his children. Even the *goyim* are his children."

Tsivia looked up at her son. Her response was immediate. "It's a test of faith, Adam. Only the righteous prevail."

"Mama, you make all these declarations. You spout out what you believe are nondebatable comments, but how much of that is because it was drilled into you, and how much of it is because you really thought it through and truly believe it?

"Why do you shave your hair off, Mama? Because it's exotic and will attract men? Yet you wear a wig that is full of beautiful hair! You look very attractive in it. Have I ever told you that? And if I'm saying it, your own son, well, has it really prevented men from looking at you?"

"How dare you speak to your mother in such a familiar way!" Nachum Goldfarb was a dragon blowing fiery smoke from his nostrils and ears.

Adam ignored his father and continued to address his mother. It was clear that if he were to make headway with anyone, it would be her. Nachum Goldfarb was just too rigid.

"And don't women look at men, too? Sure they do! Look at my hair, Mama. You've said I got these beautiful curls from you. Why don't I have to shave my head then? Why shouldn't I have to lessen my looks so women won't get distracted from their tasks in order to steal a glance at me?"

Tsivia had no answer. She looked at her husband, pleading with her eyes. He made clear with his stony stare that she was to remain silent.

"My wedding night with Teme. The whole wedding itself. The notion of you and other women going to Teme to receive a blessing. That in that moment she was somehow connected to *Hashem* and holy. Never in a million years could she be a conduit for God." Adam's tone of voice became heightened.

"And me...the groom giving my discourse on the mysticism of marriage to an entire room of men. As if I understood marriage or was an expert on it. I didn't even know how to kiss a woman properly, and still, this was what I did. That whole notion of focusing on the soul at the party. It's not about our bodies, only our souls. That's all I've ever heard.

"Yet I was teased half the night about the deed that lay ahead. Men whispering to me about the pleasures that awaited. Telling me of the delicacies behind the closed door. Doesn't sound very holy to me! And guess what, Mama! Teme is a pleasureless soul."

Tsivia put her hands to her ears. "Adam, why are you saying such private things? Nachum, speak to him!"

Adam didn't know why he was saying such things. He was rambling because he didn't know what else to do. The dam had burst, and everything wanted to come gushing out. Adam was merely spewing out his anger. Anger, in the guise of random thoughts.

"Adam, the way you are speaking to your mother is shameful. What happened to the son I raised? The things you speak of are far less important than faith in Torah. That you would even imply that personal pleasure is as important as leading a good Jewish life...I really don't understand all this."

Tsivia asked her husband, "Nachum, are we being punished for our sins?"

Here we go again, Adam thought. *My mother deferring to my father.* Adam addressed his father before he could respond to Tsivia's question.

"Papa, we're not divine. Hasids are not divine. We sin as much in this community as anywhere else. The world is not the enemy. We are, within ourselves."

"All the more reason to stay away from the rest of the world. Keep temptation away."

"Papa, I've seen it. I've felt it. We can live alongside our neighbors and interact with them and still live good lives, whether we're Hasid or not."

Adam had the ridiculous notion that he could sway his father's thinking. That somehow he'd create an ally that would help them all understand. The thought lasted merely a moment. In reality, Nachum Goldfarb had only paused to prepare himself to form his next sentence.

"But we do live aside our neighbors, Adam. We own businesses in the county, and we allow outsiders to come in and shop. We have participated in county land issues and building rights."

"Sure, Papa, but only because our community is growing and we need more property. We're practically bursting at the seams in our little village here. And as far as our businesses…we're not celebrating diversity. We're just dealing in good business. All we want is a sale. We know that to get one, we have to be nice. The world is not the enemy, Papa. We're simply led to believe that it is."

"The world *is* the enemy, Adam. It has destroyed my son. It has taken him away from me and left only a shell that looks like my Adam. You're not my son. He seems to have gone. I don't know who you are. I will never forgive the outside world for this. Never. You're living proof that everything we teach about it is true."

Tsivia added, "And I will never forgive that evil woman that started it all. Even if she didn't dare to call herself *hazzan*. She has taken you from us and convinced you to live a sinful life. I want nothing to do with her, ever." Tsivia Goldfarb began to cry once more, head buried far into her waiting hands.

Adam wanted to say so many things. He wanted to but didn't. He was a gentile as far as they were concerned.

He was a gentile of the worst kind. The Jewish kind. *My heart is breaking. I'm your son. What in heaven's name is happening here?*

Adam returned to the conversation at hand. For him in the here and now, no greater heights would be reached.

"Will you both still have those thoughts on *Yom Kippur?* When you are atoning, will you also include that you shut out your own son?"

"As of today, I have no son." Nachum's face had gone stone cold.

"Nachum, you can't mean that!" Tsivia sat with spine straight and stared past Adam. She had a wide-eyed, faraway look in her eyes.

"Papa, you can't mean that! Please tell me that you'll both still see me and my future family."

"You've disgraced our standing in the community. You've made us less desirable now. It's only by the Almighty's good graces that you are our youngest and so haven't destroyed your siblings' chances for a good match! It's a blessing that your son is with Teme. At least she will raise him far away from your crazy thinking. We will show that we, too, condemn your actions."

"Papa, Mama, you can't mourn a soul that isn't dead!" Adam looked pleadingly at his mother. "I'm alive, Mama. Alive and well."

Tsivia Goldfarb had no answer. She began to rock in her chair, wailing a repeating chant. "Adam, my Adam."

"Your Jewish soul is dead, Adam. Now please go. We can't handle this anymore." Nachum made a shooing gesture with his hands as he spoke the words. "If you don't leave now, I'll get the neighbors to help me carry you out."

Adam stood and looked at his parents, hoping for something, anything. There was nothing. No begging him not to leave. No pleading of any sort. Adam saw only a crying mother and a stone-faced father.

Adam left a house that was suddenly foreign to him. Two people sat and watched him exit through the front door. The door was closed slowly, reluctantly, by a shaking hand. Adam merely stared at his fingers as they clutched the knob. The door latch click penetrated his ears like a death knoll. He stood for a seeming eternity, though perhaps it was a minute at most. He imagined his parents running to the door, flinging it open, and pleading with him to come back in. His only ally on the cement walkway was still air.

The reality that no one was coming to the door made clear he was already a ghost. Adam, too, was dead inside. Numb, to be more precise. Somehow, he managed to return to his car and prepare to leave. As he pulled away, he saw the neighbors come out of their home and head over to the Goldfarb house. They must have been looking through the drapes all along, eager to find out what had happened. Was the outcome inevitable or a miracle? They had to know.

Driving back to Benny's, Adam was functioning on automatic behind the wheel. Only when he was safe within the walls of his room at the Kalabokas home did he unleash the beast. Adam threw himself onto the bed and cried his heart out.

Although not a Kalabokas himself, Adam was reenacting Benny's yesteryear as if they were one and the same. Once again, the loss of a mother permeated the fiber of a soul's being. Once again, the loss of a father, who was looked up to and admired, was now a reality. The loss of both parents tortured a young man who never asked for it. And worst of all, once again, the loss was for no good reason at all.

Daniella and Adam

everal things happened in the many months that followed, a strange mix of tasks that one would expect when involved in seeking a divorce. Each, part of Adam's efforts to reshape his life. Adam's existence as a mainstream man was finally solidifying. He had developed a routine that included going into the city for work at the jewelry store, bimonthly meetings with Rabbi Simon, and date nights with Danny. All the while, he was tying up the loose ends of a previous life.

In addition, he was quite actively working to ease his presence into Danny's synagogue. He was participating in events, getting to know everyone, and doing anything that would make him yesterday's news. He dreaded the gossipmongers most. How often did a Hasidic person leave the fold and seek out a Conservative synagogue? He heard many whispers about him being the cantor's love interest, and he did his best to ignore them. Some folks were audacious enough to ask personal questions.

He tolerated it all, assuming it was part of a process. A new and different test of faith to see if he could manage. Eventually he'd be old news at Beth David. The fact that he no longer dressed like a Hasid was an enormous help in the matter. The fact that everything that was happening drained his emotions, wasn't.

The technicalities surrounding his divorce were actually the easiest compared to the metamorphic experiences occurring all around him. As anticipated, the *Bet Din* of Antwerp's Hasidic community, one of the most highly respected as a Jewish court, were more than happy to end the marriage between Teme and Adam. The divorce ceremony itself happened within a matter of minutes. A mere handing over, from Adam to Teme, of the prepared divorce document. It was done in front of the correct witnesses, those men who in the eyes of the Jewish court were fit and righteous. They could confirm and give testimony to the fact that all was done in the proper manner. The supervising rabbi cut the document and assured both parties it was safe in the *Bet Din's* files.

Adam had needed to make a second trip to Antwerp when the civil divorce was finally completed. Months had turned into a year at that point, but he had no complaints. His lawyer had been correct that the civil courts would consider the proof of the matter. It was clear that Adam continued to reside in the United States, giving no solid indication that he had thoughts of reconciliation.

With the civil divorce finalized, Adam would be free. When he made this last trip, he and Teme could each receive half of the *get* document. It would be the solid and final indication that the divorce was not only given but accepted by both parties. Teme and Adam would finally be single individuals. Any notion of partnership would be gone. Adam would finally feel absolved of responsibility. He tried to put all thoughts of his son out of his mind.

Adam knew that he and Teme both, wanted it to be over and done with. Hopefully, Teme could find a man who believed in the sanctity of the Hasidic lifestyle. There was no sense of foreshadowing at that moment in time so at least in the case of Teme, the future remained unknown. Adam was grateful he had a solid plan in place.

Daniella had wanted to accompany Adam both times he traveled overseas. The sentiment was very sweet, but Adam surmised there would be abuses that he would encounter, and he had insisted that he travel alone. His gut instincts proved correct. Memories of taunting slurs from men he was once acquainted with would haunt him for months. Men that he used to respect. Men that were standing on the street as he exited the building that housed the *Bet Din*. Each of them spewing hateful comments. Supposed men of the Book. Adam had no doubt that their wives waited at home, eager for the gossip as to how it all played out.

Adam wondered what could have possibly been in the minds of those men when they taunted him. It was not the Jewish way to be cruel. It was not the Jewish way to withhold sympathy. Hasid or not, Jews lived by strict moral codes every day. The actions were quite probably the result of his father-in-law's incitement. His father-in-law remained beyond embarrassed that this was happening to his own family. Best to blame it on a son-in-law gone awry. Adam noted that his father-in-law was not among the men.

Adam smiled from ear to ear as he arrived at the airport that day. In reality, he'd have the last laugh. He was free now. He could start over. He had a loving woman waiting for him. He had opportunity at his feet and a new career about to take off. It had taken a long while for Daniella to truly believe he was there for the long haul, but persistent perseverance had paid off. Daniella was now 100 percent vested in creating a life with Adam.

Teme, on the other hand, had nothing except the task of trying to find a husband who would accept her as used goods. Used goods that also had a son. A son who may have inherited his father's crazy genes. Adam knew this as a fact. People would not say that to her directly, he knew that too, but that type of thinking was the Hasidic way. It would be a long and hard process to find Teme a new mate.

She would need to leave behind the fancy apartment, the materialistic value of every fine piece of china, the prestige of her father's place in the community. She would need to go elsewhere. Antwerp would become her past. She would have to go where someone was willing to take her as his wife. Adam knew she would resent him for this and probably even more than for the divorce itself.

In Hasidic circles, the result of a divorce such as theirs was that Teme became far less desirable as a mate. Who would want to take the risk? Everyone in the community knew about her. Odds were that the Gvirzman family would be secretly questioned too. Didn't they know better? Were they that sloppy about finding a good Hasidic man? Did they themselves drive him to such a drastic decision?

The Gvirzman family would be smarter this time. They would avoid the United States as if it were the plague. Obviously, people there were influenced by its many evils. It wasn't worth the risk. Canada would be just another round of overseas relations, so it too was out of the question. That left only Israel. Everyone knew that matches in Israel were more of a last resort than anything else.

Adam would find out two years later, through a strange telephone-line type of circumstance, that Teme did marry a somewhat older man in Israel. Apparently, the man's wife had died of illness at age thirty-two and left him childless. He wanted children. For the sake of breeding purposes, he preferred a younger bride. Teme was eager for more children. He had heard that about her and that she was truly a devout woman. A veritable jackpot, as far as he was concerned, and surely the answer to his prayers.

In time, Teme would spend countless hours caring for her brood as well as using her crafting skills to help make ends meet. Her husband studied Torah for hours on end and taught at a local school for boys. She would receive funds from her father from time to time and accept them because he always pointed out it was for the children. Good clothes, good food, and good books for the little ones.

And because of where she lived in Israel, she lived strictly by the letter of the law. Her community was cloistered within the modern country that was Israel. With rules and regulations that were religiously based, her life was rigid and unbendable. Certainly, it was outside the context of the mainstream society surrounding it. Teme had always insisted she wanted to remain away from the evils of the modern world.

Despite his lack of love for Teme, Adam felt sorry for her. And as to his son, Adam would never know what became of his life. When Teme moved to Israel, she likely brought along stories about Adam. In any case, the conviction to keep Adam out of the sacred community became a permanent one. It was as if Adam's former wife and child never existed for him, despite his insistence that they did.

In the eyes of those around him, Adam appeared successful. He seemed content and happy. He was a trooper who prevailed through the murky mud. Even so, a darker side clung to him. It stayed well hidden, and Adam kept it at bay. Adam's underbelly. A saddened side that had etched permanent scars onto Adam's hidden feelings.

Adam had left things unsaid. Things that weighed on him. Each time Adam returned to the Kalabokas home, Benny could detect a quiet melancholy about the man. He didn't want to pressure Adam into speaking his mind, but he thought that perhaps if Adam continued to live with him and Rose, Benny could somehow be a support. Benny requested that he stop by the Daily for tea and cookies.

꩜

"Adam, it's been quite a few days since your return. Rose and I, well, we've been talking about you, and we have a proposal for you. Not sure why, but you have become like the son we never had."

Benny used the term *we*, completely unaware that he was simply referring to himself. Benny had a subconscious desire to have his mother and father complete a blissful union by living a beautiful life together. Supporting Adam in every way possible was the key to making it happen.

Benny took pause to replay a memory of consulting Rose about it all. It was a way to ensure that he was actually correct to use the term *we*. Benny reminded himself that Rose indicated that she too, felt compelled to help out a young couple ready to start a life together. Feeling good about it all, Benny continued.

"We'd like for you to continue to live at the house, free of charge, until you're officially ready to start your married life with Danny. It would give you a chance to get everything in order without worrying about finding an interim apartment. Besides, it would mean saving up the pennies for much better use than paying rent to some strange landlord. It would certainly make your commute to work easier, no?"

Adam, grateful for the offer, could only say *yes* and *thank you*. He left the Daily feeling happy about the matter and headed into the city for his bimonthly get-together with Rabbi Simon. He let his thoughts ramble as he drove but decided to save the conclusions he'd drawn for his discussion with his Judaic mentor. Everything came to the forefront when he began to speak with Rabbi Simon.

"I feel pretty guilty that everything is literally falling into my lap. It's so hard on Hasids who leave. Half the time, no, more than half the time, they have no job skills, an elementary education, no family, few friends, and certainly no funds. For each of us, we're dead as far as our parents and siblings are concerned. It's only the rare few who have a brother or sister still willing to meet with them. And I even have that, with Aviva.

"Here I am, training to take over the management of a jewelry store; my future wife is already waiting in the wings; you're helping me make the transition in a way I can process; and I have people who are not my family caring for me as if I were their son."

Rabbi Simon had begun meeting regularly with Adam the moment he began his divorce proceedings. It had become a unique situation that the rabbi could hardly pass up. What Conservative rabbi ever had the opportunity to enlighten a Hasid? Now, though, they were more than student and teacher. A friendship had blossomed, and talk between them was more and more subjective. Today, it was apparent that their meeting would take a spiritual route.

"I think you're confusing guilt with heavenly nudging, Adam."

Adam laughed. "What's that supposed to mean?"

"Maybe God is trying to ensure that you don't stray from the path you have been put on. So to be absolutely sure, your life has been made a bit easier for you. Comfort, as it were, has been placed on your path so you can feel safe there. Perhaps it is to prepare you for what is ahead. Guilt is not what you should be feeling, Adam. Perhaps preparation for something bigger down the line is what is at stake here.

"You know, Adam, I've been hearing a certain phrase lately. *Pay it forward*, I believe. Maybe you're meant to feel comfortable enough in your new skin so that one day you can be a help to others who want to leave the fold. Or perhaps even to someone who wants to embrace Judaism for the first time. Just think of it. You will be able to sit down with another person and provide the emotional support they need in the same way everyone is doing for you now.

"It could be as simple as a congregant at Daniella's synagogue coming to you and saying they know of someone who knows someone. That sort of thing. Maybe someone would like to ask some questions but would be hesitant to ask. There's even the possibility of a far bigger role. Maybe someday you could start a support group of your own. Think of what a help you could be to others like yourself. And you'd be up in Epson County.

The Hasids there don't have the same safe havens you have here in the city. You told me yourself that dumb luck had brought you to your support group here in the city. Maybe the link between Daniella's synagogue and the restaurant you told me about will create that safe haven. Think of it. You're on an incredible journey, Adam. Take it, live it, and breathe it. Don't question God's motives so much."

And so, a destiny was born. Fated by *Hashem* and uttered through a rabbi's mouth. Adam arrived feeling terrible guilt and left with a purpose he never even imagined. His journey was suddenly clear. This was his destiny. He would become one of the rare breed known as the Conservadox Jew. A unique blend of his Hasidic roots turned into Modern Orthodox observance mixed with a lifestyle akin to that of the Conservative movement. How hysterical! Irony at its best! He, of all people! He couldn't help but look upward to the skies and give a hearty laugh as he walked toward the subway station.

Being honest with himself, he had to admit there were too many things he just couldn't give up. It would be hard to morph certain things into a different way of observance or even into nonobservance. That was what was so great about a Conservadox lifestyle. He would have much of what he still craved and still feel liberated. And he would do it all in the most egalitarian way he could tolerate. He would marry his *hazzan* and prove to the world that it didn't mean doom. He would make a good living, raise a family, and be a good Jew. And he would support anyone else who wanted the same thing.

He'd speak to Benny and Danny both when the time was right. One day when he was truly ready to help others like himself. Here and now, however, he needed to sort out his life with the Soblers and handle his existence in the bigger world. When he felt in his heart that it was the right time, he'd ask for permission to use the back room of the restaurant as a meeting place. Hopefully, Benny would be willing. After all, businesses and youth groups, synagogues and consumers, all had their meetings at the Daily. Hadn't Adam seen the back area cordoned off on many occasions? Would it be any different to host a support group? Tea and cookies for everyone!

He'd even get his future mother-in-law involved when the time came. Sadly, at this point in time, she wasn't fully trusting of Adam or his motives. He knew it was true because Danny had admitted as much. She had also told Adam that Marcia was feeling a bit miffed over the fact that Benny had become such an anchor for Adam. She wanted the job herself. She felt a keen need to ease Adam into his new life and see for herself that his heart was in the right place.

Wouldn't she just love the opportunity to help others, since Benny had diminished her chance to do so for him? Adam imagined her taking in young girls who needed a place to stay, letting them know that they weren't second-class citizens in the eyes of the men. He laughed, knowing she'd be thrilled and honored all at the same time. Other daughters, as it were, that she could encourage to live their dreams, just as she had done with her Danny.

Well, one thing at a time. For now, it was still a matter of reading books to catch up on basic subjects. It was still a matter of concentrating on success in business. Eventually, he would attend college classes to acquire a degree in business. He would plan his wedding in a slow but steady way. Mostly, he would win the hearts of his future in-laws and his new community. In a moment of clear cognition, Adam realized that questioning God's motives was not the problem at all. He simply had to figure out how to get so much done.

At least he had been blessed with a clear path. God gave him not one but two mentors to guide him along the way. Rabbi Simon and Benny Kalabokas. One religious and one, a much loved member of the local community. Adam couldn't help but think of them as two halves that would make the whole he could call father. Most ex-Hasids didn't have such *mazel*. Their luck was usually that they had no luck at all. They only had abandonment in every sense of the word.

Not knowing what else to do, he looked upward and said a prayer in his mind, thanking God for the kindness. At least he would have some form of a father. And it was in that moment that Adam had his epiphany. As the whooshing noise of the subway train closed in on the station, Adam understood his ultimate destiny. He would become the next Benny.

Someday, somehow, he would make this quasi-father of his proud. Follow in his footsteps. He would do for others what Benny had done for him. He'd point the fact out to Benny when he was ready to create the support group. Help him to see that, together, they'd create that beautiful concept of *pay it forward* that Rabbi Simon had mentioned. Adam ended his thoughts on the matter with a simple truth that he had heard in his Hasidic life: God works in mysterious ways.

ot that Adam had ever asked, but Benny and Rose had made it their mission to act as if they were foster parents. Never mind the fact that Adam was a grown man. They wanted to give him a safe haven in terms of shelter and food. They wanted to make sure he felt loved and accepted as he embraced his new way of life.

Adam had fallen into an assured daily routine. He got up at the crack of dawn and, along with Benny, headed over to the Daily Diner. Once there, he'd have eggs or pancakes, and Benny even prepared the occasional treat of oatmeal with fresh fruit. Upon sating his appetite, Adam would leave for the city and begin his workday.

For fun, sometimes Benny would stroke the air from right to left as if his arm were a paintbrush, timing the gesture to Adam's exit. In an even sweep across his blank canvas, Benny would gracefully move it and declare, "A daily diner at the Daily Diner. There he is, folks." The audience was typically the void of the early hours, but on rare occasion, another early riser enjoyed the humor. The result of the gesture…Adam could start his day with a smile.

Adam was riding into the city for training at Harold Jewelers. Construction for the new store was nearly finished, and Adam would be its head manager in about two more months. He was learning the nuances of good management at this point. He was tying up loose ends and preparing for the many customers he hoped would come through the doors of the new shop.

Ads were already surfacing, touting the wonderful luck that residents of the county had. Not only could they avoid having to head into the city to purchase fine jewels, but they would have Adam Goldfarb as manager. The ads presented Adam to the public as if he were king among the multitude of management. There would be a grand-opening sale to boot. A win-win situation all around.

Adam's personal life was a bit more difficult to contend with. Not in terms of the minutiae of wedding planning or apartment preparation. He left most of that to Daniella and even his future mother-in-law. It was more difficult in terms of his own transition and being fully accepted into everyday life. The Soblers were still slow to alter their conviction that Adam might turn their daughter into a fanatical observer of the faith or that he might leave her for a second time.

Hard as it had been, Adam and Daniella had both agreed to live separately until both his divorces were final. That they would not see each other except for on the Sabbath and on Sunday afternoons at the Sobler home. It was a way to ensure that no one from the congregation would dare to hint at a secret affair. To know it was all about to come to an end was an enormous relief for Adam.

Adam was staring out of the subway train window, looking at the black tunnel walls that went whooshing by. The darkness of the concrete triggered more intense thoughts and Adam was preoccupied in a thinking bubble. He pondered things that Daniella had shared. Things they discussed together.

They both knew that there was no point in dishonesty, as so many congregants knew that Adam was still married when the relationship began. Much as Daniella loved her congregation, she had warned Adam that a small handful of members speculated that she was the reason for the divorce. The rumor mill implied that somehow she had lured Adam after their fateful meeting.

Daniella and Adam hated that these people spoke as if they were privy to the details of the relationship. Implying that Daniella was the type of woman to have an affair, irked Adam to the core. There were those who said that Cantor Sobler was lessened in their eyes because there was shame in carrying on with a married man. Sadly, it all came from skewed speculation based on gossip.

At least by visiting at the Soblers', Adam ensured that their visits were supervised. Marcia, being the proud mother that she was, had no qualms about letting everyone know that the relationship was on the up and up. Her motherly defense mechanisms came into play any time she overheard people questioning her daughter's integrity. She'd also point out that this was Adam's chance to get to know Daniella's family, including her siblings. Indeed, Adam did feel comfortable in their home now, and their observances became a security blanket, reminding him of the traditions he loved.

The reality of this plan for the couple to meet at the Soblers' proved far different from the congregation's presumed intent regarding the matter. It would be a long time before Marcia and Ira Sobler truly believed in their own heart of hearts that Adam was the man he made himself out to be. And who could blame them? For Marcia, her doubt began the moment Adam had his fateful meeting with Daniella at Beth David two years back. Why did he come back? Was he using Daniella for his own personal gain? What did she really know about this man?

The fact that he still wore *tzitzit* under his shirt was not the only dead giveaway for the members of Beth David. They recognized the unmistakable mop top of curls and his smiling face. The secretary Adele had remembered him immediately. She recalled him visiting with Daniella on occasion, and she remembered the flowers and letters sent. Adam and Daniella both surmised that she began to tell others that she recognized him as the man in the cantor's office. By the time the Soblers were on board and protecting the good name of their future son-in-law, gossip was thriving.

People were hungry for details of their courtship, speculating on what they believed to be the truth, curious to know about Adam's former life. And since Adam was a source of constant speculation, to date, it hadn't stopped. Adam reflected on how he and Daniella decided to handle the matter. He smiled as he stared at the window.

They would tell anyone who asked that they became an item long after his decision to leave Hasidism. Long after his decision to finalize his divorce from his wife. That they began dating only when Adam was already exploring his new life, free and clear and simply waiting for his final divorce papers.

No one in the congregation would be privy to the fact that they had been something of a couple once before. No one would know of the heartbreak and bad decisions. There was no need for personal, private details to be put on display. Because they knew the people of the congregation would dissect each detail as if it were a savory morsel needing to be thoroughly masticated, the impetus to stick to these facts was airtight.

As to the fact that many knew the secretary's story of the day when a Hasidic man entered the building and specifically asked to speak with Cantor Sobler, well, they had an explanation for that too. Another easy half-truth in order to quell the curiosity. Adam had been exploring his options for transitioning into the bigger world and had thought that speaking to a woman who called herself *hazzan* would be an outrageous way to do so. So he had dared himself to contact the one he had heard about when asking perfect strangers to recommend a synagogue.

As to the tears that Daniella had shed that fateful day during their long-ago meeting, the explanation was one of the two small white lies in their slightly made-up story. Daniella had been overwhelmed by the fact that a Hasidic man chose to talk to her about leaving his *frum* life. That he actually entrusted a woman with his concerns. It had been an emotional overload for Daniella on that day, and she had been grateful to *Hashem* for validating her career choice in such a profound way.

The other white lie came from Adam's mouth. He told anyone who asked that he simply remembered the kindness and patience that Cantor Sobler had afforded him. He also recalled that she had been pleasant to look at and very intelligent. He had noticed that she'd had no wedding ring on her finger, only a diamond. He merely took a chance that she might still be single and willing to date him. Wasn't it amazing that they ended up being a couple and planning their marriage? He was always sure to end the encounter by posing that particular question.

In time, congregants would remember the story in the way it was presented and share it with others as if it had been the truth all along. Wasn't it fantastic how they came together? Wasn't it great that he chose Daniella's lifestyle over his own? Wasn't he such a nice man? It would take time, but eventually, even those comments would become a thing of the past, and congregants would no longer find him gossip worthy at all.

Once his lifestyle was akin to theirs, there was no excitement in it. There was nothing left to discuss. Adam would stand out in only one particular way, and it was of his own accord. He wanted to make absolutely sure that anytime someone had a question about *frum* versus not *frum*, that person would go to him. Especially if the question was vindictive. For some reason he couldn't quite explain, he wanted to make sure that people didn't harbor too much negativity about Hasids. He wanted to protect his former community. His parents and other loved ones. Those he still called friends in his heart. Adam refused to hear anyone spew cruel words.

The biggest challenge was winning over the hearts of his future in-laws and even Daniella herself. A certain level of distrust lingered for months. Silly nontruths that Adam had to battle as if slaying a dragon. For instance, they thought Adam would leave a second time. Adam would criticize the Sobler household. Adam would chide Daniella's observance choices. Adam would change his mind and revert back to his former ways.

In many ways, the battle was even tougher than leaving his first marriage. It was most certainly a blessing in disguise that Adam had the safe haven known as the Kalabokas home as he transitioned from one life into another. Benny and Rose provided his only source of strength. Foster parents for a grown man. People who loved and cared about him.

Of all the possible demons that Adam would have to face, as painful as the divorce or the prying of a new congregation had been, it was the fight within him that was the hardest of all. It's a tough battle when divine guidance clearly lights the way but everyone around you tries to snuff out the brilliance of that light, hell-bent on proving that you mean nothing of what you say or feel nothing of what you claim.

*B*enny and Adam were sitting down to a quiet meal in the Kalabokas home. Rose was in the kitchen, servicing the plates, too preoccupied with the task at hand to try to focus on what the men were saying.

"So, Adam, are you seeing any difference in the way the Soblers are treating you?"

"Yes. They're becoming kinder...more caring."

Adam dwelled on a specific memory as he spoke the words. There he was, visiting the Soblers for the first time since his return to Daniella. He was standing with Ira and Marcia Sobler. He recalled the coldness in their eyes despite the politeness in their speech. There was no trust in those eyes. How could he blame them? He had broken their daughter's heart, and that was unforgivable.

Ira Sobler kept the fury silent, as men often do. Marcia Sobler had no such qualms. Women knew it was healthy to emote, and she was more than eager to share. She found a way to get him alone that day and had just enough time to utter her frustration before Daniella came barging in. A blunt dagger shot through Adam's heart. Straight and to the point.

"For the first time, I understand, really understand, the concept of hardening the heart. You've turned me into a Pharaoh, Adam. And for that, I resent you and what you've done to me. I don't like the way it feels. It's cold and harsh. Prove to me that your love for my daughter is real. Make me believe you're here to stay. Prove to me that you are truly the person you say you are so I can change how I feel about you."

It was hard for Adam to acknowledge that the Soblers were, for all intents and purposes, on the same list as those he had left behind. People who harbored negative feelings for him. At least in the Soblers' case, he had the ongoing ability to change their heartfelt convictions. They did not shoo him out the door and ask him never to return. They had no plans to abandon him. In their case, there was at least a willingness to give him a chance. Adam responded in the best way he knew how.

"I broke a lot of hearts, Mrs. Sobler. I've lost people I love. My parents..."

There was a huge pause and a heavy intake of breath before Adam could continue.

"I've lost so much. I don't want to lose Danny as well. All I can do is pray that in time you'll believe in your heart that I'm good enough for your daughter." Adam had paused once more. "That you'll know, really know, how much I love her."

Adam returned to the conversation at hand. Benny looked as if he were waiting for more, but really, what could Adam say? Adam knew he couldn't share his deepest thoughts, not even with Benny. If he did, surely Benny would say he'd gone soft. That he was letting the demons get to him. Benny would then prod him to express them all so that the demons could be expelled.

Lately, the reality of living in a modern world was getting to Adam. Mostly because it was making clear those things he now lacked in his life. His mother. His father. His siblings. His son. How in heaven's name was Adam supposed to reconcile those truths? How was he supposed to create happiness from such sorrow? It seemed impossible. There would only be grief till the day he died.

In the blink of an eye, Adam had lost friends, cousins, aunts, uncles, parents, in-laws, and a very solid communal life. He had lost a son. Did the Soblers—or anyone, for that matter—ever stop to think about that? Did anyone really consider just how much he gave up? It wasn't even about teachings, morals, opinions, or any other nonemotional entities. Those things he wanted to give up. Needed to give up.

This was about the emotional component of his being. This was about the fact that he gave up love in order to get love. This was about the fact that he gave up a huge piece of himself. Every time Adam thought about his son, he wanted to cry. Every time he closed his eyes and heard his own mother say, "You'll always be my little *yingele,*" he choked up. Her words were those any mother would say to ensure that her son knew he'd always be her little boy, always be loved. Dearly, dearly loved.

Adam became so lost in his thoughts that he went silent. His face held a serious expression, and his eyes misted. For the moment, he forgot that Benny was sitting across from him and watching every facial change that Adam was making. He had forgotten that although the scenarios were completely different for each, Benny was his twin when it came to the experience of losing family and friends. It made Adam jolt when Benny reached across the wooden surface and took both of Adam's hands in his own. Benny's eyes were somewhat teary.

"Adam, I know it sounds crazy, but I could hear every word you just said in your head. I could hear them because I know them. I lived them, Adam. I know the pain of losing parents. I know the pain of losing everyone. Everyone, Adam. And everything that was precious and dear. I know it all the way down to losing my beloved community.

"I would never dare to compare Nazis with anyone I would call a human being, but sadly, one thing they relished is something that many of us are guilty of. They manipulated human feelings, Adam. Enough so that people who were at one time harmless citizens abiding in Europe were suddenly sure that our people needed to be eliminated."

Benny took pause and continued. "They took my parents, my extended family. They destroyed my home and everything that was my world. Gone. I had no choice but to rebuild a life for myself. Isn't it the same for you? The components are different, but the outcome is the same. Didn't you lose everything in the blink of an eye?"

"I did, Benny."

"You know, Adam, I recall hearing a phrase...I think Nate shared it with me. It went something like, when God closes a door, somewhere he opens a window." Benny nodded his head to prove to himself he remembered it correctly. He continued speaking. "Whatever is fated for us, God still gives us choices. God makes the master plan, but we are the ones to decide how the plan should be played out. It's up to us to pick the best choice from what is laid at our feet. It's up to us to find the window and open it up so we can climb out.

"God gave me my uncle and my sister. He gave me the uncle that was the ambitious one. The one that he knew would make something of our lives. God gave you Danny because she was the perfect guide into the life you were craving for yourself. I'm trying to say that it doesn't diminish the pain and hurt. Nothing will. But God made sure you had a window open. You understand?"

Benny was waiting for Adam's response, but fate had other things in mind. The mysterious workings of a higher realm took the upper hand at that moment. Benny was suddenly back in his own mind, posing the question he had just asked. *Didn't you lose everything in the blink of an eye?* Benny looked straight into the eyes of Adam. *Oh my dearest God, I know who you are.* Out of seemingly nowhere, an invisible lightbulb went on above Benny's head, and he widened his eyes and clutched Adam's hands more tightly. Wretched sobbing took control, and Benny bent his head forward and rested it on the table as he cried endless tears.

"Benny, what's wrong? Benny? Rose, please come in here."

Rose came running out of the kitchen and went straight to Benny's side. She pulled a dining chair out and over to him. She sat on it in a way that would maximize the physical connection she could make with him. She pried his body off the table and pulled him into her arms.

Adam sat in stunned silence, feeling completely helpless. He watched Benny sink into an emotional abyss.

"Tell me, my Benny. Tell me," Rose said as she stroked Benny's hair.

Rose had never encountered a scene like this before. This was deep, whatever it was. She hoped and prayed that Benny would articulate enough to get it out of his mouth and, hopefully, out of his system. As if in answer to her unspoken prayer, Benny let the words out freely, each coming between gasping breaths filled with heaving sobs.

"I understand. I finally understand. Adam and Daniella, they were my window."

"What does that mean, sweetheart?"

"They were my therapy, Rose. God gave them to me to help me. To make me see myself in them. To make me give them advice and love them. Make me care for them so I would hear aloud the very things I needed to hear. The things my own parents could never tell me."

The sentences came in choppy waves. Benny's heavy sobbing and shaking gasps between each of them only added to the difficulty of understanding what he was trying to say. Rose looked at Benny with confusion in her eyes. She prayed that somehow she would make sense of what he was trying so hard to articulate. God answered the silent request by letting Benny calm himself and speak the heart of the matter.

"I have millions of customers. I've never gotten attached to any. Not a one. Why them? Because God knew I'd see my mother in Danny. Rose, she looks like my mother. She acts like my mother. She had dreams she wanted to achieve, just like my mother."

Rose had never thought about it because, well, Danny was Danny. Thinking about it now, even she could recognize the resemblance to the woman in the photo that rested on Benny's work desk. Childhood memories locked deep inside Benny's brain had made a connection. It made sense. Rose even understood the psychology. She responded with a supporting statement.

"So somehow, Adam became your father, and you were determined to give them both life."

Benny nodded his head as he sobbed in Rose's arms.

"Rose, I think I thought that they were my parents, come back to me. I couldn't let life swallow them up again. I don't want to let life swallow them up again."

"Of course you don't, Benny. I understand, sweetheart. I do."

How strange life could be. That one moment in someone's life could completely alter the course of another's. Adam, had been listening in silent shock as he watched Benny fall apart. Nonetheless, the sentiments that were spoken were heard, considered and ultimately, put into practical sense in Adam's mind.

The result was that he looked back in his own memory banks, recalling how he thought that Benny might be a replacement for the father he'd lost. It didn't even matter that Benny equated Adam with his own deceased father. For each of them, it was obvious they were filling a void. It meant that they both loved and cared for each other. He got up from the table and walked around to crouch down at Benny's free side.

"Benny, it doesn't matter if you think that Danny and I are your reincarnated parents." Adam chuckled. "Maybe we are!" Adam reached up to wrap his fingers around

Benny's forearm. He hoped his gentle touch would convey the feelings he wanted to express.

"What it does mean is exactly what you just said to me. *Hashem* has opened up a window for us. He made us a family. Us, Benny. You, Danny, me, we're a family. That's why we care so much about each other. That's why you want us to be happy. You're doing what any loving parent would do."

Benny stopped sobbing and looked up at Adam. He smiled as he responded.

"I have been blessed with my beautiful Rose, my three lovely daughters, and my sons-in-law. Beautiful grandchildren that light up my heart. Danny became like an adopted daughter. Now she, too, will provide a son-in-law. Time will provide the grandchildren from you, God willing. Yes...I love all of you. You're all my family. You're right, Adam. You're absolutely right."

Benny gazed at Adam with a newfound tenderness. He reached up to give a loving stroke against Adam's cheek.

"You're a good soul, Adam. And the best part is that this time, I get to see you and Danny make a life for yourself. I get to see you succeed. I get to see an outcome this time."

Benny stood up from his chair and gave Adam a bear hug. Adam had no reservations about returning the affection. Rose had watched the two men embrace but kept quiet. Benny looked at her and winked. It was an unspoken message that he had more to say, and would want to do so later. Rose was a good listener and very insightful. She'd let him talk and get it all out of his system. He would certainly need to. He would reveal what he harbored inside for years.

As to Adam, well, Benny knew that Rose wouldn't mind what he had said. Adam's presence in the house had made her grow fond of him too. She was like a foster mother without really being one. She got to care for another child. Her role as mother was always her crowning achievement, and it brought her happiness. Benny knew that she cared for Adam. Rose interrupted his thoughts by offering a suggestion.

"Listen, you two. The food will keep. Why don't I leave you both alone for a while and let you talk some more. When you're ready, let me know."

Adam responded first.

"Actually, I wouldn't mind the opportunity. I do have things I'd like to say to Benny."

With all that had transpired, the epiphany about fatherhood was the perfect segue into his idea about paying it forward. He'd reflect on the fact that, in the same way he was a father figure for Benny, Benny was a father for him. And each of them was a support system for the other. He'd talk about how much they could do for others who were also lost and hurting. People who wanted out from the Hasidic community or any other situation. People who no longer had family to call their own.

Hopefully, Benny would be interested. Adam would stress that it still wasn't the right place and time, but the idea was something to think about for the future. Not even the near future. There was still too much else that needed to be settled. It was merely an idea for the years ahead. Then, after all was said and done, he'd speak to Danny about it all.

Someday, too, he'd let her know what transpired between the two today, including Benny's admission. Adam was sure it would help Danny to understand why Benny had been so involved in her life all these years. It would explain things all the way back to the time Danny and he first met.

It was hard to fathom that Benny cared as deeply as he did. Adam thanked God for opening that said window when the door was slammed shut. That window provided a way out and showed a clear view of a beautiful world equal in love to the one behind the door. For what seemed like the millionth time, Adam uttered the blessing he had come to know so well and repeated quite often in the silence of his thoughts. *Baruch atah Adonai, shomayah tefillah.* Blessed is God, who listens to prayer.

dam entered the synagogue light on his feet, a song in his heart. He didn't bother to stop at the front office. Much as he liked the ladies who worked there, nosiness was one of their strong points. He simply waved and said, "The cantor is expecting me," as he walked toward her office. Truth of the matter was that she wasn't expecting him at all, but Adam was too happy to care that he lied.

The door was closed, so he gave it a wrap as he said, "Danny, it's me."

Adam's voice on the other side of the door was the last thing she expected at that moment. She wasn't expecting him until later that day.

"Come in, Adam."

Adam entered, and Daniella immediately took note of the large manila envelope tucked under his left arm, his right hand holding it firmly in place inside the secreted nook.

"Hi, Adam. This is a real surprise. What's up?"

Adam pulled the envelope from under his arm and waved it in front of himself as if it were a white truce flag.

"These are them, Danny. I finally have my hands on my civil divorce papers and my half of the *get*. I can hardly believe it. I thought this day would never come."

Adam paused for only a moment, sighed, and looked into Daniella's eyes. "Yet here they are, and here I stand... Danny, I'm actually holding them in my hand."

Adam had flown back from Belgium two days before, but he had arrived so late in the day that the Sabbath had been only four hours away. He'd had no choice but to hustle from the city airport and arrive at the Kalabokas home before the sun completely set. Through no choice of his own, he had been forced to wait until Sunday to present Daniella with the good news.

Daniella's routine always included staying behind in her synagogue after the Sunday Hebrew School classes ended. Normally, she wouldn't see Adam until later in the afternoon at her parents' home. Adam had known he'd find her at the synagogue if he timed it correctly. He wanted to be with her outside the confines of the Sobler home. It was all he could do to get through the weekend, his nervous anxiety getting the best of him. Adam extended his arm out further, offering the papers up like sacrificial fodder.

"They're for you, Danny. My gift to you. My betrothal gift. Take them."

Daniella got up from her chair and walked around her desk. She reached out to take the envelope.

"I don't know what to say, Adam. I don't even think I should be holding these. They belong to you, not me. I really don't know what to say."

"Don't say anything, Daniella. You don't have to. I don't think words would help. Besides, I'm the one who needs to speak."

"What's that supposed to mean?"

Adam knew the process for marriage preparations in his former circles. Families made matches with the help of a matchmaker, and choices were made based on finances, family health, and genetics. Even the snobbery of looking for a scholarly line was more important than the notion of romantic love. The concept of marrying for love was so foreign in his former circles that he doubted it even existed there at all. A good match would bring love in time. The couple would grow to care for each other, and affection would follow. In Adam's new world, the Hasidic process was archaic.

Even so, Adam had learned that some old-fashioned notions remained in the secular world. One tradition, in particular, had a metamorphosis of sorts. In ancient times, daughters were considered the property of the father. Men needed to attain ownership of the daughter directly from the father. The poor girl had no say in the matter. A wife was property, plain and simple. Now, in modern times, it seemed that tradition transformed itself into the idea of men approaching fathers and asking for a blessing to propose. Women seemed to find it endearing when they learned that a blessing had been asked for.

Adam had decided to speak with both the Soblers and let them know he planned to return from Belgium with documents in hand. It would be part of a proposal for Daniella. A betrothal gift like no other. He thought that it would make the Soblers and Daniella happy. Asking the Soblers for a blessing was a good thing, a good start.

It was the winning moment between him and the Soblers. The final turn of the tide. Marcia Sobler said that the fact that he wouldn't even wait to marry meant everything. The fact that he wouldn't dillydally as a boyfriend, complaining about lack of freedom or lack of adventure in his new life, meant he was serious about Daniella. Body language didn't lie, she had said to him. She also added that only a rare few had the gift of crocodile tears under their belt and she saw truth in his misted eyes. It stood to reason that Adam meant every word he said. It was the act of asking for that blessing that had finally endeared him to his soon-to-be in-laws.

Blessings were given that day, and Adam attained two allies. He had looked at the Sobler parents with genuine affection and had said, "You have made me the happiest man on earth."

Here he was now, addressing the woman he loved more than life itself. Adam spoke from the heart. "Danny, the only thing blocking my way was my cowardice. I lost sight of the path *Hashem* was showing me and feared my family and community more than I feared God. Those stupid pieces of paper are proof of that." Adam pointed accusingly at the manila rectangle, shaking his finger in fury.

Knowing what the next step was, Adam had a simple request. "Put it down, Daniella, and come sit closer by me."

She did so, placing the envelope on her desk, and Adam pulled her over to the spare chair that was adjacent to it. He pushed at her shoulders to sit her down, and he crouched at her feet so he could look in her eyes.

"You have been my heart and soul for as long as I have known you. I was just too confused to realize it or even admit it to myself. *Baruch Hashem* that I finally woke up inside. Bless God always that I had the strength to reach this day."

Adam stopped himself from speaking and reflected on his last sentence. Without hesitation, he began to recite one of the most sacred blessings in Judaism as he stared into Daniella's eyes.

Baruch atah Adonai elohaynu melech ha'olam, shechechayanu, vihegeeyanu, vikeyemanu lazman hazeh. Blessed are you, Lord our God, ruler of the universe, who has given me life, sustained me, and enabled me to reach this day.

Adam got down on one knee like the men he'd seen in some of the recent movies he'd been watching. Men kneeling before the women of their dreams, asking them to be their brides. He even borrowed a line or two because he hardly knew what to say.

"Marry me, Daniella. Marry me and make me the happiest man alive. Your mother and father have given me their blessing, and, well, I will be blessed among men if I have you as my wife."

Adam reached into his jacket's inner breast pocket and pulled out a box. He popped the lid and showed Daniella what was inside. She stared and nodded a yes. A dumbfounded, unspoken yes as she gazed at the unique ring inside the box. Looking at it, the tears began to flow as she comprehended the meaning of the design.

The tiniest of hands formed the focal point of the ring. Made of yellow gold, the hands sat on a diagonal, one overlapping the other in a cupping gesture. Almost like the letter X. The palm of the top hand held a peridot inside. It was a pale lime green. So pale that its hue was greenish white. Almost as if it were sprinkled by the merest dab of lime juice.

Adam took the ring out of the box and slipped it onto Daniella's finger.

"I know it's not a diamond, and if you want one, you need only tell me. It's just that I thought, well..." Adam trailed off for a moment. He wanted to gather his words. State them in a way that made very clear what had motivated his choice.

"Gems tell stories. They have meaning. When I looked at peridots, long before I ever even knew you, I always thought about how gentle the August birthstone was. There is such a softness to a peridot. A kindness in its hue that is hard to describe. The gem is so unpresuming. Many a time it is a vibrant lime green. Sometimes, though, it is pale like this. Many people never give the poor stone a second thought. They find it boring. Even ugly. Especially if it is light in color. I never understood that.

"I wish you could know what I felt when I looked into your eyes for the first time. Your peridot eyes, Daniella. They were the first hint of the unpretentious soul within. The hint that true beauty was housed, unpresuming. But now, Danny, now I see that you yourself are the peridot. A peridot that I hold in my hand. Sacred. A gift, Danny. God's gift to me. I could only think that I needed to show you this somehow, and this is the result."

Daniella stared down at the ring on her finger, still unmoving, still speechless. Adam lovingly stroked her falling hair aside as he concluded his proposal.

"I picked the light hue because, just like this poor stone tries so hard to prevail despite everyone's attitude toward it, so too did you. Not only in your dream to become a *hazzan* but with your faith in me. You are my peridot."

Adam took the ringed hand into his own and gave the fingers a loving squeeze.

"Any time you have doubts, Danny, look at the ring so it can remind you of what you are to me. I want this to be the symbol of my betrothal. I want you to look at your ring and see the significance of the words that are in my heart."

Daniella lifted her hand and gazed at the ring. For the briefest of moments, she reminded herself of the previous proposal she had received. She had been presented with a one-carat round diamond, sitting atop four platinum prongs raised high for the world to see. Two lengthy baguettes graced the left and right arc of the diamond's circle. Then, it had been all about the ring. No one had ever asked about the worth of the relationship she was in. It had only mattered that she'd had such an amazing diamond. Somehow the ring had summed up Norman's own worth as a person.

Now she was wearing a ring that was certainly not what people would expect. They were sure to inquire why she wasn't even given a diamond. They would question if she was happy with the ring. They'd be tactless and thoughtless. It would be very annoying, but for the most part, she no longer cared about any comments past or possibly in the future. The worth of her engagement ring was beyond anything she could imagine. It was still hard for her to believe that any man could love her that much or think about her the way Adam did. Daniella smiled at Adam, cupped his cheek with her right hand, and surprised Adam by laughing.

"What's so funny?"

"I'm sorry, Adam. It's not you or your beautiful words. I'm so happy, but I was just thinking of my mother's reaction when she sees that you, a jewelry store manager and a former buyer of diamonds, decided to give me this ring. You, who, more than anyone, should know that a diamond was in order. I can almost hear her."

Daniella used a mocking tone. "Daniella, what was Adam thinking? What am I supposed to tell my friends?"

Adam responded in kind. "Well, I already have an answer for that, Mrs. Sobler."

"Oh, and what might that be?"

"Well, assuming Daniella will eventually move the ring over to her right hand, after we're married, I mean, I have every intention of giving her a diamond wedding band that will be the envy of everyone. As you know, I have access to the best."

Daniella responded as herself. "What if I want to keep the plain gold band that you'll be slipping onto my index finger? What if I want to move it to my left ring finger and put this ring on top of it?"

"If you prefer that, fine. Then I'll give you something beautiful to wear on your right hand. A pretty diamond that will appease the masses."

"I think you'll make my mother very happy with either offer."

"I certainly hope so! I want to keep her as an ally."

"Adam, that's all well and good, but remember, you're not marrying my mother. Just worry about pleasing me!"

He heard the joking tone in Daniella's voice, and he noted the happy smile on her face. This time it was right. That was all that mattered. Daniella rose to her feet, and Adam did too. The two left the office together that day, hand in hand and content. Their journey was about to begin. Life was an open highway, destination unknown. They began by closing the window in Daniella's office and opening the door that led to the outside known as life.

Epilogue

Benny took the last few sips of his now-tepid coffee. Only five minutes remained until he would have to open the restaurant doors. He smiled thinking about the fact that he had spent that morning reminiscing about the Goldfarbs. For some reason, he was feeling sentimental that morning and wanted to replay memories of how he came to feel so close to them. So many years had passed since the time he first met Daniella and Adam. Benny could hardly believe that time flew by so quickly.

Yes, time had flown, and now the eldest of their three children was turning twelve. Preparations were in full swing to prepare young Ezekiel for his Bar Mitzvah. Benny was sure that ten-year-old Shoshanna and eight-year-old Leah would arrive at that same milestone in the blink of an eye. Beautiful children, all of them. Each with his or her share of gemstone eyes and mop-top curls. Their parents were as happy and content as ever. A good match for sure, and a marriage based in partnership and respect. Daniella, still a successful cantor. Adam, a proud owner of his own jewelry store, nestled inside the big mall three towns away.

It took a number of years, but Adam eventually settled into the Conservative life he craved so much. Strange as it seemed, he was able to do so with an Orthodox mind-set, becoming that unique breed of Jew, the Conservadox, that he always hoped he would achieve. Tradition and ritual remained extremely important to him, and he saw to it that both were strong in his household. The fact that he was married to a cantor kept things alive in the context of his Judaism.

More often than not, Adam could be found in suit and tie, professionally assisting any and every sort that entered into his jewelry store. He was an efficient businessman, and anyone would be hard pressed to believe he had once been part of a sheltered community. Benny himself had shopped at the store on more than one occasion to buy gifts for Rose and his girls. Adam always gave him the best of the best both in value and customer service.

Adam was a doting father, and Benny often wondered if it was a personal effort on Adam's part to make up for the loss of his own father. Many a time, Benny was inundated with the latest stack of photos or quips about what each of the children was accomplishing. He didn't mind, though. They were all darling and like extra grandchildren for him. He found it a pleasure to watch them grow. To witness their happiness.

Once in a while, Adam hosted the secret meetings he had vowed to create. Benny was accommodating, allowing the use of the back-room office for those particular get-togethers. He chose that area because the door could be closed, even locked. No one need be privy to the fears of the individuals locked inside.

The meetings didn't happen all that often. When they did, only one, two, or three people at most would attend. Adam would share his personal experiences, give references, and name people who could possibly help. In time, he had a small list of willing congregants who would host these people in their homes. These families would take them to synagogue, shopping, and to schools so they could talk with administrators and inquire about an education. They were taken to every place that might give them a taste of the bigger world.

Benny looked up at the big clock on the bar-stool wall. He noted that the time was getting late. He allowed himself the briefest of moments before he stood up, in order that he could ponder the sorrow he referred to as the foolishness of Adam's parents. He often wondered what the Goldfarbs' lives were like today. Such a pity. Well, one thing he knew for sure. They were devoid of the joy that was the Goldfarb grandchildren and unaware of the blessed success of their son. As to why they gave up so much, he'd never really know. Certainly, never understand.

Next Thursday was Greek night at the Daily. Benny would see Adam and Daniella on that Thursday evening and once again, enjoy the company of his special couple. They had continued to come to the restaurant through the years and made sure to visit once a month with the children when it was Greek night. Marcia and Ira Sobler had joined ranks about three years after the wedding, making it an official family tradition. They got their own friends to attend as well. Best of all, they had become

Benny's personal pep club, letting anyone and everyone know that Benny was a *mentch* and folks needed to patronize his establishment. On those nights, he was so much more than the proprietor of the Daily Diner. He was family.

Benny walked toward the register as he looked out through the glass window nearest him. The rain had stopped, and the sun was pushing its way over the horizon, shedding daylight through the panes. Realizing the nostalgic morning had actually done him a world of good, Benny smiled, thinking it was going to be a grand day, after all. He stepped toward the front door, reached into his pocket to assure himself that his keys were resting inside, and began the same routine he'd done countless times. As Benny turned the key in the door lock, his thoughts about it all ended then and there.

It would be hours later and in another area of town, that Adam's sister Aviva would make yet another of her remote shopping trips. Her excuses were often lacking, but somehow she muddled through them. Sometimes it would be with a comment of needing to get to a certain store because the store in the neighborhood didn't carry a particular item she dreamed of sewing. "No, they don't have the velvet I had in mind. Perhaps if I take a taxi to the fabric store near that mall, I might find something. I really like that fabric shop, so I don't mind going there."

Other times she was more vague. "I'm taking care of some errands. I'll be out for a while, but I'll be back in time to prepare dinner." Always, she was cautious. Many Hasidic people were venturing out more and more for the sake of a good buy. Even so, she'd never bump into anyone in a supermarket or a restaurant far out from the community. Those places were off limits. It was more a matter of avoiding the young mothers pushing strollers through the nearby mall or shopping in the fabric store that she herself was supposed to go to. *Hashem* forbid that she would have to explain why she was using a public phone in such a secretive way.

She made her trips in order to place a call to Adam. It was getting harder and harder with each passing year, but she'd keep it up as long as she could. Public telephones were being dismantled at an alarming rate, becoming a thing of the past. Aviva often fretted as to what she would do when the time came there were none left on the streets or in malls at all. She'd have to go even farther away in order to avoid ridicule from her community. After all, she was talking to a sinner of the worst kind, and that was unacceptable.

Aviva always called Adam at his place of business. She wanted to call him at his home, but she wanted to make sure that if she were found out, at least Daniella would remain innocent of the interactions. Aviva would hear about Daniella and the children through Adam, and in turn, she always sent messages to each of them via her brother. She continually prayed that someday, somehow, she could visit their home and enjoy the loving family Adam had created. She also prayed that Daniella would forgive her for her lack of connection as a sister-in-law.

Aviva's scenario with her mother and father was consistent. She would find a way to imply that she had obtained information about Adam. She never divulged how she came across it. Would they like to hear it? They in turn would adamantly refuse to hear whatever it was that Aviva offered to say. Nonetheless, Tsivia would approach her daughter a day or two after the exchange, generally when she could get Aviva alone for a minute or two. She'd listen to Aviva's news and ache inside for the perpetual missing of her darling boy.

Knowing that her husband felt similarly in the deepest recesses of his own emotions, Tsivia would find a quiet moment when the two were alone, perhaps sipping tea or discussing the week's plans. She'd make deep and direct eye contact with her husband and simply state, *Alles is gut.* The simplest of statements to let her husband know that all was well with their boy. She even had wild fantasies of convincing her husband to drive them to the restaurant that she knew her son still frequented, just so she could see him and his family for a brief visit. Tsivia cried many a time, knowing it would never be.

In another world entirely, halfway around the world, to be exact, a young man stood close by the Western Wall with his stepfather and friends. He had a head full of mop-top curls and eyes the color of sky-blue crystals. He was waiting with bait in hand. Rotted fruit and soiled diapers were his ammunition. His name was Shmuel, and he could hardly wait to carry out God's will and deter the women who had the audacity to believe they could pray at the wall. God must surely be angry at them for outstepping their boundaries, thinking they had the right to go to such a sacred site meant for holy men.

God needed his earthly help to get that message across. Shmuel stood on guard, dirty bowel-stained diaper at the ready. He would fling it at the first woman who dared to come and try to say afternoon prayers. For good measure, he'd throw eggs too. He'd aim for those who covered themselves in prayer shawls and put *yarmulkes* atop their heads.

His own wife was at home, tending to the children as she should be. Praised be the Almighty that she knew her place. She was submissive that way, and that was how he liked it. She kept a clean home, cooked well, and gave him three sons. He was eager to get home later so he could try for a daughter. Not that he particularly wanted one, but he knew it would make his wife happy. She deserved to have at least one daughter, and for him, well, it meant he could raise a righteous woman for some other man.

Shmuel's own mother had six children in total. He was the oldest. He had been told that he was born from a different father, one who was practically evil personified. Evil enough that he had tricked his mother into marriage, feigning righteousness. He'd heard that summation repeatedly from the man he called his true father. It was a warning, to be sure, and a lesson that Shmuel felt he learned very well.

Shmuel never asked his mother if all the summations were correct. He just assumed they were. Sometimes, his mother would concur with something his father had said, but mostly, she never spoke about her prior marriage. The only thing she did divulge from time to time was that the best way for Shmuel to prevent his own self destruction was to do everything in his power to be a good and observant Jew. Yet she never elaborated on what that meant. For him, it meant following the Hasidic lifestyle faithfully. The lifestyle that he had learned to embrace from the teachings of his true father and fellow community members.

The daily brainwashing from his stepfather had taken hold when he was just five years old. It was at that age that he began to understand and remember things. Eventually, the teachings turned into an adult's solid convictions. Shmuel believed every word with all his heart. Now, an adult himself, he adored his true father's standing in the community and emulated it with a gusto that came from deep within.

He had no interest in meeting the man who gave him life or in visiting the world that man lived in. Shmuel was sure it would destroy him. He felt such deep-rooted hatred toward the man who had given him demonic genes that he could barely articulate how he felt. He could not bear the possibility that those genes could devour his *yetzer tov* and leave him only with his *yetzer harah*. Even worse, the possibility that those genes now resided within his own young sons...

Shmuel often wondered why he deserved such punishment. At least if he continued to be a devout Hasid, God would be gracious and ensure that his goodness would prevail and that his own children would not inherit the defect that could push them toward evil.

For good measure, Shmuel spit into the dirty diaper in his hand. He smiled at his father, both men harboring a look of smug satisfaction as the first woman walked toward the wall.

In the community that was Shmuel's home, Teme sat tatting. She had finally finished the day's baking and cleaning, and she could now sit and take a welcomed break. She paused for a moment and looked at her hands. Hands that were now showing signs of aging. She thought about her long-ago hands. Back when they were soft and finely chiseled, untouched by the wear and tear of raising children and running a home.

Her thoughts drifted to imaginary glimpses of her once-girlish figure. She used to be a beauty. Now, she carried about thirty pounds of extra weight. Those few times she glanced in the mirror, she could hardly believe it was herself she was seeing in the reflection. The only person she could see there was a devout Hasidic woman, chubby and boring.

Teme walked around with every conceivable form of modest clothing on. She knew that outsiders thought of her as frumpy and plain because she had heard it herself many a time when passing by gossipers. Sadly, she couldn't disagree. Her once-beautiful head of hair was now a turban-covered bald orb that diminished her looks even more. Her chiseled features devoid of make-up looked more and more lifeless. She was like every other *frum* woman in her village. There was absolutely nothing about her that made her stand out from the others.

Teme sat thinking about how she had used her good looks and her charms to gain the affections of one Adam Goldfarb. She threw herself a bone by reminding herself she had been very young and naive at the time. She was so much older now and certainly wiser. Insightfulness had increased through the years, and even some enlightened thinking had taken hold.

The secretive thinking she was sure to keep to herself. Hadn't she been a fool back then to think she even understood life? Her second husband was too pious to care about such things. He wanted to procreate for the sake of creation and nothing more. There was no tenderness when he took her to bed. Adam had tried many times to be tender, and Teme had turned it away.

She never heard many *thank yous* or even *I love yous* from her husband. Adam had tried but she had chided him for thinking about romance more than sacredness. Now, from her present day husband there was mostly piety. Supersized, over-the-top piety. Teme knew she couldn't even blame *Hashem*. She had gotten exactly what she had prayed for, and consistently at that. The mirror had been held up, and it was apparent to Teme that in many ways, her husband was a reflection of that which she herself had been to Adam all those years ago. If only she had allowed Adam's loving touch. If only she had given some consideration to his thoughts about life and the reasons we live it or even to the possibility of thinking in a different way.

In its own way, her fate was likely retribution. She finally understood what she had done to Adam all those years ago. How horrible to be shut out to such a large extent and in such intimate ways. How much better would it have been if she hadn't insisted it was her way or no way? Now, it was too late. Once more, Teme admitted that she had no right to complain. *Hashem* had answered all her requests.

In punishment, she was trapped in the very clutches of what she had hoped would bring her joy. She loved her children dearly, but she saw quite clearly that the cycle would do no more than repeat itself. Her husband was busy looking for matches for his three eldest after Shmuel, and that meant people who lived up to his pious standards. There was literally no hope that her future grandchildren would have anything different from what she lived every day.

Just for the briefest of moments, Teme felt a twinge of jealousy over the life she might have had. She had heard through the secretive grapevine that Adam owned his own jewelry store and that his wife was a successful *hazzan* in a Conservative, egalitarian synagogue. What would it be like to pray on the *bimah* or read from the Torah scroll? She could only wonder.

Teme still felt the woman had far outstepped her boundaries, yet in a strange way, Teme was proud of Daniella. Why couldn't women do more than run a house and produce children? Teme was even a bit jealous that she herself didn't have that same level of *chutzpadik-ness*. She was too afraid of her father's wrath to have ever been gutsy enough to defy him when she was younger. Now, as an older adult woman, she was wise enough to leave the judgments about it all to the true judge of life. Teme would have to be content with merely acknowledging her thoughts about it and her fantasies of what might have been.

Teme didn't like that the woman prayed with men. She had heard that Daniella was attractive, so it stood to reason that she would distract all the men in her congregation. Teme still believed that it was very important for a man to fulfill his Judaic obligations. Best not to have a woman in the way. It was too ingrained in Teme's thinking for her to consider otherwise.

Yet, as to the woman Daniella herself, being a leader who had mastered the art of *hazzanut*... Teme hoped that she was teaching other women the skills to worship. Let the women have a role beyond scrubbing and changing diapers. Let the women have their own special place in synagogue life. To Teme's thinking, there was nothing wrong with the women doing those things as long as they did them separate from the men. In a special room in the synagogue, perhaps, where the women could do everything from leading their service to reading from the Torah scroll. Teme kept the blasphemous thoughts to herself.

So long ago now, Teme had heard about Adam's life from her former in-laws. Strange stories about them happening to be on the same street as Adam and seeing him in the distance or coincidentally shopping in the same department store as Daniella when she was with the children. Teme knew better. The Goldfarbs had set up some type of spy network or some such thing. Hasids in the jewelry business who might have tidbits of information from so-and-so, who happened to have sold diamonds to Adam. Maybe information from someone who happened to shop in the same store as Daniella and was a friend to Tsivia. More likely, the information came from Adam's sister Aviva. The kind one who was always looking out for her younger brother.

Her in-laws contacted her often, at least initially. They wanted to inquire after their grandson as well as her own well-being. They divulged the information, thinking it was their duty to let Teme know what Shmuel's father was up to. What things they themselves had heard. It never occurred to them that the information might bring Teme emotional pain or even anger.

Teme often wanted to ask why they didn't contact Adam directly, despite what had transpired. Of course she never did. She knew the answer. The answer was the same one she had been taught to accept. Adam had been sucked up by the evils of the world. *Hashem* had devised a huge test, and it was up to them all to pass it. Their very own apple, which made the world their snake.

Eventually, the calls stopped, for no other reason than Shmuel making clear he didn't want a relationship with the Goldfarbs. If they were Adam's parents, he thought, his birth father's notions and ideas had likely come from mistakes in their own observances and the way they raised him. Teme visibly flinched in her chair as she recalled telling the Goldfarbs about Shmuel's decision. That had been her last phone conversation with her long-ago family. Teme wondered if it served to make them resent Adam even more.

Teme had never been brave enough to ask them the questions she desperately wanted to. Now, it was too late. They were so hurt by Shmuel's decision not to have a relationship with them that they cut Teme and him out of their lives forever. It was all too painful, they had told her during that last call. They wished her well and told her they would always pray for Shmuel. To this day, Teme didn't know if they had relinquished their anger enough to find some type of common ground with Adam. Her instincts told her that it would never be so.

Teme was kind enough not to attempt calls through the years because it would only further their pain to hear news about Shmuel and not be a part of his life. Admittedly, it was mostly because she didn't want Shmuel to find out that she dared to do such a thing. He might cut her off as well. And despite any of his adult attitudes, Teme still easily recalled the darling baby with the mop-top curls, the child she had rocked to sleep years ago. The thought of losing him was too much to bear.

He may not have wanted to inherit his father's thirst for the bigger world, but in essence, he had inherited the drive to stick to his convictions. In Shmuel's case, he followed his beliefs to a similar extreme as his father had, only toward the opposite end of the Judaic spectrum. Teme had learned enough of her own lessons at that point to know that silence was her ally. She would never do anything that would cause her son to cut her off in the same way she had done to Adam all those years ago.

Teme resumed her tatting but not before brushing her hand across the beautiful lace pattern she had created. To this day, the intricacies of the design gave her a satisfaction that was hard to describe. She hoped that, if nothing else, she honored her deceased relatives' names by producing such graceful and elegant work. As she sat and worked, a tear trickled down Teme's cheek. Simple, quiet acknowledgment that lace work was her one true happiness.

The world that was far away in the cloistered community in Israel had no affect and certainly no place in the lives of those who patronized the Daily Diner. Benny had just officially opened up for the day. He was pleased to see Sam Greenfeld walk through the doors alongside Nate that morning. He hadn't anticipated a visit from Sam that day, so it was an unexpected surprise. Benny thought it was another indication that it would be a great day. Sam was always great company.

"Benny, how's it going? Thought I'd come in since it's been a while. I hope it's a good morning for some business chat because I wanted to tell you about an article I read in *The Business Report*. Great magazine, that one. Ran a whole spread on how businesses are computerizing their inventories, registers, you name it!"

Benny looked at Nate. "If Nate doesn't mind holding the fort for a while."

"Benny, why are you even asking me? You opened up today, so go sit for a while. I'll give you a shout out if the register gets too busy."

Oddly, Sam began his conversation that morning by recalling the time years before when he had gotten his hands on a flyer that had circulated in his synagogue. Well, not inside his synagogue but rather on the windshields of every car in the synagogue parking lot. Placed there on a particular Sunday when the synagogue had produced a well-publicized community fair and all were too busy having a good time inside the doors of the building to take notice of those individuals who placed the flyers on the windshields outside.

Sam brought it up that morning as a segue to his planned discussion. Benny found it nothing less than ironic that Sam brought it up moments after he himself had reminisced about Adam and Daniella. Benny recalled those flyers quite well. They had been about the Daily Diner. They accused the Daily Diner of being an establishment that hoodwinked Jews into leaving their observances.

The flyers stated that the kosher certification was not true and was used in an attempt to lure unsuspecting Jews into the restaurant. The paper sheets stated that since it was co-owned by a non-Jew, the restaurant was a grievous blight on the good will of Jews in the county. Basically, the flyer was a nasty piece of propaganda and most definitely the result of Adam's decisions back at that time.

The community at large, including Sam, chalked it up to nonsense. Many tore the flyers to shreds, verbalizing rage and anger as they did so. The remaining papers were quickly collected and dumped straight into the trash. The relationship, or actually lack thereof, between Hasids and secular Jews of the county was becoming more and more strained, and so the paper tactic was seen as a desperate attempt on the part of the observant community to close down a beloved restaurant.

It was the pot calling the kettle black. The Hasidic community had its own share of incidences that threatened the good name of the Hasidic Jew. They were disobeying more and more zoning issues, evading school taxes, and creating housing dilemmas with an increasing population. Yet at that moment, they had only been concerned with the idea that the restaurant caused a blight on the good name of Jews.

Benny knew the real reason for the feeble attempt. It was payback. He'd never know the who, when, or how of the matter, but he most certainly knew the why. Adam's former community was trying to punish him. What Benny didn't know back then or even now, was that the source was Adam's uncle. He had been so severely chided for sending young Adam to the diner in the first place that he promised the community he would take strong action as an act of remorse.

He spoke to the elders of the community, urging them to preach the dangers of patronizing the establishment. To make sure that every teacher and parent in the neighborhood knew it was a dangerous place for any of them to enter. In turn, he himself would circulate a flyer through the rest of the county in the hopes that he could make at least some of the wayward Jews see the light.

None of that mattered because the Hasidic community never set foot in the Daily Diner to begin with, save for one or two strays that lost their way or visited from another area. Those rare few who were unfamiliar with the fact that the Hasidic community did not oversee the establishment.

In reality, the Daily Diner saw no dent in its business at all. Upsetting as the flyer had been, it had done nothing but strengthen the business. To this day, the patronage was stronger than ever.

Sam brought the topic of the flyer up to Benny because he merely wanted to show how that past event strengthened the business and the resolve of Benny's Jewish customers to patronize the restaurant. Since the restaurant was on such solid financial ground, it was time to carry it into the next century and computerize everything. Just ideas mind you, and Sam hoped that Benny wouldn't take offense at any of his suggestions.

In no time, the two were caught up in the back and forth that was their usual form of communication. Each ate a hearty breakfast while contemplating the digital age and the possibilities that computers held for the future. What might it be like to have all the registers, as well as all the business records, computerized? Benny was excited about the idea.

Benny was so engaged in conversation that he didn't see when Molly Abramowitz came in for breakfast or when she sat down in the back booth of the diner. After saying his good-byes to Sam and heading to the register to relieve Nate, Benny spied her in the remote corner.

She was sitting with papers, pen, and texts all askew around her plate of eggs and beef fry.

This was at least the sixth time he'd seen her there. How ironic that twice now someone or something he'd thought about this morning happened to show itself at the diner. Hadn't he thought about Sam when he first sat down? And wasn't it odd that Sam brought up the flyer just to make the point that the business was stronger than ever?

Hadn't Benny also thought about Molly when he began to reminisce? About how she, too, seemed to be attracted to the back booth and up to something? There she was again, furiously writing once more. Maybe she was preparing for an exam? That seemed silly because she had become a licensed nurse years ago. Benny fought every temptation to head over there to quell his curiosity.

Whatever it was she was doing, it was another adventure, to be sure. Molly had the look of one mesmerized by deep thoughts. She was there physically, but her mind was elsewhere. She'd look up and stare and then write in her notebook once more. There was something about that booth! Benny couldn't understand it. Was it because it rested in a corner? Was it just more comfortable or private? Technically speaking, it was just a booth.

Benny and Nate both served many a couple sitting in it through the years, as well as individuals who, like Molly, seemed to be handling important matters. Secret matters. Certainly, it had been a haven for people like Adam and Daniella who were dealing with the business called life.

Benny was beginning to think that there was divine manipulation at hand. He could think of no other reason for seeing both Sam and Molly after such a pensive morning. Perhaps it was the good Lord's way of showing that he was listening to Benny's remembrances.

Benny looked over at Molly and smiled. Wasn't it nice that Molly was there on this particular morning? She was a living symbol of everything he had remembered before the sun came up. It was truly ironic that Benny started all his thoughts by thinking about Molly's mother...one of his four synagogue ladies from yesteryear. It was almost as if Molly had known that he had wondered about her during the gray hours of the morning and so had decided to come and sit in the booth.

Whatever it was, Benny would let it be. Let Molly have her secret adventure without his running interference. Besides, he'd learned his lesson with Daniella and Adam. More so, the psychology of his own emotions had been soothed and healed by the good Lord's act of simply putting Adam and Daniella his path. He certainly needed no more healing, and for sure, he wanted no more possibilities in regards to rocking anyone's boat!

They say that God works in mysterious ways. In an effort to put an end to Benny's story, several things happened in succession, beginning at that very moment. The first being that Molly signaled her waiter that she'd love more coffee. She did look tired to Benny. He knew she was a nurse. Perhaps she had just finished a rough shift the night before and was still lacking in sleep. Coffee would be just the thing. Benny would make sure his employees kept the coffee fresh.

Given his summation, it should have been no surprise that Molly opted to lean over and open the window adjacent to her booth just a crack. Merely a hair's breadth so she could let in some of the cool air from outside, to help wake her up a bit. It would hit her face and give her a bit of pep.

It was the next sequence of events, however, that made Benny understand that God was always there, always watching, always guiding, and always talking to us.

A customer was leaving the restaurant. He dropped his keys on the floor and bent down to pick them up. The act must have made him forget where he was for the moment. Perhaps it even made him think he was actually at his own home and about to leave. Benny thought this because, for some unknown reason, the customer felt compelled to close the inner door to the restaurant and try to slip his own key into the lock before stepping into the front entryway that led to the outside door.

The inner door that Benny and Nate always made sure stayed open during business hours was now shut solid. The customer had pulled it hard and made the key-turning gesture just before realizing his error. The customer laughed and gave himself a bump on the forehead as if calling himself an idiot. The one thing he did not do was reopen the inner door before leaving through the outer one. It was at that precise moment when Molly had leaned over to open the window at her side. Benny watched it all and smiled. He nudged Nate in order to get his attention.

"Nate, ever think that God is talking to you?"

"So that came from left field. What the heck are you talking about?"

"What's that phrase, you know, the one that was in *The Sound of Music*? The one you told me a long time ago.

I think it was, 'When God closes a door, somewhere he opens a window.'"

"Yeah, it was something like that. What are you going on about, Benny?"

Benny decided to shrug his shoulders and let it go. Whatever was in store for Molly, he wished her well. He'd likely find out about her goings-on, because she seemed to be the newest of his daily diners. One of the servers would ask her what she was doing, and that server would share the information with Benny. That was the way it always seemed to happen.

Benny wouldn't pry, though. He'd be patient and wait. Knowing how thoroughly God had seen to all of Benny's needs, he knew that Molly would be guided well. God was the true judge. God was the puppeteer. Whether we admit it or not, each of us is continually nudged in a certain direction by a divine hand. Benny turned his head in the direction of the back booth.

He whispered under his breath. "Your turn, Molly. Best of luck, sweetheart."

Benny rang up the next customer.

About the Author

M. Marmer Verhoeff is a happily married mother of four children and grandmother of two boys. She has been a registered nurse since 1979 with a subspecialty in oncology and HIV. In her last two years before retirement, she worked in functional medicine.

She is the director of her synagogue's choir, as well as one of the Torah scroll readers, and finds great meaning in both of these endeavors. Dance is her favorite form of exercise and she enjoys performing tap dance with other adult women.

Verhoeff has passions for reading, writing, and every form of needlecraft and loves jigsaw and crossword puzzles.

Her colorful imagination has finally led her to a second career as a writer. The author of *When Fishes Love Doves* and *The Daily Diner*, Verhoeff is currently working on her third novel.

For more information, please visit www.mmarmerver hoeff.com.

Made in the USA
Columbia, SC
18 January 2018